STEPHEN COONTS'
DEEP BLACK

By Stephen Coonts

Liberty
America
Saucer
Hong Kong
Cuba
Fortunes of War
Flight of the Intruder
Final Flight
The Minotaur
Under Siege
The Red Horseman
The Intruders

STEPHEN COONTS'
DEEP BLACK

*Written by Stephen Coonts
and Jim DeFelice*

ORION

First published in Great Britain in 2003 by Orion Books
an imprint of The Orion Publishing Group
Orion House, 5 Upper St Martin's Lane, London WC2H 9EA

A CIP catalogue record for this book is
available from the British Library

ISBN (hardback) 0 75286 049 6
ISBN (trade paperback) 0 75285 730 4

Printed and bound in Great Britain by
Clays Ltd, St Ives plc

*To the men and women at the National Security
and Central Intelligence Agencies, who do it
better than we could ever say*

Author's Note

The National Security Agency, Central Intelligence Agency, Space Agency, Federal Bureau of Investigation, National Security Council, United States Special Operations Command, Air Force, Delta Force, and Marines are, of course, real. While based on actual organizations affiliated with the intelligence community, Desk Three and all of the people in this book are fiction. The technology depicted here either exists or is being developed. Liberties have been taken in describing actual places, organizational structures, and procedures to facilitate the telling of the tale.

1

Taxiing on the ramp at Novosibirsk in southwestern Siberia, Dashik Flight R7 looked like any other tired Russian jet, weighed down by creditors as well as metal fatigue. Anyone glancing at the exterior of the Ilyushin IL-62 as it bumped toward the runway would easily see that the craft was preparing for its last miles. Aeroflot's faded paint scheme was still visible on the fuselage though the Russian airline hadn't operated or even owned the craft for nearly a decade and a half. Shiny metal patches lined the lower wing and fuselage where repairs had been made, and there was a rather conspicuous dent next to the forward door on the right side of the plane. Though converted from passenger to cargo service aeons ago, the plane retained its windows. About half had been painted over halfheartedly; the rest were still clear, though a third of these were blocked by shades, most stuck at odd angles. A close inspection of the four Soloviev D-30K engines below the tail would reveal that they had recently been serviced, but that was clearly an anomaly—the tires on the landing gear had less tread than the average Hot Wheels car.

According to the details of the flight records filed with the authorities, the onetime airliner was now used primarily to fly parts west of the Ural Mountains. Tonight its manifest showed three crates of oil pumps and related machinery were aboard. They were bound for Vokuta, from which they would be trucked to their final destination, about thirty miles farther east. The crates had been duly inspected, though as usual the inspector had been somewhat more interested in the unofficial (though definitely mandatory) fee for his services than in the crates themselves.

Perhaps because of the weather, the inspection had been conducted in the airport cargo handling area before the plane was loaded. Had the inspector ventured into the aircraft itself, he would have found nothing unusual, except for the sophisticated glass wall of flight instruments lining the cockpit. Such improvements were out of place in an aged and obviously worthless craft, though since the inspector knew little about airplanes it was doubtful he would have drawn any such conclusion. Nor would he have been surprised to find that the door on the compartment aft of the flight deck could not be opened. Such doors and compartments were the rule rather than the exception. On discovering the door, his next step would have been to elicit an additional fee for overlooking it.

Dashik R7's locked compartment held neither *mafiya* cash nor drugs, as the inspector would have guessed. Instead, a small fold-down seat and a long metal counter dominated the space; on the countertop were two large video screens, stacked one atop the other. They looked as if they had been taken from a home theater setup, but in fact the thick bundle of fiber-optic cables extruding from the sides was attached to a computer system whose parallel processing CPUs and flash-SRAM memory lined the full floor of the cargo bay. This computer system had no keyboard, accepting its commands through a special headset that could be used by only one person in the world. The beaked band at the top of the headset included sensors that analyzed both the operator's voice and retinas; it would only communicate with the computer if they matched the configuration hard-wired into the computer's circuits.

By no coincidence at all, the man the headset had been designed for sat in the locked compartment, waiting patiently as Dashik R7 gunned its finely tuned and subtly modified

Solovievs a touch more aggressively than a casual observer might have expected. For the first thirty yards down the runway it might properly be described as lumbering; from that point on, however, it moved with the efficiency of a well-tuned military jet, leaping rather than faltering into the sky.

Stephan Moyshik—more accurately known as Stephen Martin, though only to his ultimate employer—breathed slowly and deeply as the plane took off, willing his consciousness to remain locked in the Zen meditation exercise he had practiced for months. The Dramamine he had taken a half hour ago calmed his stomach, but there was no cure for the claustrophobic feel of the small compartment, nor the sensation of helplessness that crept across his shoulders as the Ilyushin climbed. Martin knew that his anxiety would pass; it always did. But knowing such a thing could not completely erase his fear. When Martin had come to Russia at the start of the Wave Three missions three months before, he felt mildly agitated at takeoff and landing. Now his heart pounded and sweat poured from every part of his skin, his breath the erratic cacophony of a dozen pneumatic drills firing at once. Ironically, he was himself a pilot, though not qualified on multiengined craft.

Martin spent the first twenty-seven minutes after takeoff tonight in high panic. Two large blades, one black, one white, twisted in the middle of his chest, their dagger points entwined around his heart.

Twenty-eight minutes after takeoff, a low tone sounded in his headset. Martin took a long breath, then reached his fingers to adjust the mouthpiece. His fingers trembled so badly that he had a great deal of difficulty setting it in place.

Yet once it was there, the panic ebbed. "Readying start-up," he told the pilot over the interphone.

"Roger that. We are fifteen minutes from Alpha."

Martin looked up at the blank screens for a moment, then reached to the counter and placed his hand on a highly polished rectangle at the right. The sensors below read his fingerprints; red dots appeared in the middle of the screens.

"Command: System activate. Diagnostics One," said Martin.

The computer did not acknowledge directly. Instead, a pink light flickered at the center of both screens, and then their dark surfaces flared with a barrage of color. A mosaic of different shades—actually a diagnostic screen for the video components—materialized in mirror images, one atop the other. Martin settled his hands into his lap, thumbs together over his thighs. The computer spent the next five minutes testing itself and the discrete-burst communication system it used to communicate with the outside world. When that was done, it turned its diagnostics to the intricate grid embedded in its wings, fine-tuning the induction device so that it could pick up the presence of a discarded compass magnet at 50,000 feet.

The computer had to get considerably closer to the ground to pick up the magnetic patterns on a spinning disk drive—15,000 feet, though they would fly at 12,000 to give themselves a margin for error.

"Alpha in zero nine," said the pilot just as the tests were complete.

"Yes," said Martin, his eyes focused on the pattern of colored dots on the top screen. The computer could easily filter very strong magnetic fields as Dashik R7 passed over them; the great difficulty was dealing with subtle sources. For some reason, discarded telephones presented the greatest difficulty; all of Martin's tweaks—delivered as voice commands and prods on the touch-sensitive screens—barely screened 50 percent of the devices from their net. Given that they had a limited capacity to transmit the data to the collection satellites above, and the fact that they had to fly without arousing suspicion, every mistaken capture was costly. On their last flight, Martin had recorded the data of a fax machine apparently belonging to a dentist; he suspected that colleagues would now refer to him as "the Periodontist" in derision.

Martin pointed to a magenta cluster at the right-hand side of the screen and made a circular motion with his index finger. The cluster zoomed into a white-lined box with a black legend at the edge—a twenty-megabyte hard drive, probably belonging to a laptop. Had they been transmitting, a tap in the middle of the cluster would have uploaded all of the magnetic patterns into the capture satellite above; from there it would have been beamed back to the U.S. for analysis. Within twelve or fifteen hours, depending on the shift, the contents of the drive would be available for detailed inspection.

Satisfied that he had the gear tuned as well as he could, Martin ordered the computer to display a sitrep map on the lower screen. The map, using GPS input and an extensive map library updated by daily satellite input, showed Dashik R7's position on a simulated 3-D image as it approached the Iachin commercial complex, the small R and R facility west of Kargasok operated by Voyska PVO that was tonight's target. Martin was neither privy to the intercept nor briefed on the precise significance of his target, but he would have been dull indeed not to know what the high-tech NSA sniffer was looking for. The Russians had lately been trying to perfect their long-range laser technology, creating a weapon that could conceivably replace conventional antiair and perhaps antisatellite missiles. Two complexes containing laser directors— the units that actually emitted the high-energy beam—either were being constructed or had been constructed east of the Urals. Not only had Martin seen them on the satellite images included in the flight briefs, but also their instructions included strict language to avoid those areas. The facility they were targeting was located about halfway between them; he assumed that the computers were connected by dedicated fiber-optic cable to the facilities and contained information about the tests. (Had the connection been more conventional, it could have been penetrated by easier means.)

The sitrep showed Dashik R7 over a wasteland about two minutes from the stretched elliptical cone where information could be swept into the net. Martin raised his head from the screen, a wave of relief flooding over him. It was downhill from here, just a matter of punching buttons.

"Shit," said the copilot over the interphone. "Company."

"Bogey at twenty thousand feet, coming right over us," explained the pilot, his voice considerably calmer than the copilot's. "MiG-29 radar active. No identifier."

Martin ignored them, concentrating on the top video screen. He pointed to a bright red cluster in the left-hand quadrant. This belonged to a rather large disk array a few miles from their target area. It had the sort of profile he'd seen from units used by banks for financial records, but since their briefing hadn't identified any large computer systems here—and the sitrep showed they were still over a largely unpopulated area—Martin decided it was worth starting the show a little early.

"Command: Transmit. Command: Configuration Normal One."

The computer gave him a low tone to confirm that it had complied.

The copilot drowned it out. "That son of a bitch is targeting us!"

"Keep your diaper clean," said the pilot. "He's only going to hit us for a bribe. He's alone. He's obviously a pirate. Hail him. Tell him we'll agree to terms. His squadron probably ran out of whore money—or jet fuel."

"Nothing on the radio. He thinks we don't know he's here."

"Hail him."

Martin once more tried to ignore the conversation. Air pirates were rarely encountered by Dashik since they freely paid the protection fees in advance, but there were always new groups muscling in. Legitimate PVO units obtained quite a bit of "supplemental funding" through their Air Security fees; occasional freelancers got in the act for a few weeks or as long as they could get away with it. The agreement to make a certain credit card payment to a specific account upon landing generally precluded being diverted; if that didn't work, naming a specific PVO general as their protector inevitably got the pirate to break off. Russia's chaos had grown considerably over the past few months; the country's economy, never strong, was once more teetering. Part of the problem had to do with an increase in military expenditures to develop new weapons and deal with insurgencies in the southern parts of the country, but Martin thought the country would have been far better off putting the money into things such as housing or even subsidizing agriculture.

Not that anyone would have been interested in his opinion.

The red clusters on the video screen pulsated as their contents were transmitted. A white dialogue box opened to their right, the computer sniffing a significant sequence. A run of hexadecimals shot across the screen; Martin tapped them to stop the flow of numbers, then pointed below the box.

"Command: Open Delphic Fox translator. Access: Compare."

The computers took the intercepted sequence and examined them for signifiers that were used in the current Russian military telemetry and data storage. As smart as they were, Dashik's onboard computers did not have the capacity—or time—to translate the information, let alone hunt for cipher keys or do anything to "break" an encryption. But that wasn't the point. By identifying the way the information was organized, the system helped operators decide what to capture. Its significance was determined elsewhere.

Fox Blue, Variation 13, declared the computer.

Martin had no idea what Fox Blue, Variation 13, was, only that it was on his list to capture. He directed the system to concentrate all of its energy on tapping the source rather than continuing to scan for others. He debated asking the satellite image library for a close-up of the target building, which looked like a small shed on the bottom screen. But the library wasn't kept onboard, and requesting the information from SpyNet and having it beamed back down would narrow the transmit flow.

An overflow error appeared—clearly this was a very large storage system; the plane's equipment couldn't keep up with the data it was stealing.

"Slow to minimum speed," Martin told the pilot. "We

may have to circle back on this one. This is something interesting."

"Impossible. Hold on—"

In the next second, Martin felt his stomach leave his body. The aircraft plummeted, twisting in the air on its left wing. As it slammed back in the opposite direction, the seat belt nearly severed his body. The computer sounded a high tone that meant it was losing its ability to reap magnetic signatures; the signal grew sharp and then was replaced by a hum—they were no longer collecting.

The copilot shouted so loudly Martin could hear him through the bulkhead.

"Missiles! Missiles! Jesus!"

The next thing Martin heard was a deep, low rattle that traveled through the floor and up into his seat. He felt cold grip his shoulders but had enough presence of mind to issue a command to the computer.

"Command: Contingency D. Authorization Alpha Moyshik Moyshik. Destruct. Cleo—"

Cleo was not part of command sequence; it was the name of his six-year-old daughter, whom he'd lost to his wife after their divorce five years ago. It was also the last word he spoke before a second missile struck Dashik R7—aka NSA Wave Three Magnetic Data Gatherer Asset 1—and ignited the fuel tank in the right wing. In the next second, the aircraft flared into a bright meteor in the dark Siberian night.

2

William Rubens pushed his hands slowly out from his sides as the two men in black ninja uniforms approached. Palms upward, he looked a little like an angel supplicating heaven; he waited patiently while one of them took a small device from his belt and waved it over Rubens' body. About the size and shape of a flashlight, the device scanned Rubens' clothes for circuits that might be used to defeat the next array of sensors, which were positioned in a narrow archway a few feet away. Satisfied that he carried nothing electronic, not even a watch, the ninjas nodded, and Rubens stepped forward through the detector.

The fact that Rubens had led the team that developed both the archway and the circuitry detectors did not exempt him from a thorough check, nor did the fact that, as the head of National Security Agency's Combined Service Direct Operations Division—called simply Desk Three—Rubens was the number two man at the agency. If anything, it made the men work harder. The ninjas, as part of the NSA's Security Division, ultimately worked for him. Anyone leaving Black Chamber—the massive multilevel subbasement facility bureaucratically known as Headquarters/Operations Building National Security Operational Control Center Secure Ultra Command, or OPS 2/B Level Black—was subject to a mandatory search. Had Rubens not been searched, these ninjas would have been summarily fired—after serving a one-year sentence in the NSA detention center for dereliction of duty.

Cleared, Rubens continued from the basement levels of OPS 2 upstairs into the main operations building (known as OPS 2/A or just OPS 2), ran another gauntlet of security checks, and finally emerged outside where a Chevrolet Malibu waited to take him to his appointment in Washington. He slid into the front seat, nodded at the aide behind the wheel—an Army MP in civilian dress—and then leaned the seat back to rest as the driver pulled away from the curb.

Two other similarly nondescript vehicles, a panel van and a pickup truck, followed as they headed through Crypto City—known to the outside world as Fort Meade, if known at all—to get on the Baltimore–Washington Parkway. Both carried ninjas, whose dungarees and work shirts covered lightweight body armor; their vehicles were equipped with a variety of weapons that ranged from handguns to a pair of shoulder-launched Stingers, though the only things they would be tempted to use this afternoon were the M47 Dragon antitank weapons to cut through some of the traffic.

The trip from the Maryland suburbs where the NSA's Puzzle Palace was located to the West Wing of the White House took roughly fifty-five minutes. Rubens spent it eyes closed, head back on the rest. His mind focused on a one-syllable nonsense word a yoga master had given him years before to conjure energy from the kundalini, a point somewhere near the lower spine that the master believed was the center of Rubens' personal (and potentially transcendent) soul.

By the time he arrived at the suite where the National Security Director was waiting with the president of the United States, the thirty-two-year-old mathematical genius and art connoisseur felt rested and refreshed. He also felt he had centered his often rambunctious energy and clamped hold of his ego.

It was a good thing.

"The Wave Three mission was not authorized by Finding 302," said National Security Director George Hadash as Rubens entered the Blue Room, a secure meeting room in sublevel two of the building. "Losing that plane was a screwup."

Rubens had known George Hadash since MIT, where he had been Hadash's student in a graduate seminar on the use of science in international relations. He was used to the blunt blasts that substituted for proper greetings. "The target was discussed," he told his onetime professor. "The protocol for Desk Three is that it is to operate autonomously once broad objectives are outlined. Wave Three was the best asset for the job, and it was under our control."

"The laser facilities were not important enough to risk that asset," said Hadash.

"I beg to differ. Contrary to the estimate from the Air Force Special Projects Office, the weapon is near an operational state. The CIA analysts believe it's more advanced than our own Altrus. And there is no question that if it were operational, it could completely eliminate our satellite network over central Asia."

Hadash's cheek twitched slightly, but he said nothing. The tic indicated to Rubens that he had made his point.

"We haven't finished analyzing the data yet," added the NSA official.

"You're going to have to explain to the president," said Hadash.

"Of course. If he wants to know."

Hadash gave him one of his most serious frowns, though Rubens hadn't intended the comment as impertinent. The issue wasn't plausible denial; compartmentalization was essential to successful espionage and covert action, which were Desk Three's raison d'être.

"He's not happy," added Hadash. "The CIA has been all over this, and DOD is reminding him that the NSA has *no* operational experience."

"Not true," said Rubens mildly. Silently congratulating himself on the earlier mention of the CIA—which would convey an open-minded neutrality in sharp contrast to the paranoid backbiting of his bitter intelligence service rivals— he took a seat on the couch. Hadash went to see if the president was ready to meet with him.

Both the CIA and the military had made plays to control Desk Three when it was created at the very start of President Jeffrey Marcke's administration. Both were disappointed that the NSA was given primacy over the operation. CIA and military assets assigned to Desk Three, either on permanent "loan" or for temporary missions, were under Rubens' direct command until released. This inevitably led to jealousy. While Rubens had foreseen this, it did present an ongoing problem that a man of lesser intellect and ability—in his humble opinion—would have had great trouble controlling.

The idea behind Desk Three was relatively simple in outline: New technologies such as satellite communications, miniaturized sensors, and remote-controlled vehicles could revolutionize covert action and direct warfare if used properly. The CIA, the NSA, the Air Force, the Navy, the Defense Intelligence Agency, the Army—all had expertise in specific areas but often could not work smoothly enough to leverage that expertise. It was no secret that the different groups charged with national security tended not to cooperate; any number of fiascoes, from the infamous *Pueblo* incident in the 1970s to the attack on the World Trade Center in 2001, could be at least partly blamed on this lack of coordination. And at a time when advances in technology were making all sorts of things possible, coordination was essential.

Desk Three's evolution could be traced directly to the CIA's former Division D, which had worked with the NSA in the 1950s and early '60s planting sensors, stealing codebooks, "turning" crypto experts—and assassinating foreigners, though this was not necessarily an NSA function. It was succeeded by the Special Collection Service, or SCS, which had essentially the same job, sans assassinations, which were outlawed by Congress following scandals in the 1970s. In both cases, the arrangement had the CIA working essentially as a contractor to the NSA; the SCS headquarters was not in Crypto City, and the field agents were never, or almost never, under direct NSA control.

Desk Three was different in that respect. It was intended

to represent a new, cutting-edge force to be used for not only collecting data but also, when the situation demanded, taking action "ad hoc" to meet objectives outlined by the president. It could tap into the full array of sensors maintained by the NSA, as well as the processed intercepts from those sensors and data analysis provided by all of the major intelligence agencies. It could call on its own air and space assets, including twelve Space Platforms, or ultralarge satellites that could launch customized eavesdropping probes, and eight remote-controlled F-47C robot planes that were arguably as capable as F-22s, with twice their range and about one-third of their size. Underwater assets gave Desk Three similar capabilities in the ocean. And a small team of agents, drawn from a variety of sources, gave it muscle.

Several agencies could have "run" Desk Three. Besides the CIA, the military's USSOCOM, or U.S. Special Operations Command, had been a lead contender. But the NSA was chosen primarily because it was used to working with the high-tech gear that formed the backbone of the force concept. It also lacked some of the political entanglements that plagued the others.

And, of course, it contained William Rubens.

Rubens was critical for several reasons beyond his outsize abilities. One was his friendship with Hadash. Another was his demonstrated skill at melding the disparate talents required for such an enterprise. Last but not least, he had conceived the concept. He personally wrote the report outlining it, well before Marcke's election. Titled "Deep Black," the report formed the blueprint for the operation and was still among the most highly classified documents in the government archives. The report title had become an unofficial name for Desk Three and its operations.

Rubens had long ago learned the difficult and distasteful lesson that sheer intelligence, culture, and genetics often mattered little in Washington, let alone in international affairs. The trick was to use these assets to maintain one's position and thereby accomplish one's goals. It took eternal vigilance and, perhaps, a touch of paranoia.

Rubens cleared his mind of external distractions, preparing himself to speak to the president. The room's spartan furnishings made it look as if it belonged in a suburban tract house. A large video display sat behind a set of drapes where the picture window would be; otherwise the Blue Room was refreshingly devoid of high-tech gadgetry.

The door opened so abruptly Rubens barely had time to get to his feet as the president burst into the room, his hand thrust forward.

"Billy, how are you?" said Marcke, playing the hail-fellow-well-met politico. Marcke was an inch taller than Rubens, who at six-four was not short; though in his early sixties, Marcke had an incredibly strong handshake and was said by the media to work with serious weights every afternoon.

"Fine, sir."

The president released him and sat on the couch. Hadash and the secretary of defense, Art Blanders, entered belatedly. Both remained standing as the president leaned toward Rubens.

"How's your boss?" asked Marcke.

"Admiral Brown is still traveling, sir."

Vice Admiral Devlin Brown was a recent appointee to head the agency; he'd only been on the job for a few weeks. Rubens didn't know Brown very well yet and, frankly, didn't feel he'd be much of a force. It would take considerable ability to outperform the previous head of the NSA, in Rubens' opinion—though if the opportunity presented itself, he certainly would be willing to try.

"All right, Billy," said the president with the air of a favored uncle. "Tell us what happened to your airplane."

"The Ilyushin carrying the Wave Three magnetic data reader was targeted and shot down for reasons that remain unclear," said Rubens. "We haven't been able to identify where the MiG came from, which has complicated matters."

"How is that possible?" asked Blanders.

"We're not omniscient," said Rubens, managing a smile to keep his tone mild. The secretary had come to the administration after serving as CEO of a bank; it was difficult to take him seriously. "More than likely, it was a renegade PVO unit working out some sort of dispute over 'fees.' But the possibility that both the program and Wave Three itself have been compromised cannot be ruled out."

"The lasers," prompted Hadash.

Rubens launched into a quick but detailed summary of the Wave Three target, a data center related to the Russian-directed energy program.

"The Russian president denied there was a laser program in an interview with the BBC two weeks ago," said Blanders.

The defense secretary was obviously interested in pushing DoD's own laser program, but that wasn't what motivated his comment. Rubens noted for future reference not only Blanders' disdain for Alexsandr Kurakin, the Russian president, but also the hint that Blanders believed Marcke trusted Kurakin too much.

"Perhaps you should bring it up with President Kurakin when you speak with him tomorrow," added Blanders, alluding to the president's biweekly telephone conference with the Russian president.

Doing that would inadvertently reveal quite a bit about the agency's capabilities. But before Rubens could find a way to point this out semitactfully, Marcke cut him off.

"Of course we're not going to do that," said the president. "Why show him our hand? The question is, will he ask about our aircraft?"

"I don't believe so," said Rubens.

The Wave Three compartment was rigged to self-destruct. According to protocol, none of the crew carried parachutes, though there was always a possibility that some had been carried anyway. Still, transmissions from the plane indicated that there had been no survivors.

"How can you be sure?" asked Blanders.

"The plane went down in a fairly remote area," said Rubens. "We have one possible site that we're keeping track of, and I have a team en route to survey it."

"You didn't see it on satellite?" Blanders asked.

Was that a criticism or a play for the comprehensive optical survey satellites, which would give the U.S. worldwide around-the-clock coverage? Rubens decided to interpret it as the latter.

"At the moment, we don't have the resources for complete coverage," said Rubens. "That would be very desirable. We did, however, pick up the explosion. We have data on the possible wreckage. Now we send someone there to look at it and make sure it was destroyed. Routine."

Hadash cleared his throat and began speaking in the slightly loud, slightly rushed tone that indicated he'd been rehearsing what he was to say for some time. "Given the controversy—"

"What controversy?" asked Rubens.

"Given the controversy, I—we—feel there should be someone outside of Desk Three along."

"What?"

"A neutral observer," said Hadash. "Just to see the wreckage and make an unbiased report."

"I don't see why that would be necessary." Rubens had been taken by surprise, but he labored now to hide it. More difficult to suppress was his anger at Hadash for failing to warn him.

He remembered his yoga mantra.

"You don't understand the political situation," said Blanders.

"What political situation?" said Rubens.

The president put up his hand. "Billy, here's the problem. The CIA wants to chop off your head. They have some friends on the Senate Intelligence Committee. The committee wants a briefing. George is going to give it to them based on what his personal investigator finds out. We need to be able to tell them definitively that the plane was completely wrecked, that there was no screwup."

Collins, the deputy director of operations over at the CIA. She was responsible for this. The bitch.

"There was no screwup," said Rubens.

"It's for your own good, William," said Blanders.

"Sir, we're talking about something that's at Level Five VRK," said Rubens. *VKR* meant "very restricted knowledge"—the ultimate compartmentalization. "The team I'm sending in doesn't even know about the technology, and they're my top team."

"George's man won't know anything about it, either," said Blanders. "What's the big deal? Assuming the plane really was trashed."

The president's gray eyes met Rubens' and held them. Did he want Rubens out? Were they going to use this as a pretext to bag him?

"This isn't a matter of trust, William," said Hadash.

Rubens turned slowly toward him, deciding not to answer or debate the point—it was obviously already settled.

"If the politicians have any reason to run with this, they'll compromise Desk Three and a great deal else," Hadash added. "We don't want that."

"You have someone in mind?" said Rubens.

"I do. His background has already been thoroughly checked. We can trust him. All he needs to do is confirm that the plane was destroyed. He won't even know about the original mission, just that he's to tell me what he sees."

"We don't need more CIA people with axes to grind."

"He's not. He has no axe to grind; he's a complete outsider."

It was possible, just possible, that Hadash was trying to help Rubens. A neutral observer could be trotted out for the Intelligence Committee and then turned out to pasture without jeopardizing anything.

On the other hand, he could do serious damage gathering ammunition for someone like Collins.

"Who is he?" asked Rubens.

"Charles Dean," said Hadash.

"Dean? As in *Jihad* Dean?"

Hadash nodded.

Dean had been used on a cooperative venture with the French some months back. An ex-Marine, he had proven himself brave and resourceful. His background had been thoroughly checked, and he had proven able to keep his mouth shut.

He'd also been a bit slow to figure out what he'd gotten himself involved in. And the project had been opposed by Collins.

So maybe Hadash was helping him out after all.

Or not. Collins might have feigned her opposition. Rubens would have to reconsider what had happened carefully and review Dean's background.

Dean didn't like the CIA—wasn't that in the transcripts of his conversations?

A cover, perhaps.

"He'll have to pass the security protocols," said Rubens. "Briefing only on a need-to-know basis."

"Of course," said Hadash.

"If he passes our security tests, fine," said Rubens.

"Make sure your team waits to examine the plane's wreckage until he does," said the president. He rose, and as he did, he smiled broadly and his shoulders seemed to roll a bit. "So talk to me about wine, Billy. The French ambassador is upstairs and he's always trying to one-up our California reds. Walk with me, gentlemen."

3

"Name?"

"Charles Dean."

"Middle name?"

"Aloysius."

"*Real* middle name?"

Dean pursed his lips, hesitating to answer.

"If you think this is hard," said the man in the black business suit near the door, "just wait."

"My middle name is Martin," Dean said. "Charles Martin Dean."

The technicians sitting in front of him nodded. Dean sat on an uncomfortable wooden chair in his undershirt. A web of thin wires ran from sensors taped to his chest, back, neck, and both arms. A headband held larger arrays of sensors to both temples. He felt like an actor in a '50s Disney movie, transferring his consciousness to a chimp.

Or maybe Mr. Black Suit by the door. Same difference.

"Place of birth?" asked one of the technicians.

"Bosco, Missouri. Population 643, not counting the cows."

"It would be better if you answered the questions simply," said the technician on the right. "The process is automated, and anything the machine can't interpret will be held against you."

"Let him ramble," said Black Suit. "We've got nowhere to go."

Dean started to fold his arms to his chest before remembering the attachments. He put his palms on his thighs instead, willing himself into something approaching patience while the techies continued with their questioning. As Black Suit had hinted, this wasn't the actual interview; all the technicians were doing was calibrating their elaborate lie detectors.

It took them nearly forty minutes to do so. When they were done, Dean asked for a break to hit the head.

"Not now," said Black Suit. "You're a Marine. Cross your legs."

Three hours later, Dean's bladder had displaced his lungs and was working its way toward his throat. It gave him a bit of an edge on the questions about his sexual relationships and carried him through the little game Black Suit and the head-shrink played, peppering him with accusations about how he must really consider himself a failure. But it started to become painful when they began asking him detailed questions about his belief in God.

Dean wondered what part religion might play in his assignment as George Hadash's photographic memory. Hadash hadn't been particularly profuse in describing what Dean was supposed to do before sending him up here, saying only that he wanted someone he could trust to take a look at something unpleasant.

Dean had met Hadash years before, back when both were considerably younger. As a Marine, Dean had been assigned to accompany a young Pentagon visitor around Da Nang for a few days. Hadash proved to be considerably smarter than most of the suits who came out to look at what Vietnam was all about. He'd also proven himself relatively brave, if somewhat naive, volunteering to go out in the bush with Dean. Dean took him—a decision that caused him considerable grief with his commander.

But it wasn't like he and Hadash were best of friends. Hadash got in touch with him a few times after the war, once to tell some students over at MIT what the jungle was like. Until yesterday morning, he hadn't even realized Hadash was the country's National Security Director.

"You can take a break, Corporal Dean," said Black Suit finally.

"Yeah, real funny," said Dean, who had left the Marines as a gunnery sergeant, not a corporal.

Black Suit smiled—the first time he had for the entire session. "Actually, I thought you might finally pee in your pants."

"I'll tell you something truthful. When I was a corporal, that was probably the best time of my life," said Dean as they unhooked him from the machine. "I should have refused the promotion."

Dean was taken down the hallway, flanked by two men who accompanied him into the men's room. They said it was impossible to go anywhere here without an escort, and under no circumstances to lose his badge with its "V" insignia—someone without a badge might very well be shot. He thought they might be exaggerating, but he didn't intend on testing it.

Dean hadn't volunteered to help Hadash, exactly. Hadash simply called and told him he had a job he needed done immediately. He just assumed—just *knew*—that Dean would drop everything and do it.

And Dean, for reasons that included $2 million in a Swiss bank account, agreed.

Bladder finally relieved, he emerged from the men's room feeling invigorated. He girded himself for the second round of questions as he entered the room, but the shrink and technicians had left. Only Black Suit remained. He looked at the guards and lifted his forefinger. They nodded like a pair of matched robots, then backed through the door.

"Dinnertime?" Dean sat in the wooden chair.

"Not for you."

"This where you slap me around a bit, ask if I'm going to come clean?" Dean asked. "Or do you toss down a pack of cigarettes and offer to split the loot if I talk?"

"You're a real funny guy, Sergeant."

"You know what? I'm not a Marine anymore." Dean stopped himself from saying that he didn't really care to be reminded of his days in the service; no sense giving the guy a stick to hit him with. "I'm guessing you were in the Army. I can tell you weren't a Marine. And you were an officer. Maybe you still are. A major, right? They always had something up their butts."

Black Suit smiled.

Dean stretched his legs and wrapped his arms across his chest, starting to feel a little cold in his T-shirt. "So all right, you asking me more questions or what?"

"We're done."

"Same time tomorrow?"

"No. You're on the job, starting now."

"You mean I'm hired?" said Dean sardonically as he got up from the chair. "We going to go meet the boss?"

"You don't have time to meet anyone," smirked Black Suit. "You have a plane to catch."

"Where am I going?"

"Eventually, to Surgut."

"Surgut?"

"You're a businessman. Your passport and luggage are waiting for you in the foyer upstairs. Your driver will take you to the airport."

"Where the hell is Surgut?"

"Don't ask questions. Just follow the program."

"Surgut," Dean demanded.

"It's in Siberia. But don't worry; it's not the really bad part of Siberia."

4

Eight hours and several time zones later, Charles Dean found himself at the counter of Polish National Airlines in Heathrow Airport, waiting as one of the ten ugliest women in the world pecked his *nom de passport* into the reservations computer. His handlers had chosen "John Brown" as his cover name, matching it to a cover story claiming he sold metal and plastic fixtures used for filling teeth. Undoubtedly they knew of his fear of dentistry, though if they had really wanted to be perverse they might have given him the first name James and sent him out as a record salesman.

"So, Mr. Brown," said the reservation clerk. "How long will you stay in Warsaw?"

The woman attempted a smile. Dean realized that his initial assessment was incorrect—she must rank among the *five* ugliest women in the world.

"Not long."

"Business or pleasure?"

"Business."

"I have a brochure of restaurants," she said, reaching below the counter.

Dean took the pamphlet stoically, unsure whether the woman was moonlighting for the Polish travel board or— and here was a frightening thought—trying to pick him up. When he looked at the pamphlet a few minutes later in the boarding area, he saw that two words separated by several paragraphs in the densely packed jungle of ungrammatical English had been underlined—"King" and "Street."

His instructions had been to simply use his plane tickets and he would be contacted along the way. This couldn't be their way of contacting him, could it?

King Street?

But what else could it be?

Dean took the brochure and stepped away from the desk. Was King Street a destination or a code word?

He made a circuit around the mall of newsstands, fast-food shops, and currency exchanges, walking slowly to let anyone interested in contacting him do so. When no one stopped him, he went across to the baggage check-in area, checking the suitcase he'd been given. Upstairs, he cleared through security and walked down the hallway to a duty-free area that reminded him of a massive department store. As he headed toward the airline gate, he realized that "King Street" might refer to a display of some sort—booze or perfume, maybe. So he went back through more carefully, perusing the pyramids of Chivas Regal and Baileys, stopping by the Bulova watches, sniffing the Chanel. The only one who came close to him was a three-year-old German girl trying to escape from her mother. He made his way down the tunnel to the gate, where the stiff plastic seats were about a quarter filled. His carry-on baggage contained sales material relating to his dental cover story; he'd managed to read through it twice on the flight over. He was just debating whether to try a third time when a middle-aged doppelganger for Porky Pig—had Porky Pig worn a goatee—pushed down into the seat beside him. Dean noticed that the man had a wire-bound street atlas of Krakow in his open briefcase.

"Hate Polish National," said Porky, in what to Dean sounded like a Scottish accent. His light tan loafers were made of thin, expensive-looking leather, but the material of his blue suit pants had begun to pile.

"Yeah," replied Dean.

"Have you flown it?"

"Never before," said Dean. "First time to Poland."

Which was about the only part of his cover story that was actually true.

Porky told Dean that he was a barrister for a reinsurance company, heading to Poland to depose witnesses in a negligence case. He frowned slightly when Dean gave him his fake name and cover. Few people wanted to talk about dental fixtures, though Dean wondered what he would do if he ran into a dentist.

"Staying in Krakow?" asked Porky.

"Just a quick business meeting."

"Then where?"

"Russia," said Dean. "It's wide open for braces. And cosmetic fillings—we have no quality competition. Our crowns are among the best."

"I'll bet." Porky changed the subject to the weather.

As they were talking, a petite Asian woman took a seat across from them. Her pale white hose pulled Dean's eyes up her legs to a short red miniskirt. Above it she wore a mostly unbuttoned black silk shirt beneath a faded denim jacket. Her milk-white neck and slim face managed to look somehow vulnerable and bored at the same time.

Their eyes met; the woman's frown deepened instantly. Dean smiled. The woman got up from the seat, shaking her head as she walked away.

"Mostly what I do," said Porky, who had changed the subject once more as Dean indulged in a little gratuitous lust, "is take depositions. Industrial cases. Defective jackhammers, faulty pressure valves, that sort of thing."

"Intriguing," said Dean.

"Yes."

Porky started detailing his current case, concerning a railroad company that was being sued by passengers, or rather the survivors of passengers, after a coupling failed on a brake system, with horrific results.

The story was about as interesting as dental fillings. Was this guy the agent who was supposed to contact him?

Dean interrupted a finely wrought description of pneumatic couplings to ask if he could look at the street atlas in Porky's briefcase.

"Sure." Porky's sandwich-sized hands jammed against the sides of his briefcase as he unwedged it. The atlas had a few pages creased over, but Dean got the distinct impression the creases had been added to make it look used. He studied the city.

"Maybe I can help," said Porky. "What are you looking for?"

Dean said, "King Street," and waited for Porky to tear himself out of his fat suit and reveal himself as an American agent. But he did neither, instead scratching his thumb against his temple. "King in English or Polish?"

"Don't worry. Somebody's meeting me at the airport," said Dean.

He glanced at his watch, then decided he'd hit the gents' before boarding the Polish plane. Excusing himself, he wandered across the waiting area to the hall with the rest rooms. He entered the men's room and was just positioning the strap of his carry-on against his shoulder when someone else came in; the sharp click of heels against the floor caught Dean's attention and he glanced over his shoulder.

It was the Asian woman.

"Hey," he started to say.

"Into the stall," she said.

"What the hell?"

The woman leaned toward the sink and waved her hand in front of the faucet. Its motion sensor clicked and water spewed from the tap.

"The stall," she said, pointing.

"Wait up."

The door opened once again. As Dean glanced toward it the woman took two quick steps to him and wrapped herself around him, her mouth seeking his.

Even if her accent hadn't given her away as an American, Charlie Dean was hardly the sort to forgo a kiss, even if it was offered in a men's room. Still, he wasn't entirely comfortable with the situation.

Nor was the man who'd come in to use the facilities for their intended purpose. He retreated hastily, the door slamming behind him. In the meantime, the woman had begun pushing Dean backward toward the last toilet stall.

"Uh, what's go—"

She slapped him.

"Idiot," she hissed, reaching over and waving her hand in front of the flush sensor.

"What the hell's the story?"

"Idiot," she repeated. She reached into her jacket pocket and pulled out a small, round makeup case. "Here."

Dean took the case. He turned it over and then opened it. There was nothing inside, so he started to give it back. She grabbed it from him, opened it, then pushed it in front of his face.

"What, my five o'clock shadow?" he asked.

"Just shut up."

Something about the mirror wasn't right. The woman tilted it slightly, clicked something on the back, then frowned and shook her head as she pocketed it.

"Retina scan?" he asked, finally catching on.

"Did they recruit you off the street?" the woman asked. "Or is it just that you're from Texas?"

"Do I sound like I'm from Texas?"

"You sound like you're from the planet Moron," said the woman.

"Well, don't let that stop you from explaining who the hell you are," Dean told her.

"Santa Claus. Now why the hell are you talking to a Russian agent?"

"Who?"

"You idiot. The fat boy sitting next to you in the waiting area works for the Russian Security Service."

"He does?"

"Listen, do me a favor and go home, okay? I don't have time to baby-sit an NSC wanna-be."

"Fuck you."

"Gee, Chuckie, what a clever comeback. That wow 'em back in Houston?"

"I don't come from Texas."

"I know where you're from." She glanced toward the door of the rest room, as if she heard someone coming. "Yeah," she said to herself. "Yeah, yeah, I know. Okay."

Dean strung his carry-on bag over his shoulder. Except for the fact that she obviously knew who he was, he might have thought the woman psycho.

Not that those were mutually exclusive propositions.

"Just go catch your flight," she told him, turning back around and pointing. "When you get there, in the terminal, go to Gate Two. Gate Two—you can count that high?"

"Ha-ha."

"I'm not joking."

"I don't have a ticket beyond Poland. I'm supposed to be going to Surgut, but no one gave me a ticket."

"You *are* from Texas. Just buy a ticket on the first flight on the board."

"That's going to take me to Surgut?"

"Buy a ticket on the first flight on the board." She pushed open the door to the stall. "Good-bye."

The door to the men's room opened before Charlie could grab her. "Ooo-la-la," said the newcomer, watching her leave.

"Yeah, ooo-fucking-la," said Dean.

5

Rubens straightened and walked down the narrow aisle behind the row of consoles, glancing toward the back of the room where the technical people were monitoring relevant intercepts and other real-time intelligence. Jeff Rockman, who was assigned to communicate with the field agents on the operation, leaned from the station Rubens had just been hunched over.

"You were right," Rockman told Marie Telach, who as watch commander was supervising the mission. "She went into the men's room."

"Did she dunk his head in the toilet?"

"No."

"She must like him," said Rubens acerbically. Lia De-Francesca—shanghaied from the Army Special Forces Delta unit—was one of his best field agents but had a personality that the Wicked Witch of the West would have admired. "And what's with the miniskirt?"

"Tools of the trade," said Telach.

"Which trade is that?"

"Boss." Telach gave him the same look a teenager's mother might use to ward off an overprotective father.

"All right," said Rubens. He turned back to Rockman. "The Russian take the flight?"

"They're just boarding," said Rockman. One of his computer screens showed the Polish flight's manifest, which was being updated passenger by passenger as they boarded. "There goes Dean."

"One of George Hadash's best men," sneered Telach.

"We can leave Mr. Hadash out of this," said Rubens. "Dean is doing us a favor, even if he doesn't know it."

"Classic deer caught in the headlights," she answered.

"He's not that bad." Rubens had reviewed Dean's file again. He had been a competent—maybe more than competent—Marine sniper, no mean feat. He had nothing but disdain for the CIA operatives he'd worked with, which made it extremely unlikely he would knowingly help Collins. And the fact that he hadn't just decked DeFrancesca spoke well for his self-control.

"All right, they're aboard," said Rockman. He began pumping the keys on one of his computers. "You want to listen to the plane and tower?"

"That won't be necessary," said Rubens. "What about Lia?"

"Just made her flight," said Rockman. "Gave one of the male attendants a wedgie."

"No doubt."

Located on subbasement three of OPS 2/B in the heart of the Black Chamber, the Art Room was the center of operations for Desk Three. An improvement over the original War Room—officially known as OPS 1 Room 3E099—the Art Room allowed a small group of specialists and former field agents to run operations all across the globe. Sitting at three banks of consoles, Rubens' people—called runners because they "ran" the field agents—could access real-time data from satellites and other sensors. If their own library of scripts and programs couldn't get them into target computers or security systems, they could call on Desk Three's hacking operation, which was housed in a separate facility. Besides tying into the Defense Special Missile and Astronautics Center (DEFSMAC), which maintained an array of satellites, they had their own satellite and UAV (unmanned aerial vehicle) force available, controlled from a bunker down the hallway.

Rubens had handpicked the runners from former CIA as

well as NSA officers. (With the exception of Collins, Rubens had a high opinion of the agency and most of its ops.) The majority of the runners had some science or technical background as well as experience in the field. Jeff Rockman, for example, had started with the NSA as a cryptographer. Assigned to the Moscow embassy, he had begun working with some CIA agents there and helped turn a low-level field clerk into a major conduit of Russian cipher keys. Loaned to the agency, he'd distinguished himself in Afghanistan before returning to Crypto City to help Rubens set up some of the procedures for Desk Three. Telach had led a clandestine mission into North Korea, sabotaging a nuclear research facility during the Clinton years. She had then come back to the NSA and helped work out the bugs in Predator 2.1 and Predator 3.0, two programs that Rockman could unleash with hot keys from his station. (The differences in the versions had to do not with the basic coding but with the ways the programs disguised themselves. Depending on the configuration, both programs could either act as sniffers, gathering data, or simply destroy the targeted computer.)

Rockman and the other runners could speak directly to agents such as Lia through a secure satellite communications system. An ear-set chip was embedded in Lia's inner ear; the chip was just small enough to escape detection by a metal detector. But the most critical part of the system was contained in her jacket, whose studs and zippers were actually an antenna and the miniaturized radio gear. Unfortunately, the communications system itself was not perfect; the need to not only keep transmissions secure but also limit them so they couldn't be used to direct others to an agent meant that there were generally only small geographic and time windows when it could be used. The direct-link satellite had to be almost directly overhead; this wasn't always possible. The field agents often fell back on small, secure satellite phones and a wireless transmitter built into handheld computers they used for a variety of tasks.

Rubens had two teams working on upgrading the implant com system; it was just a matter of time, they predicted, before they could implant his thoughts in his agents' heads on the go.

He believed they were joking, though that wasn't necessarily a given.

Besides Rockman and Telach, there were three other men on duty. All top-shelf geeks chosen from other NSA areas, they handled and coordinated the various intercepts funneling in from the NSA's vast outer reaches. The team was still small because the mission was just getting under way; by the time Lia got Dean into Russia at least a dozen people would be on duty. Literally hundreds more, toiling at their various jobs in the Puzzle Palace and associated military agencies, could be called on to lend expertise and backup in an emergency.

Rubens took a quick tour around the room, then told Telach to page him if he was needed. He gave Rockman and the others a wave, then entered the decompression chamber.

The chamber had nothing to do with atmospheric pressure, though the process of clearing its scans seemed to take nearly as long. The original designers had wanted to make the Art Room a full-blown "clean room," meaning that anyone entering would have to wear a special suit inside, doffing it on leaving. Rubens had personally nixed the idea, but as he stood waiting for the various sensors to do their work, he wondered if the showers and bio suits wouldn't have been more expedient. Finally satisfied that he harbored nothing he hadn't come in with—and it *did* remember what he came in with—the automated security computer cleared Rubens into the vestibule, where he was met by two men in black from the Security Division, who'd picked this moment at random to do a PASS check. He submitted; there was no choice, not even for the director himself. He was directed to sit on a metal folding chair while one of the men took what looked like a small Palm Pilot from his pocket, along with a set of wires. The handheld computers were made by a company formed solely to work on NSA gear; a wide variety were used for an array of functions by NSA employees and field agents. In this case, the small computer was optimized as a

lie detector, running a miniature version of the updated
PASS, or the Polygraph Assisted Scoring System, that was
the primary lie detector software used at the agency. The
wires were taped to his palm and temples. Rubens was next
asked a dozen questions drawn at random from the computer's list. Most, though not all, had to do with security
matters, but there were others thrown in to keep subjects off
their guard, such as: "Have your sexual preferences changed
in the last two weeks?"

They hadn't. The two men showed no emotion whatso-
ever; Rubens could have told them that he was a pedophile
and they would not have cared, as long as the machine said
he wasn't lying.

Cleared, he headed back upstairs to the eighth floor of
OPS 2/A, where he had his office next to the director's. He
was running late—his cousin had invited him to her seven-
year-old daughter's First Holy Communion party, and while
he ordinarily avoided such events, he had accepted this in-
vitation partly because the guest list included Johnson
Greene, a congressman on the Defense Appropriations Committee. The congressman was expected to run for Senate; if
he won, he would be a likely candidate for the Intelligence
Committee within two years. It was never too early to cul-
tivate someone with that kind of potential—especially since
he had been a critic of the agency in the past.

A mild and uninformed critic, the best kind.

After checking his messages and making sure his computers and office were secure, Rubens ran the security gamut
and left Black Chamber. Traveling without a driver or bodyguard, he took his agency Malibu out of Crypto City, through
Annapolis Junction. After a brief jaunt on the Baltimore–
Washington Parkway, he turned to the west and headed toward a rather inconspicuous suburban enclave of yellow and
white raised ranches. Rubens took a right turn past a stone
fence where the words "Sleepy Hills" had been enshrined in
floodlit mock stone; a short distance down the road he took
another right and then a left, entering a cul-de-sac. He pulled
into the third driveway on the right, where a sensor in the

garage read his license plate and automatically opened the second bay door.

Rubens was out of the car as the garage door came down, sidling across the narrow space at the front to a vehicle more in keeping with his personal preferences—his own black BMW M-5. The garage and car, and in fact the entire house and block, were under constant surveillance, but this did not keep Rubens from making his own discreet check, taking a small container of powder from his pocket and sprinkling a generous portion over the locks and handle, as well as part of the hood and the door for the gas cap. The powder contained a chemical that interacted with oil residues less than twenty-four hours old. When he was sure that no one had touched his car he used his key to unlock it, got in, gave the interior another check, then left the garage.

His next stop was a car wash. The fingerprint powder supposedly didn't harm the car paint, but Rubens didn't trust the guarantees. Besides, he didn't particularly care for anything associated with him to be dirty, not in the least.

No one else at the NSA went to the length of keeping a safe house as a car drop. It was almost certainly unnecessary, and the bureaucracy's attitude toward the arrangement could be seen in the fact that Rubens paid for the safe house himself.

That was shortsighted of them, in his opinion. There was no such thing as too much security, especially when you were head of Desk Three. But then he took other precautions that the bureaucracy undoubtedly scoffed at, including not one but two cyanide capsules implanted under his skin, which he was fully prepared to break if the circumstances required.

As for paying for the house himself, Rubens considered it almost an investment, given the continual rise in real estate prices over the past few years. Besides, he lived independently of his government salary—and in fact regarded it as something less than a gratuity. It did not quite cover the amount of money he spent each year on clothes.

Car washed and dried, he got back on the highway and

headed south toward Washington and his cousin's home. When Rubens arrived, the party was just about reaching its height. A band that looked vaguely like 'N Sync and sounded like a cross between country pop and thrash metal, with the occasional rap beat thrown in, held forth on a stage in front of the pool.

The swimming pool and surroundings had been shaped to look like a bamboo sanctuary. The bamboo was rather obviously plastic; Rubens, whose own pool looked like the contemplative pond of a Zen monastery, smiled wryly at his cousin's poor taste as she thanked him for coming.

Greta Meandes was related to him on his mother's side. Greta had money, of course. No one related to Rubens did *not* have money; it was part of their genetic structure. But the bulk of it came from her husband, who worked as a CEO. As if that weren't bad enough, his company made paper products, one of which was—naturally—toilet paper. It seemed to Rubens a grotesque satire on the decline of the family's American branch, and he tended to keep Greta at arm's length, even though she held a relatively important job as counsel to the House Defense Appropriations Committee.

"Sylvia looks very sweet," said Rubens, who in fact had not seen the girl yet.

"She'll be so glad that her favorite uncle could make it," said Greta, as phony as ever.

"Yes," said Rubens. The girl was actually his cousin once removed, but it was typical of Greta to be imprecise.

"I was talking to your mum just the other day," said Greta. "She called with regrets."

"Switzerland can be difficult to leave this time of year," said Rubens.

"That's exactly what she said."

Rubens nodded politely as Greta began telling him how perfectly tuned the communion ceremony had been—balloons for the children, a sermon that included references to Chuckles the Clown.

A server approached with champagne. Five-five, she had a bright, beautiful face. Her curly shoulder-length hair was held back by a ribbon, accentuating her lightly freckled cheeks. These, in turn, complemented her very round breasts, which swelled from the black cocktail outfit like the glorious chest of Venus offered to the youth Adonis in the obscure but exquisite *Estasi* by Giorgione, one of Titian's teachers. The painting hung in Rubens' bedroom, a constant source of inspiration.

Some might translate the Italian title of the work as "Ecstasy," others as "Ravishment" or "Rape." All three ideas occurred to Rubens as he took a drink from the tray.

"Congressman Greene is here," said Greta, probably hoping to break his stare as the girl walked away.

"How very nice," murmured Rubens.

"He's over by the pool, getting ready to take a dip. You should talk to him later—he's running for senator."

"He is?" said Rubens, feigning not to know much about him. "Greene is from Kentucky, right?"

"He's on the Defense Appropriations Committee," said Greta. "You didn't know?"

"I can't keep track. Honestly."

Greta nodded. She knew that her cousin worked for the NSA, though they never discussed it. He doubted she knew what he did. More than likely she thought him a career paper-pusher, an image Rubens did his best to reinforce. He even doubted she knew Desk Three existed, though it was possible she had caught references to the supporting infrastructure through her work.

"Maybe I'll say hello to the congressman," said Rubens. "After I mingle."

"Good." Greta gave him a peck on the cheek and slipped away, leaving him with a perfect view of the waitress, who was now serving drinks to a cluster of leering white-haired business associates of Greta's husband. Rubens sidled into a position to watch her pass back to the bar, feigning interest in the band. He tilted his glass up in her direction as she went by as a signal that he wanted more. She nodded; it seemed a professional nod, however, and after smiling in response he turned to look at the stage, determined to be discreet in his ogling.

Which meant he had a perfect view a moment later when the lead guitarist did a full-gainer off the stage into the nearby pool, guitar and all.

Unfortunately, the guitar was still plugged into its amp and power source. Even more unfortunately, Congressman Greene had just gone in the pool himself. The enormously loud pop and the massive blue spark that enveloped the stage appeared to some in the audience as just another part of the band's act, but the odor of ozone and fried gristle that followed permitted no such delusion.

6

The first flight on the board at Gate Two proved to be a flight to Rzeszow, a city in southeastern Poland. Dean dutifully bought his ticket, though he had begun to have his doubts about both the woman from the rest room and the mission itself. Hadash had said it would be easy; Dean had doubted that, but he had at least thought it would be straightforward. So far it had been anything but.

Looking at the plane did nothing to assure him. The aircraft could be charitably described as a torpedo-shaped screen door with propellers attached. In fairness, the Ilyushin IL-14 had been a serviceable transport in its day; unfortunately, its day had come and gone fifty years before.

As Dean strapped himself into the thinly padded seat, two Polish nuns took the row in front of him. Undoubtedly their presence was beneficial, because the plane made it to Rzeszow in one piece.

Dean followed the others out the cabin door, down the stairway to the tarmac, lit in the darkness by a pair of distant lights. The passengers had to retrieve their own bags; Dean hesitated for a moment before grabbing the blue-and-brown suitcase he had been given back in the States. He snapped out the handle and began pulling the suitcase behind him toward the nearby terminal building. He had taken only a few steps when a Polish customs agent materialized from the shadows, demanding in good but brusque English that he follow him back to his office. Dean's muscles tensed and his eyes narrowed into wary slits as he studied the shadows for the most likely ambush spots. But rather than shanghaiing him in the customs office, the Polish officer led Dean through a narrow corridor at the side of the terminal to an outside door. He grinned and held it open.

A wave of paranoia flushed through Dean, but there was nothing to do but go through the door. For a moment he feared that the man's coffee-stained teeth would be his last memory of the world.

They weren't. A car waited a short distance away. In the driver's seat was the woman he had seen in Heathrow.

"In," she said.

"You want to pop the trunk so I can put my suitcase in?"

"Leave it," she said. "It's junk. Same with the carry-on. Clothes probably don't fit anyway."

Dean hauled the suitcase around to the other side of the car anyway. He might have thrown the bags in the back, except that the woman pressed the accelerator as he opened the door. He barely got inside in one piece.

"Did I do something to you, or have you been a bitch all your life?" asked Dean.

"Listen, Chuck, there's one thing we have to get straight," she started.

She didn't finish, because Dean had his hands around her throat.

"Enough is enough," he told her, nudging his right hand against her neck. His fingers held a small, very sharp blade made of a carbon-resin fiber he'd smuggled aboard the plane in the back of his belt. The material was only 90 percent as strong as the steel used in the best class of assault knives, but 90 percent was more than enough to slit a throat, even a pretty one.

"Your call," said the woman, whose foot remained on the gas.

"Pull off the road gradually," said Dean.

"I don't think so. We're being followed."

Dean pushed the knife blade ever so gently against her

neck, tickling her common carotid artery. It wasn't the best placement, but it was adequate.

"Have it your way, Chucky boy."

"Hit the brakes and you'll bleed to death in thirty seconds," he warned.

"Don't be so dramatic." She eased off her speed and pulled to the right, driving past a row of trucks. "It would take two minutes for me to die, if not three or four."

A blue light began flashing behind them.

"See what I was saying?" said the woman.

Dean nudged her throat one last time as a warning, then slid his hand down to the back of the seat rest as she stopped the car. A pair of policemen approached with flashlights. Dean noticed that she not only kept the car running but also had her foot hovering over the gas pedal.

He also noticed that she had changed her miniskirt for a pair of multipocketed cargo pants, which seemed a bit of a shame.

The woman waited until the policeman was at the side of the car before rolling down the window. When she did, the policeman said something in Polish; the woman answered with a laugh and the policeman laughed, too. Then the man became very serious, apparently asking for her papers. She dug into her jacket for them. It occurred to Dean that the policeman's angle gave him a pretty fair peek at her breasts, a view that she did nothing to discourage. Finally she handed over a thickly folded set of papers. The policeman frowned some more, took something from the middle, then gave them back. He and his comrade retreated to their car. When they were inside, she started forward slowly.

"What did you say?" Dean asked.

"That we're American spies and would kick his butt if he interfered with us."

"Seriously."

"I am serious."

"What did you really say?"

"He *is* nosy, isn't he?"

"Who are you talking to?" said Dean.

"Voices. I hear voices. I'm Joan of Arc. Didn't they tell you that, Chuck?"

Dean grabbed her neck again. "Never, ever call me Chuck, Chucky, or Chuck-bob."

"Chuck-bob?" She started laughing uncontrollably, and didn't even stop when he pressed the knife harder against her flesh. "Chuck-bob?"

"Explain what's going on."

"Hang on. I have another bribe to pay." She pulled over to the side of the road, which had narrowed somewhat since they left the warehouse area of the airport. It looked deserted, but it wasn't—a pair of headlights appeared on the opposite shoulder. They belonged to a Toyota pickup, which revved across the pavement. The driver pulled close enough to their car that Dean could smell his breath when he rolled down the window. Joan of Arc handed him an envelope and the truck flew away. She put the car in gear immediately, continuing down the long, dark expanse. After about a minute and a half, she took a turn onto what seemed to be a dirt road; fifty yards of potholes later they whipped onto a highway, just in front of a panel truck.

"One damn truck on the road for miles and it nearly flattens us," she said after accelerating from the squealing tires and piercing horn. "You're bad luck, Charles Dean."

"My friends call me Charlie," he told her.

"I'm not your friend."

Dean slid the knife blade back up his sleeve and brought his arm back to his lap. "What's your name?"

"I told you. Joan of Arc."

"You're not much of a comedienne."

"True. I like the meaty tragic roles." She shifted a bit in the seat. "Lia DeFrancesca."

"Funny, you don't look Italian."

"My parents are second-generation Italian-Americans. I'm adopted. No bullshit, Charlie." She glanced at him. "Look, we have certain ways of doing things, okay?"

"Like barging into men's rest rooms?"

"Got your attention. And I knew it was secure."

He couldn't tell whether she was smiling or not.

"Look, your only job here is to watch what we do," she said. She sounded as if she was making an effort to be nice, though it fell short. "You're just a baby-sitter. So don't get in the way and we'll be fine."

Before Dean could say anything, Lia jammed on the brakes and spun the car into a one-eighty. Then she started accelerating back in the opposite direction.

"Now what?" asked Dean.

"Now we board another flight," she said.

"Another flight?"

"They did tell you we were going to Siberia, didn't they?" she said. "They didn't tell you that?"

"They told me Surgut."

She made a face. "Not exactly. In any event, we need to take a plane. We've already lost a lot of time."

"What was all the business at the airport?"

"What business?"

"In the bathroom."

"You happened into a Russian agent."

"Seriously?"

"Yes."

"Was he tracking me?"

"We don't think so." Lia touched her ear. "No, we don't think so. So what if he knows? That's bullshit."

"Who are you talking to?"

"God, Charlie. God."

"Look—"

"I have a radio hookup," she said. "I talk to the Art Room. Fuck yourself."

"You talking to me or them?"

"Anyone who thinks it's appropriate," Lia told him. "You've got a lot to learn, Charlie. But at least you'll learn it from the best."

It was lucky for her, he thought, that he'd put his knife away.

7

Rubens stepped back as the sparks continued to arc above the bamboo of his cousin's swimming pool. He saw immediately what had happened and realized the grisly consequences—the guitarist had jumped into the water still connected to his amp, freakishly electrocuting himself and the congressman in what would undoubtedly become the lead item on the evening's news broadcasts. Rubens saw headlines and news magazines, articles and pictures, video interviews, innuendo, rumors, *Nightline* specials, and debates on *Crossfire*.

It was time to leave.

As discreetly as possible, he walked through the house to the front door, down the long driveway to his car at the curb, got in, and started away. As he turned onto the main road, he thought he heard a siren in the distance. He punched the CD selector, calling up a collection of piano sonatas from Mozart.

Hours later, resting at home in his den, he put on the television. CNN greeted him with a special graphic and musical interlude, just coming back from commercial break during a half hour devoted to what it called Congressman Greene's Unique Life. Rubens flicked the remote to MSNBC, where a pair of talking heads argued about whether guitars should be banned from poolsides. FoxNews used the occasion to roll out clips from other bizarre deaths, including one where a man had been gored by a rhino and carried for a mile, impaled on his horn.

The local television station showed a shot of police interrogating witnesses. His cousin Greta was being comforted by her husband in the background. Rubens felt a slight pang of sympathy—it was unfortunate that anyone had to be connected with such a bizarre media parade. As for Greene— well, he hadn't been the agency's most reliable supporter; hopefully his successor would prove more pliant.

Rubens pushed the remote again. A&E was just beginning a broadcast of *Carmen,* the opera based on Prosper Mérimée's classic story of love and betrayal. He settled back to watch.

8

The word *Siberia* had an almost magical ability to conjure a thousand images, none of them particularly pleasant. Yet the reality was infinitely more complex, as Dean realized scanning the vast plains below from the copilot's seat of the Antonov An-2 that had brought them from Rzeszow across the Urals, with two brief stops to refuel in between. A seemingly infinite pattern of green and black stretched forward over the horizon, blotches of land that, from the distance, seemed oblivious to human intrusion, let alone any predictable pattern of development characteristic of modern *Homo sapiens*. As they descended, the blurs and blotches of color gave way, first to brown and blue, then to complicated dots and swirls. As Dean focused his bleary eyes, the dots and swirls revealed themselves as roads and towns and clusters of factories and oil fields. The vast whiteness that Dean had imagined Siberia to be was nowhere in sight; this did not mean that it did not exist, only that it lay beyond the horizon of his imagination.

Dean put his hand against the dash as the An-2 began banking sharply. If the Ilyushin he'd taken earlier was old, this aircraft seemed to date from the very first days of flight. It was a single-engined biplane, with portions of its exterior covered by fabric rather than metal. Its large—and loud— 1,000-horsepower Shveston Ash-621R engine grumbled below Dean's feet, the swirl of its propeller at the nose of the plane a haze before his eyes. But the An-2 was in fact a steady, extremely dependable aircraft, and while its wings harked back to an ancient era they gave the craft amazing stability and maneuverability, factors not to be taken lightly when hunkering through mountain passes such as those they had taken through the Urals. These wings also allowed the plane to land on makeshift fields, which it did now, touching down on a dirt strip that seemed too short and narrow for a game of football. Dust and grit flew in a small tornado as they turned and taxied back; as the prop feathered, the pilot, who hadn't spoken a word on the flight, looked expectantly at Dean. Dean took this as a signal that he should get out; he undid his seat belt and squeezed back into the rear cabin.

Lia was already outside. As Dean landed, the engine whipped back up and the plane shot forward, almost instantly lifting into the sky.

"So?" he asked Lia as it circled away.

She didn't answer.

"This is Surgut?" he asked.

"No, we're a little north of Surgut."

"How far?"

"Two hundred miles."

"That's a little?"

"It is out here." She stopped, spun around slowly for a moment as if checking her bearings, then took what looked like a small cell phone from her pants pocket. Unlike most women, she didn't have a handbag.

"What about the radio in your head?" Dean asked.

He meant the question sarcastically, but she took it seriously. "Doesn't work everywhere or all the time. Here, we're out of range." She punched some buttons, waiting for a connection. "It's a satellite phone, Charlie," she said sarcastically, as if he had asked. "Yes, it's very small. Yes, it's secure."

Lia shook her head, as if he had said something stupid.

"Hey," she said into the phone. Whoever was on the other end must have told her something, because she answered by saying, "Well, kick ass then," and hung up. She slipped the phone back into her pocket

"All right, come on," Lia told Dean.

She began walking along a path crusted with thick tire tracks, the sort a tractor would make in mud. The field lay at the edge of a swamp and, in fact, had drainage ditches nearby; it had obviously been part of the swamp at one time. Lia's shoes were low-slung affairs, the sort that might be called sensible on a city street but here were barely up to negotiating the clumpy dried mud and ruts on the scratch road. Still, she labored on. Dean grabbed her once as she lost her balance; she pulled away without thanking him, and the next time she slipped he let her fall.

The road curved out from the field through a set of green rushes, past a scummy pond to a larger road. This road wasn't paved, but it was wide and flat, or at least flatter than the one they had taken from the field. As they walked along it, a swarm of bugs flew up so thick that they seemed like rain. Dean swatted and batted them away, but the swarm was thick and persistent; bugs flew into his eyes and nose and against his mouth. Finally he broke into a trot, running ahead, then twisting and turning like a kid playing keep-away on the school ground. The swarm was not easily dodged, however; finally he got away from the thickest part of it by running full blast for about twenty yards and dropping to his knees.

"They're a bitch, aren't they?" said Lia when she caught up.

"You have bug spray?" he asked.

"No." She kept walking. It might have been his imagination, but the swarm didn't seem to be bothering her.

"You get used to them?" he asked.

"Are you crazy?" She stopped. The land around them had gradually become drier; on their right a long, narrow field stretched to the horizon. Dust rose in the distance, a cyclone bent on its axis.

"You're the only woman I ever met who doesn't carry a pocketbook," said Dean.

"You don't get around much, do you?"

A small van materialized in front of the approaching cyclone. Except for its oversize double tires and a raised suspension, the truck looked like a standard GM panel van, the type a small florist in the States might use for deliveries. Its radiator grille had a symbol made of Cyrillic characters; otherwise it had no markings.

"Took you long enough," said Lia, who had to reach up to pull open the door when it arrived.

"Hello to you, too, Princess," said the driver.

"You're in the back," said Lia when Dean tried to follow.

"Don't worry. She's always on the rag," said the driver, a large blond man of about twenty-three wearing a Yankees cap. Dean walked to the back of the truck, half-expecting that it would take off and leave him stranded. He opened it and got in; cabbage leaves were strewn across the floor and there was an old wooden vegetable crate, but otherwise the rear was bare. Dean shut the door behind him and made his way toward the front, which was open except for a wide double bar with hooks for securing cargo.

"Name's Magnor-Karr," said the driver, twisting around from the back. He stuck a thick hand out to Dean. "First name's Kjartan, except nobody calls me that."

"What do they call you?"

"Asshole," said Lia.

"Tommy," said the driver. "Or Karr." His hand was callused, as if he did heavy work. His accent sounded as if he were from Hoboken. He reminded Dean of a kid who'd worked the counter for him at one of his gas stations before his overextended business went south.

"Charlie Dean."

"You're our baby-sitter, huh?"

"Not really," said Dean.

"Can we please get moving?" said Lia.

Karr rolled his eyes for Dean, then turned and put the truck into reverse. He didn't seem to use the mirrors and wasn't going particularly slow.

"If we go off into the swamp, I'm not pushing," said Lia.

"Not a problem," answered Karr. "We'll sink so fast you won't have a chance to escape."

"Hmmmph," said Lia, crossing her arms.

"You up to speed?" he asked.

"Of course," she said.

"I meant you, Charlie Dean," said Karr. "You like 'Charlie,' right?"

"If you're a friend," said Lia, in the sarcastic tone of a fifteen-year-old girl dissing friends at the mall.

Karr laughed. He turned around—not to look where he was going but to talk to Dean. "You follow baseball?"

"Sometimes."

"Man, I wish the Yankees would bring that kid Rosen up, don't you think? Kid throws ninety-seven miles an hour, and he's a friggin' lefty. I mean, what are they waiting for?"

"If you're going to talk about baseball, I'll just barf now," said Lia.

"Don't do it on your clothes," said Karr. "We don't need to see you naked."

"You'd give your right nut to see me without clothes."

"Trashy mouth, too. All the ugly ones are like that. Some sort of compensation thing going on there," said Karr. He turned and whipped the wheel of the van so hard Dean flew against the side. As he struggled to regain his balance, Dean realized they hadn't tumbled off the path but merely come to a paved road. The van's tires squealed as they accelerated down it.

"You're some driver," said Dean.

"Thanks. I can cook, too."

"A real man's man," sneered Lia.

As if in answer, Karr veered sharply to the right, following the road. Dean once more lost his balance, this time slamming against the back of the seats.

"God, kid," he said. "Give me some warning. Jeez. You drive like that for your boss?"

Tommy laughed.

"Is that where we're going?" added Dean, sitting back up.

"How's that?" asked Tommy.

"Are we going to see your boss? The person running the mission," said Dean.

Karr laughed again. "I'm the boss, Charlie. I know you've been in the dark the whole way out," he added. "Don't take it personally. It's kind of a culture thing, you know?"

"Not really," said Dean.

Lia turned around. "You wouldn't think they'd put a jerk like this in charge of sensitive operations, would you? He looks barely competent to handle a candy store."

"I'd love a few hours in a good candy store," said Karr.

"He's the head of operations in Russia, Charlie Dean," said Lia. She had a self-satisfied smirk on her face. "Looks like you put your foot in it, huh?"

"Ah, give the guy a break," Karr told her. "He's probably jet-lagged all to hell. You slept on the Antonov."

"How do you know?"

"You always sleep on it."

Dean felt as if he'd hitched a ride with a couple of college kids heading back to the dorms. He told himself he probably wasn't quite old enough to be their father. He also told himself he'd made a mistake agreeing to help Hadash.

"This isn't like the desert thing you were involved in," Karr told him over his shoulder. "This is just a quick look at some metal."

"What do you know about the desert?" Dean asked.

"Charlie, I know everything about you. I can tell you how much money you owed when the banks foreclosed on your gas stations. I can even tell you which companies were working together to put you out of business." Karr looked back and smiled. He seemed to believe that looking where he was driving was optional; he looked at Dean as he continued to speak, though the van must have been doing at least fifty miles an hour. "You helped nail a bunch of scumbag terrorists in the Middle East. Which proves you're resourceful."

It also proved that he was a sucker—Dean had signed on to the job because he'd bought a sob story from a woman who claimed her parents had been killed by the terrorists and she was looking for revenge. In fact, the hit had been set up by French and American intelligence services—probably, he now realized, including the NSA.

"It also proves he's a mercenary," said Lia.

"Nah. The gas stations were in hock and he needed the money," said Karr. "Right, Charlie?"

Dean shrugged. It had been more than that.

"See, the thing you don't know about Charlie Dean," Karr told Lia, "is that he's an honorable guy. When one of his part-timers needed an operation, he put him on the full-time payroll and paid his health insurance. Of course, the guy never really came to work at all, because he was too sick by then."

"What a sport," said Lia.

"And then the case blew the crap out of his insurance rating, so he ended up having to pay even more. That's one of the reasons he went under. Right, Charlie?"

"No."

Truthfully, it hadn't added much to the general downward spiral of his business, which had in fact managed to eat through most of the two million he'd gotten for the Middle East assignment. The stock market took care of the rest.

"I'm just not a very good businessman, I guess," Dean said.

"What are you good at?" Lia asked.

"Come on, Princess, stop riding the guy," said Karr. "She's just busting your chops because she has a crush on you."

"Fuck off."

"See if I'm lying," laughed Karr.

Part of him liked Karr. He was a big, garrulous kid, the kind Dean would have hung out with as a young man. But he was a *kid,* and his offhand manner implied to Dean that he was more than a bit full of himself. Dean had seen first-hand what happened to such types—and, all too often, the people who were following them on a mission.

And frankly, it rankled a bit that someone so young would be in charge of anything important. Dean wasn't sure he would have let Tommy run one of his gas stations.

Well, maybe.

"I sold my business," Dean said. "It wasn't foreclosed."

"Not a problem," said Karr.

"So you know who I am—who are you?"

"I wouldn't tell him jack," said Lia.

"Why not?" said Karr.

Lia didn't answer.

"Relax, Princess. Dean's straight up or he wouldn't be here. Right, Charlie?"

"Yeah."

"I came to Desk Three from the men in black, security team. Actually, I have an engineering degree, but I haven't used it in, I don't know, a million years."

"He designed toilet seats," snickered Lia.

Karr ignored her. "They told me they wanted me for the degree, but I think it was because I'm bigger than the average bear."

Karr laughed.

"You're pretty young to have an engineering degree," said Dean. "Isn't that a master's?"

"Very good, Charlie. I got into RPI when I was fifteen. What sucked, though, was that I missed the high school base-ball team. I'd screwed up my knee anyway."

"So what are you, twenty-five?"

"Charlie's writing a fucking book," said Lia.

"Twenty-three. How 'bout yourself?"

"Twice that," answered Lia. "Just about."

Dean, suddenly feeling defensive about his age, let the error stand. "So what are we doing?" he asked.

"I'm kinda getting to that," said Karr. He took off his baseball cap and ran his fingers through his thick hair. Not only did he consider looking where he was going optional, but he wasn't doctrinaire about having his hands on the wheel, either. "Basically, we have this problem. We lost an airplane the other day, and we're not entirely sure why."

"Maybe it broke," said Dean.

"It wouldn't have just broken," said Lia.

"Maybe it broke," said Karr, putting his cap back on and returning his hands to the wheel. "Anyway, what we have to do, number one, is make sure it was fried to a crisp on the way down. That's mission one—look for one major crispy critter in the tundra. Mission number two—maybe—is see if there's any clue about who or what shot it down."

"Why maybe?" asked Dean.

"Well, because if the plane really was burned to a crisp, there shouldn't be any clues left, you follow?"

"Your fancy gizmos can't figure it all out for you?" said Dean.

"Meow," said Lia.

"You a Luddite, Charlie?" asked Karr.

"I'm not a Luddite."

"Technology," said Lia in a sententious voice, "is a force multiplier, not a replacement for human intervention."

She began to laugh uncontrollably.

"She's making fun of the boss," explained Karr.

"Who do you really work for?" asked Charlie. "The CIA?"

Lia's laugh deepened.

"I figure you're the Special Collection Service, CIA working for the NSA," said Dean.

"Wow, he knows his history," Karr told Lia.

"I know Division D," said Dean. Division D was the CIA group charged with assassinations. He had worked with two members of it back in Vietnam and immediately afterward, though only as a "trainer" in sniping techniques. If the truth be told, the men he worked with knew at least as much as he did. Dean was a bit hazy on the connection between the Special Collection Service and Division D, but he believed that the Special Collection Service was an arm of Division D. Or vice versa.

"Well, listen, Charlie, if it makes you feel more comfortable, think of us as Special Collection on steroids," said Karr.

He turned around and stuck out his hand. "Welcome to the club."

Not sure if the kid was kidding or not—he seemed to

be—Dean took Karr's hand and shook it quickly, hoping he'd turn back around and pay attention to where they were going.

"We're one big happy family," said Karr.

"Pull-ease," said Lia.

"Except for the Princess. She's a loaner from Delta Force."

"I didn't know they let women in," said Dean.

"They don't. She's a transvestite."

"Hardy-har-har," said Lia. "A lot's changed since you were in the service, Charlie Dean. Who was your commanding officer, George Washington?"

"I think it was U. S. Grant."

They had come to an intersection, the first Dean had noticed. Karr stopped the truck. "Okay, Princess, you need freshening up or what?"

"No."

"Charlie, you got to take a leak?"

"No."

"Good. Then we'll go straight to Numto."

Karr threw the truck back into gear and kicked onto the road, spitting mud and gravel as he did. Dean had learned by now to hang on, and managed to keep his balance as Karr steadily and quickly brought the van to cruising speed. Dean couldn't see the speedometer from where he was, but he figured they must be going eighty at least.

And that was miles per hour, not kilometers.

"What's in Numto?" Dean asked.

"We think a piece of our plane. Actually, it's about ten miles beyond Numto," added Karr. His voice had become subtly more serious. "We'll stop in an hour or so and get some food. It will taste like shit, but you're going to want to eat it. After that, you want to try and catch some sleep back there. We work mostly at night, except when we work during the day, so your body clock is going to be fried, if it isn't already. Makes some people grumpy. Unless they were born that way. Oh, one more thing. I have a request."

"What's that?"

Karr turned around and grinned. "Don't get bumped off, okay? I'll never hear the end of it."

"I'll do my best," Dean told him.

"Good man."

9

William Rubens shifted on the ornate seat in the White House Map Room, doing his best not to glance once more at his Rolex. This was the reason he hated meeting the president, especially here; overbooked, Jeffrey Marcke ran perpetually behind schedule.

He had been summoned without explanation, though Rubens suspected it was for an update on the mission to check the Wave Three plane's wreckage. Two senators had made a polite though terse request to the CIA for information on the Russian laser system that had been Wave Three's target; the request had undoubtedly been kicked over to the White House, where the president himself would make the final call on what to tell the legislators.

A mountain of projects awaited Rubens back in Crypto City; Third Wave was the most prominent but hardly the only one. To have to kill a half hour sitting across from ancient but nonetheless tacky furniture and shellacked maps did more than waste Rubens' time—it offended his sense of aesthetic balance.

George Hadash entered the room, sweating so badly that he wiped his brow with a handkerchief. "Decided to hold a press conference on the new Energy Bill," said the National Security Director. "What a nightmare. Come on."

Hadash led Rubens around and out to the south lawn, past a cordon of aides and Secret Service agents, and down to the horseshoe pit, which was not far from the tennis court. The president had doffed his coat and tie but was otherwise still dressed in his standard work clothes: well-tailored suit and broadcloth shirt with sturdy-soled, rather plain black shoes. The pit dated back several presidencies, though it hadn't gotten much publicity until Marcke remarked in a *Time* interview soon after taking office that tossing the iron around was as therapeutic as "punching a wall."

Which apparently he regarded as a special pleasure.

"Naturally," said Marcke as his last horseshoe fell away from the post. "How are you, Billy?"

"Fine, Mr. President."

"Better than me, I suspect." Marcke smiled wanly, then retrieved his horseshoes. He pitched all four—he played without an opponent—before speaking again as he walked back to the other end of the pit. "We're waiting for Bob Freeman."

"Oh," said Rubens nonchalantly.

Freeman was the head of the FBI. Meeting with him could mean any of a number of things—most deliciously, that the Bureau was trying to track a double agent in the CIA and needed technical assistance.

Of course, it could also mean that a member of his own agency had gone bad, but Rubens dismissed the far-fetched notion out of hand.

Marcke let the horseshoe fly, nailing a ringer. "Have we recovered Wave Three yet?" asked the president, sizing up another toss.

"Still working on it, sir." He didn't bother correcting the president's misstatement—the mission was not to recover the Wave Three plane but merely to make sure it was sterile.

The president's shot sailed high, bouncing at the end of the box.

"Here's Mr. Freeman," said Hadash, pointing back toward the lawn.

"Very good." The president continued to pitch his shoes.

Rubens was surprised to see that accompanying Freeman was his own boss, Admiral Brown. Brown had just returned from South America. Rubens wasn't sure whether he had been summoned to the meeting as well or was just stopping by to report on the trip.

Probably the former, Rubens decided. Undoubtedly Freeman had gone to him first, not realizing the way things truly worked.

"Mr. Freeman, hello," said the president as the horseshoe clanked against the metal pole. "Admiral Brown—you're back from your trip."

"This morning," said Brown. He nodded to Rubens.

"Did you catch the press conference, Bobby?" asked the president.

Freeman said something about how remarkably well it had gone.

"Very nice of you to lie," said Marcke. He tossed another ringer. "It went over like a fart in church. They're going to hammer me on the Energy Bill. Not a doubt about it. Bob, you know Billy Rubens, right?"

Rubens grimaced—the president's use of "Billy" would now make Freeman feel as if he were entitled to use it as well.

"Mr. Rubens." Freeman stuck out his hand.

"Mr. Freeman."

"I'm a great admirer of the NSA," said Freeman.

"The FBI does a fine job as well," said Rubens.

The president retrieved his horseshoes. "Now that that's established—Mr. Hadash?"

"There have been some questions raised about Congressman Greene's demise," said Hadash, starting in an unusually roundabout way. He paused to add a few qualifiers, then said something about Congressman Greene's contributions to the country.

Rubens folded his arms across his chest, utterly surprised by the topic, though naturally he endeavored not to reveal anything except boredom. He listened with half of his brain and turned the other half to self-examination: How could he have allowed himself to be blindsided?

Obviously because the matter was absurd. The accidental

death of a congressman, even from the president's own party, was hardly a ripple on the ocean compared to the weighty matters the administration faced.

But surely that was one of the earliest lessons he had learned—Washington ran on absurdity. He should have anticipated this.

"What George is getting at," said the president, cutting him off, "is that some people don't think Greene's death was an accident."

"Nonsense," said Rubens.

"You were there, Mr. Rubens?" asked Freeman.

It was obvious that he already knew Rubens had been there, and the obsequious note in his voice undoubtedly registered with the others as totally bogus. There was therefore no need to underline it.

"Greta's my cousin," said Rubens. "It was her daughter's communion. I saw the guitarist jump into the pool," he added, cutting to the inevitable chase. "It was an accident. Bizarre, freakish, unfortunate—but definitely an accident."

"You weren't there when the police arrived," said Freeman.

"Really, do you think I should have stayed?" Rubens let his contempt peek out, ever so slightly. "There were plenty of other witnesses."

The president's horseshoes clunked against each other. He'd scored four ringers in a row.

"There are some legitimate questions," said Freeman. "Reporters have theories. You know what happens."

"Why don't you spell them out?" said Brown.

Freeman told him that there were rumors that Greene had been preparing to use his influence to have Greta fired as committee counsel.

"So she picked up the guitarist and threw him into the pool?" asked Brown.

Freeman held up his hands.

Rubens looked through the trees toward the south fountain, its white water furled into a rectangular mist by the wind. It was counterproductive to say anything; his boss had actually done an admirable job defending him.

Perhaps that was intended as a blind, though. Perhaps Brown had put Freeman up to this.

Paranoia. Rubens realized he was overreacting because he had been taken by surprise. It was important not to overcompensate.

"Congress is concerned about the circumstances of Congressman Greene's death," said Freeman. "And there's likely to be a call for an independent investigation."

"I'm sure it will prove to be a freak accident," said Rubens.

"One of my pathology experts says there should have been no electrocution," said Freeman.

"Then I suppose it was poisoning that he died of," said Rubens dryly. "Just like the media to get it wrong."

"My point is, maybe the guitar or pool was tampered with," said Freeman.

"By whom?" asked Brown.

Freeman shrugged. Rubens knew that as ridiculous as this all was, it could not be summarily dismissed. During the Clinton administration, the media and antagonistic congressmen had made quite a hash of Vince Foster's suicide, basically accusing the president of pulling the trigger. At the time, Rubens was a young buck in the collection operations area, but he remembered the controversy well. If such a controversy tainted him, he would undoubtedly be asked to resign. The NSA depended on its image.

A thought occurred to him: This must all be the work of Collins, the CIA DDO, trying to make a power play for Desk Three. She had all sorts of media and congressional contacts, and she wanted his job. It was even conceivable that she had set the whole thing up. She'd murder her mother to move ahead.

More paranoia. But not necessarily misplaced.

Marcke threw his last horseshoe—another ringer—and then walked a few steps up the hill. He held out his hands and a member of the White House staff ran down with his suit jacket.

"Our problem here is crazy rumors," said the president. "We all know that this was an accidental death. But in Washington, the more bizarre something is, the more plausible it becomes in the public mind."

"There were rumors that Congressman Greene pressed for information about NSA operations and was denied," said Freeman.

"Baloney," said Brown.

"Actually, if you recall the hearings, he did make a bit of a fuss," said the president, pulling on his coat. He looked directly at Rubens.

Surely the president did not believe that Rubens would assassinate a congressional opponent rather than let him join the Intelligence Committee.

However tempting that might be. Besides, Greene was hardly an opponent.

Now, someone like Senator Katherine Hilton . . .

"Anything else, Mr. Freeman?" Marcke asked the FBI director.

"We would like to interview Mr. Rubens informally."

"Not a problem," said Rubens. "If I can help the Bureau in any way, I'd be glad to."

It was an immense lie, as most lies in Washington were, and Freeman accepted it with a smile twice as phony. "Very good."

"Next appointment?" the president asked the man who had helped him with the coat.

"Education secretary for lunch."

"I'd like him roasted and turned on a spit, with maybe a light gravy on the side," said Marcke, starting back toward the White House. Freeman, walking beside him, gave a forced laugh.

"Take this seriously, Billy," hissed Hadash, who had taken hold of his jacket to hold him back.

"It's absurd and obnoxious," said Rubens.

"Agreed. But if the press finds out you were at the scene of a crime and then left, there will be fallout."

"Please," said Rubens, though he knew Hadash was in

fact correct. Still, it would have been bad to be there when they arrived.

Rubens turned back to find Admiral Brown frowning at him.

"Make this go away," said the admiral, starting toward the front.

10

Malachi Reese unclipped his MP3 player from his waistband and held it in his hand as the chemical analyzer took its sample in the torture chamber leading to the Remote Piloting Chamber down the hall from the Desk Three Art Room. The sniffer was ostensibly designed to detect the small range of chemicals involved in the manufacture of explosives; Malachi figured that it was actually intended to keep cyborgs out. Which was why he had thumbed "Cyborg Trash," an XeX^2 tune, into the player and cranked the sucker to 10.

The black suits didn't catch the irony, but that wasn't their thing. Malachi stepped forward as the green panel flashed near the door and entered the empty room, which looked like a cross between a flight simulator and a dentist's examining room. Dull blue lights in the floor led to the control seat, which was canted back about twenty degrees from vertical. Sensors snapped on soft yellow lights from the side of the room as Malachi sat in the chair, adjusting it to his preferences—he liked to sit upright, as if he were at a desk.

Which, in a way, he was. The controls in front of him included three keyboards as well as an oversize flight stick, which he wouldn't need for this mission. At the front of the room was a large, configurable plasma screen; immediately in front of the seat were three large LCD panels. At the left of the seat were several smaller, dedicated tubes with an assortment of affiliated knobs, sliders, and dial controls. On the right were two more screens. The top tied into the Art Room down the hall, feeding either a general shot or a picture of whoever was speaking to him over the dedicated circuit. The bottom tied into either SpyNet or whatever was on the main screen at the Art Room; a simple toggle switch chose the view.

Malachi set his music player on the small shelf at the left side of the seat, then slid his headset over the player's ear buds, fiddling with the arrangement for a moment to get the proper alignment. When he thought he had it, he reached beneath his T-shirt and took the small metal key from the string around his neck, placing it into the inset below the keyboard. The key, which had a chip-based random number generator in its small cylinder, allowed him to enter his two passwords into the keyboard. Given the elaborate security procedures required to get in here, the system designers had decided only a few modest protocols would be required to operate the controlling unit; the screen flashed immediately with the main feed from Orbital Platform Three, which the twenty-one-year-old had come to operate.

At the same time, the other screens popped to life. Marie Telach, who was in charge of the operation, popped onto the Art Room video screen.

"Hey," said Malachi to Telach.

"Hey yourself. You're late."

"Yeah, my shirt set off one of the alarms upstairs. Too much bleach—sniffer thought it was C-4."

"There is a dress code, you know."

Malachi grinned. She was undoubtedly referring to his jeans and T-shirt, which were a bit scruffy even for the NSA. Malachi relished his role as a bit of a rebel, albeit one with a patriotic cause. He could play the rebel because he was undeniably one of the best Ree-Vee ops on the planet, able to handle not only the complicated satellite platforms and their Vessels but also the high-speed F-47C and naval assets as well. (*Ree-Vee op* came from *Remote Vehicle operator*. The Vessels were like one-way space planes that were configured and launched from the satellites.) Ironically, Malachi had first attracted NSA attention for his math skills—he'd been accepted to Princeton as a fourteen-year-old—and had only stumbled into the occupation after an interviewer found him playing a version of AirCombat XXVII he'd hacked into a GameBoy cartridge.

"Our team is almost in place," Telach told him. "We need those sensors down. Now."

"That's why I'm here." Malachi popped the 3-D "sit-grid" supplied by the Art Room onto the screen in the center of his workstation. The grid was a computerized map showing his target. Based on satellite images, it could in theory be only a few minutes old. In this case, however, it had been constructed from the image library and was nearly a year old. There were not enough satellites and, frankly, not enough need, to have high-quality images of every corner of the Earth available 24/7. Malachi studied the view for a moment—it looked like a junkyard with some outer buildings—then keyed in the target destination.

The Vessels were essentially space-borne dump trucks, preloaded with different payloads. Three basic configurations were stored at the satellite platforms. All looked and operated the same. One held three dozen small sound sensors, bugs about the size of a quarter that could transmit back to the satellites for about four hours. Another held two dozen slightly larger motion sensors with roughly the same endurance. The last held a combination of both. The Vessels looked like small pipes with a sharp nose cone and blisters halfway down the side. The boosters had steering fins similar to those found on a standard air-to-air missile.

As the computer made its launch calculations, Malachi brought up the smaller panels on the left side of his console. He punched up a weather radar in screen one, updating himself on the progress of a storm he'd been briefed on earlier. Screens two and three had radar images of both the target area and a wasteland nearly a thousand miles to the northwest where the Vessel's parts would scatter after destruct. Neither of the images was particularly fine; objects less than two meters in length, such as the Vessel he would be piloting, were essentially invisible. But they were enough to give Malachi a decent idea of what was going on.

At least one of the previous Vessels had refused to blow itself up, and the operators had been instructed to make sure they landed in as remote an area as possible if, in the irreverent slang favored by the tiny coterie charged with controlling the space weapons, they didn't "go jihad." It was therefore important to know that he wasn't flying his self-destruct pattern into Army maneuvers. By the same token, he'd need to know if anything dramatic happened at the target area before making his drop.

By the time he returned his attention to the forward screens, the computer had calculated its launch, wing inflation, and ignition points, showing them in color-coded symbols on the main screen.

"Ready or what?" asked Telach.

"Almost," he said, picking up his MP3 player. He slipped the RCA plug into his console and togged the number three preset. G*ngs*rfx's "Buzz" ripped up and down his back, the bass good enough to set off a hum in the NSA earphones. "Ready to fly," he said. "I need a target time."

"Yesterday," said Telach.

"Can't you play some classical music?" asked Jeff Rockman. Rockman was in the front row of the Art Room, running the agents on the ground. "Springsteen or something?"

"Baby, we were born to run," said Malachi, typing in his command password to unlock the platform.

"How's the Civic?" asked Rockman.

"Chip's supposed to come today. We'll see how we do," said Malachi. "I got the Monsoon speakers in, though. Sounds awesome. Whole town shakes."

"Cool."

The computer queried for his mission authorization number; Malachi pounded it in, starting to catch the hard beat of the rap-metal song he'd dished into his buds. Malachi did a quick inventory check of the platform's available bugs—it was due to be restocked by Shuttle next week—then selected one of the Mixed Bag Vessels as his entry vehicle. The main screen morphed to a video view of the interior chamber—the top of the platform was covered by a solar array, as much to avoid observation by other space vehicles as for power. He turned to screen two and toggled a preset to put the 3-D mission profile there. The computer was suggesting a class one fuse—actually, a solid-propellant rocket motor—but Malachi, working from experience and still worried about the weather, chose class two. He had to confirm his suggestion twice with the computer—an annoying nudge installed by designers who basically didn't trust human pilots. Finally he watched on the main screen as the stubby motor rode down a track to the back of the selected Vessel.

The satellite platform's parts were not unlike those in the sophisticated plastic-and-electronic Lego sets Malachi's father had bought the prodigy when he was three, and if Malachi had been the nostalgic type he might have flashed on a scene or two of his dad, who had died in a traffic accident when Malachi was nine. But he wasn't particularly nostalgic; he popped off his headset, grabbed the MP3 player, and got up, walking to the back of the Chamber, where the small galley included a large refrigerator. He bent to the bottom and took out a Nestlé's strawberry drink (stocked here at his request), then took a straw from the counter and went back to his station.

"Today?" asked Telach.

"I was thinking today." Malachi slipped back into his seat. The engine had been strapped to the Vessel. The computer indicated it was ready to launch and, in fact, had started to count down for him, albeit at ten minutes.

"Move countdown to sixty seconds," he said, opening the bottle. He poked the straw through, still watching the screen. The computer ferried the missile from its assembly point, extending the long arm that held it until it was twelve feet from the bay. It then swiveled the missile slightly to obtain the proper launch angle. Platform Three was roughly twenty-four hundred miles to the southeast of the Vessel's target and, in fact, was closer to Tehran than Moscow. The rocket would propel it toward Earth at speeds approaching Mach 6;

it would hit the target area in just about an hour.

Or two and a half strawberry drinks.

When the countdown hit twenty seconds, the computer paused to ask Malachi for the go/no-go command. He quickly typed "GO"—it had to be capital letters, or the computer would freeze, yet another safety feature.

At fifteen seconds, the computer again asked if it was allowed to launch. This time, Malachi gave verbal authorization, as did Telach from the Art Room.

The frame jostled up and down as the main screen filled with pure white tinged by red and yellow. By the time the video camera adjusted its aperture, the rocket was gone. Malachi left the image on the screen long enough to confirm that the launch had gone smoothly; the rail was intact, with no visible scorching. He then thumbed exterior camera two into the screen. The yellow diamond of the burning motor dominated the bottom left-hand quarter of the screen; he knew from experience the launch was a good one. He tracked it from the camera for a few seconds, then took one last big sip of his drink and set it aside.

An old Beck song from *Odelay,* "Where It's At," rammed through his ear buds as he quickly worked through the instrument readings. Malachi watched the rocket's actual and projected trajectory on screen two, fingers starting to get twitchy. His control at this point was minimal, for all practical purposes limited to the rocket motor itself; it was like controlling an on-off switch that could be used a total of five times. The computer turned the dotted projected course into a solid line as the Vessel moved along, comparing it to a projected 3-D path that looked like a long tube of yellow spaghetti on the screen. Malachi watched as the rocket began dipping from the top of the tube toward the bottom; as it passed through the yellow into the black he killed the engine. Five seconds passed before the dotted line once more found the proper course; Malachi waited another three before initiating the relight. There was a slight delay in acknowledgment, almost enough to make him bite the inside of his cheek. The rocket engines had a mean failure ratio of something like .003, and the restart wasn't a sure thing. But the delay was due to a tracking glitch on SpyNet, which was ferrying over information from DEFSMAC satellites—just working out the initials alone was a hassle—and after a slight hiccup the main screen showed the Vessel was now perfectly in the middle of the spaghetti tube. Malachi leaned back in his seat, soaking in "High 5" as the computer baby-sat the Vessel toward Point Hydra, where the winglets would be deployed and he would gain more control over the flight.

"Looking for an ETA," said Rockman over sonic drone.

"On course and on time," said Malachi. He clicked in the main flight screen—similar to a HUD that might be found in a fighter, it gave a crosshairs and artificial horizon against, in this instance, a simulated backdrop of space and Earth. The forward video camera wouldn't transmit until much later in the flight.

"So you're ready to put the new exhaust in?"

"Yeah. Gonna be wicked hot."

"I'm thinking about buying a Camaro," said Rockman.

"A Camaro?"

"Classic '68. Has a rebored 302 in it. Engine is probably for shit, though. I've seen the driver and maybe I might trust him with a skateboard."

"Can we have an all-around update, please?" asked Telach, who was addressing the entire team involved in the mission.

The chatter dissolved as the analysts tracking various developments gave terse briefings. Malachi fenced the updates off in a corner of his brain, concentrating on his space plane. He leaned toward the control screens, gradually falling into the zone. Once he was there, everything would be automatic. It was like typing; he wouldn't have to look at the keyboard to know where his fingers were.

Five minutes from Hydra, the onboard computer did a series of system checks. They were all in the green.

He came over the Urals. Telach had to give the final okay to drop the sensors from the Vessel. He updated her regularly on the flight, even though she could track it from the Art Room.

"Preparing to deploy wings," he told her, edging forward in his seat.

The blare of another new tune from G*ngs*rfx—a heavy metal–rap piece that found a way to incorporate a tuba—nearly drowned out Telach's acknowledgment. Malachi got the view in his main screen; the computer helped out with a white box showing the Vessel. The streaking pipe was only forty-four inches long, counting the rocket motor. While theoretically detectable by three different Russian ground radars, the programming on all three would reject any returns from it as errors.

Malachi knew that for a fact, since he had helped develop the virus that placed the code into the systems.

The computer began counting down the seconds to Hydra. At H minus forty, Malachi cut the rocket motor but left it attached; the standard contingency plan called for using it to attempt to complete the mission if the winglets failed to deploy.

Not that they would. But you always had to have a backup.

At H minus three seconds, the computer flicked a small switch located nearly at the midpoint of the Vessel. This moved an actuator into position at the opening of four long tubes connected to the blisters on the pipe's body. At precisely H zero, a small nanotrigger activated. A flood of hydrogen gas shot into the blisters. The thin metal around them, already partially burned and worn by the friction of the flight, burst away. Hydrogen, under somewhat less pressure, flowed into what looked like a compressed paper bag directly beneath the ellipses where the metal had blown away. Like a butterfly emerging from its cocoon, the pipe sprouted a set of composite wings and steering fins from the bulges. Malachi got a tone from the computer that indicated the winglets had been properly deployed, then glanced quickly at the instrument data on screen one. There wasn't time to scan the numbers—he looked only to make sure they were all green, rather than yellow or red. He saw green, then quickly typed the command to lose the rocket motor. As he did, the Vessel began sending its video image back to the platforms above, which in turn gave them to Malachi, supplying a real-time image for his forward display.

The separation pushed the nose up and the Vessel began to jitter, not only making it difficult to steer but also hampering the pilot's ability to stop its spin and fly it like a normal aircraft. Malachi's fingers flew to the right side of his keyboard, thumbing the bat on the bottom and then poking the large red arrow at the right, initiating commands to deflate the rear fin and push out the leading edge on the starboard wing. His fingers flew back and forth for nearly thirty seconds, until the craft was completely stable and on course. At that point he began controlling it using the yoke, which operated like a standard pilot's control stick. His left hand rested at the base of a pad that could control the limited maneuvering rockets as well as the attack angles and dimensions of the winglets.

"Sensor launch in ten minutes," he said.

"Hallelujah," said Telach. "I thought I'd be filing my retirement papers before we got there."

"They let you retire from this outfit?" asked Rockman. "I thought they just took you out back and shot you."

"That'd be too easy," said Telach.

Malachi was too busy to joke. Stabilized, the Vessel was now gliding through 200,000 feet at about Mach 5. The optimum speed for dispensing the sensors in the Vessel's belly was just under Mach 1, and the computer showed they'd be going at least three hundred knots too fast. Folding the middle and fourth fingers of his left hand into his palm, he hit the top triangular buttons on his control pad simultaneously, telling the computer to inflate the leading edge pieces two degrees, the standard way to slow down the probe's descent.

Ninety-seven percent of the time, the procedure worked perfectly. This time belonged to the other 3 percent.

The inflatable membrane on the winglet was made from a sandwich of metal and thin plastic alloys. One layer of the sandwich was pure copper, and while it had a number of advantages over other materials that had been tried in its place, it also had a tendency toward hairline creases that caused problems under high-stress regimes. Pretty much by definition, the entire flight was a high-stress regime, and when the leading edge inflated now, the crease caused a dent in the winglet geometry. Within seconds, the dent created a strong vortex on that side of the Vessel; the new stress point made a hole in that part of the wing.

The hole was less than a millimeter, but it allowed a fair amount of hydrogen to escape. The winglet was constructed in small tubes or pockets, so structural integrity could be maintained, at least for a while. But even with the computer's help, Malachi knew he was going to lose the battle to keep the Vessel from sliding into a spin.

"Problem?" asked Telach.

"I'm out of milk," he told her, struggling with the controls.

Within a few more seconds, the control panel on the left went from yellow to red. Malachi opted for a trick he had practiced several weeks ago on the simulator—he jettisoned the winglets, guiding the probe entirely by the fins as if it were a missile. While doable, this complicated the sensor launch pattern.

"We're going to be a little off-target," he said.

"How much?" asked Telach.

"A little."

In the simulations, he had managed to get about 75 percent of the sensors within five miles of the target.

Something moved behind him. Malachi jerked his head around, a shudder of shock running through him.

It was Telach. She came over to him and crouched next to his station. "You're my man, Malachi. Do it."

"Hey," he said. While he appreciated the verbal stroke, her presence made him nervous. He tapped the keys with his thumb and pinkie, sweat pouring from his fingers.

"Ground team has to know—go or no go," said Rockman.

"It's getting toward day out there. Should I bag it for tonight?"

"Hang on," said Telach.

Malachi pushed his head down toward the keyboard, tilting his head toward screen two, where his course was projected. He was below the spaghetti tube by a good hunk.

"Go or no go?" asked Rockman.

"Just hang on," said Telach.

The computer had calculated new launch data, recommending a sweeping arc as he approached the site. The pattern would rob so much momentum that he'd have to find a new self-destruct site, but he'd have to worry about that later. Malachi got a tone from the computer, counted another three seconds, then hit the keys as the diamond-shaped piper in his main screen glowed bright red.

Twenty-eight sensors shot out from the belly of the Vessel as Malachi applied just enough body English to slip the spinning pipe through a pair of drunken-S maneuvers. They fell in a jagged semicircle around the target area, hitting it like a hail of rocks.

They were supposed to form a circle, but this was going to have to do.

"All right," said Telach, standing up. "Jimmy, you have the sensors?"

"Just starting to bring them in now," said the Art Room techie charged with hooking into the bugs Malachi had dropped. "Got a couple of dead ones."

"Enough for a profile?" she asked.

"I think so—got a couple of dead spots."

"All right, ask Tommy if he can work with it." She slapped Malachi on the back hard enough to make him lose his breath. "Good work."

"Thanks, Mom," he told her, scanning for a place to blow up his high-tech dump truck.

11

The canvas bag hit Dean in the back as he stood a few yards from the van, his hands on his hips, admiring the moon and wondering what the hell they were going to do next.

"Put 'em on, cowboy," said Lia.

Dean picked up the bag and held it as she walked toward the edge of a stone wall about eighty yards away where Karr was watching the nearby highway with a starscope. The moon was so bright it was possible he didn't even need the device. Karr gave her the scope and walked back toward the van.

The bag contained a thin vest and a pair of black pants. Dean stripped down and put on the pants, which were a little loose and stiff-legged. He pulled the vest over his black T-shirt. It looked and felt like the thin vest a hunter or skier might wear for additional warmth beneath a jacket. Karr explained that beneath the quilted fabric were flat tubes made from a boron alloy; the tubes could stop a bullet from an AK-47 at twenty paces.

"What's the deal with the pants?" Dean asked Karr. "They shielded?"

"Nah, just black. Princess is very fashion-conscious. That and they have a locator in them. If you get lost I can find you."

A car passed on the highway nearby. Dean watched the

vehicle move past, its headlights making a long arc across the empty lot and the building.

"Another hour they usually send a guard around," said Karr. "But we should be inside by then."

"What are we waiting for?" Dean asked.

"Just waiting. You a big coffee drinker?"

"Cup or two a day. Why?"

"You ought to give it up. Makes you too jittery." Karr walked over to the van and got in, emerging a short time later wearing a vest similar to Dean's. As Karr walked toward him, something sparkled in the northern sky.

Dean stared up at it. "Shooting star," he said.

"Nope," said Karr. "Not even close."

Karr stretched his arms and put them behind his head, staring in the direction of the meteor. Dean decided that he must be listening to something over the complicated com system that was partially implanted in his head.

He couldn't imagine working with something like that. You'd feel like a psycho, hearing voices.

It was a damn good thing they didn't have that in Vietnam, he realized. There was no telling what the people back at headquarters would try. He imagined being on patrol and having Dick Nixon whispering in his ear.

Dean laughed. Karr turned around, gave his own laugh, then went back to staring into the night.

The next step would be using pure robots, thought Dean. Maybe that was a good thing—better a machine got broken than a man killed. Still, it didn't feel entirely right.

Could've used this vest in Nam, though. Lightweight sucker.

Karr turned abruptly and walked toward him. As he did, he put his fingers to his mouth and whistled very loudly.

"They hate when I do that," he told Dean, tapping him and heading back to the van.

"They had some problems putting out the sensor net, but we're good to go," Karr said, opening the door. "Hop in. Princess can ride in the back."

He started the motor, then took a small handheld computer

from inside his shirt. He clicked a switch and a grid map appeared; another flick and a white-and-black diagram filled the screen.

"Are we going or what?" said Lia, opening up the back.

"Keep your shirt on." Karr slid the van into drive and they started rumbling toward the highway. "Here's the layout," he told Dean, handing him the handheld computer. "This part here is a set of pumps and piping for underground oil tanks; don't worry about it. We go through this fence, down through this storage yard to this compound. It's like an auto salvage place, a junkyard. Except the cars are hot, and generally new. That's where our parts are. If they're ours. We don't think there's guards, but we'll know in a minute or two."

"How?"

"That flash of light was a space-launched plane self-destructing. Before it did that, it dropped a bunch of little sound and motion detectors, okay? They're on the ground, and our people back home are using them to augment the other data they have. We wait until they're sure they have all the players set, then we move out."

"They can see what's going on in there?" asked Dean.

"Not exactly. There wasn't time to move the optical satellite that covers this region, and besides, it's night, right? Can't see in the dark. You're going to ask me about infrared, right?"

"Not really," said Dean.

"Not precise enough, not for this. This'll do; don't worry."

Karr cranked onto the highway.

"You can shoot, right?" said Lia from the back. "I mean, you *are* a sniper."

Dean turned to find Lia holding a submachine gun on him.

"Take it," she said. "I know it's a piece of shit. Just take it."

"Nah. Solid gun," said Karr. "Just old. Like Dean. He's not a piece of shit."

"Remains to be seen," said Lia.

The gun looked like a shortened AK-74, with a folding metal stock and an expansion chamber on the muzzle to control the gases when fired. It had a long banana-style clip and an oddly shaped flash hider.

"AKSU. Basically a sawed-off AK-74," said Karr. "We have to go native. But it'll do the job."

Lia had a similar gun in her hand and was piling up clips from a hidden compartment in the truck bed.

"Uses a five-millimeter bullet," continued Karr.

"Five-point-forty-five," said Dean.

"Very good. You've fired it before?"

"I've handled AK-74s," he said.

"Same thing except different." Karr turned toward him and smiled. He actually seemed to be paying a little more attention to the road now and turned his head back before adding, "Gun flies up more when you fire it than an AK-74. But it's pretty sweet."

"I think I can handle it."

"Hopefully, you won't have to. We want to avoid it, actually."

"Not to the point of getting killed," said Lia. She finished stacking the clips, then handed six to Dean. The boxes held thirty bullets apiece—a lot of lead considering they didn't want to fire them. Dean put one each in his front pockets, then stuffed the others in his pants.

"Smoke," said Lia, handing him two small grenades.

"Flash-bangs would be better," said Dean.

"Let *us* run the mission, baby-sitter."

"We have flash-bangs," said Karr. "You won't need them. This is all about subtlety, Charlie. Subtlety. We're not in Vietnam."

Under other circumstances, Dean might have told him to go to hell—or he might have laughed at him. Karr sounded like the typical know-it-all second lieutenant fresh from the States lecturing troops who'd been in the field taking shit for six months.

Dean shifted his clips around to get the grenades into his pockets. The vest did not contain pockets.

"Okay, boys and girls, show time," said Karr, pulling the truck off the road. A tall fence topped by razor wire stood thirty yards away; there was a second one just beyond it. Dean reached for the door.

"Hold on, cowboy. Put this on first," said Karr, reaching to the glove compartment. He took out a small tangle of wires and dropped it into Dean's lap. Unraveling it, Dean found that there were ear buds and a mike that clipped to his shirt. A long wire ran down from it, ending in a micro-plug.

"Where do I plug in?"

"Back of your pants, believe it or not," said Karr. "Kind of a designer's in-joke, I think."

Dean fished around and found a small receptacle on the back side of the waistband.

"Hear me?" whispered Karr. His voice had a slightly tinny sound to it.

"Yeah."

"It works through our satellite system, but you're locked off from the Art Room. Sorry about that." The NSA op reached down to a panel in the door and took out what looked like a thick set of skier's goggles. The sides were thick metal rather than plastic, and they weighed two or three times as much as goggles.

"Starscope," explained Karr. "Range is a little limited, but you can't have everything."

Dean slid it over his head, pulling the rubber strap at the back taut. The interior of the van looked like a gray, washed-out video feed. The aperture adjusted automatically.

"The image won't be as bright outside," said Karr, who took out a similar set for himself. "They auto-adjust. The brains who designed them probably thought we'd break them if we had a knob to fiddle with."

"Are we going or what?" asked Lia over the com system.

"Keep your shirt on, Princess." Karr held up his small computer for Dean, who had to slide the night visor off to see the screen. "Lia's point, I'm next, you're tail. We go over the fence, avoid the minefield, move across, and get to the big shack." Karr traced the path with his finger, then clicked on the button in the lower left-hand side of the screen. Displays of the layout of the facility flashed on, showing each member of the team as a green circle moving across the target area. "You're always in the back. You watch our butts."

"There people in there?" Dean asked.

"Oh, yeah," said Karr. "They're at the far end, though. I think we're cool."

"What do I do if they kill you?"

"That won't happen," said Lia, opening the rear of the van.

"Just remember, you're paid to watch," said Karr. "Come on. This is easy stuff compared to what you did in the Marines."

"How do you know what I did in the Marines?"

"I keep telling you, Dean, I know everything there is to know about you." Karr gave him a shoulder chuck and started away.

The way George Hadash had explained what he needed Dean to do, it had sounded more or less like glorified tourism. Dean had realized, of course, that there was more to the situation than what Hadash was saying and that there was a possibility of at least some danger. But until this moment he hadn't actually considered how much danger there might be. He didn't particularly relish the idea of being shot at, much less dying in the Russian wilderness.

Fear began creeping up his back as he walked across the field. It felt like a small monkey, nails poking slightly as it curled itself up on his shoulder. The ground was a little wet and Dean slid slightly with each footstep. The visor, though light, sat awkwardly against his cheekbones. The assault gun had an oddly unbalanced feel, seemingly all in the stock. Dean pushed it against his side, reaching up to his ear to adjust the com set.

"Keep your spread," said Karr.

"No shit," muttered Dean. He stopped, checked six, then crouched, trying to relax. The visor gave the sky a purple glow where the clouds cracked to let the moonlight through.

The sheds and warehouse looked like a shot used in a movie to set a scene.

A dark, foreboding scene.

Dean thought he heard a helicopter. He lifted out the ear bud to listen better, then realized it was just an odd effect of the com device.

"Don't fall asleep back there," said Karr. "We're at the wire."

"Not charged," said Lia, testing it for electric current.

"Go for it."

Dean heard a soft clang of metal as she started to climb the fence. He stopped about five yards from Karr, then turned to face the van. He didn't look back until he heard Karr's grunts going up the fence.

Lia was already inside the complex, probably at or even beyond the building closest to the fences. Karr pulled himself over the razor wire—Lia had covered it with a blanket—and went down the other side so quickly Dean thought at first he'd fallen.

"Your turn, baby-sitter," said Karr, after topping the second fence. "Keep in touch."

The Kalashnikov swung as he climbed. Dean paused at the top of the fence, examining the blanket covering the wire. It was made of a metal mesh and something similar to Teflon. He found he could grip the sharp wire strand through it without cutting himself as he pulled himself over the fence.

The second fence, much lower, had three strands of barbed wire on the top. Lia had secured these with a pair of what looked like carpenter's C-clamps, flattening them down. Even though Dean was careful, he caught the side of his pants leg against the barbs.

At the bottom of the fence, he checked his six once more and scanned forward and back along the fence line. Maybe their high-tech gear was worth something, he realized; without it he would have been worried about the bulky shadow to the left, wondering whether there was a gun emplacement there.

He left the fence for the back of the building, moving

toward the spot Karr had shown on his handheld. The position gave him a view of the yard beyond the structure as well as the approach to the fence and the field behind them. He crawled the last few feet, peering around the corner from the bottom. The steel warehouse had been constructed on a large cement pad. The foundation sagged about midway, and the warehouse wall hung down at a slight bow. There were some small floodlights at the front of the building, aimed toward the side. Their oblong circles of light left more than two-thirds of the alleyway in the dark. Across from the warehouse sat a brick wall that had once been part of another building; now it was just ruins. The back wall no longer existed, but the front remained almost completely intact, with a large metal garage-type door and two windows that seemed, at least in the night viewer, to have glass.

"More fuckin' razor wire," said Lia over the com set. "What the hell—do they make it here?"

"Eyes on the prize," said Karr.

"Dogs!"

Dean could hear barks in the background, then a faint *whiffff*. There was a whine, another *whiffff*.

"Shit," cursed Lia. "What the hell—they couldn't find them? Shit."

"Eyes on the prize. I'm on your left."

"Right, right—truck!"

Dean heard the vehicle and saw a pair of headlights moving well beyond the building. He moved up the alleyway to the front of the warehouse building, but he still couldn't see the truck. Karr and Lia exchanged a terse pair of curses, then stopped transmitting. Dean pulled out one of the ear buds, listening for the truck. He heard the motor somewhere on his left, beyond a row of squat shadows that had been drawn as one-story buildings on Karr's handheld. Then he heard something else considerably louder—the crackle of three or four automatic rifles working through their magazines.

12

Lia cursed as the bullets began to fly. The idiot Russians didn't have a clue where they were but were putting so much lead out that sooner or later they were bound to hit something. She had gotten her knife into one of the dogs as it came at her, and used the rifle butt on the second, crushing the Doberman's skull and killing it instantly.

Damn shame to hurt dogs. She felt like shit.

The Russians stopped firing. They had flashlights, and she saw them flickering about ten feet away, near the entrance to the fenced-in yard where she was. Then they put the lights out.

"You see where they are?" said Karr in her ear.

Something moved very close to her and she froze, not even daring to answer.

"Damn," Karr cursed in her headset. Obviously he was pinned as well.

Okay, Marine, Lia thought to herself. This is where you show us you can live up to your résumé. Get your cute butt in here and show us you're more than gray-haired eye candy, Charlie Dean.

13

Dean plunged across the large circles of gray-yellow thrown by the spotlights, running across an access road into a level field strewn with gravel and weeds. Three or four huts sat at the other end; the fenced yard where Lia and Karr had gone was just beyond it. At the near-left corner was the truck he'd heard.

What he couldn't see were people.

So all the high-tech bullshit was just that—bullshit. It was a liability now—if one of the other team members were captured, the Russians could probably figure out how to use the gear to locate the others.

Like him.

Kneeling, Dean unclipped the mike from the collar of his shirt and put it as low as it would go on his shirt, where he folded the fabric over to cut down as much as possible on any ambient noise. He'd continue listening over the headset; it might give clues on what else was going on.

If it came to it, he'd have to take off the pants and their locator device. Stinking high-tech toy crap.

Dean took one of the extra clips from his pocket, holding it in his hand as he moved to his right, flanking the truck and the small buildings. The perimeter fence stood on his right, near what seemed to be a generator shack; a motor hummed inside it and there was a faint glow from under the door, as if a night-light were on inside. Beyond this was a lagoon of muck, which extended beyond a chain-link fence. Inside the chain-link fence sat a row of old cars.

Or not-so-old cars. They looked to be Mercedeses. Dean still didn't have a good read on where his team members were or who'd fired the guns. He began edging toward the truck, moving parallel to the fence. Finally he saw something move on the other side of the truck and he froze.

A man with a rifle.

Short, five-six or -seven. Bulky, maybe because of a vest.

Dean watched the man walk to the front of the truck, scan down the fence line, then walk back. Thinking he might start the truck and turn on the headlamps, Dean lowered himself to the ground and waited a few moments. When nothing happened, he got up and strode as quietly but quickly as possible toward the truck, aware that he was exposed to any-one in the huts on his left.

There'd be at least one other person working with the guy at the truck. Otherwise, he would have left.

About twenty feet from the truck, Dean's boots splashed into a shallow puddle. He stopped, leveling the AKSU slightly lower than he'd normally aim, figuring it would ride up when he fired. He was worried, too, about the vest.

But the Russian didn't hear the noise, or at least didn't check it. That bothered Dean—maybe the man had moved away from the truck. Dean stepped through the puddle as quietly as he could, moving into a crouch. He slid the second clip back into the back of his pants, scanned around to make sure he wasn't being flanked himself, then edged backward, taking an elliptical approach to the rear of the truck. When he was less than five feet away, he saw the Russian standing a few feet from the tailgate, zipping up after taking a leak. The man glanced over his shoulder, then reached into his pocket to light a cigarette. He had his gun under his arm.

Dean flew forward. He was a step and a half away when the Russian heard him and started to spin around, bringing up his rifle. The short wooden stock of Dean's AKSU smacked the Russian in the side of the skull so hard he fell out of Dean's reach. Dean jumped after him, hammering the man's chin with his boot but losing his balance and falling backward on the ground near the rifle the Russian had dropped. Dean rolled to his side, levering himself up and throwing out his elbow to protect against the attack, but the sentry lay limp nearby.

Dean waited on one knee, momentarily unsure of his bearings. The sketch from Karr's handheld had shown an opening along that side of the fence, but he couldn't remember how far up it was.

He could hear something.

Feet on gravel. Inside the fence.

Dean moved behind the truck, then circled around. He saw a figure emerge from the fence line about twenty yards up. As he brought his AKSU up he felt something sting him hard in the side, an errant fastball catching him in the ribs. He spun, catching a muzzle flash a dozen yards away. The submachine gun on Dean's hip barked, the recoil easier than he'd thought.

Dean threw himself to the ground as the figure by the fence fired. He touched the glasses, steadying the image. The man he'd fired at had gone down and didn't seem to be moving. As Dean twisted his head toward the other Russian, he saw a shadow retreating away from the fence.

Still on his belly, Dean began following. Before he reached the fence, two figures carrying rifles appeared on the other side, back near the truck. Dean cut them both down, aiming high enough to hit them in the necks or heads above any armor they might be wearing. As he fired, the man he'd been tracking began to shoot as well. Bullets whizzed in the dust; Dean managed to crawl into a shallow gully and reload.

He lost track of the gunman for a second as he started to crawl out. Thinking the man had retreated, Dean climbed to his feet. Almost immediately, two bullets bounced off his vest. They barely hurt, but before he could return fire he lost the man again. Dean dived back into the ditch.

Most likely the Russian had a nightscope or something similar. Dean thought of the smoke grenades Lia had given him—they'd work just as well against a night device as they would in daylight. He took one from his pocket, thumbing off the tape. As he went to toss it, the gunman began firing again, this time with a much heavier weapon.

Adrenaline screamed in Dean's veins. He curled his body and leaped from the ditch toward the fence. The Russian had moved to a PKU machine gun a few yards from his original position. The smoke may have blinded him—his shots were wild and high—but also made it difficult for Dean to see.

Best bet, he thought, was to flank the sucker while he was focused on the smoke. Dean crawled sideways to the fence, rose, then shouldered the chain links until he got to the opening. As he dashed across, something grabbed him from behind and yanked him to the ground. In the next second, there was a loud explosion from above.

"About fucking time you got here," said Lia when the ringing in Dean's ears stopped.

14

Rockman studied the sensor grid. "They got them all," he told Telach finally. "Tommy took out the machine gunner with a grenade. Got him right in the head. Big mess."

"How'd you miss the dogs?" asked Telach.

"The spread," he said. "They must have been in the back of the truck sleeping. We just weren't close enough to hear. We knew where the people were. They would have stayed in the shed and the truck if the dogs hadn't gone crazy."

Telach frowned.

"Got movement on the road," he told her.

"Tell them."

"I'm about to."

15

Lia began trotting toward a pile of wrecked buses farther back in the lot.

"Is Karr hurt?" Dean asked, running to catch up.

"Nah."

"Where is he?"

"He started circling around to ambush them when you didn't show up," she said. "He just took out the machine gun. He's looking to see if there's anybody else our friends in the Art Room missed."

"Aren't we going to back him up?" asked Dean, grabbing her arm as they reached the closest bus.

She jerked her arm away. "He can handle it. Just watch my ass, okay?"

"She's got a cute one," said Karr in his earphones.

Dean reached to his shirt and undid the muffle, putting his mike back in place. "What happened to you?" he asked.

"I had to go deep. You did a good job, Charlie Dean. Noisy, though."

"They fired first."

"I've heard that before." Karr laughed. "Stick on Lia. I'll come over and play tail gunner. I always like the dirt road."

Dean walked past a row of Mercedes S sedans. There was a break in the row about ten cars down on his left; he turned up and walked past another two rows of pickup trucks, these mismatched among Fords, Chevys, and Toyotas. Beyond the second row sat a decrepit bus. Dean walked to the right and saw that the rest of the yard was laid out with various pieces of machinery and pipes. He nearly tripped over the bodies of two dogs, then saw a figure working at a piece of metal ten feet away, beyond a large Y-shaped piece of metal piping. A small blue flame appeared and danced in the air.

"Lia?"

"What?" she snapped without turning around.

"Just making sure it was you."

"No, it's Mr. Midas." She went back to cutting the metal.

Dean, his left hand on the clip of the gun, scanned the area to make sure they were alone. Lia kicked at the metal, removing a rectangle about twelve inches long. She worked at the remaining piece almost as if she were a sculptor, burning the edge into a wavy pattern.

"What are you doing?" Dean asked finally.

"Baking a cake," she said. "I think this is it."

"Okay, Princess, let's move," said Karr.

"Coming."

"Dean?"

"I can hear you," he said.

"Grab her and pull her out of there."

"Fuck you," said Lia, jumping up and grabbing the piece of metal she had cut off. She kicked the dirt around in what seemed to Dean a fairly useless attempt to scatter the bits of burnt metal that had fallen off and then cover her tracks. Then, as Dean moved backward toward the old bus, she started to run full speed toward one of the pickups on the right, tossing something in the back.

"Come on, Chuckie," she said, catching up on a dead run.

Dean started to run after her. "What's up?"

"Two trucks," announced Karr. "Mile away. Meet me at the perimeter fence where we came in."

Dean followed Lia out past the buildings, through the marshy field, and back along the alley where he'd originally been posted. Lia sprinted hard and threw herself about eight feet up the fence, hustling upward seemingly without breaking stride.

"Separation," she hissed as she hit the top and twirled over.

"Screw separation," said Dean, starting up after her as the headlights of the approaching truck swung across the far side of the fence.

"Charlie, take the blankets and clips with you," said Karr. "Don't forget them."

Dean had trouble with one of the clips, and the blanket on the razor wire was hooked on the inside of the fence. He tugged and almost lost it over the side, which would have meant going back in. Finally he got it and, barely holding his grip with his left hand, managed to drop it below. Just as he started down, gunfire erupted beyond the lot where they had left the van. Within thirty seconds, Kalashnikovs were roaring all along the fence line. Dean couldn't tell from where he was what was going on, and he didn't stop to observe, dropping the last eight feet from the fence, grabbing the blanket and tucking it beneath into his pants as he ran. A flare shot up from the access roadway, lighting the night. As Dean squared his AKSU in the direction of the gunfire, he heard a loud hush, the sort of sound a vacuum might make in a sewer system. It was followed by a crinkling explosion and then a loud rumble; one of the trucks had been hit by a small antitank missile, which ignited its fuel tank and a store of ammunition.

A second later, the compound they'd just left erupted with a series of explosions. The loudest came from the pipe area Karr had told him earlier to ignore—the underground tank exploded, spewing fire into the air.

Dean stared at it for a second, then realized the van was starting to move. He ran to it, grabbing at the rear door as the truck veered suddenly to the left. Somehow he managed to throw his weapon and then himself inside. One of the AKSUs fired from the front cab and then a grenade exploded nearby. Smoke and the acrid smell of burning metal filled the back. The van slammed to a stop and then quickly began backing up at high speed. Both Lia and Karr were shooting now—Dean fished for his gun but lost it as the truck tipped hard to the right, wheeled around, and sped erratically over the field, bouncing wildly over ruts and through a ditch.

And then it was over. The gunfire stopped, the ride smoothed out; they were on the highway. Dean couldn't even see the glow of the burning flares through the window.

"How you doing back there, baby-sitter?" snarled Lia from the front. She was in the driver's seat. "Pee your pants yet?"

"I thought he did pretty well," said Karr. "Sorry about the big bangs at the end, Charlie. That was mostly for effect."

Dean looked up at the top of the truck. Several rounds had come through the walls.

"Some effect," he said.

"The problem with dealing with the Russians is that you have to act like the Russians," said Karr. "You have to be as totally obnoxious about things as they would be. Otherwise they get suspicious."

The agent explained that they had made the operation look like a rival *mafiya* gang had hit the storehouse of another, blowing up most of their vehicles with a Russian version of C-4. Hitting the trucks on the way out was necessary, since a rival gang would not have missed such an easy opportunity.

"Plus we wanted to get rid of the part from our airplane," added Karr.

"Was it your airplane?" Dean asked.

"Looks like it."

"Now what do we do?"

"See, they found the wreckage and scavenged the engines," Karr explained. "But they also brought along a little piece of the tail with some Russian serial numbers. The Art Room will check it out, but in the meantime we're going to go to the place where they found it and see if anything else is left."

"Why didn't we go there in the first place?" Dean asked.

"Not my call," said Karr. "But I assume they had it under surveillance, saw that these guys took something, and wanted to find out what it was. It was the motors, right, Lia? I mean, you do know the difference between motors and wings."

"Oh, har-har."

"If you hadn't taken out the guards, we might have just snuck out," Karr told Dean. "But that kind of committed us. Better to blow all the shit up anyway. Plus I can't resist using the Russian bazooka. What'd you think of the pyro shit at the gas tanks? Wasn't that cool?"

"If I hadn't taken them out they would have killed you," said Dean.

"Water over the dam now."

"Wait a second. You're criticizing me for bailing you out? I saved your butts."

"I'm not criticizing you, Charlie," said Karr. He sounded almost hurt.

"We almost got killed. Your high-tech gear isn't worth shit," said Dean. He began surveying his body to see if any of the various aches and pains he felt were serious wounds. "And your plan sucked."

"Oh, please," said Lia.

"Well, the support team didn't cover itself with glory," said Karr. "I'll give you that. But we weren't almost killed."

"You got ambushed. If I wasn't there, you'd be dead."

"If you weren't there, we would've done it differently."

"I suppose the Marines have a better way," said Lia.

"A Marine operation would have had more people."

"And less dogs," said Karr brightly.

"Yeah. Your high-tech gizmos were outsmarted by dogs," said Dean. "Shit."

"Nobody in the Art Room has pets. That's the problem," said Karr, stepping on the accelerator.

16

Alexsandr Kurakin nodded as his adviser continued, talking about how Kurakin might refine his image for the coming elections. American-style election consultants with their polls and slick advertising styles had been mandatory since the 1990s; Kurakin himself had first used the consultants to win election to the state parliament. But there was a great deal of witchcraft involved, and he trusted these men even less than he did the parliament.

"Your popularity in the countryside remains strong," said the consultant, whom Kurakin privately referred to as Boris Americanski. The man gestured toward the chart he had projected on the wall, the gold of his pinkie ring catching a glint. He talked like an American consultant, but he dressed like a Russian gangster. Kurakin hated both, though necessity at times demanded they be used.

More and more he found himself a prisoner of necessity. Not since the breakup of the Soviet Union had Russia been so ungovernable, so at odds with itself. By any economic measure, by any social indicator, it was in chaos. The future promised by the democratic reformers had proven to be the stuff of a child's fairy tale. No, crueler—a parent's promise of a plentiful Christmas when foreclosure loomed instead.

Kurakin felt the bitterness more deeply than most of the people he governed. He himself had been one of the reformers; many of the now-empty promises had emanated from his own mouth.

He had been a true believer. He trusted in the people and the system to bring a better life to ordinary Russians—to his parents and brother still living in the east beyond the Urals and still, by any definition, ordinary Russians.

The president strode around the room as the consultant continued to speak. Some months ago Kurakin had moved his offices from the Senate to the Arsenal as a security measure. His quarters were cramped, altogether inadequate, but the move had been necessary. It was, to him, an important symbolic concession to reality, and to the course that he knew he must pursue.

Kurakin had lost faith, not in the people, not in the future, but in the system. Democracy did not work, at least not here. Special interests blocked true reform. Graft and corruption diverted energy and resources from where they were needed. Old hatreds—some even dating from Stalin's day!—poisoned the legislature. Rivalries in the military drained morale. He saw and understood everything, and it was his responsibility as president to fix it.

He would do so, but with his own methods. In parliament, a bill suggesting that the sun rose in the morning would not make it to the floor for a vote if it was whispered that he supported it.

The rebels in the south were an even more enduring and obstinate irritation. But he could not deal with them forcefully, as Putin had dealt with Chechnya, because of the Americans.

Indeed, Kurakin felt checked at every point by the U.S. The American president professed to like him—Kurakin kept his own opinion of the man well hidden—yet blocked Russia from taking its proper place as partner in NATO or the Middle East. More critically, the Americans threatened to call in their loans and end a long list of programs if Russia punished China for aiding the southern rebels or dealt too severely with the rebels themselves. The Americans had recently taken to monitoring the Kazakhstan border. It was a particularly egregious slap, considering how Russia had assisted the U.S. in its war against the Islamic militants in Afghanistan.

"The good news is, no other likely opponent polls higher than fifteen percent," said Boris, who'd been droning on, oblivious to the president's disinterest.

"The bad news is, I poll fourteen," said Kurakin dryly.

"It's not quite that bad."

"I still have my sense of humor," the president told the consultant. His approval hovered between 35 and 43 percent and had since the election.

"Historically, it's not bad. Look at Yeltsin. Russians love to hate their leaders."

Yes, thought Kurakin, unless they give the people a reason to hate them. In that case they love them.

The phone on Kurakin's desk buzzed. His appointments secretary was trying to keep him on schedule; his 7:15 A.M. appointment had already been waiting ten minutes.

"Our time is up," Kurakin told Boris abruptly. "Your check will be sent."

The consultant gave him an odd look.

"Yes, I'm terminating the contract," Kurakin said. "I've decided to go in another direction."

"You haven't hired one of the German firms, have you?"

"I'm not going to work with a consultant," said the president. "I'm going to handle things on my own."

Boris clearly didn't believe him, but there was little else for him to say. He shrugged and was still standing by the door when the president's next appointment was ushered in.

17

Rubens folded his arms in front of his cashmere sweater, staring at the distant hills that undulated beyond the glass wall of his house. The dawn was just breaking, and from here the dappled hills looked like perfect little mounds of untouched greenery; if you discounted the odd pockmark or two, they presented an image of untamed and untouched nature. But Rubens knew there were houses and roads all through those hills, and if the area wasn't nearly as developed as the geography immediately to the south and east, it was anything but pristine.

That, unfortunately, was an excellent metaphor for Representative Johnson Greene's death. From the distance—even from the ten or fifteen feet away that Rubens had been standing when it happened—it was a bizarre, ridiculous, and ultimately coincidental tragedy. Up close, it was something more complicated.

Rubens had been interviewed by two FBI investigators in the presence of an NSA attorney and a representative from the agency's Office of Security yesterday afternoon. It was clear from their faces that he told them absolutely nothing that they had not known already. It was also clear that they were very disappointed—obviously, they wanted to prove that the death had not been accidental. They undoubtedly saw the investigation as a ticket to better things, assuming they could prove it was something more than an accident.

This, of course, presented an enormous danger. Ambition was forever the wild card in Washington. At no level, in no walk of life, could it be ignored. Channeled, yes, but never ignored.

And so, having been blindsided once, Rubens had taken steps to find out everything he could about the investigation, his cousin, the band, and the congressman. Of course, he did not use the agency's resources, most especially the black computers at Crypto City. Anything he did there could be tracked and recorded. He had even eschewed his home phone and computers, even the gray one, which was equipped with a scrubber program. (Powerful, but not quite at agency-level standards.)

Instead, Rubens—William Madison Rubens—had gone to a public library to conduct most of his grunt research over the Internet. It was a good exercise, the sort of thing he would encourage a young operative to do to stay sharp. Deriving information without Desk Three's resources was a tonic, even an end in and of itself.

Actually, Rubens had gone to two libraries and made use of phone booths in three different diners. Were it not for the dishwater coffee he'd been forced to drink as a cover, the whole experience might have been considered oddly thrilling.

The results were somewhat less so.

The kid with the guitar went by the name of Trash, a fairly accurate appraisal of his station in life. Before joining the band his hazy history extended only as far back to his days as a teenage street person in New York City. He'd been recruited into the band when some of the members heard him playing guitar at a shelter they were volunteering at. A regular Horatio Alger story had ensued, Trash turning out to be a guitar genius with a special appeal to nubile prepubescent girls. Of course, to get the high gloss you had to ignore certain calculated self-promotional behavior, as well as a serious drug habit that leaned toward Ecstasy and an odd, if original, mix of Quaaludes, "crank" speed, and double-olive martinis. Rubens believed the martinis probably hinted at the young guitarist's actual pedigree, though he hadn't bothered to pursue that, and the young man's credit reports contained no hint of rich relatives bailing him out.

Prowling chat sites dedicated to the music scene, Rubens had picked up considerable gossip on the band. The guitarist's death had made the group a very popular topic of discussion in the extremely small world of people interested in following such things. Rubens was able to find a former devotee who called herself EZ18 but was actually a thirty-five-year-old schoolteacher in Edison, N.J. In an IM conversation that lasted three hours, EZ18 helpfully pointed out that the band's rise began when a middle-aged woman had befriended them while they were playing at a small but obscure club in New York City's East Village. She had given them considerable money, recommended a manager, and in other various and sundry ways pushed their career.

The middle-aged woman was Greta Meandes.

Rubens turned from the windows and began to pace. He was not shocked that there was a connection between his cousin and the guitarist. She was the family's token liberal and probably saw him as a reclamation project. There might even be some sex involved, though frankly, Rubens had never had that high an opinion of her.

Rubens paused at the corner of his room, staring at the massive Matisse that hung on the wall opposite the windows. It was an unknown and uncatalogued piece from the dancer series; six red figures (not the five in the better-known paintings) swirled around the green-and-blue field. The painting always looked somewhat off-balance to him, which was one of its attractions.

One of his phones buzzed. He let it ring.

What he had not determined, however, was who was behind spreading the rumors. They appeared sourceless, which naturally led him to suspect Collins. He had heard that she had had lunch with Freeman two days before. His informant suspected a tryst; Rubens concurred—pillow talk was very much her style.

If Collins was involved—he was admittedly not 100 percent sure of his source, a CIA underling who wanted her job—well then, perhaps she was doing more than whispering. Perhaps she had arranged for the guitar or pool to be tampered with, then drugged and hypnotized the idiot band member, programmed him to take the leap.

Child's play.

Unlikely, surely. Ah, but if he could prove that—if he could find the smoking guitar, so to speak, he might be through with her forever.

The idea was too delicious to avoid. A ridiculous long shot, yes—but it would bring such indescribable joy.

Now he realized why poor people played the lottery.

His next step was to find out if the guitar or the pool had been tampered with. Obviously the local police would attempt to do so as well; quite possibly they already knew the answer.

Or not. He doubted their inquiry would be expert.

There were pedestrian reasons for finding out, reasons that had nothing to do with Collins. If he had a report that declared everything in order, it could be leaked to the press. It would end their interest abruptly. The rumors would dry up; there would be no reason for anyone to find out that he was at the scene, et cetera, et cetera—problem quashed.

How could he examine the guitar and the pool without involving the NSA?

He might suggest the idea to the police, arrange the technical help, then get access to the findings. That could be done quietly if he recommended the company, one that did work for him.

But the FBI would then get access to the report. Freeman would see it.

Of course. The FBI should do the work in the first place. He would hold Mr. Freeman close—very close.

Not quite as close as Ms. Collins was, certainly.

But then he wouldn't want the lab to be easily connected to him. Hadn't there been a Division D project to electrocute a KGB agent in a backyard pool during the 1960s?

That was before Collins' time, but still, she'd know about it. She always did.

The phone rang again. This time the programmed ring pattern told Rubens that it was his driver, waiting outside to take him to Crypto City. He'd arranged to use the driver—who doubled as a bodyguard—for the duration of the mission to make sure the Wave Three plane had been destroyed.

Rubens walked to the kitchen and bent to the refrigerator drawer in the cabinets. He took out one of his bottles of Belden bottled water, then went down to meet the driver.

An hour later, Rubens passed through the security gauntlet and entered the Art Room, where Telach updated him on the progress of the Wave Three team. At the bottom of her eyes were hanging bags so deep, she looked like she was growing a new face. But if he asked her if she was tired she would have insisted she wasn't, and she would have fought—probably with her fists—any suggestion that she catch a nap in one of the nearby "comfort" rooms. She never wanted to leave the Art Room, much less go off-duty, once an operation was under way. It was a quality Rubens prized highly in selecting Art Room staff.

"The wreckage at Slveck is ours," Telach told him.

"Svvlee-veck," said Rubens, correcting her pronunciation.

"The team is en route. They're meeting with Fashona and the Hind."

"The Petro-UK Hind?"

"We don't have another, do we? Besides, they needed an acceptable cover. The weapons are boxed and hidden in the hold."

"What about the satellite images?"

"Inconclusive." She made the face of a woman who had just tasted the world's most sour grapefruit. "It absolutely burnt to a crisp, but the bastards at the CIA are sitting on the goddamn analysts and telling them not to sign off. That's what the problem is."

Rubens nodded. Petro-UK was one of the shell companies

Desk Three had established for operations in Russia and the Middle East. It was thought by most intelligence agencies, including Russia's, to be a front for the Chinese.

"I'd hate to lose the Hind," said Rubens.

"Hopefully it won't be compromised, but we seem to be star-crossed on this one." Telach told him what had happened at the auto yard.

"They should have used a Bagel," said Rubens, referring to a small UAV surveillance system.

"They didn't have one with them," she said.

Rubens said nothing, realizing it was counterproductive at this point to criticize or second-guess. The UAVs were cached in kits the ops referred to as S-1s and were rather bulky to transport; having one with them increased their security concerns, especially in a place like Siberia, where even a pickup truck stood out. Besides, the Space Platform/Vessel system had been designed exactly for that type of operation in a relatively remote area.

"How's Mr. Dean doing?" Rubens asked.

Telach shrugged. "He hasn't gotten in the way. Karr seems to like him."

"Tommy likes everybody," said Rubens. "What does Lia think?"

Telach gave a snort. "She hasn't castrated him yet. That's a plus."

"Well, see that she doesn't."

"Karr wants to know if it's OK to implant him."

"Is that necessary?"

Telach shrugged. "We're having some difficulties with communications out there anyway. It'd probably just be a waste of time."

"Then don't. He's not ours."

Implanting was slang for surgically placing the small com and locator devices on an op's body. Coverage in some areas was limited by satellite position as well as active government interference programs, even though they weren't aimed specifically at the NSA's system. It was almost impossible to use the devices in Israel and a good portion of the Arab countries near it. Both Russia and China were obviously studying and applying some of the Israeli techniques. A new system relying on laser technology was being readied, but it, too, had limitations.

Rubens glanced at the board in the front of the room, which showed a large map of north-central Siberia. The team's position and target were marked by blipping lights, blue and red respectively. They were nearly two hundred miles apart.

"They're on the Hind?" Rubens asked, noting that the blue light was moving.

"Yes. Just refueled."

"Tell them not to break it, will you? It cost a fortune."

18

The helicopter was a stripped Mi-24W Hind E, in its day one of the most formidable attack helicopters in the world. Unlike American Cobras, Apaches, or the new Comanche, the Hind had a cargo compartment that could hold at least eight fully armed men. While vulnerable to even primitive heat-seeking missiles, the helicopter nonetheless had proven itself a fearsome weapon, most notably during the Russian–Afghanistan War.

This particular model dated from roughly that time period, though it had served with a Polish Army Aviation unit. It had been stripped by the government for private sale, which meant that when it was sold its nose did not include its nasty chain gun and the large wing pylons could not operate weapons. It also lacked advanced night navigation equipment and a host of other gear that would have been considered de rigueur on any of the machines still serving with several eastern armies, including Russia's.

A thin coat of gray paint covered its green-shade camouflage; the name Petro-UK, the NSA cover company that owned it, was stenciled in bright white on the fuselage. Externally, there seemed to be few other improvements from the condition it had been sold in, but as with anything associated with Desk Three, appearances could be quite deceptive. With some slight adjustments and the removal of two thin screws, the hard points could host a wide variety of missiles and rockets. The choice was in fact greater than what was available to the helicopter's Polish commanders. The navigation system included GPS gear with a comprehensive CD-ROM topo library of all Russia. The FLIR in the helicopter's nose could reliably see a mouse on a hot stove at 3,000 yards.

The interior accommodations were more spartan than those of the Hueys and Blackhawks Dean was familiar with. He took a seat on the thin bench opposite one of the fuselage windows, holding the nearby brace—a painted pipe—as the rotors began to spin. The engine coughed a few times, then seemed to smooth out, and finally stalled.

Dean looked over at Karr, who was peering through the narrow door to the pilot's cabin. The team leader turned toward him, gave him a thumbs-up, then looked back toward the cabin as the rotors once more began to revolve. This time the engines ripped into a fury. The chopper tipped forward and lifted away in seconds.

"So at some point," Dean said to Karr when he sat on the bench next to him, "you're going to lay this all out for me."

Karr glanced at him. "Basically, we're going to look at the wreckage, make sure it's really wrecked."

"Where is it?"

"Couple hundred miles from here, in a field or a bog near a road. We take a look at it; maybe we pack up some of the wreckage and send it home with you. Good enough?"

Dean shrugged. "I guess."

They settled in for a while, Tommy on the other side of the bench, Lia back at the rear of the cargo hold. Dean, exhausted from the workout at the junkyard, dozed off for more than an hour. When he finally woke, he saw that Lia was watching him. She scowled, then got up and walked toward him. She held an odd-looking box in her hand; at the bottom was a grip and trigger, as if the bottom half of a pistol had been melted into the metal. She handed it to Dean, who didn't know what to make of it. "Careful, sniper boy; it's loaded," she said.

"This is a G11?" he asked, recognizing that it was a high-tech gun.

"Give me a break," said Lia, turning and going back to the chest.

"No, actually, you're close," said Karr, twisting around. "It's a caseless machine gun designed by H & K, with a little help from our technical section. That's a laser dot at the top port there. Depress the sighting trigger on the right." He reached to the side of the long box behind the pistol grip, where a large gray button sat. "The targeting laser will stay on, showing you where to hit. There are two modes. One's standard op, which means basically that anyone can see the light. The other is infrared. You need to use it with your glasses. To be honest, I wouldn't bother with that. Someone sees the light, they're dead anyway, right?"

Dean turned the gun over in his hands. It was just over three feet long, a bit shorter than an M16, but a few inches longer than a G11, which was the first—and, as far as Dean had known until now, only—caseless assault rifle in the world.

The G11 had been designed by Heckler & Koch to answer an age-old army requirement—increasing the probability of a first-trigger hit. The physics involved in firing a bullet inevitably affect the aim of a gun. While there are many advantages to using an automatic weapon that can spit a number of bullets with one press of the trigger, some of those advantages are offset by the natural reaction of the gun. Even in well-trained, experienced hands, an assault rifle will begin to climb as the first shot is fired, so that on three-shot burst mode there will almost always be a wide spread of bullets—in other words, a good chance of not hitting what you're aiming at. True, the fact that you get three cracks at your target with a single press of the trigger is a definite plus. But an inexperienced soldier in combat—actually, most soldiers in combat—can't control even a superb weapon like the M16 sufficiently to guarantee a first-trigger hit.

Examining the problem, the Heckler & Koch engineers decided that the best way to improve first-hit probability was with a three-shot burst that wasn't affected by recoil at all. They therefore decided to design a rifle that could fire three shots before the gun's recoil could affect them. The design necessitated caseless ammunition, which at 4.7mm was significantly smaller than the ammunition used in M16s. That led to the G11.

"A hundred and two rounds," said Karr. He pointed to the front of the box. "This slides back by turning the piece here. It's not easy under fire. That's the main drawback. You've used the G11?"

"No," said Dean, still examining the gun. "I heard of it."

"This is pretty similar, except you can select five-shot bursts as well as three- and full automatic. Even full there's almost no recoil. Seriously. They call it an A-2, but I don't know if there was ever an A-1. Pretty loud. The bullets sound like they're one long cannon shot. I'd leave it on three-shot unless the entire Russian army comes over the hill. Very, very accurate. If you're any good, all three bullets right into the dot at three hundred yards. If you're terrible, the spread's maybe a half an inch. Give or take."

"I only need one bullet."

Karr grinned. "Yeah, but you have to fire three. Guess they didn't figure NSA dweebs would be much good at shooting."

"They got that right," said Lia.

"Does the small caliber stop anybody?"

"Well, you won't stop a tank," said Karr. "But it's close to a NATO round and you get a muzzle velocity out near nine hundred, nine hundred thirty meters a second. That's better than an M24. Right? And it's three bullets, on the dot."

Dean grunted. The kid did know a few things about guns, at least. Dean held the A-2 up. The laser danced around the interior of the helicopter.

"Would have made more sense to activate the laser by touching the trigger," he said.

"I gather the trigger assembly is tricky," said Karr. "Besides, it's not a sniper weapon; it's an assault gun."

Dean wondered what they might give a sniper these

days—probably radio-guided bullets. The A-2 felt more like a toy than a gun. He put its muzzle down and clicked off the sighting device.

"Don't shoot unless you have to," Karr said.

"I never do."

The helicopter began to bank. Karr got up and went to the cargo door, looking through the large window at the top. Lia, with a binocular and one of the guns in her hand, came and stood beside him. The helicopter took a wide circuit, orbiting around their target area. Karr wrestled with the door mechanism, pounding a few times with his fist before rearing back and kicking. The door unfolded downward with a thick *clunk*. The helo completed two more turns, then settled into an unsteady hover. Dean gripped the bottom of his seat, worried that he might spill forward. Lia pulled a small digital camera from one of her pants pockets and began taking photos.

The front end of the helicopter suddenly pushed forward and down. It rammed hard against the ground and Dean found himself sprawling on the floor. He rolled to his feet, expecting to see a fire or smoke or something, but the cabin was empty; the others had hopped out. Apparently the jolt was nothing more than a routine landing, as the rotors were still spinning and the helicopter seemed intact.

Which was more than could be said for the aircraft sprawled along the ground in front of him.

Not that it looked like an aircraft. Twisted sheets of metal lay in different jags in the mushy tall grass. Odd wires, shards of glass, and toothy spars that looked like chewed-up I-beams dotted the ground. Dean walked along the trail of metal, gradually catching up to Karr and Lia, who were standing over what looked like a black shroud about twenty feet long. Karr appeared to be talking to himself, but Dean realized he must be using his com device to talk to the NSA support people in what they called the Art Room. Dean adjusted his ear buds and mike, calling to Lia to make sure his unit was working.

"You're supposed to be watching the road," she told him.

"Why don't you watch it, Princess?" Dean told her.

"Don't *ever* call me that," she hissed.

Dean hung back near the road as she circled the wreckage area. Most of the ground was solid, but there were large patches of muck and deep mud. In one or two places water puddled in shallow pools a few feet wide. Dean walked down toward the road a ways, checking to see if there were any parts here. He'd heard stories about people finding intact luggage, wallets, shoes, and clothing at crash sites, and wondered if he would find any.

He also wondered if he'd find anything more gruesome.

"Here," said Lia, calling to him. Dean trotted over, thinking she'd found something, but she was pointing to empty grass.

"What?"

"One of the engines was here. They saw them from the road, see?" She pointed.

"OK."

"The other one they took—there." She pointed again. This time the marks were more obvious—there was a gouge in the dry earth. The tail fin had probably lain right next to it.

They checked around but found nothing else. Lia straightened suddenly, said "OK," and began jogging toward the helicopter. Dean watched her, thinking again how pretty she was. As he stared, she got into the Hind and it lifted off.

Karr slapped him on the back as he watched it go.

"I want you to work from this side over," said Karr, handing him what looked like an oversize electric tester with a microphone instead of a set of probes. "Tell me if the needle moves."

"What am I looking for?"

"That's a sniffer. If it detects certain chemicals, the needle will move."

"So what am I looking for?"

"Human remains. Preferably incinerated."

19

When he reached his office, Rubens found a note on top of the blanket he routinely threw over the desktop to cover any classified material inadvertently left there. It was from Admiral Brown, in his usual shorthand—"Me ASAP."

It meant Rubens should see him immediately. Rubens folded the note and then inserted it into one of his shredders; it was an unnecessary reflex.

There was a whole list of calls to make, projects to check; each was undoubtedly more important than whatever his superior wanted, in Rubens' opinion. But demanding an immediate audience was his superior's prerogative, and so Rubens left his office and went down the hallway, sticking his head through the portal so the admiral's administrative assistant could see him.

Connie Murphy had served under three different directors and probably knew more about the agency than anyone else. She also was pushing seventy, at least.

"Mr. Rubens." Connie sounded like a third-grade teacher nipping off trouble in the back row. "We've been waiting."

"I just saw the note."

"You were paged."

"I was in the Art Room." The security precautions prevented the paging system from reaching him there; the system would have automatically rerouted to his voice mail.

"Yes." She picked up the black handset on her desk and tapped on the intercom.

"How's the bingo?" asked Rubens, waiting for the admiral to pick up the line.

"Proceeding," she said. "Five cards yesterday evening."

Rubens wasn't sure whether that meant she had won on five cards or merely played them. "Is that good?"

"Better than would be expected."

The admiral finally picked up on the other end. She said one word—"Rubens"—then looked up at him. "You may go in," she said.

Inside, he found that Brown already had someone in his office—Collins of the CIA.

Rubens was too well practiced to reveal his true feelings to the DDO, though she undoubtedly knew what they were. He bowed his head graciously to one side.

"Ms. Collins, so nice to see you today. Admiral." Rubens helped himself to a chair. As a gesture of strength, he pushed it so close to hers that it nearly touched. She repositioned her legs—which were in rather ordinary blue pants—as he sat.

"The CIA has a theory," said Admiral Brown. "The deputy director came here to explain it in person. They believe a coup is being planned in Russia."

Here was a dilemma. Rubens and George Hadash had discussed the possibility of a coup just a week ago when analyzing the frustration of the hard-liners in the Russian parliament. Rubens thought it not only possible but perhaps even probable; in fact, he had had a team sifting the tea leaves for evidence that they were right.

Evidence that had thus far eluded them.

To admit this, however, could be interpreted as saying that the agency not only was correct but also had beaten him to the punch. On the other hand, denying the possibility of a coup would be arguably worse, most especially if his own people did come up with evidence.

The straight play was to admit everything. But he dared not do that with Collins until he fully understood her agenda.

Rubens straightened his shoulders, then moved his legs, momentarily brushing Collins. He felt her jerk back.

"Hard evidence?" he asked.

"There are . . . indications," said Collins.

"Hmmm," said Rubens.

They had nothing more than guesses, he decided.

Or was she being coy?

"We're going to the president with an estimate tonight," she added.

"Of course," said Rubens, who now had to assume that they did have evidence. "Can we see it before then?" The estimate would be a high-level intelligence summary of the situation.

"It's not ready. The team is working very close to deadline. I'm here to ask for more help."

"If it's in my power, it's yours," said Rubens. He couldn't help but sweep his arms.

"Thanks." There was just the slightest twinge of sarcasm in her voice. "Amy Gordon and Bill Kritol are with the Sigint and Collection people."

"Sounds like you have it under control," said Rubens.

"I do." She rose. "Mr. Director, William, thank you for your time."

Rubens watched her leave. Whatever her age, she had the hips and butt of a twenty-year-old swimsuit model. Even in pants.

"Pretty cold," said Brown.

You'd be surprised, Rubens thought. But he simply nodded.

"What do you think?"

"It has been a concern. I discussed it with George Hadash last week in an offhanded way."

Brown's eyebrow shot up involuntarily.

"It was purely theoretical," added Rubens. "We are, however, looking at intercepts. The normal thing."

"Collins was practically gloating," said Brown. "She thought she had stolen a march on you."

Rubens smiled. Anyone else would have denied it, shaken

his head, said, "Absolutely not." But the feigning humility was considerably better. It was a gesture people remembered and valued.

"She may have beaten us," said Rubens, confident that Brown would think exactly the opposite. "Did you two have a long chat?"

"Hardly."

There was no subtle way to get him to elaborate, and so after a suitable pause to make sure the admiral had nothing else to say, Rubens rose and said good-bye.

"Is she always that . . . frigid?" Brown asked, having trouble finding the right word.

"Not always," he said. "Not nearly."

20

By the time Dean heard the truck coming, Karr had already begun walking toward the road. Dean trotted up to him, A-2 rifle parallel to the ground. Karr put his hand out to lower it. "Ours," he said.

Maybe it was, but it looked like a Russian Ural-375, the ubiquitous 6×6 that was to the Russian Army what the M35 series once was to the U.S. It had rather garish red stars on its dull white cabin, and a canvas top flapped loosely over the slatted sides. The truck stopped on the road, then backed off toward Karr, stopping when the muck reached halfway up the deep treads of the tire.

"Gotta load it on the highway," said Karr.

The truck whined and groaned as the driver ground the gears and shoved it forward to the drier ground, stopping on what passed for a shoulder to the narrow two-lane road. The cab door opened and Lia jumped out.

"Find anything?" she said, going to the back.

"One hit, up near the edge of the swamp," said Karr. "A little metal there. Nothing beyond that."

"They must've been fried. The sniffers aren't that sensitive."

"Hmmph. Maybe. One definitely. Maybe two."

"You're getting too paranoid. You're going to be like Rubens soon. Show me where it is."

Karr pointed to the area where the sniffer had registered

something. Lia climbed onto the tail end of the truck and hauled back the canvas, disappearing inside. When she returned, she had a large boxy device that looked a little like the leaf blower a parks maintenance worker might use.

"High-tech vacuum," Karr explained to Dean. He held him back. "Damn thing's louder than hell. Just let her do her thing. When she's done, we'll load the pieces into the truck. Then you take them back for analysis."

"Back where?"

"The farm," said Karr. "Home."

"Home being the States?"

"Who says you're slow, Charlie Dean?"

The vacuum revved up. Dean's eardrums rattled so badly he put his hands over them. Karr, meanwhile, went around to the front of the truck. He returned with a brown paper bag, from which he took out a pair of sandwiches. Before Dean could unwrap his, Karr had swallowed the other whole.

A metallic oily smell filled Dean's nose as he opened it.

"Some kind of sturgeon they stick in oil," explained Karr. "Goes good with the egg. Beer, too, but we don't have any."

Dean looked at the sandwich doubtfully. He brought it up to take a bite, then thought better of it. Just the smell was enough to wrench his stomach.

"It's good," insisted Karr, even as he took the sandwich back.

When Lia finished her vacuuming, Dean helped Karr cut the long pieces of blackened metal so they could be easily piled into the truck. The metal had obviously been burned by a serious fire; pieces of plastic and other material had adhered to it, and in sections were thicker than a phone book. This, along with scattered clumps of congealed plastic and metal, was all that remained of a top-secret elint-gathering section that had been part of the aircraft.

Karr, though he professed to know nothing of the mission, said that the high-tech gear would have been rigged to self-destruct if anything went wrong, incinerating itself. There would have been no way out for the pilots and operators.

"You don't think they could get around that?" said Dean.

Karr shrugged.

"If it were me, I'd find a way," Dean told him.

"Good thing it wasn't you, then," said Karr.

"Maybe your gear doesn't work right."

"Hey, look around. Definitely. I'm not thrilled with the results myself. Like I told Lia, I doubt there were more than two bodies fried into the mush there."

"Maybe they were there and left."

"Nah. Doesn't work that way. The sniffer—" Karr jerked his head around midsentence. Lia was already running across the road, taking a position on a knoll that overlooked the wreckage.

"Just a car," Karr said. "Keep working. She'll cover us."

The vehicle, which looked as if it dated from the end of the Soviet Union, slowed but did not stop. Dean stripped off his shirt as it passed. This might be Siberia, but the afternoon had turned remarkably warm. Karr had given him an ointment to ward off the flies; it had an overly sweet citrus smell but was infinitely better than having to swat the things away.

"Jesus, put your shirt back on," squealed Lia from her vantage across the road.

"Hey, I like his pecs," laughed Karr.

"Why don't you take off yours, Lia?" said Dean.

"You'd like that, wouldn't you?"

"I wouldn't," said Karr. "My stomach's not strong enough."

They finished removing the blackened classified section of the aircraft around three o'clock. Lia, meanwhile, had been looking at a piece of the tailplane that had been left behind. As Karr tied up the rear of the truck, she announced that the plane had been taken down by a radar-guided missile.

"How do you know?" Dean asked.

She ignored him, repeating the information for Karr, who only shrugged and went to sit in the shade next to the truck. Sweat had soaked his shirt, and the skin exposed at his neck and arms was beet-red from the sun.

"How do you know it was a radar missile?" Dean asked. "Are you an expert?"

She made a face and tapped her ear. Obviously the people in the Art Room had been feeding her data.

"How do they know?"

"Number one, because the engines were intact," Lia told him. She went to the driver's side of the truck, returning with a large bottle of Gatorade. She gave it to Karr, who polished off about half before handing it to Dean. To Dean's surprise the liquid was so cold it hurt his back teeth.

"Don't drink it all," said Lia.

Dean glanced at her and realized she was trying not to be caught staring at him. He held the bottle over toward her, then started to jerk it away, but she was too quick, grabbing it from his tired grip.

"If it had been a heat-seeker, it would have hit one of them. There also would have been burn marks on the tail," she said. "And there weren't, at least not that we saw. That confirms that the shootdown was done from a reasonable distance."

"And?"

"No visual ID. They knew what they were firing at."

"Or maybe they didn't," said Dean. "Maybe they were too far away to see but assumed they were right."

"True."

"Or maybe the mission was compromised," said Dean. "So they were targeting it all along."

"Then why is it still here?" said Karr. "If we shot down a spy plane in Nebraska, would we leave it sitting on the ground until someone else came and picked it up?"

"Another car," said Lia. She grabbed her gun and ran back across the road.

"Art Room warns us," said Karr. "They sowed small detection units along the approaches before we got here."

"They're not watching us from space?" said Dean.

"Not in real time. We're too low a priority," said Karr, who could dish out sarcasm but obviously had trouble detecting it, at least from Dean. "Besides, you can only get stills every sixty or ninety seconds, and they tend to lag even further. Real-time video from space doesn't really work too well."

Dean wanted to ask why they weren't high-priority, but Karr had taken one of the A-2s and surreptitiously crouched behind the truck in case it was needed. A small Fiat approached from the north, slowing as it came close. Two men, both so large they seemed comical in the small car, stared at him. They were wearing suits and ties.

Dean glanced toward the ground, making sure his own rifle was nearby. For a moment he thought the Fiat would stop, but the driver downshifted and it picked up speed.

"Not good," said Karr. "But we're leaving anyway."

By the time they got to the small airport where Fashona was waiting with the helicopter, it was close to 6:00 P.M. Karr and Dean had changed into military fatigues that bore no insignias, and sat in the cab of the truck. Lia had managed to wedge herself among the wreckage and curled beneath a tarp in the back. Their weapons were hidden beneath the seat of the truck, with the exception of a miniature pistol that Karr passed to Dean as they pulled up to a post guarding access to the cargo section of the airport.

Karr took some papers from the dash and spoke to the police officer in a tired voice. Dean had no idea how fluent his Russian was, but undoubtedly the stack of euros he'd passed with the papers spoke eloquently enough. Cleared through, they rounded a dusty access road past a row of military transports, then headed across weed-strewn concrete to a row of hangars that looked big enough to house a Saturn rocket. Their Hind sat in front of one, so dwarfed it appeared almost forlorn.

"Everybody's corrupt here," said Dean.

"Everybody's hungry," said Karr. His face was serious for a second, as if contemplating that fact; then it shifted back to its usual bright smile. "This used to be a big military base. They had IL-76s in the hangars, along with some weird-looking planes with their engines on top of their wings. Big mo-fos. When they decided to rent out the hangars, they took the planes and pushed them off into the field over there. We're thinking of buying one. Apparently they're real dogs, though. Pilots don't want to fly them. Don't even mention them to Fashona. He'll bite your ear off, no shit."

Karr backed the truck around to the helicopter, whose cargo doors were open. While Lia went to find Fashona, Karr and Dean loaded the chopper.

"College education," said Karr as they hauled the piece in, "and I end up a schlepper anyway. My father always told me, you can't do much with math."

The salvaged wreckage formed a pile about five feet high and almost eight feet square. They strung a large heavy-duty net in front of it to secure it, though Dean was dubious.

Lia returned with Fashona, who in the space of a few hours had managed to grow what looked like a three-day-old beard. They'd been introduced before, but the pilot didn't seem to remember. He stuck his hand out.

"Fashona," he said.

"Dean."

"Don't call me *Fashone*. Or none of that shit."

"I won't."

"Nice helicopter, huh?"

"Looks OK."

"Want to sit up front?"

"Up front where?" asked Dean.

"Gunner's compartment," said the pilot. "No gun on this flight, though. Our weapons are packed away until we need them. We look like we're civilians. Well, almost."

Even without weapons strapped to its hard points and no chin gun, the helicopter hardly looked innocent, but Dean didn't argue.

"But the front is the best seat. Great view," added Fashona.

Dean shrugged but then remembered the rough landing at the field. How well could they possibly tie down the jagged metal in the back?

He walked with the pilot to the nose cabin, which looked a little like an upside-down fishbowl. A sensor boom protruded from the top of the cabin like a spear, its four winglets looking like knives.

"They took the cannon out before they sold it," said Fashona, pointing to the underside of the nose.

"Bummer," said Dean.

"Yeah, big-time. There's something about a nose gun, you know what I mean? We have podded cannons we can slap on if the going gets tough, but they just don't have the same, the same something, you know—"

"Savoir-faire?"

"Yeah. I mean, they are thirty-millimeter Gats, so don't get me wrong, plenty of firepower. More than the Commies had. But still . . . suave. It's lacking."

"Sure."

"I'm lobbying to get it back. Plus, some of these have shark's teeth, you know? Right here?" He swung his hand up the front of the fuselage. "That would be intense."

"Very," said Dean.

"OK." Fashona pulled open the door. Dean climbed up and then slipped in, feeling a little as if he were climbing down a sewer hole. The seat restraints were so thick, donning them felt like putting on a quilted vest.

"Headphones," said Fashona. "They work."

He pointed to a headset at the side, then slammed down the canopy, which failed to latch. He slammed it again—apparently the pneumatic prop was broken, since it bounded up. Dean managed to grab it from the pilot and close it gently, latching it shut. He pulled on the headphones just in time to hear Lia ask, "So what are you going to tell them when you get home, baby-sitter?"

"I don't know that I'm going to tell them anything," said Dean.

"Just tell the truth," said Karr. "They'll have you on a lie detector anyway."

"Probably right."

"Probably ask if the Princess put out," said Karr. "In that case, you probably want to lie."

The blades started to whirl. Dean felt the helicopter shaking back and forth and heard the engine whine—it seemed only slightly more distant here. Just like before, the engines revved, coughed, and died.

"Stinking fuel," grumbled Fashona. "They piss in it, I swear."

The rotors spun again. The blades seemed awfully close to the canopy, and Dean found himself staring down at the ground as the helicopter began to move forward, rocking up and down. There was a cough from the engines, but they kept running, the Hind moving steadily down an access ramp that led to the runway. Dean listened as Fashona exchanged barbs with the controller—in English.

"I'm a contract pilot," he told Dean over the interphone circuit, which could not be heard by the tower. "Part of my cover. Work for Petro-UK. That's why I talk English."

"Uh-huh."

"It's obvious I'm an American. And the aircraft, you know, it's traceable. So it's not a security breach or anything."

"Don't be so paranoid, Fashona," said Lia. "They're not after your ass."

"I'm *not* paranoid," said the pilot. "I just want the guy to know what's going on, that's all. For his report."

"We'll all get raises; don't worry," said Karr.

Dean could see that there were no planes in front of them. Nor did it appear that they were waiting for any to land. Nonetheless, the controller kept them waiting more than fifteen minutes before finally clearing them to take off. By then the sun had set and everything was turning gray.

As the engines revved and the helo began to skip quickly along the pockmarked pavement, Dean realized that sitting in the front seat was a mistake. Whether it was because of the physical location or just the clear bubble, every move the chopper made seemed amplified up here, ten times worse than it had been in the back. The helo pitched forward sharply as it came off the ground; Dean felt as if they were going to do a somersault right into the tarmac. It turned sideways into a bank and he swore he'd fall out. A sharp rise and then another bank and Dean wondered if his internal organs had rearranged themselves.

"Quite a ride, huh?" asked Fashona.

"Oh, yeah," said Dean. "The best."

His stomach was still unsettled ten minutes later when he heard the pilot curse and call Karr.

"What?"

"MiG-29s, hot, on our tail," said the pilot tersely. "RWR says they're scanning. Shit—we're spiked!"

Before Karr could answer, the helo pitched hard toward the ground.

21

Nothing in the world was more depressing than a pure mathematician at middle age. Young, they were full of vim, vigor, and fresh answers to Fermat's Last Theorem. When they hit thirty, however, they inevitably began tumbling downhill. In Rubens' opinion, it wasn't that they lost mental acuity. Instead they started to question things outside of math, and that threw them off. Questioning the sequence of prime numbers was one thing; questioning whether to change a haircut or have an affair was something else entirely. By the time they hit forty, the questions had done serious damage to the certainty required for top-level math.

And then, most devastatingly, they would ask the Impossible Question. This might be phrased many ways, but its most terse expression found its way to coffee cups throughout the complex: *If I'm so smart, why ain't I rich?*

In a few cases, the result of asking the question was relatively benign—a bath in the stock market. Too often, however, Rubens had watched it lead to ashrams and mass marriages in baseball stadiums.

Or stadia, as a mathematician would insist they be called.

John Bibleria—"Johnny Bib" to his co-workers—was fifty-one, and a prime candidate for the stock market/stadia stage. He had joined the NSA out of Princeton. His area in the government was cryptoanalysis, but his true interests involved string theory, and during the early years of his career he had published several papers with impressive titles and even more impressive arrays of Greek letters in the text. He had also been responsible for realizing the Chinese were using a fractal code in the early 1990s.

The days of one individual "cracking a code" were long gone by the time Johnny joined the agency. "Codes"—lists of word-for-word substitutions—had been obsolete for a hundred years or more, and even the more complicated ciphers of the early Cold War seemed quaint. Modern encryption was done by translating plaintext into data streams through mathematical algorithms or formulas governed by keys. Teams of cryptoanalysts, cryptologists, mathematicians, computer scientists, and programmers with overlapping abilities and responsibilities worked with cutting-edge computers to "solve" a cryptosystem.

But even with all that, Johnny Bib came as close as anyone to being a one-man show. To Rubens, his genius had little to do with his math, at least not in the way most people thought about math. What Bib at the height of his powers did as well as anyone in the world was intuit the significance of sequences. You didn't need to know the precise words being used in a sentence if you knew that the sentence told a missile to launch. Simply knowing that allowed you to answer many questions. Did you want to know how many missiles there were? Count the sentences. Where they were? Look for the sentences. How they were aimed? Study the events before the sentence was uttered. Bib not only spotted the sentences; he also could come up with questions no one else had thought of that they would answer.

But Bib's heyday had passed. Officially an Expert Cryptologic Mathematician, Johnny Bib was now an excellent team leader and an invaluable member of Rubens' inner circle. But he was no longer a star's star. Rubens, a connoisseur of genius, hated to see diminution. He looked at Johnny Bib and felt pain for the true heights the man's mind might have reached.

Rubens had hopes, however—a few mathematicians were able to enter remission following the question stage. Whether this had to do with advancing senility or not, Rubens hadn't yet decided.

Johnny Bib, standing over Rubens' desk, pointed to the status sheet he'd just put down. The color of the sheet matched Johnny's jacket.

"Now if you want my analysis," started Bib.

"Actually, I don't," said Rubens. "We have plenty of analysts."

"It's the pattern that's interesting," said Johnny Bib. "Ten units, fuel purchases, obscure encryption, connection to Anderkov. Bingo."

"Bingo," said Rubens sarcastically.

"Russian coup," said Johnny Bib.

"Bingo," said Rubens.

"You can see it?"

"Not really."

Johnny Bib blinked his owl eyes, then pushed back his longish hair, which had a habit of falling over his forehead and covering his right eye.

The E-mails that Bib's group had selected from the vast array of intercepts harvested in the NSA's Russia Military Project were, individually and collectively, benign—they were reports of fuel reserves in ten different Russian Army units. The fact that all of the units were east of the Urals did pique Rubens' interest, as did the fact that they used network addresses formerly reserved for diplomatic channels. Most interesting, however—and this was Johnny Bib's actual point—the messages used a very sophisticated but cumbersome asymmetrical or double-key encryption. Why go to so much trouble with information that was of relatively little strategic value?

"You really don't see it?" asked Johnny Bib.

"Assume I'm playing devil's advocate," said Rubens.

"Ah," said Johnny Bib, nodding knowingly.

"The CIA draft estimate doesn't say who is organizing the coup," said Rubens. He had obtained a copy of the draft from one of his usual sources even as Collins was leaving the Puzzle Palace; she had undoubtedly said it wasn't prepared as a personal challenge to him.

Johnny Bib wrinkled his nose, fighting back a sneeze. He seemed to loathe the CIA people so badly he had an actual allergy to them.

"Are they holding back?" Rubens asked.

"They're not smart enough to hold anything back."

"Smart and devious do not go hand in glove, John. Who's the leader of the coup? Vladimir Perovskaya, the defense minister?"

Johnny Bib stifled another sneeze by burying his nose in the crock of his arm. Rubens wondered if the agency ought to add etiquette and manners classes to its basic training regime.

"If you gave me access to the Wave Three findings," said Johnny Bib finally, "perhaps we could pinpoint the players then."

It was a variation of a common refrain—the intelligence expert asking for more intelligence. Wave Three, the program to take information off hard drives via aircraft, had not targeted government officials yet and, in fact, was currently on hold because of the shootdown in Siberia. But Johnny Bib wasn't authorized to know that, which meant that the program represented a kind of Holy Grail to him—if only he had that information, he could solve the problem.

"You're looking at me as if I don't know about the program," said Johnny Bib. "I was the one who invented the process for discerning significant magnetic wave patterns in real time. You've forgotten."

"What wave patterns?" said Rubens. "And you're exaggerating your role."

The mathematician began shaking his head violently.

"Relax, Johnny. Relax." Rubens realized he had gone a little too far. "Nothing in the data contributes to this."

Johnny continued to shake his head. Rubens sighed.

"You are an important contributor to our operation," Rubens told him. "Need I say more?"

Though still pouting, the mathematician stopped shaking his head.

"Do we have anything at all about our aircraft?" Rubens asked. "The PVO intercepts—that's what we need."

"It was a renegade unit. It's one of the ones that sent the E-mails."

"Now that's interesting. What else do we know about it?"

Johnny pushed his hair back, then stuffed his arms into his pockets. A good sign—it meant he was thinking about something he hadn't considered before.

"We have no other data at all," said Johnny. "No intercepts from the unit." Something had suddenly clicked in his complicated mind. "Yes. Well, yes. Yes. A subunit—if we go far enough back in the library, if we look at its creation— perhaps the person who created it: Perovskaya?"

"Don't jump to conclusions," said Rubens. He slid back in his seat. He still wasn't sure about the coup prediction, but they were definitely making progress. A light began blinking on his phone console. "I have to answer that."

Johnny Bib scowled but then nodded. "I'll update you when we have something."

"Two hours," said Rubens. "Every two hours."

Johnny nodded, then closed the door behind him—a good sign.

"Karr's team is being tracked by a MiG similar to the one that took Wave Three down," said Telach when he picked up the line to the Art Room.

"I'll be right there."

22

The Hind whipped downward, the momentum snaring Dean's body in the seat restraints like a flailing shark caught in a tuna net. The helo pitched right and he flew in the opposite direction, his arms smacking the side panel so hard they went numb. The Hind leveled off, spun, then zipped through a figure eight before plummeting another thousand feet in the space of a breath. Dean remembered the warnings they gave in commercial airlines about crashes and somewhat confusedly fought to tuck his head down, though the restraints kept him upright.

Somewhere around twenty feet off the ground, the helicopter stopped its tumultuous descent. Its path, however, ran toward a rise, and just as Dean thought the worst was over, the undercarriage smacked against some trees. The top branches hit the nose so hard Dean thought they'd been whacked by a cannon. In the next moment, he felt himself thrown back in the seat, the pilot yanking on his yoke to get over the rise, then flailing left.

"We're clear," said Fashona, even though they continued dodging left and right across the rough terrain. "They may have seen us, but they never fired at us."

"So what happened to the MiG?" asked Karr. His voice sounded as nonchalant as ever.

"Uh, looks like, uh, they're tracking another aircraft, I think. Escorting."

"Escorting what?"

"An IL-62, passenger plane. Um, you know the identifier section on the—"

"You sure they're escorting it?"

As Fashona began to respond, there was a warning beep in the pilot's cockpit.

"Missiles in the air!" Fashona jerked the chopper hard left.

"They're firing at the passenger plane," said Karr calmly.

The team leader's assessment proved correct. Fashona reported that their radar—a vast improvement over the unit the Poles had removed before selling the aircraft—showed the Ilyushin plane descending rapidly about fifteen miles away. The MiG, meanwhile, had curled off to the south and hit its afterburners.

"Damn," said Fashona. "He's going in."

They were too far away to see the crash. Fashona said the pilot thought he had regained control of the plane, but then it disappeared from the screen. "Down," he concluded. "Not sure how he went in—possibly there are survivors."

"Maybe," said Karr. "I don't know that anyone's going to get there, though."

"Well, we can."

"Negative," said Karr. "Get back on our course."

"Wait a second," said Dean. "You're not going to let those people die out there, are you?"

"How do you know there are any survivors?" Karr asked.

"Fashona just said so. Let's check it out," said Dean.

"Listen, baby-sitter, no offense, but this is my gig, right?" For the first time since they'd met, Karr's voice seemed actually a little strained—not quite angry, but at least mildly displeased.

"We can't let those people die."

"Maybe he's got a point," said the pilot. "There'll be nobody around to help them."

"Guys, look, whatever happened to those people, our mission's more important."

"We have burnt metal in the cargo hold. What's so important about that?" asked Dean.

Karr didn't answer.

"How long would it take us to get there?" Dean asked.

"Eh, four or five minutes," said Fashona. "A little more."

"I say we go. It makes sense to check this out anyway, right? From a mission point of view—see if the shootdown is similar to ours."

"We've lost contact with the Art Room," said Lia, speaking on the circuit for the first time. "The Russians are running some of their jammers, and the satellite's position changed. We're at the far end of the range."

"I say we go for it," said Dean.

"We're supposed to go back to Surgut," said Lia. "And that's quite a haul."

"Princess, don't you know it's fashionable to be late?" said Karr, back to his buoyant self. "Fashona, get us out there now. But that MiG comes back, anything comes back or around, bug out. Got me?"

"Loud and clear, boss."

Dean's night glasses worked fairly well even through the thick helicopter glass, and he could see the crash site when they were still two or three miles away. Unlike the other plane, this one seemed relatively intact.

The chopper dipped downward, its nose pointing like a dagger at the destroyed Ilyushin. The left wing had separated and lay in several pieces. One of the engines had fallen off on the right side and most of the tail and rudder assembly seemed to have simply disappeared. But the main fuselage seemed unscathed, at least from the distance.

"Nearest road is about a half-mile, call it southwest of the wreck," he told the others.

"I'm going to circle once, then swing down near the cockpit area," Fashona said.

"No, land on the road," said Karr. "We'll hike in. We don't want any marks from the helicopter, and if it's wet we get stuck."

Dean found that he could get a more focused view

through the night glasses by holding the frame with his hands. The terrain seemed like black-and-gray soup, with odd pieces of vegetables sticking up here and there. The road ran ruler-straight into the horizon in both directions.

"Going down," warned the pilot, tipping the nose forward and descending quickly.

Dean braced himself, but the landing still rattled everything from his shinbones to his teeth. By the time he had stopped shaking and unhooked himself from the cockpit, Karr and Lia had trotted in different directions down the road about a quarter-mile. Unsure what they were up to, Dean started for the plane. As he did, the helicopter's blades whipped up behind him. The wash as it took off bent him forward and nearly knocked him down.

"What the hell?" he said over his com system.

"Just a precaution," explained Karr. "He'll watch from the distance. We're putting little mines along the road in case we need to keep anyone back," he added.

Dean took one of his ear buds out, expecting he might hear someone crying or screaming in pain. But the night was quiet, except for the Hind in the distance. He smelled jet fuel and burnt metal.

The cockpit glass had been shattered on the pilot's side. Dean kicked something as he walked and turned back, bracing himself to see a body. But it was just a log petrified into stone.

"Here," said Lia, who was on the left side of the plane. "Radar missile again. Hit very close to the wing root."

"Hey, there's something alive in there," said Dean. He saw something, or rather someone, moving in the cockpit. He started to run, but as he reached the nose of the plane something grabbed him from the side and threw him down. Dean rolled to his feet with his left arm forward and his right cocked back.

"Easy," said Karr. "It's just me."

"What the hell are you doing?"

"We can't touch anything."

"We have to get those people out before there's a fire or something."

"Relax. If it hasn't caught on fire yet, it's not going to catch on fire now. Just slow down. We can't compromise the mission."

"We have to save these people."

"Slow down," said Karr. "We're not in Vietnam."

The remark struck Dean as smart-ass bullshit. And what the hell was the sense of coming here if they were going to let the survivors burn to a crisp?

"Couple of bodies in the field here," said Lia over the circuit. "I can see inside. Two or three people moving."

"Let's get them out," said Dean. "There's jet fuel all over the ground."

"Wait," snapped Karr. He put his hand to his ear. "Back to the road. Lia, grab the mines. Go south to the second pickup point."

"We have to save those people," said Dean.

"Someone else already plans to," said Karr. "Fashona says there's a helicopter on a direct vector five minutes from here. If you want to help, slip these on the bodies out near that wing. Put this glove on first."

He pulled a thin latex glove from his pocket and held it out, then retrieved a small test tube. The glass seemed empty; it was only by staring at it very closely that Dean discerned four or five tiny specks at the bottom. They looked like ticks.

"Flies," said Karr. "They're just tracking devices. One on each body if you can. No fingerprints, no sweat, no spit, if you can help it."

"What are you going to do?"

"You wanted me to help them, right?"

Karr disappeared around the other side of the airplane. Dean made his way around to the wing area but had trouble finding the bodies. Finally, he saw one—a woman facedown in the muck, her long hair splayed to the side. He bent toward her, then slipped down to one knee. As he unscrewed the top of the test tube, his hands started to shake and he had to stop for a moment. He'd touched corpses before—more than his share—but the woman's body unnerved him somehow. He shook his head, silently scolding himself, then tipped the tube gently to work one of the flies into his palm. Two or three tumbled out, bouncing across his palm onto her body.

There was a screech of pain.

Dean jerked back, completely overcome by shock and fear. It took him at least ten seconds to realize that the cries he heard were coming from someone else.

Someone nearby. He scanned the area quickly, saw a piece of white near the plane but not attached to it. As he stepped toward it he realized the white belonged to the body of a man—or rather, the top half of a body of a man. The legs were missing.

As Dean looked away, he glimpsed a shadow writhing on the other side of him. He couldn't help but think he was going to see the dead man's legs, but he went to it anyway.

Legs, yes, but tiny. And attached to a body, a kid, a small child no more than five years old. And alive.

Dean bent to the kid, turned him over. There was a thread of blood across his forehead, but his eyes were wide open. They closed, then opened again. The child screamed. Dean saw a pair of thick blankets nearby. He pulled them over, arranging them to make the kid comfortable. The boy seemed to realize that the stranger wasn't going to hurt him and stopped screaming, though his expression remained somewhere between suspicion and complete bewilderment. He looked almost comfortable—Dean saw no obvious broken bones or other injuries—but he'd need an expert to check the boy over.

"Dean. Time to go," said Karr in his ear bud.

"I got a kid here."

"They'll save him. Go."

"I'm taking him with us."

"Don't do it."

"How do you know they'll find him?"

"Look, we got to go," said Karr. "You hear the helicopter. I promise, if they don't take him, we'll come back. But not now. Most of these people are dead, or will be soon."

"We can save this kid," said Dean.

"You sure about that? You have a trauma center handy? One that won't ask questions?"

Something inside Dean resisted the logic of the argument. Nonetheless, he tilted his hand, tilted the small test tube, showering the flies over the child's body. Then, with the helicopter rotors pounding the ground and a searchlight playing over the broken, discarded wing, he began trotting south, following Karr's outline against the open terrain.

23

By the time Rubens got to the Art Room, the helicopter had disappeared from the screen. Telach hunched over Jeff Rockman, hitting different feeds; they had an image from a Space Command satellite on the main screen at the front of the room, but it was blurry and full of clouds.

"Did you lose them?" Rubens asked.

"They were flying at the edge of our broadcast circle and the Russians started to jam. It's one of their new systems," said Telach.

The com system satellites had very restricted broadcast ranges, sometimes called shadows or arcs, to make them more difficult to intercept. Telach looked distressed, even worse than when the Wave Three aircraft had gone down. Rubens told himself he'd order her to go on a vacation as soon as this assignment was over.

"Were they shot down?" Rubens asked Rockman, the runner.

"We're looking at radio intercepts," said Rockman. "The MiG wasn't targeting them. Probably the satellite can't get them with the jamming. They might also have turned everything off because of the MiG."

"Not the locators," said Telach.

"We were having trouble with them earlier," said Rockman.

The locators were essentially small pieces of very slightly

radioactive iodine, whose isotope could be detected by a specialized system of detectors, including some mounted in a satellite system. While the system worked fine under perfect circumstances, the thinner the satellite coverage the less reliable the detection. The area where the team was now was actually covered by a satellite focused on China. Even a good-sized cloud bank could interfere with the reception, and so it was not surprising that they were off the grid.

"Where's the MiG?" asked Rubens.

"They shot down another plane and took off," said Rockman. "We think it's the same unit, but it's going to take a lot of work to make sure."

"Who was shot down?"

"A civilian flight," said Telach.

Rubens went to the empty station next to Rockman and pulled the infrared and imaging radar images up. Unfortunately, the imaging process took time; the data was more than five minutes old.

"That may be them," Telach said, pointing to a tear-shaped blur in the middle of her screen.

"Let's not worry about them for a second," said Rubens. He agreed with Rockman's assessment that they must be alive but still hiding from the MiG. "Instead, let us consider why the MiG shot down the plane. They'll show up, Marie," Rubens added. His assurance didn't soften her glare. "The plane's course. Can we compare it to ours?"

"To the Hind's or the Wave Three aircraft?" she said. Her bottom lip quivered slightly, but she reached down for the keyboard.

"Wave Three."

"OK. Hang on." The aircraft had taken off from the same airport and their courses had about an 80 percent overlap—not a coincidence, since the Wave Three mission had been purposely laid out to look like one of the common flights through the area.

"They must have thought it was one of ours," said Telach. "They must have incomplete information, half-rumor, half-guess."

Rubens harrumphed. It was possible.

The ELF transmissions from the Wave Three plane were detectable, though the equipment needed to measure them was extremely sophisticated. The working theory on the shootdown as a premeditated, targeted attack on the spy plane was that the transmissions had been detected with the use of that equipment. This wouldn't fit that theory. On the contrary, it validated the random, renegade attack profile.

Which was exactly the finding Rubens most desired, since it meant that his program hadn't been compromised. He had to, therefore, reject it out of hand.

"New flight company," said Rockman, pulling up data on the civilian that had been shot down. "Maybe they just didn't pay the grift," he suggested.

"Maybe," said Rubens. "Or maybe the Russians are trying to convince us that they didn't actually target our plane."

"Heck of a way to confuse us. There must've been over a hundred people aboard."

"Could be an acceptable price."

He could order up an F-47C mission, have transponders on a kite or mini–remote plane, see if the MiG came out. They could study the response, pinpoint the detection system.

Why would the Russians go to such lengths to protect information about the lasers? Hitting the U.S. plane was one thing, but their own?

When operational, the lasers had the potential for changing the balance of power between the U.S. and Russia by blinding U.S. ABM satellite monitors. Of course, a preemptive strike would certainly initiate a war or at least serious retaliation.

What would the circumstances have to be to prevent that?

None. Hitting the U.S. satellites would trigger a violent, immediate response. No one would plan such a thing.

Of course, in the context of the American response, a hundred or so lives would be nothing.

"Boss?" asked Telach, bringing Rubens back to the present.

"What's been the military response?" he asked.

"None." Rockman brought up the SpyNet page on the PVO administrative unit responsible for the area. The page, which summarized decoded intercepts from the unit over the past twenty-four hours, showed only routine communications, most of which were weather reports. The self-defense squadron had six planes, all ancient MiG-25s, assigned to the Surgut area, a good distance away from the shootdown. There were several encrypted intercepts on the docket for automatic translation, but the times did not correspond to the shootdown and Rubens saw no need to push them out of the normal queue.

"Do we have radar intercepts available?" he asked.

"Too deep," said Rockman. The area self-defense radar was too far from the country's borders to be monitored directly by the standing NSA programs, though of course it could be specifically targeted for a mission. Communications intercepts ordinarily provided more than sufficient information about their operation.

"News media?" Rubens asked.

"Plane's not due yet," said Rockman. "Far as we can tell, there hasn't been an alert. We know from the Third Wave missions that this area isn't under direct civilian radar and has only spotty PVO coverage."

Rubens closed his eyes and saw the list of bases Johnny Bib had given him. None were along the flight path.

"We'll want a passenger list," he told Telach. "And a cargo manifest."

"Yes."

"CIA is on this?"

"As of ten minutes ago. We alerted them."

Protocol called for an interagency team to be assembled to report on the shootdown. Rubens would want his own person on the team.

"Maybe you're right," said Telach. "Maybe they are OK. Karr's pretty capable."

"He is," said Rockman.

Reports on fuel reserves. Bulky encryptions. Random shootdowns. Wave Three. Laser program.

Hard to find a common thread.

Assume they weren't random. Assume the laser program wasn't related to this.

Why would they shoot the planes down?

Protect other data at the lab.

What would that have to do with a coup?

Niente.

Skip the coup. Assume the laser was ready to be used.

Still nothing.

Rubens turned and began walking toward the door.

"Boss?" said Telach behind him. "What do you want us to do?"

"When Karr reestablishes contact, see if he can observe the crash site. We're going to want information on who goes there, everything we can get on the reaction, who was on the plane, everything."

"They have the Third Wave wreckage aboard the helicopter."

"Surely they can deal with that," said Rubens.

"But—"

He didn't wait to hear the rest of her objection.

24

Dean followed Karr through the marshy tundra for nearly three miles, once or twice losing sight of him. Water from the boggy soil soaked through his boots and well up his pant legs. The dampness and fatigue began to tighten his muscles, and he felt a massive knot forming between his shoulder blades.

They walked parallel to the highway, for the most part along what looked like an abandoned farm path or perhaps the original road before it was improved and paved. No vehicles passed; Dean realized the area was about as desolate as any he'd ever been in and wondered how much emptier the extremely cold northern stretches of Siberia must be.

Karr finally began angling toward the road, and Dean saw that the terrain rose toward a knoll that would give them a fair vantage point. Sure enough, Lia was already there, watching the wreckage and the Russians who had come to inspect it.

"They're not helping the survivors," she said.

"Why not?" said Dean.

Lia ignored him, talking directly to Karr. "They went into the cabin. I haven't seen them come out. Two men."

"What kind of chopper?"

"Helix, I think. I can't tell if it has a star on the tail or not. Could be civilian."

"Out here?"

"One man in the cockpit. If it was military, there'd be more. Besides, Helixes are normally assigned to the Navy."

"No way it's a civilian. Gotta be Army or something."

"Or something."

Karr took out a PRC radio to communicate with the Hind. The discreet-burst unit was similar to those used by Spec Ops and downed airmen. Dean went over to Lia and asked for the binoculars she was using.

"It's polite to share," he told her.

Somewhat to his surprise, she passed the binoculars to him. "You don't sound like you're from Missouri."

Dean tended to be defensive about his home state; in his experience, most people who brought it up did so only to put it down. But he simply grunted, trying to arrange the binoculars in front of the night gear and get them to focus.

"Hold them directly on the lens, at the exact center of the eyepiece. It's calibrated to focus." She pushed them onto the glass. "It takes a second."

It felt awkward, but it worked well enough for him to see something coming out of the plane.

"Got a bag," said Dean.

Lia grabbed the binoculars back, taking a step forward on the knoll. "He went in with that."

"What are they doing?" he said.

"Going back to the helicopter."

"There's a kid in the field on the other side of the plane," Dean told her. "He's alive."

"Really?" Her voice was sincere and surprised.

"Little kid."

"Blades are turning. They're taking off."

Dean put his hands on the sides of the glasses, steadying them, as if that would help him see farther. But the helicopter was nearly three miles away, and all its running lights had been extinguished.

"They're leaving them to die?" he asked.

"They're probably the ones who killed them," said Karr. "We'll follow them once Fashona picks us up."

"What about the kid?" said Dean.

"What kid?"

"Dean wants to play Florence Nightingale," said Lia.

"Oh, *that* kid," said Karr. "Yeah, Dean, just one fly, OK? You used like four on him."

"How do you know?"

Karr took his handheld and showed it to him. There were pinpoints of light on a grid—the locations of the small bugs.

"They took the flight recorder," added Karr. "That's what they went in there for. To make sure there was no indication who shot down the plane. Probably unnecessary, but they didn't want to take any chances."

"We going to help those people or what?" demanded Dean.

Karr ignored him. "Who do you think they were?" he asked Lia. "PVO?"

She shrugged.

"Probably not the GAI or *militsiya*," said Karr, referring to police agencies. "They wouldn't have come by helicopter."

"Probably not."

Dean was about ready to punch both of them.

"Closest town is fifteen miles away," said Karr. "And it's not much of a town. But maybe that's our best bet."

"Well, let's just do it." Lia took her satellite phone out from inside her vest.

Dean finally realized that they were discussing how to get help. "You have the number memorized?" he asked.

Lia scowled. The Hind was approaching from the south, its throaty TV3s considerably louder than the engines that had powered the other helicopter.

"She's calling home," explained Karr. "They'll handle the details."

"We have to help that kid," said Dean.

"Charlie, we're going to have to take our chances on that one."

"It's his chance, not ours."

Karr slapped his back and nodded grimly, but he'd made up his mind.

• • •

They lost the helicopter somewhere near Sym, a city that passed for large in the central area of Siberia on a tributary to the Jenisej. Running low on fuel, they finally set down about a mile from a hamlet called Sitjla, a good hundred or so miles due north of Tomsk.

"Run the engines dry," Karr told Fashona.

"No way, man," he replied. "We'll never get them started again."

"I don't want the helicopter stolen if we have to leave it."

"Who the hell's going to steal it?"

"It's worth more than the whole damn village."

"Shit, they won't fly it. They'll take it apart and sell it for scrap."

Fashona finally convinced him that leaving only three or four minutes of fuel in the tanks was good enough. He killed the engines the second the gear plopped onto the ground. It was still night, and Karr decided they'd take shifts standing guard and napping until morning. He left Dean conspicuously out of the rotation. Dean said he'd take a spot, but Karr told him not to worry.

"Age before beauty," Karr told him. "Just sleep."

Dean, angered by the reference to his age, told Karr to screw himself. He just laughed his usual laugh.

"Don't be stubborn," said Lia a while later when she saw Dean wasn't sleeping. "You're going to be sorry later."

"Right," he snapped, but he did bed down and fell asleep for a few hours.

The next thing he knew, Fashona was tugging at his feet. "Time to hit the road," said the pilot. "Let's go check out the big city."

Dean, his muscles knotted and stiff, followed Fashona unsteadily. The sun poked through some of the mist rising from the ground, shafts of yellow swirling in the humid air.

Karr and Lia had just finished stowing the team's gear away from the helicopter, hiding the A-2 guns and some of the high-tech equipment in the nearby field. They took a GPS reading, then returned to the aircraft. The first order of business, Karr told the others, was to find some food. They were no longer using the com system to communicate with the Art Room, relying on the sat phones instead for periodic updates.

"Hey, Charlie," said Karr as they started to walk. "Your kid's in a hospital. Fair condition."

"Good," grunted Dean.

"Don't sound so enthused, tough guy." Karr laughed. As they continued to walk toward town, he told them that the Art Room had changed their mission priorities.

"They want to know about the Helix," he told the others. "So that's our gig."

"What about the trash in the chopper?" asked Fashona.

Karr shrugged. "They want it eventually, just not right away."

"What about him?" Lia jabbed her thumb toward Dean.

"I think they forgot about you, Charlie," said Karr. "Didn't even mention you."

"Then I'll just walk home."

"Go for it," said Lia.

"So how come with all their satellites and other gadgets they lost track of the Helix helicopter?" said Dean. "How come they can't just push a button and find out about it?"

"Man, you've been hanging around Princess too long," said Karr.

"Don't blame him on me," said Lia. "He was whining when I found him."

"Truck," said Fashona.

It made no sense to hide—the helicopter was clearly visible, and in a place like this, the fact that it had landed would undoubtedly soon be common knowledge. So Karr turned and waved.

The truck looked like it had been made in the 1950s or even earlier. The driver stopped; it took less than a minute for Karr to talk him into giving them a ride into town. It wasn't particularly hard, the op explained as they climbed into the back; the fifty rubles he offered the driver amounted to more money than the man would make that week and perhaps that month.

Downtown Sitjla consisted of a dirt road bordered by a trio of sheds, a few piles of bricks that had possibly once been houses, and a two-story building covered by the large asbestos tiles common in the States during the 1950s. The building's facade, off at a slight angle to the street, had a wooden door and no windows. It proved to be a combination restaurant, inn, and meeting place for the local inhabitants. A collection of trailers sat about a half-mile farther down the road, but there were no oil derricks or factories or anything else nearby that showed why anyone would live here.

A large woman in her early twenties met them inside the open hallway of the cement building. It was difficult to tell from her appearance whether she was the manager or a cleaning lady. She wore a thick polyester dress that didn't quite reach her bulging knees, but her hands were covered by rubber gloves and her hair pulled back in a scarf that looked like a dust rag. Karr did the talking for the group, explaining in Russian that they were Westerners working for an oil company whose helicopter had broken down and would need repair. The woman smiled, frowned, shook her head, and finally said something about providing food, impressed by either Karr's patter or, more likely, the wad of rubles he produced from his shirt pocket. Within a half hour, they were sitting at a tin folding table in a whitewashed room sipping a very hot and very bland red-tinted water that may or may not have been vegetable soup. Dean was so hungry he asked for a second bowl, which seemed to make the woman think he was flirting with her. About midway through the meal, Karr excused himself to go to the rest room.

"Olive says there's a bus due soon," he told them when he got back. "Fashona and I are going to take it to Tomsk. We should be able to buy fuel for the helicopter there. If not, we'll be able to make other arrangements."

"How long's that going to take?" Dean asked.

Karr shrugged. "The bus was supposed to be here this morning. Sometimes it's a whole day late. They stop a few more times along the way south. In theory it's a four-hour trip. My guess is we'll be back by tomorrow night."

"We can get some sleep, at least," said Dean.

"Actually, no," said Karr. "Desk Three wants you two to find that helicopter ASAP. I was talking to them in the men's room. They have some leads."

"What?" snapped Lia.

"Olive says we can rent a pickup from her brother-in-law. There's only three places the helicopter can be, according to the Art Room," he added.

"What's my cover?" asked Lia.

Karr shrugged. "Whatever you feel like, Princess. Far as I'm concerned, you can use the traveling prostitute bit. Dean can be your pimp."

"Screw yourself, Tommy. Just screw yourself."

Fashona was suppressing a smile. Olive—her actual name was something like Olenka, which would be Olga in English—returned, offering tea. This proved to be a green liquid that tasted as if it had been made from moss. Fashona and Karr downed theirs, but Dean tried only half a sip.

"Look, if you have a better idea, talk to them," Karr told Lia when Olive had retreated. "You know the number."

"Hardy-har."

"She can't just hear them talking in her ear?" said Dean derisively.

"Not too well. The Russians are picking up their jamming. They're really getting obnoxious," said Karr.

The communications system had high-orbit stationary satellites that provided coverage in important areas. The rest was supplied with low-earth, purpose-launched satellites that tied into the system. Partly for security purposes and partly to keep them small and disposable, their range was fairly limited. Jamming by the Russians made things even more problematic.

"How do you know the Russians aren't listening in?" asked Dean. It was a serious question, not like his earlier sarcastic remark.

"Yeah, exactly," said Karr. "That's why we don't want to

overuse the system. Although it's pretty good. I mean, any-thing can be broken," said Karr. "But this one is very hard in real time. Besides the encryption, the frequency skips dur-ing the transmission. There are two different noise streams mixed in. In other words, if you're intercepting it, you get three different conversations, and you have to figure out which one is real."

"They're *I Love Lucy* reruns," said Lia.

Fashona laughed.

"They're actual conversations," said Karr.

"Having Washington talk in your ear isn't a pain in the ass?" asked Dean.

Karr shrugged. "It's not Washington." He rose. "Supposed to be able to buy smokes down the road. OK, Princess, go find Olive's brother-in-law. We'll see you probably the day after tomorrow."

"They give me a map?"

"They promise to download. Didn't say when, though."

"You know, screw them. Screw Rubens."

"I hear he's got a monster wad," said Karr.

25

The truck wasn't as old as Dean had expected. In fact, by Russian standards, it wasn't old at all—a 2000 Toyota 4×4 pickup that had, according to the odometer, 157,132 miles on it.

Four large drums were included in the deal, along with a hand pump, two spares, and a jack that looked half-stripped. Filling the drums with gasoline from a pump at the back of the asbestos-shingled building took nearly an hour, and left Dean's stomach twisted on its axis, though that may have been from breakfast. The truck's springs were looser than a mattress in a whorehouse, and Dean hit his head once or twice on the liner as they drove. The first order of business was stopping and getting some of the gear they'd cached near the chopper. The big helicopter looked a little forlorn in the fading light, its rotors drooping toward the ground.

"Stay here," said Lia, who took the keys and jumped from the truck before Dean could say anything. He got out of the cab and walked down the road, looking for a good place to relieve himself. There wasn't much cover beyond the rubble of whatever building the lot they'd landed on had once belonged to. Finally he decided he was so far out in the wilderness it didn't make much difference where he took his leak. He was about halfway through when he thought he could feel someone's eyes looking at him. He glanced around quickly, saw nothing, then glanced back and forth again, as if trying to shake the paranoia away. Something about peeing in unfamiliar territory made him feel extremely vulnerable, but he couldn't get rid of the feeling even after zipping up. He took a few steps farther from the road, then crouched down, staring in the direction of the helicopter, which was now beginning to blend in the shadows. He couldn't see Lia.

Something moved about fifty feet from the helicopter. It was low to the ground, an animal. It began moving roughly in Lia's direction, disappearing in the darkness.

"Hey!" yelled Dean.

Lia didn't answer, nor did the dog or whatever it was.

Dean went back to the pickup and fished around behind the drums of spare gasoline to find the tire iron. He couldn't see it in the dark, and when he heard something else moving in the field, decided to take the long notched pole from the jack instead. The animal was undoubtedly some sort of dog and probably harmless, but Dean's instincts wouldn't let him leave Lia alone. He began flanking the general area where they'd put the gear, not quite sure of where it was, debating whether to yell again. Something low and oddly shaped lay on the ground a few yards from the helicopter, in a shallow ravine.

He stared at it for a few moments before realizing it was a bicycle.

"Lia! Lia!" he shouted, trying to warn her. There was a loud growl and then an even louder explosion, the sound a cherry bomb makes in a garbage can. Dean hit the ground; when he looked up he saw Lia dragging a figure toward him, cursing.

It was a girl, fifteen or sixteen, with close-cropped hair and a bruised, dirty face, eyes closed.

"Did you kill her?" said Dean.

"Fuck you, did I kill her? Of course not. Shit." Lia dragged the girl back to the pickup, where she dumped her on the ground. "Watch her."

Dean crouched next to the kid. Her pants were torn at the knee and she had a fat lip, but otherwise she didn't seem hurt. Petrified, yes.

Dean realized he still had the metal jack piece in his hand. "I'm not going to hurt you," he said.

"She doesn't speak English," said Lia, returning with two knapsacks and a long metal box. The box held one of the assault guns. Lia ripped off something in Russian to the girl, who didn't acknowledge it.

"Put her in the cab," said Lia.

"Why?"

"We can't leave her here. She was trying to steal some of the gear."

"What are we going to do with her?"

"We'll dump her off somewhere down the road."

"Let me get her bike," said Dean.

"What are you, the fuckin' Red Cross?"

Dean retrieved the bicycle. As he pulled it upward, he realized a pair of eyes were watching him. He could see the whites clearly, less than ten yards away. He picked up the bike, took a step toward them—they didn't move.

"Rah!" he yelled, taking another two steps and holding the frame over his head. The eyes disappeared.

Another kid?

No, it was cowering—a dog, definitely a dog.

Dean bent down. "Come here," he said, though of course the dog had even less idea than his mistress what Dean was saying. He lowered himself into a crouch, but the dog didn't approach. Finally, he started back toward the truck and heard the animal starting to follow.

Lia had the truck running already. Dean picked up the bike and put it into the back. As he turned, the dog appeared a few yards from the helicopter, barking at him. Dean whistled, then opened the tailgate and whistled again. Maybe it was a universal dog language—the animal bounded forward, jumped into the truck, and squirmed through the barrels to bark at his mistress's head in the back. She turned and tapped the window, smiling as Dean got in.

"The fucking dog, too?" said Lia.

"Why didn't you kill it?" said Dean, guessing that the sound had come from the A-2.

"Maybe I'm a rotten shot," she said, stomping on the gas pedal.

None of them spoke for several hours. They drove north on the highway, stopping twice to refuel and once when Lia ran into a small store and bought food while Dean watched the girl. The temperature outside was dropping steadily by four o'clock; an hour or so later it felt so cold they turned the heater on.

"There's snow on the ground," said Dean, looking out the window.

"Just frost," said Lia. "You forget how far north we are. Some nights it gets cold, even in the summer."

"We gonna freeze to death?"

"Don't be a sissy."

"Where are we going?" he asked.

Lia scowled but didn't answer.

"How far are we taking her?" Dean asked.

"Far enough that she can't get back in a day," said Lia. "If we didn't take the bike and the dog, we could have let her go by now."

"Pretty far to ride a bike from here."

"You'd be surprised." She looked at him. "You could ask, Charlie Dean. You don't know everything."

"I didn't say I did." He looked at her frown. She was pretty, but she had an attitude the size of Minnesota. "It's my fault, huh?"

"You got that straight."

Dean pushed his leg up against the dash. The truck's seat was a bench and Lia had it all the way forward so she could reach the pedals. There was no way to stretch out his legs.

"Want to let me drive for a while?" he asked.

"What are you going to do when someone stops you?"

"Who's going to stop me? We haven't seen anybody for hours."

Lia didn't answer.

A while later, when she was sure the girl was sleeping,

Lia explained that their cover story was an extension of the one they'd used in the town; they were trying to keep an appointment in an oil city near Nahym.

Not *in* Nahym, but near it.

"Did that kid really go to a hospital, or did Karr just tell me that?" said Dean.

"Tommy doesn't lie," said Lia.

"How do you know?"

"Jesus, Charlie Dean, you're a pain in the ass."

Dean took another shot at conversation. "So you were with the SEALs?"

"Do I look like a fuckin' SEAL?"

"Special Forces."

"Delta, asshole."

"I thought Delta Force was part of Special Forces."

"The problem with jarheads is that they try to think."

Dean started to laugh. "Jarhead? What's that from, a John Wayne movie?"

"The problem with *Marines*," said Lia, "is that they think their shit doesn't stink."

"Mine does."

"Tell me about it."

Dean gave up trying to make conversation. Eyes heavy, he felt his head drooping off to the side. Finally he gave in to fatigue and fell asleep, his shoulder resting against the young girl's.

There was a time in Dean's life when he'd had vivid, angry dreams, dreams obviously inspired by some of the things he'd been through—sniper missions, an assassination, firefights, a hostage situation he'd become part of. It was as if his subconscious had to work some of the violence out, decipher the contradictions, and bridge the gap between what should have happened and what actually did. Dean hated the dreams when he had them; many nights he'd tried to stay up in a vain attempt to keep them away.

And then one morning he realized he didn't have the dreams anymore. In fact, he didn't dream anymore at all. Had he worked all that stuff out?

Truth was, Charlie Dean wasn't the kind of guy who spent a lot of energy working things out. Not in a formal way. He liked to think of himself as a guy who went on instincts, who trained his body—and his mind—to do what had to be done without hesitation. It's what had made him a decent, better than decent, sniper.

Maybe. Or maybe it was just that he was a pretty good shot no matter what the circumstances were. In any event, he didn't believe in analyzing it.

So when the dreams stopped, he didn't complain about it, nor did he celebrate. He didn't dream now, either. But as his body jostled back and forth in the pickup, he did feel a vague sense of unease brushing around his face and hands.

When he woke, Lia and the girl were gone. It was dark out; his watch told him it was close to two in the morning. There were taillights and a large shadow just in front of them. He stared into the darkness and realized they were in the middle of a large parking area near a highway, a much different road from the one they'd been on.

Dean was freezing. He rubbed his arms and waited. Finally, Lia and the girl returned, lugging several plastic grocery bags.

"Ah, Sleeping Beauty is awake," said Lia. She reached into one of the bags and took out a jar. "Coffee. Almost, anyway."

The warm liquid did taste somewhat like coffee. The girl had a large loaf of bread and chewed at it ravenously, pausing every so often to smile at Dean. Lia sorted the bags, then produced a large revolver from one. It looked like a Smith & Wesson .44, though it had no markings on it. Three of the six cylinder chambers were filled; the bullets were Magnums, and the gun was indeed a very good clone of the S & W Model 29.

"Best we could do," she said. "It has to be fifty years old, and I doubt it's been fired in the last ten. Clean it. The bullets are in the bag."

Dean took the gun and the bag, which contained some tools and small tubes of different types of oil, Vaseline, and graphite besides the bullets. There seemed to be a whole set of burglar's picks as well.

"Package deal," said Lia, shrugging.

There was a knock on Lia's window. Dean pulled the bag up, hiding the gun behind it.

Dean could smell the vodka on the man's breath as he exchanged words with Lia. She waved him away; he seemed reluctant to go and for a second Dean thought he'd have to show the gun.

"What was that all about?"

"Wants to buy Zenya." Lia started the truck. "Time to go."

Zenya, the girl, turned abruptly toward the back of the pickup. Lia told her in Russian that the animal was fine, then repeated the information for Dean's benefit.

"They buy kids?" Dean asked as they got onto the highway.

"They buy anything. These guys got more money than we do. And we have a printing press."

Zenya and Lia talked in Russian for the next hour or so. Dean figured it was the girl's life story, but Lia didn't share it. Among the items Lia had bought were a wool sweater and a parka; Dean put on the sweater, though it was a bit tight, and used the parka as a pillow, leaning against the door. His brain settled into a state of half-sleep, as if his consciousness were a crocodile with only its snout peering out of the water.

Eventually Lia turned off the highway onto another well-made but narrower road. Within a mile this had given way to well-packed gravel, twisting and turning through what seemed to be a swampy forest. Rectangles of dim yellow light broke the darkness on their right; the road curved gradually to reveal a fairly large city set on what seemed to be a pile of peat moss above the surrounding terrain. Lia and the girl exchanged a few words. As soon as they came into the city, Lia took her first right and parked in front of a low-slung building made of concrete blocks. Fluorescent light flowed from the narrow casement windows at the building's front, set about six feet high.

"Time to eat," said Lia.

The glass door at the side of the building opened into a short hallway blocked off by a thick metal door. This led to a stairway; at the top of the six steps was another glass door. Inside was a rustic diner or restaurant, the sort that in the States used to be found near third-rate resort areas before the days of McDonald's and Pizza Hut. Ten of the twenty tables were already filled, even though it was only a few minutes past four; three-quarters of the counter stools were also occupied.

The crowd was exclusively male. Lia's scowl did little to ward off the stares. Zenya blushed as they sat down.

Afraid that speaking English might cause trouble, Dean said nothing. His breakfast came quickly—a large order of pancakes and coffee, which was instant. There was no milk or creamer.

"They know you're not Russian, don't worry," said Lia. "They're used to foreigners. Or at least their money. That's why they have pancakes."

Both Lia and Zenya had ordered some sort of pastry with bits of meat in it, but whether it was ham, beef, or something more exotic, Dean couldn't tell. The girl ate hers quickly, then, looking at Lia, asked her something. Lia nodded, and Zenya got up from the table, taking her things and going out the door.

"Bathrooms out there?" Dean asked.

"She's hitting the road."

"We're far enough away?"

Lia shrugged. "She'll probably go back to the truck stop. She was pretty impressed."

"That's OK with you?"

"We're in Russia. Remember? And I'm not her mother."

Dean got up and walked out, trying to hold himself back from running. When he got downstairs, Zenya was just getting on her bike. She'd smuggled some food out to the dog, who jumped up and snared it when she threw it to him.

"Hey!" yelled Dean, starting toward her.

Zenya looked at him, waved, then realized he wanted to stop her. She began pedaling away. The dog trotted behind, still chewing.

"Hey! Hey!" Dean took a few steps but saw it was hopeless, worse than hopeless—even the dog had trouble keeping up with her.

"Save the world yet?" asked Lia when he came back. She had her handheld computer out and was tapping on it.

"You just going to let her go back there? She'll become a prostitute."

"You think she's not already?"

"She's fifteen or sixteen."

"You don't know where we are," said Lia. "It's different out here. We're not in Moscow, let alone the States. Think of it as the Wild West."

"This isn't hell," said Dean.

"It's close."

"Bullshit."

"I'm glad you're such an expert. How long have you been here now? It's not a whole week, is it? Time just drags when we're together."

Dean sat back in the chair, curling his arms together in front of his chest.

26

His name was Laci Babinov, and his death clinched it for Rubens. He hated—loathed—admitting the CIA was right on anything, but Babinov's presence on the airplane that was shot down was a smoking gun.

An obscure one, certainly, but good intelligence was often a matter of making the obscure obvious.

Babinov was the number two man in Moscow's OMON, or *Otryad Militsii Osobgo Naznacheniya,* the riot police. He'd been appointed by Kurakin and would undoubtedly have been loyal in a coup.

Assume the Ilyushin had been targeted to get Babinov. Was the strike on the Wave Three plane then a mistake?

Rubens wanted badly to think it was. But he couldn't let himself reach that conclusion, not yet anyway; he wanted it too badly and there was no supporting evidence. It might just be a coincidence—which happened just enough to keep conspiracy theorists in business.

As soon as he saw the manifest, the NSA deputy director picked up the phone and called Hadash. In the time it took for Hadash's assistant to run him down, Rubens had retrieved Babinov's dossier and copied the information Johnny Bib had given him onto a small device the size of a key fob. The flat plastic housing covered a chip of specially designed flash ROM; the chip would flush its memory clean in eight hours, leaving no trace of the information recorded on it.

"Hadash."

"We need to talk about Russia," said Rubens. "The CIA's estimate may be correct."

"All right," said Hadash. "How quickly can you get here?"

"I can leave immediately."

"Yes, wait—" Hadash held his hand over the mouthpiece of his phone, checking with someone about a schedule. "Go directly to the White House. The president wants to talk to you as well."

An hour and a half later, Rubens found himself on the back lawn of the White House trotting alongside one of the staff people as they hustled to board *Marine One* before the president emerged with the mandatory entourage of media people.

Like its Air Force equivalent, *Marine One* was simply the designation for the Marine Corps helicopters transporting the president. For years, *Marine One* was an ancient, spartan Sikorsky used essentially as a flying taxi to take various presidents (and sometimes their dogs) on short hops, often to catch *Air Force One*. The S-58 model was a superb aircraft in its day, but that day actually passed back in the 1950s. President Marcke had decided to upgrade, and out of the Marine Corps' impressive stable of aircraft chose arguably the best—a CH-53D capable of taking him over two thousand miles on literally a moment's notice. The interior was nearly as well equipped as that of *Air Force One*. And if the three-engined monster helicopter wasn't quite as fast as the Osprey, its performance record was considerably better.

The interior of the helicopter was cordoned off into three different spaces. The first included the doorway and bench seat pretty close to the simple slings used on many military aircraft. The next, which was generally occupied by the Secret Service detail and whatever staff people were aboard, had cushioned vinyl seats that could have been pulled from a bus stop and spray-painted a tasteful gray.

The third compartment, the president's, had a thick though admittedly synthetic Persian carpet and very real leather chairs. These were bolted to the floor and had special three-point seat belts (never used, in Rubens' experience) and small pockets at the side with splash guards. Of considerably more interest to Rubens were the fold-up panels that flanked the seats; two seventeen-inch TFT screens were tied into a hard-wired LAN that could be connected with all of the government's secure computer systems. The panels also had keyboard and assorted ports for plug-ins, including the memory device Rubens had loaded with the information he believed pointed to the coup plot.

The stations also included television feeds. Rubens turned his on, cycling among the cable news networks to see what they were reporting on. It was a mistake—all three featured live feeds from a press conference called by the House Judiciary Committee to announce that it was going to hold hearings into Congressman Greene's death. The head of the committee, an ambitious Democrat from California named James Mason, smiled and stared portentously at the screen as he declared that any elected representative's demise was a matter of primary concern for the public.

"So you believe it wasn't an accident?" one of the reporters asked Mason.

The congressman bobbed and weaved, giving hints of his true political potential.

Yesterday morning, Rubens had called one of the FBI agents who had interviewed him to discuss what he called "speculative ideas." Along the way he suggested how they might go about checking the guitar and the pool to make sure this was a freak thing. The agent not only thanked him but also asked if he happened to know anyone who could do the work.

Naturally, he demurred at first. But within a few minutes an assistant called back with information about a company in Virginia that might be able to help. Coincidentally, the company did not hold a contract with the NSA. Not so coincidentally, its vice president had been one of the midlevel analysts who got a soft landing during the infamous wave of layoffs in the 1990s—a soft landing Rubens had helped arrange.

The findings were already en route to the Bureau: *"Bare wires and a short in one of the pickups. Alterations to the amp the guitar was plugged into, causing it to supply an outrageous amount of electricity to the guitar. Alterations to the fuse circuitry. Fraying on the pool heating elements that seemed suspicious or at least out of the ordinary. All told, a bizarre, fatal combination."*

Purposeful? The lab didn't say, though the implication was clear.

Rather than short-circuiting the investigation, Rubens had made things worse. The inconclusive report would encourage speculation once it was leaked—inevitable now that Congress was involved.

"Gilligan's Island again?" said President Marcke, pushing into the compartment.

Rubens rose from his seat as Marcke, Hadash, Blanders, and James Lincoln, the secretary of state, came in.

Followed by Collins.

"Ms. Collins," said Rubens.

"NSA finally realized we were right, huh?" she said, smirking as she sat. The helicopter whipped upward.

"We're headed for Camp David," said the president. "I'm going to guess you can't stay, Billy."

Rubens hadn't planned to, but could he afford to let Collins and the CIA have the president's ear?

God, he thought to himself, what if Marcke is banging her?

God.

"No, sir, I, uh, have a full agenda. Things are popping," said Rubens.

"Next time," said the president. He glanced at the television screen. "Mason announcing his inquiry, eh?"

Rubens nodded.

"You know, I think he's related to *the* James Mason. Not the actor, the Virginia statesman."

"Could be."

"Mr. Rubens has data confirming the CIA assessment," said Hadash.

"Go for it, Billy."

"We've been studying intercepts relating to various troop movements, status states, that sort of thing. They've been building very slowly," said Rubens. "And this lines up with the analysis by the CIA people. Which I'm sure the DDO could talk about if necessary."

"I already have," said Collins.

Would Marcke really give it to her? Rubens momentarily felt a wave of nausea.

"In the past few days, we harvested communications via an E-mail network used, at least until now, strictly by diplomatic personnel." Rubens explained that the odd thing about the E-mails wasn't the information—that was fairly routine—but the fact that they were so heavily encrypted in a back-channel or even off-channel communications line. He then ticked off indicators—fuel, leaves allowed, even the assignment of medical personnel to sick call—that showed all of the units were getting ready for some type of campaign. As he spoke, he inserted his memory device into the keyboard in front of him and punched up the data on the screens.

"And it's not a fresh move against the southern rebels?" asked Blanders.

"The units are mostly near Moscow and in Siberia," said Rubens. "Two armored battalions have been moved within a twelve-hour drive of Moscow, and there's another about the same distance outside of the dachas south of—"

"The southern units are also within range for an offensive in the Caucasus," noted Blanders.

"True," said Rubens. The defense secretary was a potential ally, and so Rubens made sure to concede the point graciously. "If it were just those units, I'd agree."

"There is overlap with the units we tagged," said Collins. "Of course, we have additional humint."

She said "humint"—short for *human intelligence,* or old-fashioned "spy information"—as if it were potting material for an exotic houseplant.

Rubens brushed aside her attempt to steal back the spotlight. The CIA might have made the first guess, but the NSA had done the hard work to show what was really going on. "Most interestingly," he said, "they've killed Laci Babinov."

"Babinov is who?" asked the president.

"The leader of the riot police in Moscow," said Hadash.

"Actually, the number two man, but he's really the one in charge," said Rubens. "He was on the aircraft shot down by the unmarked MiG."

They all knew which plane he was talking about, so Rubens didn't have to explain. Collins took another shot at bringing the attention back to the CIA by saying that two colonels who worked as military attachés in the Kremlin were missing from their posts, but the others ignored her. Rubens had clearly supplied the key.

"It does line up," said Hadash. "But who's behind it?"

"Perovskaya," said Collins. "Has to be."

The defense minister was an obvious choice, and Rubens would have suggested Perovskaya himself if she hadn't. But now he made a face. "No intercepts support that."

"Who else could it be?"

"I don't know, Christine, but until I have evidence, I can't say."

Using her first name was a slip and he knew it; Rubens went silent.

"What about the shootdown?" asked the secretary of state. "The plane was similar to yours. Maybe they simply thought it was another."

"Doubtful," said Rubens. Lincoln should not have known that the planes were similar. Who leaked that to him? Collins? But she shouldn't have known, either.

Hadash? Blanders? The president?

"The Russian media are playing it as if it were an accident, and there were no intercepts at all about it," said Rubens, subtly changing the subject. "No transmissions at all. Highly unusual. As far as we can tell, the MiG that shot it down didn't even get a tower clearance to take off."

"So the consensus is that the military, or part of the military, is planning to revolt," said the president. "Do we know when the coup is planned for?"

"Impossible to know," said Rubens.

"Within a week," said Collins.

"What do we do?" asked the president. He pushed back in his seat.

"We should tell Kurakin," said Lincoln. "Head it off."

"That might not be enough," said Collins.

"We should squash it," said Rubens.

They all looked at him.

"You have a plan?" asked Hadash.

"No," said Rubens. He saw Collins' mouth twist—she did, or at least was going to claim she did. "Not a specific plan. But if we're concerned about a coup, obviously we could interfere with it. Desk Three has the capability."

Rubens knew he was overreaching, but he felt he had to stake out the ground quickly. Desk Three was supposed to be the country's preeminent covert intelligence organization—it couldn't afford to sit on the sidelines.

He wasn't overreaching. Desk Three could disrupt communications among the different military groups quite easily. Providing the Russian president with real-time intelligence would be child's play—they did it all the time for their action teams on the ground. The Russian president would have to do the heavy lifting himself, of course—but with judicious assistance, surely he would prevail.

"A coup would be disastrous," said the secretary of state. "But we can't get directly involved."

"True," said Hadash. "On the other hand, it would be very risky. We still don't know exactly who's behind the coup."

"We're working on it," said Rubens.

"So are we," said Collins.

"I can't see helping Kurakin, or any Russian," said Blanders. "It's galling."

"I don't necessarily disagree on an emotional level," said Rubens. "But of course, it may be to our advantage."

"Maybe," conceded Blanders, still clearly reluctant.

"Billy, put together a plan," said the president.

Rubens let himself bask in the rarefied air of presidential approval for a few seconds, then turned his mind toward a plan that would justify it.

27

The weapon was simplicity itself. A stainless steel barrel, an aluminum frame, a plastic stock. The bolt eased bullets into firing position, treating them like the perfectly selected hand-prepared rounds they were. The sight itself was not particularly powerful at 6×42, but it was more than adequate and perfectly matched to the weapon. With the proper preparation, the assassin could guarantee a hit at 600 meters. Even at that range, the 7.62mm bullet would slice through a man's skull as easily as if it were an overripe cantaloupe.

Once, the assassin's commander had objected to the fact that he preferred the British gun—an L96A1, procured at a ridiculous cost that included two lives—to the more readily available and homegrown Snaiperskaya Vintivka Dragunov. The SVD was not, in fact, a poor weapon and, depending on the circumstances, might surpass the L96A1. If the assassin still did his work in the field, for example, he would perhaps have preferred the SVD for its reliability.

But he did not do his work in the field. He was stationed now in the second story of a hotel in Doneck on the Black Sea, waiting for his target's limousine to appear on the street. He had waited here in fact for two days. Another man might think, after so long a wait, that the information that had been provided to him was incorrect. Another man might have sought other instructions.

But the assassin did neither. This was, in large part, his

great value. He did not need to sleep—a bottle of blue pills, one every six hours, took care of that. He kept a large chamber pot and never drank or ate while waiting. He had been at his post for eighteen hours straight and could stay for at least another twelve, if not eighteen or twenty-four. He had waited three entire days to kill a leader of the Chechnya criminals, so this was nothing.

The assassin had killed twenty-three people, not counting the men he had slain as a paratrooper. Besides the L96A1 zeroed in on the entrance to the hotel across the street, the assassin had a submachine gun at his feet. This was not intended for his target—the L96A1 was more than adequate. But the assassin did not trust his employers—for good reason, he knew—and in fact much of his preparation had involved finding an acceptable escape route.

The phone on his belt began to vibrate. Still watching the window, he reached down and pressed the talk button.

"Yes?" he said.

"It is postponed," said the voice on the other end. "Go to Moscow. Be there the day after tomorrow."

Without saying another word, the assassin punched the end button and began to take down his weapon.

28

When they returned to the highway, Lia and Dean went back in the direction they'd come for about ten miles, finding another highway running to the southeast. Just after turning off they stopped and refilled the truck's gas tank, hand-pumping it. They had passed at least two gas stations, but Lia told him the gas sometimes couldn't be trusted.

"Everybody's out to make a ruble," she said. "Country's going to hell."

With the girl out of the truck, Lia told him where they were going. All three locations they had to check were near the Kazym River, the first about a half hour's drive. Dean looked at the map on the handheld. They were more than two hundred miles north of where they had left the Hind and well to the east; they'd followed a rather twisted route to get here.

"How do you know the helicopter's still there?" he asked.

"May not be," said Lia. "We'll just scout around, see what we see. Kind of your job description, isn't it?"

"It wouldn't have been able to get to any of these spots without refueling," he told her. "And if it refueled, it could have gone anywhere."

"The Art Room coordinates all kinds of data, Charlie. Eavesdropping, signal captures, satellite pictures. Just relax."

"Garbage in, garbage out."

"Gee, that's original."

"Well, your gadgets and gizmos haven't done too well so far."

"Sure they have."

Dean scoffed. "Why don't we look for the MiG?"

"That's not our job."

"Somebody should."

"Did you do this in the Marines?"

"Which?"

"Question every stinking thing."

"All the time."

"Good."

Surprised by her answer, Dean pulled himself upright in the seat.

"The girl will be OK," said Lia, as if they'd been discussing her. "Really, she'll be OK."

"You told her to go become a prostitute."

"*I did not.*" Her face lit red. Then, in a much lower voice, a voice close to a whisper, she repeated herself. "I did not. She'll be OK."

As Lia shook her head, Dean noticed two very small creases near her eyes, aging marks she wasn't old enough to have.

"It's not my job to save people, not like that," said Lia. "It's not why I'm here."

"I think it is."

"You know, Charlie Dean, that's the same attitude that got a lot of people killed in Vietnam," said Lia.

"What do you know about Vietnam?" he snapped.

"My dad was there, my adopted dad," said Lia. "He told me what it was like."

The last thing Dean wanted to hear was warmed-over Vietnam stories. They were all well-constructed set pieces of horror. People trotted them out to show that they had been *touched, moved* by war. They still had nightmares. They still thought about it.

Except that most of the people who spit out the stories were full of shit.

He liked her better when she was being an asshole, he decided.

The first spot they were supposed to check out was an oil machinery plant, which dealt with companies like Petro-UK. It lay right off the highway. Lia saw the rusting fence and the sign with its Cyrillic letters as she passed, hit the brakes, and wheeled through a one-eighty, narrowly missing the only other vehicle they'd seen for the last fifteen minutes or so.

"Jesus," said Dean as the large tractor-trailer whipped about an inch from their bumper.

"They're not used to other drivers on the road here," said Lia. She glanced at her watch. It was before seven, but already there were people in the building. "Here's the deal. We're looking for a helicopter. You're the new accountant from Australia. I'll do most of the talking."

"I can't do an Australian accent," said Dean.

"I doubt they can, either."

Lia parked the car in a muddy lot, then hopped from the truck. They locked it; Dean adjusted his pistol under his sweater and followed her inside.

Accountants held a more important position in Russian businesses than in most Western companies. One token of this was the fact that they were the ones who tended to be arrested when the required permits or bribes weren't paid. So it wasn't surprising that when Lia mentioned Dean's cover to the man they met in the front room, he bowed deeply, put up his hands, and practically ran to the back to get the big boss. Lia's story was that they needed a helicopter. The boss protested that they were not in the business of selling aircraft—but then he proceeded to add that they did, as a matter of fact, have several available. He led Lia and Dean outside to a small jeeplike truck and drove them out through a yard filled with rusting tractor blades to a packed gravel yard filled with large pumps, pipes, and vehicles at least twenty years old. At the center of the field sat a thick cross of asphalt that obviously functioned as a helipad. Large plastic barrels sat at the far side, half-buried in the ground—obviously a fuel farm of some kind.

Lia pushed out her story, complaining that they needed a heavier helicopter than the Alouette the manager showed her. That led to two identical rather tired-looking machines parked at the farthest end of the large yard. They were squat, with two sets of rotors, one atop the other, and a double-fin tail. Dean could guess from looking at the machines that neither was what they were looking for, but Lia played through, checking the craft and even asking if one could be started up. The manager didn't know how and the pilot wasn't available. Perhaps they'd come back, Lia said.

As they were walking back to the truck, she stopped to tie her shoe. The manager began talking to Dean in English about the difficulties of doing business here. Dean simply shrugged. He worried that he might have to eventually say something about Australia and decided he would divert the manager with a story about being educated in America—he could bullshit plausibly about that, he thought. But Lia caught back up with them and it wasn't necessary to say anything else.

"We have more stops," she said, taking the manager's card. "We will be in touch."

"Those were Helixes we looked at?" Dean asked as they got back in their truck.

"Kamov KA-27s," she said. "Match the pictures the Art Room gave me."

"How do you know the Art Room's right about what kind of chopper it was?"

"You really are a Luddite, aren't you?"

"No. I just don't trust everything I'm told."

"They're the right kind of helicopters."

"So civilians have military helicopters?"

"Well, civilians *do* have military *type* helicopters, even in the West," said Lia. "But here there's a bit more flow back and forth. You have to trust us on this one, Charlie Dean."

"If they don't sell helicopters," said Dean, though he knew he was being stubborn, "why do they have so many?"

"Oh, they always say that," said Lia. "See, if they sold helicopters, they would need certain licenses. We might be from Moscow instead of spies."

She laughed and started the engine.

By the time they reached their next site, the morning had turned almost balmy, which brought the bugs out in full force. A swarm seemed to attach itself to them as they drove into a small town. Several rows of fairly large houses sat in a staggered semicircle next to the main road; beyond them were oil fields. The town gave way to a tall fence, which at first seemed to contain empty land. Nearly a half-mile from the start of the fence it veered toward the road. A hundred feet farther down it crossed at a gated cul-de-sac. A large building sat at what would have been the middle of the road had it continued. There were other buildings behind it; the complex seemed to stretch a fair distance. A guard stood in the middle of the road; there were others beyond him. All had AK-74s, and there was at least one machine-gun post inside the gate.

"I think it's time to turn around," said Dean.

"Yup," said Lia, who nonetheless drove right up to the guard and started talking to him. He didn't buy whatever she tried to sell. He gestured sharply for them to turn around and finally showed his anger by raising his gun. Still chattering, Lia put the truck in reverse and backed down the road.

"Not much for chitchat," she said after they had gone back through the town to the main highway.

"What'd you say to him?"

"I asked if he knew someone who wanted to get laid."

"What'd you really say to him?"

She laughed. "Why don't you think that's what I said?"

"What'd you really say to him?"

"I told him I was looking for my brother. Didn't even break the ice."

"This has got to be the place."

"You think, Charlie? But what if the Art Room agrees? Then what? They can't be right."

They refilled the truck's gas tanks. Lia consulted the map on her handheld, then got back on the highway, heading to another town about five miles farther south. As they drove, Dean took the binoculars and looked back at the area, trying to see something beyond the forest of oil pumps and fences.

"It's some sort of school," said Lia. "They used to send KGB officers there for what we'd call SWAT training. That was fifteen years ago."

"Now what do they do there?"

"I don't know yet," said Lia. "We'll ask when we check in. In the meantime let's go see what's behind door number three."

29

Foreigners throwing around wads of cash attracted several different types of attention in Russia. The most dangerous was the fawning, sell-my-brother-for-a-ruble attention; Karr realized that anyone being overly nice to his face was more than likely calling a *mafiya* connection to tip them off to a potential kidnapping candidate. The Russian gangs were considerably more difficult to deal with than the security police simply because they were unpredictable. Not even the NSA had the resources to track the myriad groups that operated throughout the country. A few were aligned with fairly well-known political or business figures, and a couple were essentially military units moonlighting in the open season for graft. But the vast majority of Russian gangsters were small-time hoodlums with very small operations, many of which either were quasi-legal or would be entirely legal if the proper permits were obtained.

The corruption pained Karr, even as he took advantage of it to do his job. The price for the jet fuel and the two large drums to transport it was so low that the fuel was either watered down or stolen.

Fashona swore it wasn't watered down, and since they pumped it themselves, they got reasonably close to the amount they had paid for. They rolled the barrels up the single wooden plank into the back of the ancient Zil they'd hired, and moved out of the airfield. Karr fingered his pistol as they passed the guards, but he could tell from the men's faces they were too depressed to even bother stopping them to ask their business.

His mother had come from Russia as a young girl, the daughter of a refusenik. Though she loved America, she still talked fondly of Russia and often spoke of going back to visit now that the country was a democracy.

He wanted to tell her about the country, but security concerns absolutely forbade him to. It probably wouldn't have done much good; she wouldn't believe what he'd tell her. At best, she would blame the woes on the Communists.

Karr wouldn't completely dismiss that. But it seemed to him that the problem had more to do with greed—a disease imported from the West. As Russia tried to catch up to America, it had lost something of its nobility.

Most people had a depth and warmth that hardship only enhanced. But others were deeply infected with greed and cynicism. It was if it were one of the mosquito-borne viruses plaguing the new oil fields.

Heading back toward Sitjla, the driver of the truck became somewhat talkative. In his early thirties, he owned the truck with his brother, who was riding in the back and carried a small pistol concealed—or at least intended to be concealed—on his calf.

"I can tell my children I helped the CIA," said the driver, whose name was Varnya.

"If I was with the CIA, I wouldn't have run out of petrol," laughed Karr. "And I would have paid you twice as much."

The man laughed, though he insisted he knew that the two men were both American and members of the Central Intelligence Agency. According to Varnya, the CIA ran Russia, but this was an improvement from the days when the KGB had. Varnya's grandfather—it may have been his great-grandfather, as Karr couldn't quite stay on top of the accented and slightly drunken Russian—had been a political prisoner in one of the camps. After twelve years, he had been released with the understanding that he would stay out of western Russia. A similar story could have been told by half of the local inhabitants, if not more.

Varnya began to speak of things that his grandfather had told him—bodies in the river, a forest of skulls. His anger started to build. He offered to share his vodka. Karr agreed, knowing that to refuse would be a serious insult. He blocked the mouth of the bottle with his tongue every time he tipped the bottle back. The sting of the liquor helped keep him awake on the long ride.

It was dark when they got back to the helicopter. Varnya and his brother volunteered to help roll the barrels toward it. Then, as Karr knew they would, the two men pulled out weapons and tried to rob them.

"What would your grandfather think?" said Karr, shaking his head.

Varnya's chest inflated, alcohol-fueled anger rising within him. He looked at Karr as if he were the KGB man who'd locked his grandfather in exile and tormented the family for three generations. He raised his pistol to fire, pushing his arm toward the American.

Fashona's first bullet caught him in the side of the head. He didn't bother firing another. By the time Varnya dropped, Karr had shot the brother twice in the forehead with a Glock 26.

"Motherfuckers," said Fashona. "I told you they'd wait to see if we really had the chopper."

"Yeah," said Karr. He slid the Glock 26 back into its hiding place up his sleeve. "Kinda pains me that they didn't believe us. Nobody trusts anybody these days."

30

The third site Dean and Lia checked was a civilian airport. Several new Fokkers sat amid a smattering of older Russian types in neat rows beyond the terminal building. When they found the Helix they saw it had been plumbed for crop dusting. Lia took several photos of it with a digital camera about the size of a cigarette lighter. Back in the truck, using her handheld computer she compared it to pictures of the Helix that had inspected the crash site. They didn't seem to be a match, though the program she used on the handheld would only say the results were inconclusive.

By now it was early evening. A Western-style motel sat near the airport. They went there and took two rooms, then had dinner in what amounted to a cafeteria on the basement level. Lia had to go outside to get the phone to work. Dean sat at the table sipping a vodka, the first alcohol he'd had since getting the assignment. He rolled the liquor around his tongue, letting the sting loosen his sinuses.

The mission Hadash had sent him to do was over. The plane was obviously destroyed, and sooner or later the material they'd loaded into the Hind would be returned to the States for analysis to prove it.

That was all he was here for. Hadash had said something along the lines of "you'll just be a tourist."

Or a baby-sitter. They needed one.

Not really. Lia was a bit much, and Tommy Karr had

rubbed him the wrong way, a little too easygoing for his own good, Dean thought—but they were competent in their own way, comfortable with technology in a way Dean would never be.

Not that he was a Luddite, for christsakes. What the hell was a stinking Luddite anyway? Some sort of nineteenth-century English revolutionary worried about losing his job to a machine. Which Dean definitely wasn't.

Dean watched as two young men came into the room with overloaded trays of food. They were loud, obviously drunk; he couldn't understand what they were saying, but it was obvious they were pretty full of themselves. Both wore track pants and Nike basketball shoes; their shirts were opened several buttons down and they had rows of gold chains around their necks.

"Credit card thieves," Lia said, sliding in across from him. "They broker numbers."

"How do you know?"

"You figure things out after a while. Karr'll meet us in the hotel. Let's go get some sleep."

Upstairs, he had started to go to the room across the hall when she opened her door. She grabbed the sleeve of his sweater.

"Where are you going?"

"Get some z's."

"We stay together. Don't look at me like that—one of us sleeps, the other stands guard. We sweep the room first." She took her handheld out and slid a small silver bar into an expansion slot at the top. "Talk," she told him.

"About what?"

"Your sex life. Just talk."

Dean began reciting the alphabet. Lia held her computer in two hands and swept up and down the walls, looking a little like a supplicant worshipping the god of hideous wallpaper. Dean followed as she worked her way around to the bathroom.

"No bugs," she said finally. She started the shower. "Which doesn't mean we can't be bugged."

"How?"

"Walls are thin and there's plenty of glass. Picking up the vibrations off them is child's play."

"So what do we do?"

"Don't say anything and we won't have a problem."

"How about sneezing?" The bathroom smelled like week-old mold and was getting to his nose.

"I wouldn't worry about it. I'll keep watch," Lia added. "But first I want to take a shower."

She pulled off the heavy black sweater and undershirt she'd been wearing, leaving only a thick gray sports bra between Dean and her breasts. They weren't large but stood out well against her flat belly. "Excuse me, can I have a little privacy?"

"Don't flatter yourself," said Dean, squeezing out the door and into the other room. He picked up the A-2, deciding it would be more useful than the pistol if they were attacked. There were two locks on the door—a fairly useless chain and a better dead bolt—though anyone who really wanted to get in would have the door down in about five seconds. Dean pushed the room's chair against it but couldn't find a way to wedge it home. Finally he moved the chair against the wall so that it would keep the door from opening more than half-way.

"What are you doing?" Lia asked, emerging from the shower.

She was completely dressed—somewhat to Dean's disappointment, he realized.

"Making it harder for anyone to get in."

"Yeah, that'll slow 'em down." Shaking her head, she reached back into the bathroom and took a towel to wrap her wet hair in. Then, palming a pistol so small it looked like a preschooler's toy, she went out into the hallway. Ninety seconds later, she was back.

Dean watched silently as she took her handheld and hit a quick set of keys. A blurry window opened up on the screen, then split in half. Dean realized it was a video feed from two cameras in the hall.

"They're the size of nickels," she said. "I mounted them under that hideous light fixture. It'll do until morning." She put the small computer down on the bureau top, then finished toweling her damp hair. "You gonna take a shower?" she asked.

"Nah," said Dean.

"Suit yourself." She pulled over the chair so she could sit, positioning it near the bureau and holding the A-2 in her lap.

"What was the gun?" Dean asked.

"Which?"

"The little gun."

Lia reached to her sweater and pulled a small pistol out like a magician making a bouquet of flowers magically appear. "It's a Kahr," she said, holding it out in her palm. "Custom-made. Here."

The silver steel gun looked like a K9 with its stock and clip sawed off. The trigger and guard were a little too small for Dean's fingers.

"Nine-millimeter?" he asked.

"Nine-millimeter."

"This small it must be hard to aim."

"If I have to use it, I'm not going to miss," she said, taking the gun back. "I'm going to be right on top of whoever I'm shooting."

"So you get the high-tech weapon and I get the rusty old six-gun."

"First of all, that's a .44 Magnum," said Lia. "Second of all, you're the one who's always putting down high-tech gear."

She returned the weapon to its hide, a pocket in the sleeve of her sweater where it could nestle undetected.

"Better get some sleep," she told him. "Karr'll be here in a few hours, and he always wants to party."

31

Malachi Reese slid his headset off, put both hands at the center of his scalp, and began to scratch. His fingers cut a symmetrical pattern across the top of his head, ending finally behind his ears.

He'd read somewhere that this increased the blood circulation to the brain. It was probably complete pseudo-scientific bull, but Malachi liked the tingle it left. He bent his head back, then down, zoning for a moment on the tiny red light of his MP3 player. Then he pulled the headphones back and looked at the status screen.

"Decision time," he told the Art Room, studying the computer's proposed trajectory from Platform 2. "You have sixty seconds left in this launch window, and the next is three hours away."

"We need listening devices on Site B," said Telach finally. "That's it."

Malachi turned to the screens on the left, paging up a computer-rendered diagram of Site B, the facility in north-central Russia that the NSA ground ops had been turned away from. This was obviously a military base, not the best application for the Vessel-launched listening devices—they were small and looked like rocks but could be detected by a trained counterintelligence officer.

"We really should line up the RS-93," he repeated.

"I know you want to fly the plane," Telach told him. "But

this isn't worth the delay—or the expense. Do what you can."

"Yes, ma'am."

Malachi uploaded the mission information into the flight computer, selected the proper configuration—all listening devices—and began the launch countdown as his MP3 whipped into a section of tunes from a Bob Dylan tribute. The Vessel whipped out from the satellite station in a sharp downward angle, and he had to sit on the retros to angle it into the proper path.

"Platforms, we're going to need a diagnostic on Two," he told the maintenance group when he was finally confident that he had the Vessel on course. "Hey, Baldie, I had a bad angle on the launch, dude, and it's all your fault."

Malachi sipped his strawberry-milk drink while the maintenance tech debriefed him. The bad launch meant he was going to have trouble getting the Vessel into a recovery zone following deployment; he'd have to red-button it.

"Gotta go," he told Baldie as the computer flashed its five-second countdown to Hydra.

"Hey," said Rockman over the NSA line.

"Hang tight, Rock." Malachi hit his commands. He had good telemetry from the Vessel—the wings had deployed—but the track on SpyNet disagreed with his own data. The difference was only two meters—but at this altitude and speed, two meters would translate into several miles at the target. He tried two refreshes but couldn't get them to agree. There was no time to run a diagnostic to find out which was right.

"Yo, Mom, listen, I have a disagreement on my course position," he told Telach. "What I'm going to do is split the drop. I think I can hit both projected sites."

He said that before doing the calculations.

"What kind of coverage are we going to have?" asked Telach.

Duh.

"A quarter of what we planned," said Malachi. "Half the

devices over half the area. I'll jack the power if you want, but you'll kill the endurance."

"Acceptable," said Rockman.

Malachi pounded the keyboard and got the two drop points worked out. The extra maneuvers left him with a self-destruct point only twenty miles from the second drop, which called for a verbal override not only from him but also from Telach.

"Go for it," she said.

To interpret the voice intercepts provided by the miniature bugs, Desk Three used specialists from the NSA's translation section, who were fed the intercepts in real time over a dedicated network. The translators used a version of Speaker ID—a neural network computer program based on the Berger–Liaw Neural Network Speaker Independent Speech Recognition System developed at the University of Southern California for the agency and the Defense Department. Speaker ID could separate recorded conversations into dialogue transcripts almost instantaneously; the exact speed depended on conditions and what the program's mentors sometimes referred to as interference from the human linguists working with the gear. An uncorrected transcript appeared on one of Rockman's screens in near real time; a more polished draft could be called up on a sixty-second delay. The runner preferred to rely on the translation supervisor, who could summarize developments quickly. The supervisor was with the translators in another part of Crypto City, though he could take a station in the Art Room for important missions.

"Macho talk," said the translation supervisor, Janet Granay. "A lot of conversations. General stuff. We'll start harvesting in a few seconds." The corrected transcripts were entered into a computer program that searched for key words such as cities or military commands. The program would then flag the conversation streams, highlighting them for the supervisor. While the program was definitely useful, in practice Granay could probably keep up with what was for her a limited number of conversation streams without its help.

"We're looking at a Marine base then?" asked Rockman. "That's my main question, if I can confirm my background."

"We're still working on it. We have only six conversations here. A lot of snoring. It's nighttime over there."

"I can wait," said Rockman. Site B was a bit of an interesting mystery. The most recent satellite photo showed equipment ordinarily associated with Marine units, even though this was deep in Siberia, not a place known to house the extremely small Russian amphibious forces. A vehicle analysis put the force strength just short of a battalion—which would make it the largest concentration of Marines outside of naval bases in the Far East.

Telach theorized that they were looking at an Army unit that had inherited Marine gear, but NSA's researchers could find no evidence of that. Large military units were routinely tracked across the globe, so the appearance of a fairly significant size force here was interesting in and of itself. So far no reference to it had been found in the mountains of daily intercepts out of the Kremlin and defense ministry.

Lia's data didn't provide much illumination. Her images of the men, transmitted over the phone hookup, showed that they were probably wearing Marine uniforms.

Rockman studied the eavesdropping data; one of the flies was close enough to pick up what seemed to be a conversation at the main gate. It consisted largely of a debate over how much vodka could be drunk without pausing to take a breath.

"So let's say the helicopter belonged to them," suggested Telach, sitting at the console next to him. "What's it mean? Units operating independently of Moscow."

"Private force, answerable to the defense minister," suggested Rockman. "Big, though."

"Why the defense minister?"

Rockman shrugged. "Who else? Yeltsin's ghost?"

"Could be a *mafiya* network. Or something we haven't tracked yet." She rubbed her finger along her chin, considering the situation. "We'll have to send Karr up there to see what he can find. It's too big to ignore."

"Yeah. Mr. Rubens is going to want to know."

"Definitely."

"What do you want to do about Dean?" Rockman asked.

"Have Fashona fly him and the metal back, pack it into a transport, and get it home."

"Karr's going to complain about having the Hind taken away."

"Who's running this operation, us or him?"

"You know Tommy."

They were interrupted by Granay. "You ought to listen to this," she said. "Line Four. And it matches, I checked it."

Rockman punched the feed button, bringing up the raw intercept in his earphones. He was about to key in a translated overlay when he realized he didn't have to: the voice being picked up by the tiny bug was speaking English.

American English. Reciting, in fact, a passage from the Bible—one so well-known that even Rockman, who was about as religious as Rin Tin Tin, could recite by heart.

"The Lord is my shepherd," said the voice shakily in a low whisper. "I shall not want."

Telach and Rockman looked at each other. They didn't need the audio library to know the voice belonged to Stephan Moyshik—aka Stephen Martin.

32

Favors begat favors. In exchange for the information that the consultant provided to the FBI on the guitar—information that would be forthcoming from the FBI anyway—Rubens had managed to obtain access to the local police department's complete investigation file on the Greene murder.

It was a shockingly easy transaction, though it required Rubens to go to the police station in person. The investigator clearly didn't know who he was. He had accepted the rather bland declaration that Rubens was "looking into the matter on an informal basis for the administration" far too easily. That didn't speak well for the quality of the investigation, but then, he'd never thought very highly of them to begin with.

And yet, the file was fairly thorough. The interviews with the surviving band members indicated that the guitarist had never jumped into a pool while playing before, with or without his guitar—but then again, they'd never played anywhere there was a pool. He did do bizarre stuff, no question. Plunking himself into the water, wire and all, was completely in character.

The band members didn't know much about Greta Meandes and were vague on whether she even worked, let alone what she did. Rubens got the impression that they had been playing up the drugged-out airhead band thing for the police, but in any event they had added nothing of substance. One suggested the guitarist had been "boffing" her; the investigator's notes said specifically that he doubted it.

The notes suggested there was plenty of opportunity for the guitar to have been tampered with. The detective had attempted to put together a time line, but it was full of gaps. Obviously working on the assumption that it was a freak accident, he hadn't even bothered to speak to everyone on the guest list, though Greta had provided one.

Rubens' name, of course, was on it. He had to exert every bit of his self-control not to grab it from the file. He surely would have if the detective had left the room.

Not that it would have done much good. By now the congressional committee would know he had been there, though no one had made an issue of it.

Yet.

It required no imagination and even less paranoia to envision the scene:

> **Congressman Mason:** By the way, did you see Representative Greene the whole time he was in the pool?
>
> **Witness:** No, actually. William Rubens was in my way.
>
> **Congressman Mason:** William Rubens? [pretends to be shocked] Is that *the* William Rubens who works with the NSA?
>
> **Witness:** I wouldn't know. . . .

By the end of the hearing, the papers would be printing that the death was an NSA plot. They'd have it all figured out.

Rubens, waiting to clear the last check into the Art Room, wondered how he could prove that his cousin had murdered the SOB. That, and only that, would end the investigation.

But there was no proof. If this were a Desk Three mission, he could have such proof manufactured—a security video showing her playing with the guitar would suffice.

Of course, this wasn't a mission, and it was his cousin he was thinking of railroading. Nor would he break the law by manufacturing evidence.

Still, if he was convinced his cousin committed the murder, if he had real evidence, he'd definitely give it to the police. That was his duty.

Especially if it would ward off potential embarrassment.

Not that it wasn't embarrassing to have a cousin accused of murder. But that was preferable to being accused yourself.

Rubens cleared the matter out of his head as he waited for the computer to admit him to the Art Room, substituting his yoga mantra instead. He needed to clear his mind so he could focus on the Russian coup and his plan to thwart it.

If he could only *prove* Greta did it, he'd save everybody a lot of grief.

Not everybody, but definitely himself.

The Art Room door opened. Telach looked like she was about to explode.

"Martin's alive," she blurted. "We have his voice pattern at Veharkurth."

"Martin?"

"The Wave Three op. Yes."

"You're sure?"

"Matches exactly. We have a possible location. We have the facility sketched out, but we're going to update. We'll have a satellite on-station in twenty minutes."

Rubens' skepticism grew as Telach detailed the situation. The voice they thought was Martin's had spoken only for a minute or so, saying a short prayer apparently to himself. Analysis put it in one of two buildings about equidistant from the bug's location in the northwestern corner of the facility.

"Is it a prison or what?" asked Rubens, looking at the satellite details.

"It's two things," said Telach. "One is a base for a Marine unit that Defense Intelligence says is attached to a Black Sea naval force."

"Black Sea?"

Telach smirked. "Obviously, something's wrong somewhere. Look at the right side of the complex. Serious SAM defenses."

"Unit protection?" asked Rubens.

"Well, I wouldn't rule anything out," she said. "But this

deep in Russia, not, as far as we know, connected to the standard defense network."

"Not connected?"

"Doesn't show up in our inventory," she said. "Again, not to jump to conclusions."

"So what else do they do there?" Rubens asked.

"My bet is it's a lab or a research facility connected to their laser operation," said Telach. She reached to the console and punched up a new set of satellite photos on the main board. The series showed a thin blue rectangle along roads and wasteland. "There's a dedicated fiber-optic line between one of the Wave Three targets and the facility."

The NSA had studied the possibility of breaching the network linking the laser facilities nearly a year before, ultimately deciding that it could not be penetrated without detection. Rubens did not remember this site as part of the network, though of course he could not expect to.

"There were no Marines here then," said Telach. "Not when the line was built. It was originally tagged as a supply depot and possibly a backup laboratory. I have a call in over to the laser specialists; they may be able to fill us in."

Rubens looked at the situation map. The Wave Three aircraft had been shot down nearly three hundred miles away; the plane's target was another hundred or more to the south. The actual weapons facilities were between the Marine base and the Wave Three target. Four other buildings believed to house associated research facilities were within the same grid. The project had probably been scattered to increase physical security.

Obviously, they had a lot of work to do. The connection between the Marines and the laser project was intriguing and had to be fleshed out. But the coup took precedence.

"How are we going to get Martin out?" said Telach.

"It can't be him," said Rubens.

"It is."

"No. There's no way he got out of the plane."

"Boss, it is," said Rockman, from his station. "Trust me."

"It's not a matter of trust," Rubens told them. "It's physically impossible for him to have escaped from the Wave Three package."

"The voiceprint is perfect." Rockman's voice was un-characteristically sharp and loud. "He must've gotten out before he hit the self-destruct. And you know as well as I do that the contract people on some of our aircraft have packed parachutes. Martin probably did as well. And the pilots."

It was, regrettably, true.

"Karr found traces of human remains in the wreckage," added Rockman. "So obviously someone went down with it. But not Martin."

"We have to get him out," said Telach.

"If it is Martin, I agree," Rubens said. "But we need more information. And regrettably, we have something of a higher priority. I need the team in Moscow."

Telach started to object.

"No, I need them in Moscow," said Rubens. For the moment, he couldn't explain why. "We don't have anything definite and I really need them in Moscow. Tell them to pack up and get out there."

"If that's Martin, we have to get him," said Telach. "And we're there now."

"The team isn't there," said Rubens, who pointed to the locator map that showed them a good twenty miles farther south.

"Boss, I'm begging you," said Telach.

Rubens clamped his lips together. He was not an unreasonable man. And truly if Martin was alive, retrieving him was very important. But the coup was more important, ultimately.

Still, he could not appear to be unmoved by his team's plea. It would undermine their effectiveness.

"Six hours to gather more information," said Rubens. "Anything beyond that needs my personal authorization. I want them in Moscow."

"Thank you," said Telach.

There was so much relief in her voice that Rubens decided to leave quickly, before she had a chance to do something foolish—like rushing over and kissing him.

33

Dean felt her moving toward him even before he heard her. He kept his face down on the bed, turned away from her.

For a second he let himself fantasize that she was coming to slip into bed with him. His desire surprised him, not least of all because he knew she wasn't coming to slip in beside him.

He opened his right eye, the one closest to the pillow. The lights were still on and the sun shone through the nearby window.

She touched the end of the bed.

"Can't resist me, huh?" he said. He pulled himself up.

Instead of a torrid comeback there was a shriek. A maid stood near the end of the bed, her face blanched in surprise. A stream of Russian—the tone showed it was not necessarily an apology—left her mouth as she backed from the room.

Lia was gone. The cushions from the seats and the curtains from the windows were piled next to him on the bed, which might have explained why the maid didn't realize he was there. Light streamed through the windows; it was now past eight o'clock, according to his watch.

Lia had taken all their gear from the room. She didn't answer when he knocked on the other door. Unsure what else to do, Dean walked out to the lobby area, slowly enough so the clerk could stop him if there was a message but, on the other hand, not trying to look as if he were expecting one. He went outside; the truck was gone.

A small building next to the motel looked like a restaurant. Inside, Dean took a place at a small table; the rest of the room was empty. The woman who came out from the back frowned when she saw him. Somewhere in her rapid-fire greeting he thought he heard a word similar to *coffee,* and so he said, *"Da."* This elicited more words, which sounded like questions. Dean nodded and said "Da" again, but apparently this didn't suffice as an answer.

"I'm just a dumb American," he told her, shrugging. "Bring me what you got."

The woman didn't laugh, but her answer didn't seem particularly belligerent, either. She tried her question again, this time speaking very slowly.

Dean nodded, having no clue what he was agreeing to.

The woman shook her head, then retreated into the back.

"Saying you're a dumb American rarely works, because they figure it's pretty much a given. You know what I'm saying?"

Dean slid around in his chair, trying not to look surprised as Karr walked over with his big grin and pulled over a chair from a nearby table.

"When did you get here?" Dean asked.

"Couple of hours ago." As if to emphasize that he'd had little sleep, Karr rubbed his eyes with the middle finger of each hand. It looked like a not-so-subtle obscene gesture, the kind kids might make to a teacher soon after learning the significance of the middle finger. "Some shit irritated my eye," said Karr. "Think the damn eye duct's clogged or something."

"Looks red."

"Yeah. Have to find something to throw in it. I'd go to a doctor, but all they'd offer is vodka."

"Where's Lia?"

"I told her to call the Art Room and see what the hell's going on. Fashona's doing some business with the helicopter. Let's have some breakfast."

The woman reappeared with Dean's order—a shallow bowl of fish covered with a thick, oily white liquid. Karr choked back a laugh, then began conversing with the woman. She frowned but soon retreated into the back, leaving the dish.

"What is this?" Dean asked.

"Got me. I just ordered some potatoes and *chay*. We can share."

"What's *chay*?"

"Tea."

The woman soon appeared pushing a cart with a monstrous bizarre-looking urn made of steel. She fussed quite a bit with large glass cups, placing them before Karr and Dean and adjusting small saucers of jam next to each one. Then she fetched a tin teapot from the bottom of her cart and poured water from the spigot of the urn. She then retreated into the back.

"She getting us bread?" Dean asked.

"No, the jelly's for the tea."

"The tea?"

"This is a high-class place," said Karr. He gestured at the urn. "Samovar and everything."

The woman soon returned with a pitcher. She poured small amounts of dark tea into the glass cups, then took more water from the samovar and added it to the cups.

"The *pelmeni* is probably really good here," said Karr, who added about half the jelly to his tea. "But I'm not all that hungry. *Pelmeni*—they're dumplings. Try 'em with vinegar sometime. Blow out your taste buds."

Karr could've been a college kid talking about the local diner. Hell, he looked like he was in high school, with his golden hair and offhand smile.

"You're pretty good with Russian," Dean said.

"Nah. I screw up the accents. Because of my mother. She was Russian."

"Blond Russian?" asked Dean.

"My dad's Norwegian." A big Karr grin. "Lia's actually

better than me. Don't tell her I said that, though. Go to her head."

"She wouldn't believe it if I did."

"Sure she would. She's got the hots for you. Princess is in looooove."

"Fuck you, too."

"I'm not busting your balls. She does."

Dean shook his head. Karr really was a kid, still raw, still jokey, not sure where the line was between being serious and goofing around.

When Dean was Karr's age, he'd known the line. He had to. He spent his days pushing through jungle as thick as a Persian rug. His life was stark and simple, focused on an uncomplicated goal—kill a specified Vietcong operative or officer, expected to be at a specific place and a specific time.

Of course, those specifics usually turned out to be fiction. The only thing you could really count on was fear. It boiled in the middle of your chest and came out in your piss and sweat; it kept you from sleeping and then made you sleep too well. At twenty, Charlie Dean was an old man in Vietnam. He'd grown considerably younger since.

Dean tried the tea without sweetening it. It was very hot and bitter, but the caffeine had an immediate effect. He pushed his fish dish to the very edge of the table, waiting to share Karr's potatoes.

The door opened, and Fashona came in, his face creased downward in a deep frown.

"Problems," said the helicopter pilot.

"Sit down," said Karr, pulling over a chair. "Have some mud."

"Nah."

But Karr's eyes seemed to cast a spell over Fashona, and he sank down just as the Russian appeared with a large platter of potatoes. They weren't the home fries Dean had expected. Rather, they seemed to have been boiled in some sort of thick white sauce. It tasted something like mayonnaise, slightly acidic. Probably an acquired taste, thought Dean, who was nonetheless so hungry he quickly ate about half the plate.

"Problem getting fuel for the Hind?" Karr asked Fashona.

"Nah, easy. That Helix came from a Marine base, and they want us to check it out. Lia's still getting the whole story." Fashona stopped as the woman reappeared with a teacup and a large round of very black bread. The table shook as she cut through the bread, which proved to be a country rye—tough on the teeth, Dean thought, though Karr raved about it.

A half hour later, Lia still hadn't appeared. Karr got up, taking a few bills from his pocket without bothering to wait for a check.

"More than enough, don't worry," he told the others, waving to the woman and bowing as he told her the food had been wonderful.

They found Lia in the truck, bent over her handheld and scowling. Dean watched her as Karr opened the driver's side door and leaned in.

"What the fuck are Marines doing in Siberia?" Karr asked.

"The Art Room doesn't have a fucking clue." She glanced at the others, her eyes holding Dean's for half a second. "They think Stephen Martin is in there."

"Who?"

"Wave Three. The operator in the plane."

"No way," said Karr. He laughed.

"No shit."

"Well, I guess we can have a look. Can we get the helicopter down near there without the Marines shooting us down?"

"We have five and a half hours. Then we have to leave for Moscow," said Lia.

"Moscow? You kidding?"

"No. Rubens gave the order." She held up the small computer to him. "According to Rockman, Martin is somewhere at the top left corner. There are two buildings there. They think they're either labs or prisons, maybe both. They might also be barracks."

"Good thing they narrowed it down." Karr handed the computer back to her, then took his out from his pocket. He held it near hers, obviously getting a download via the infrared connection. "They're sure it's Martin?"

"They heard him praying and they got a voice match. I think Rubens is skeptical, though."

Karr turned serious for a moment. "Five hours isn't going to give us enough time to get him."

"They don't want us to get him. They want us to go to Moscow."

"Ah."

"Ah yourself."

"Go pay off the hotel. I'll meet you all back at the helicopter."

"Where you going?" Dean asked.

"To tell the boss to eat shit," said Karr, starting the engine. He smiled, then threw the truck into reverse.

34

Rubens pushed back in his office chair, listening as his stereo played the first act of *Don Giovanni*—the scene, in fact, where one of the Don's lovers is warned of his treachery.

On his desk were two code-word classified, eyes-only papers. The reports were so secret that each one of their pages was imbedded with metal foil that acted as a tracking device. The reflective ink of the words and the fiber pattern in the paper itself made them difficult to read and harder to copy, although this was not impossible.

The top report was a twenty-page summary of the Russian coup plot, courtesy of Johnny Bib. The report expanded on the CIA estimate, backing it up with more specific information about the units that might be involved. Most notably for Rubens, Bib had managed to track down the MiG that downed the Wave Three aircraft, which belonged not to an IA-PVO or air defense unit but an IAP or Frontal Aviation squadron—the portion of the Air Force that ordinarily operated either outside of the country or, as the name suggested, on the front lines, not deep in the heart of Mother Russia. From the radio intercepts examined so far, only one Army unit was clearly involved, but it was a division of armor headquartered southwest of Moscow, within an easy drive of the Kremlin.

Like the CIA, however, Bib's group hadn't been able to pin down who was behind the coup. While the best guess was Defense Minister Vladimir Perovskaya, none of the very large set of intercepts concerning him—including literally thousands of phone calls he had made over the past few months—had so far yielded any trace of a coup. There were some materials still to be translated, and Bib had just directed one of his teams to review a series of digital images thought to contain encryptions mixed into the image data, but the only thing halfway incriminating was a series of instant messages sent in the clear with somewhat ambiguous statements: "Big Boy will fall" was about the worst.

Not knowing for sure that Perovskaya was behind the coup complicated the plan contained in the second paper on Rubens' desk, a plan to deal with the coup. Code-named Bear Hug, it included two phases: Phase One was to monitor the coup as it progressed, pretty much a no-brainer decision, though there were some intricacies involved in selecting and moving around assets. There were never enough satellites or platforms when something like this happened, and everyone in the intelligence community seemed to have their own perspective on what the priorities ought to be.

Phase Two outlined a strategy to stop the coup. Coordinated by Desk Three, the plan called for a massive attack on the command and communications systems of the plotters, cutting off their leaders, crashing their computers and other electronic gear. At the same time, Desk Three would provide intelligence about the coup to the Russian president and his loyalists. Clear lines of communication would also be provided to the government. Bear Hug followed strategies developed during war games played during the second Bush administration, updating them with some new computer weapons—most notably Piranha IV, an automated virus that had already been implanted in the Russian defense system— and new remote vehicles, including the F-47C.

Rubens' plan did not call for the direct involvement of any American force, since such a move might easily backfire. Field agents would be needed to monitor the situation in Moscow, augmenting the thick network of sensors. In addition, they would probably have to provide the Russians with radios, a delicate task Rubens wanted Karr and his team to handle.

Rubens, along with Admiral Brown and Johnny Bib, would present the plan at the White House in a few hours. While he would naturally defend it aggressively, Rubens did have some doubts. Not about whether it would work—surely it would. But like Blanders, he didn't trust Kurakin. The Russian president had his own agenda, and his intercepts showed he didn't think much of Marcke. Marcke had seen the intercepts, of course; even if they weren't so blatant, there were plenty of other examples of Kurakin's duplicity such as the laser system, which Kurakin continued to insist didn't exist.

Perhaps he didn't know. Perhaps Perovskaya had developed it on his own.

Highly unlikely, even in Russia.

The Federation might very well be part of NATO, but its history and relative strength still made it a serious threat. For all the concern about Islamic extremists and Chinese nuclear sales and rogue South American drug dealers, Russia remained capable of ending civilization at the push of a button.

The button on Rubens' black phone for the direct line to the Art Room lit. He picked it up.

"Karr needs to talk to you," said Rockman.

"OK," he told Rockman. A second later the agent's chronically overenthusiastic voice nearly broke Rubens' eardrum.

"Hey, what's happenin'?" said the team leader.

"You tell me," said Rubens.

"I'm going north to check this base out where Martin is. How the hell did he get out of the plane alive? It was burned to a crisp."

"I assume you're the one who's going to answer those questions," said Rubens.

"Yeah, but the only way I can do that is by grabbing his butt out of there. Rockman says we have like five hours now?"

"I gave them six."

"Not enough for us, boss. We need more time."

"Tommy, I need you in Moscow," said Rubens.

"When?"

"Tomorrow or the next day the latest." Rubens wasn't sure; the estimates on when the coup might begin were nebulous at best. "We're working out the details."

"Ah, we got plenty of time."

"You don't have the resources to take on a Marine brigade."

"Relax, it's just a battalion."

"I doubt that would make much of a difference."

"True. But the Russians would feel better with bigger odds," said Karr.

"I want you in Moscow."

"I'll get there." Karr's voice became instantly more serious. "If it's our guy, we have to get him. Got to."

The truth was, Rubens really didn't disagree. If Karr really did locate Martin, and really was convinced that it was him, he had to try to get him. They might not have the opportunity again.

Six hours was, in fact, too short.

"I need you in Moscow the day after tomorrow," said Rubens finally. "Get the Wave Three wreckage to the transport point. Scout the site. Be prejudiced toward caution."

"My middle name," said Karr.

"Tommy, I'm serious about you being careful. I don't want you going in there and up and getting slaughtered by a battalion or whatever it is of Marines. And I need you in—Tommy? Karr?"

He'd already hung up.

35

Kurakin waited until the cabinet ministers were rising before signaling that the defense minister should stay. Perovskaya reacted the way the Russian president knew he would—a self-important grin flickered across his face before he nodded solemnly and pretended that this was what he had intended all along.

Among other things, the meeting had touched on the death of Laci Babinov in an officially unexplained—and unpublicized—shootdown beyond the Ural Mountains. The death of the head of Moscow's riot police was a blow to Kurakin, an unfortunate accident, because Babinov was a supporter.

The shootdown had been necessary, however. Without it, the Americans might have realized the significance of the earlier attack.

"The unit responsible for the attack will be discovered," said Perovskaya after the others had gone. He was repeating word-for-word his earlier pledge. "I will find it myself."

"I'm sure you will," said Kurakin, who was actually sure he wouldn't. "But we have a more important matter to discuss."

Perovskaya looked at him with a mixture of surprise, caution, and disdain. His scalp seemed to glow beneath his thin hair, and the corner of his mouth curled just short of a sneer.

"The American ABM system must be neutralized," said Kurakin. "Until it is, we have no leverage. We cannot deal with the southern insurgents as they should be dealt with. We cannot punish the Chinese for helping them as we should."

Perovskaya surprised Kurakin by saying nothing. The president had not expected that. He had thought—hoped, assumed—that Perovskaya's native animosity toward the Americans would result in something suitably bombastic. Standing no taller than five-six, Perovskaya made up for his slight stature by blustering and talking the bully. But whether because he was caught so completely by surprise or genuinely thought the idea of blinding the Americans too belligerent even for him to suggest, he said nothing.

"We have discussed the ABM system many times," continued Kurakin. "The problem is well-known. But until now the idea has been to attack it directly, which of course would be suicidal. An indirect attack on only those satellites that can detect our launches—that is safer and more feasible. Without those satellites, the Americans could not warn the Chinese, much less stop an attack. Once the Chinese realize that, they will stop helping the rebels. They will realize this is aimed at them."

"The Americans won't—they'll interpret this as an act of war," said Perovskaya.

"Why?"

"Because it *is* an act of war." The defense minister practically crossed his eyes, obviously trying to discover whether Kurakin was tricking him in some way. "If the Americans knocked out our satellites, we would respond harshly."

"We couldn't," noted Kurakin. "Not with the ABM system in place. With it blinded, well, such things then might be possible—they would have to take that into account. We would have more leverage with them."

"You're thinking of the *Becha*," said Perovskaya, using the code word for the laser weapon.

"Of course."

"To strike the satellites, even in their parked orbits—the lasers are untested. It would be difficult."

No tests had been conducted, since doing so would tip

the Americans off. But Kurakin had seen the results of four different computer simulations; it would work.

Perovskaya was not privy to the simulations, which Kurakin had ordered using his envoys. So rather than citing them, the president merely said he was confident the weapons would work—and then asked pointedly if the troops manning the weapons were incompetent.

Perovskaya's face turned red, and finally he reacted the way Kurakin had foreseen.

"There are no more potent weapons," said the defense minister. "They could destroy the American satellites—they could eliminate missiles, aircraft—they are as effective as the Americans' own system. More effective."

Perovskaya caught himself. He was proving considerably more mature than Kurakin had believed he was. "Using them would be provocative. And of course, we would have to succeed."

"They would destroy their targets in seconds."

"From the time the order was given, three minutes. Four or five minutes between salvos. But no. It is far too risky."

"You feel an attack would be suicidal?" said Kurakin.

"Against our interests. Not suicidal. No, it would succeed. But the consequences."

"We need to stop the rebels, and the Chinese from helping them."

"Yes. But this—no."

Kurakin got up from the long table where he'd been sitting and walked across the room. He paused near the window. Through its glass he could see a line of tourists in the distance near Trinity Tower.

"No. I was rash," he told Perovskaya finally. "The rebels have me frustrated, and the Americans block us from dealing with them properly."

Perovskaya eyed him warily, clearly sensing that this had been a performance but not sure to what end. It was possible, Kurakin thought, that the defense minister would question others in the government about Kurakin's sanity. Hopefully

those conversations would take their usual belligerent tone—
and be remembered.

"I'm feeling very out of sorts," added the president. "The
election is only a few months off. Democracy is a stressful
thing."

"Yes."

"Thank you."

"That was it?" asked Perovskaya.

"Should there be more?"

When Perovskaya was gone, Kurakin picked up the phone
set and dialed into the private line of his security chief.

"So?" he asked.

"We can use it. He seemed reluctant at first."

"That can be edited out."

"In a sneeze."

"Make it happen," said Kurakin. "We will need the tape
in a few days."

36

While they waited for Karr at the helicopter, Lia propped herself against the pile of metal in the hold and tried to take a nap. She had her legs tucked up against the helicopter's sidewall and her jacket beneath her head as a pillow. Her right breast drooped ever so slightly, and Dean could easily imagine it bare.

Karr sailed into view, a big smile on his face. Dean and Fashona took a few steps away from the helicopter to meet him.

"Where's the Princess?" Karr asked.

"In the Hind sleeping."

"Ah, leave her a minute. She needs all the beauty rest she can get." Karr turned to Fashona. "Raymond, you and the Princess cart the wreckage down to the railroad head as planned. Paul Smith is on his way out to meet you. You know him?"

"CIA."

"The same. Come back with an S-1 pack. We'll be up checking out the Marines or whatever the hell they are. Did they tell you it's called Arf?"

"I think it's more like Veharkurth," said Lia, emerging from the Hind.

"Hey, Sleeping Beauty. *Arf* sounds better," said Karr. He turned back to Fashona. "When you bring the Hind up, I don't want them to see you, OK?"

"Really? No shit."

"I wouldn't shit you. You're my favorite turd."

"You're both so clever," said Lia.

Within a half hour, the helo had clattered off the runway. Dean and Karr were back in the truck, heading toward Veharkurth, or Arf, as Karr insisted on calling it.

"What's an S-1 pack?" Dean asked.

"Kind of a standard surveillance set of tools kind of thing," said Karr. "A lot of good toys; you'll like 'em. Even if you are a Luddite, baby-sitter."

"I'm not against technology," said Dean. "How are they going to get the helicopter close to the air base without being detected?"

"They'll figure it out. Stuff kind of comes to you. You know what I mean?"

"No," said Dean.

Karr looked at him and laughed. "You're a real ball-buster, Charlie Dean."

They were still about five miles from Arf on the main road when Karr suddenly pulled off it. He cupped his hand over his ear, obviously listening to a transmission from the Art Room. As he waited, Dean saw a small puff of dust on the horizon.

Karr said nothing but threw the truck into reverse. He did a one-eighty and headed back south.

"What's up?" asked Dean.

"Gomers are moving on us. There was a crossroad back about a mile, wasn't there?"

"Yeah."

They sped down the road toward it, fishtailing onto its barely packed surface. Karr charged down the road about five hundred yards, looking for a rise or some other vantage point from which to observe the approaching caravan. He finally spotted what looked like a trail leading to a hill on the right; twenty yards in, it turned into a bog. He jammed the brakes too late to avoid skidding about hub deep in the water but managed somehow to get the truck backed up onto more solid land.

"Out," he told Dean, jumping from the truck with the motor still running.

Dean followed through the water and mud to the rise. By the time he got there, Karr was on his belly, watching the trucks with his binoculars.

They were close enough that Dean didn't need the glasses. Twenty-three KAMAZ 5320 6×6s passed, doing about forty miles an hour. The backs were covered and it was impossible to know how many men were in each truck, but it was obvious there were plenty; Dean saw a few hanging off tailgates as the convoy passed.

"So, what's that tell us?" asked Karr, turning over when the procession had gone by.

Dean shrugged. "They're deploying somewhere. They have no heavy weapons. Twenty-three trucks, could be as many as two dozen guys in a truck. Five hundred men. Two whatever those were at the end, like Land Rovers. Company commanders, maybe."

"Good, baby-sitter, right up until the end. You're thinking in U.S. terms. That's just about an entire Russian Marine battalion we watched go by. Maybe the whole thing."

"Five hundred men is a battalion?" Dean asked.

"Marine battalions are bigger than the Army battalions," said Karr.

"An American battalion is over a thousand guys, and once you start talking about support—"

"This ain't America. In theory, the Russian Marine brigades have close to a thousand men, but I don't know of any force in the country that's at more than fifty percent strength, so I'm guessing that was the whole shooting match, give or take."

"If that was a full battalion, there'd be more support, more gear," said Dean.

"Maybe they left their ships home," said Karr. "We'll find out soon. Come on, before our truck sinks into the swamp."

• • •

A second convoy passed them as they drove, this one with only five trucks, all of them much older Zils. Dean told Karr these probably included backup gear and extra supplies for the main group.

"Could be, baby-sitter," he said.

"You ever going to stop calling me that?"

Karr just laughed. They drove for another two hours before coming to the town where the base was. It was still heavily guarded, and there didn't seem to be an easy way of looking inside or even examining the perimeter without being seen. The small settlement nearby offered no cover. There was a long stretch of fence near the highway; Dean saw a stake and a ribbon flag and guessed it was a minefield.

"We'll have to get the latest satellite download, then wait for Fashona and the Princess," said Karr. He gunned the truck off the muddy path they'd been on back onto the main highway. "There's some sort of old building up the road about two miles. Satellite pic shows it's deserted."

"Looks like your satellite's a little whacked," said Dean as they approached the building. Two dozen small tents were pitched near the cement-block structure; several campfires burned. "Maybe somebody should go up there and clean the lens."

"Could be we're hallucinating," said Karr cheerfully. Slowing to a stop, he rolled down the window and gazed at the small city for a moment, then turned off the engine. "Let's check it out."

At least a dozen men were staring at them. Dean couldn't see any rifles, but their ragged clothes could easily hide a myriad of weapons.

"Be a little safer to leave the engine running, don't you think?" said Dean. "One of us stay in the truck?"

"Don't be paranoid." Karr shut the door behind him nonchalantly.

Dean pushed out reluctantly, adjusting his pistol under his belt. Two of the men who'd been watching them walked toward Karr as he shambled forward and did his hail-fellow-well-met thing. Dean came around the back of the truck slowly. Something flashed on the left; instinctively he drew out his gun, dropped into a crouch, and yelled a warning.

In the next second, he realized it was simply a glint of light bouncing off a steel fry pan.

"Lighten up, baby-sitter," said Karr.

He said something to the Russians and they laughed. A few eyed Dean apprehensively, but they seemed to take his suspicion in stride. He slid his pistol back into his belt and tried smiling, but it was a weak effort at best.

One of the Russians walked up and offered him a drink from a water bottle. Dean, who hadn't had anything to drink since breakfast, took it.

And nearly choked on the homemade vodka.

"Don't spit it out," said Karr, pounding him on the back. "That's a big-time insult."

"Tastes like gasoline," managed Dean.

"White lightning, with a vodka tint," said Karr. "Never accept a drink in Russia. Once you do, you have to swallow it all and ask for more. Otherwise they'll think you're a wimp."

The man who had offered the bottle to Dean was now gesturing that he should have more. Dean tried giving him back the bottle, but the man waved him off. Dean tried to insist, but the man waved him away, his expression starting to cloud. Karr saved the situation by grabbing the bottle and taking what looked like a huge swallow, which elicited a happy remark from the Russian. Karr answered and they bantered a bit.

"Says I'm drinking my weight," the NSA op explained finally. "At least I think he is. Can't get the hang of their accents."

"Why are they here?"

"Yeah, good question." Karr scratched the side of his head. "They're some sort of gypsies. I think they're native people who got into some sort of argument with someone a lot more powerful than they are. I'm not going to get deep into it. Here, pretend you're drinking."

"Don't you think you ought to figure out what the hell they're up to?"

"Not good to act too nosy, baby-sitter." He took the bottom of the bottle and pushed it up, as if urging him to drink. "What you do is put your tongue on the opening, choke it off. Let it dribble down your cheek if you want. They won't notice after a while."

"Burn a hole in my tongue."

"Better than in your stomach. Keep them amused, OK?"

"How?"

"Show 'em your gun. I told them we'd trade it for food, if they can rustle up anything less than a week old. I'm going to mingle."

37

"They'll take Kurakin out," said Collins, helpfully keying a picture of the Russian president onto the data screens around the conference table in the White House situation room. "They'd have learned their lesson from the aborted Yeltsin coup, and they'd take him out right away."

"Possibly," conceded Rubens. "I would point out, however, that we have no intercepts on it, and no evidence."

"There are no direct intercepts on the coup at all," she volleyed back—a not-so-subtle suggestion that the NSA wasn't doing its job.

Rubens refused to take the bait, continuing to argue that it would be difficult for the plotters to hit Kurakin. "His bodyguards are all exceedingly loyal—most of them either are old friends or are related by blood."

"They'll take him if they can," said Blanders, the defense secretary. "They'll use an assault force and, if all else fails, a sniper."

"Can we protect him?" asked the president.

"Should we?" said the defense secretary, making one last play at keeping America on the sidelines. "Should we even try and interfere with the coup at all?"

Rubens sat back and listened as the others debated the matter. It was clear that the president had already decided to do just that, calculating that above all else the democratic system in Russia must be preserved. He said twice that he neither liked Kurakin nor trusted him—Rubens thought the former wasn't true, even if the latter was. But President Marcke clearly believed that long-term, democracy in Russia was preferable to a return to dictatorship, especially if it was run by the military.

Rubens' gaze met Collins'. She'd aged quite a bit in the last three years, but she was still attractive.

In two more years she wouldn't be worth another look.

Be director of the agency by then.

"What do you think, William?" asked the president.

"Kurakin would be a high-priority target," he said. "They would need a rather large assault team with heavy firepower to get past his bodyguards. As for a sniper . . ." He gestured with his hands. It was certainly possible. "The best way to protect him is to tip him off to the coup."

"If he believes us," said Marcke.

"That would be up to him," said Rubens.

"Tipping him off is the best way to protect him," said Collins. "But revealing that we know about the coup will tell the Russians a great deal about our capabilities."

Rubens hadn't expected the note of caution. Obviously she was positioning herself for any contingency—no matter what happened, she would be able to say she'd been right.

So like her.

"There are many trade-offs," said Hadash. "I would recommend telling Kurakin that he's a target once we're sure, but leaving out details of our own attack. If we jam the rebels, ID the loyal units, and keep his communications lines open as Mr. Rubens has outlined—if all of that does not ensure his success, then he does not deserve to be president."

"Assuming he's alive for us to tell," suggested Collins.

She was baiting him, Rubens finally realized—the agency had humint on a plot they hadn't shared.

It could not be very reliable if there were no intercepts. Nonetheless, Rubens saw his best move—his only move: feign some vague understanding of it already.

"You haven't briefed the president on the assassin theory," he told Collins. "Perhaps you'd better."

She hesitated ever so briefly. Rubens felt as if he'd won the point, if not the set.

"As Mr. Rubens hints, it is just a theory," said Collins. "But a strong one."

She detailed humint gathered within the past six hours that indicated a highly trained member of the Russian military had cased out part of Bolso in the Caucasus region last week, examining part of the city where President Kurakin was supposed to have been this week. When Kurakin's schedule changed, the man disappeared.

"We call him the Wolf," Collins added with an unbecoming smirk. "He was involved in the Georgian operation last year and has assassinated two leaders of the southern Islamic movement."

Rubens did not know who "Wolf" was, and Collins didn't pop up an image on the screen. Whether this meant she didn't know either, or she was deliberately holding back information from him was anyone's guess.

He fully suspected the latter.

"Why didn't you share this information earlier?" asked Hadash.

"We just developed it," said Collins. "And I'm still not convinced it's significant."

"William?" asked Hadash.

"There are no intercepts to back it up," said Rubens. He resisted the temptation to add a subtle dig about the CIA not sharing, deciding it was best not to provoke her. "But I agree in principle. It's very possible."

"Where is he?" Hadash asked.

"We believe Moscow," said Collins.

"Desk Three can attempt to find and intercept Wolf as part of the operation," said Rubens. "If we can get data on him. Still, informing Kurakin is our surest way of protecting him."

The secretary of state began to argue that they should go completely public with the information immediately, putting the whole world on notice. Rubens rolled his eyes.

It was obvious that the president didn't take that seriously, but he did pay attention when Blanders suggested that the entire country's electrical grid be disrupted. This could be accomplished largely through a software attack similar to the one planned for the communications networks, but there would have to be a physical attack on at least two parts of the grid. Desk Three did have assets to launch the attack; it controlled two groups of remote F-47C attack planes, which could be fitted with bombs. But Rubens believed shutting down the grid would ultimately hurt the loyal forces more than the plotters.

"You'd have considerable suffering in the general population," Hadash said, making the argument for him. That allowed Rubens to speak up with what seemed like a reasoned counterproposal—it could not have been a better setup if it had been scripted.

"We do have the option for some selective, temporary blackouts, if necessary," he told the president. "And we will have assets in the air in case it's deemed necessary."

"I envisioned more comprehensive forces," said Blanders. Having made his last stand, he was now belatedly trying to carve out a piece of the pie for his people. "Delta and some Rangers could be there within twenty-four hours."

"Too risky," said Marcke. "A large force could easily complicate matters."

Johnny Bib nudged Rubens' leg under the table. He was looking at his alphanumeric pager and scribbling furiously on his yellow pad. Rubens tried to look discreetly at the notes but couldn't make out what Bib was writing.

"I will choose the moment to inform Kurakin," said the president. His voice was firm; the decision was irrevocable and it was time to move on. "Billy, I want you to make the assassin a priority. Can you do it, Billy?"

He'd need Karr and his team and some of the CIA people.

The CIA people were already in place; they'd have to take point.

Change the satellite priorities.

Revamp the signal intercept schedule.

Stretch everyone to their breaking point.

Impossible.

"Yes, of course we can do it," Rubens said.

Bib slid over his pad. Rubens had to squint to decipher the words, and even then it was tough going. Bib had filled the page with chicken scratch that would make a doctor's prescription look like forty-eight-point block letters.

"Bear Hug will execute at my command only," said Marcke. "George, I want you at the command center to keep me updated. We'll use the dedicated line."

"Excuse me, Mr. President," interrupted Rubens, rising. "The units we've been watching are on the move. I would estimate the action will begin in forty-eight hours, or less."

38

Karr clicked through the different magnifications of the photographs, though he was no longer paying any real attention to them. Most of the vehicles that had been at the base yesterday were gone, which probably meant that the bulk of the troops that had been located there had left with them. The question was, Had Martin?

There seemed like only one way to find out—go in and look. But that wasn't going to be easy.

The bug that had heard Martin had landed between two low-slung buildings near the northwestern perimeter of the base. Two guard posts were situated within fifty feet of the buildings along the fence line. Even if there was no surveillance equipment to supplement them, their sight lines not only overlapped but also were visible from another set of posts farther away. Because of the way the buildings were arranged, Karr doubted there were mines between them and the fence—but since the satellite archives showed there were minefields just to the south, it would be difficult to be sure without checking.

Less than a hundred yards from the buildings sat a small airstrip, probably intended solely for helicopters. Six Helix and two Hip choppers were dispersed around it. The strip was heavily guarded. A pair of ZSU-23 antiaircraft guns were set up in shallow revetments at either end of the field; there were at least two other netted areas south of the helicopters where 23mm guns might also be hiding. Mounted on tank chassis, the weapons were primitive but deadly, and not just against aircraft. Farther to the south, just off the main road into and through the complex, was an SA-6 missile launcher with its associated vans and radar. The air defenses could hold off a pair of F-16s, let alone the Hind.

A bit of a knot, but probably doable.

"So what do you think, kid?" asked Charlie Dean, leaning in the truck window. He smelled of the rotgut he'd been pretending to drink.

"I think we need a clandestine insertion, a major diversion, and a Marine division."

"No high-tech miracle force multipliers?"

"Actually, all we need is a pair of pliers." Karr pondered the image, then clicked the handheld's keys and had the computer conjure a simple outline from the photo. He knew they could get in; the plan to do it was hovering somewhere in the back of his brain but just hadn't come forward yet.

"We're not getting in," said Dean.

"Sure we are," said Karr. Something in Dean's sarcasm finally coaxed the idea into the conscious part of Karr's head. "We slip across here, come right over the road, then find our guy. We need a serious diversion down on this end at first. Then again at the end."

Dean looked at him as if he were insane. "This looks like a minefield."

"That's because it is."

"How do we get across it?"

"Fly," Karr joked.

"The chopper will be a sitting duck."

"I'm kidding, Charlie Dean. Man, you're a lot of fun, but sometimes you're way too serious."

"I'm always serious where my life's concerned."

Karr laughed. "Listen, I want you to come in with me. We're going to need Princess out here in case we get nailed, and besides, watching her butt while you're getting through a minefield is extremely distracting."

"You're out of your fuckin' mind."

"That's what they tell me." Karr gave him a fist to the shoulder. He liked the geezer; working with him kept him on his toes. "Let's go find some food. All this thinking makes me hungry."

On the one hand, Dean agreed that they had to rescue their man, no matter the odds. He admired that; it was, after all, the Marine Corps way. On the other hand, what Karr had sketched out barely deserved to be called a plan.

They'd been ambushed at the junkyard because they put too much stock in their high-tech gizmos, but at least that plan could be defended based on the available intelligence. This one couldn't. Forget the satellite photos. Even just driving around it told Dean it wasn't going to be infiltrated. Best to go in there with a couple of companies and serious firepower.

As in six or seven tanks.

They drove back to the gypsy camp, Karr bopping up and down to some tune only he could hear, Dean trying to come up with some kind of alternative plan.

There weren't any.

Nor were the gypsies or whatever they were at the building. Instead, a black car sat in front of the building ruins, a man in a suit sitting with his arm out the window, smoking a cigarette. Karr kept a steady pace as they passed.

"What's up?" asked Dean.

"Looks like the police pushed them on," said Karr. "So much for a cheap meal."

"It cost me a decent pistol," said Dean.

"Lia'll bring you another; don't worry. Couple of nice little hideaways in the S-1 pack—these little Glocks."

"Plastic."

"Strong and light."

"Still plastic."

"You only like six-guns, right, Wyatt Earp?"

"I'm not against technology. When it's appropriate." Dean leaned against the dashboard as he turned toward Karr, bending his head so that it was almost in his face. "You don't really think we're going to get in and get out alive, do you?" he asked. "Even if most of the soldiers are gone, the perimeter is well protected."

"Nah. That minefield's wide open."

"How do we get across it?"

"Pogo sticks."

"Very funny. You're going to have to lay it out for me, step by step. Otherwise I'm not coming."

Karr turned to look at him. The look that crossed over his face combined disgust, anger, derision—and fear. Then it dissolved in a laugh so hard the truck shook.

"You're a lot of fun, Charlie Dean. Truly."

39

Even Malachi balked at the plan when they conferenced in the Art Room with the Desk Three team. The team needed to get by an SA-6 missile battery with a helicopter—not an easy prospect without eliminating the battery, but doing so seemed almost impossible from the ground.

"So let's get it from the air," said Tommy Karr cheerfully.

"Can we?" Telach asked Malachi, who was sitting in the Art Room for the conference.

There was no time to get an F-47C into position, let alone the larger A-7 space plane. That left the Space Platforms' Vessels.

Which weren't armed.

He could put one through the radar van. Smack through the side with the processing gear—all he'd have to do is fry a transistor or two and the unit would be dead.

Shit, yeah.

"I can take out the SA-6 with a Vessel," he told them.

"How?" asked Telach. Pacing in front of the blank screen at the front of the room, she looked exactly like his third-grade teacher, Mrs. Woods.

Malachi tried to ignore that. He'd had a bad experience with Mrs. Woods.

"I'll put one of the Vessels through the radar van," said Malachi. "Sizzle-boom, it's gone."

"What about the ZSU-23s?" said Rockman.

"What, the guns?" asked Karr. "Screw 'em. Fashona'll nail the closest suckers with missiles off the Hind when he comes in."

"Timing's going to be tight," said Rockman. "You have to take out the SA-6 just before the helicopter pops up to clear the fence, then get the guns."

"You're telling me the helicopter's going to be on the radar screen at six feet?" asked Karr.

"The fence is twenty," said Rockman. "And they have a second dish outside to cover just this contingency."

"Ah, the SA-6 can't hit shit under a hundred and fifty feet," said Karr. "We just stay under that."

"I can take out the processing van," said Malachi. "Tell me the time and it's gone."

"That's what I'm talking about," said Karr.

"Yeah, but what about the guns?" insisted Rockman.

"Those Zeus suckers?" asked Karr. "If the helo comes in right, they won't be a problem. They don't have a good line of fire, and besides, Fashona'll splash them."

"That's not entirely true," said Rockman. "There's about ten seconds' worth of exposure in and out."

"Ah, what's ten seconds?" said Karr.

"You know how much lead that translates into?" asked Telach.

"Enough for a coffin," said Karr cheerfully.

Malachi leaned back in his seat, sipping his strawberry milk. A diversion in the air outside the fence, opposite the direction of the helicopter, would divert the gunners long enough for the Hind to wax them. He could self-destruct a Vessel out there, but there wouldn't be much of a bang— the whole idea of the process was to be as unobtrusive as possible.

What if he crashed two together?

Still not much of a bang. Unless he had the boosters on them.

"I got it," said Malachi. "Rather than using one Vessel and self-destructing, we fly two down, then have them crash into each other. Should cause some sparks."

"How much?" asked Karr.

Malachi wasn't sure. "I'm going to have to talk to the design people," he told her. "May run some sims, too, see where the best impact would be and—"

"Run what you want," said Karr. "Just as long as it happens in two hours."

"Two hours—that's tight, dude." Malachi turned to the screen where he'd punched up a course earlier. "Two hours— I'd have to launch within five minutes."

"Sounds good to me," said Karr. "We'll look for the bang. Update us on times when you're ready."

40

Dean and Karr rendezvoused with the Hind in a deserted field about five miles north of their target area. Fashona had had to scrape his belly against the ground for nearly ten miles to be sure of missing the SA-6's radar and was in a foul mood, not even helping them unload the gear.

Dean remained dubious. The key to the plan was getting across the minefield using a scanning device attached to the handheld. The problem, though, was that it wasn't designed to find mines, just explosives.

"Works like the sniffers at airports," Karr said. "Nothing to worry about."

"I heard those things don't work," said Dean.

"Ah, sure they do, baby-sitter. The only problem is I have to calibrate it for one explosive at a time, say C-4 or gunpowder, or what have you. Not a problem, though, because the Commies only have one kind of mine."

"Bullshit," said Dean, who'd dealt with mines in Vietnam. "And these guys aren't the Commies."

"You've been hanging around with Lia too long," Karr told him. "You're getting very negative."

Lia, carrying a duffel bag of gear from the Hind, snorted in derision. Dean glanced momentarily at her sleek, muscled body, her sweaty T-shirt clinging tightly to her breasts. Then he turned back to Karr.

"How do we get from the minefield to the buildings?" asked Dean.

"We cross the road."

"Real funny," said Dean.

"He's a riot, isn't he?" put in Lia.

"A comedian."

"We just duck the patrol, that's all."

"We going to time it?" asked Dean.

"Nah. Take too long, and besides, you can't count on these guys. Their watches are always off. Cheap Commie workmanship," said Karr. "We'll watch them and go when they're not there."

"How?"

"The Bagel, baby-sitter. The Bagel."

The Bagel looked like a kid's hovercraft toy. Round with a hole in the middle—hence its name—it had two engines on either side and a long twin-rudder tail. It carried five kilograms of fuel and could fly for about an hour and a half, feeding its video to a receiver in Karr's backpack. Though very slow, it was extremely quiet, and once in hover would stay at its designated spot even in gale-force winds.

Dean looked at the thing doubtfully. Even its rotors were plastic. The front had a small clear panel; the rear featured a thick set of baffles where the exhaust was muffled.

"Georgia uses these for traffic control," said Karr. "Check out accidents, that sort of thing. They get better endurance because they don't worry about the noise."

Karr took the Bagel and put it into the back of the truck. It didn't quite fit and he had to angle it.

"Lia and Fashona can strap the weapons on the Hind. You and I have to get going," said Karr, looking back to the helicopter. "Long walk ahead of us. Get your vest, headset, gun, knife, the works."

"I'm not a kindergartner, kid," said Dean, picking up the lightweight armor.

"Sorry, graybeard." Karr laughed and walked over to Lia near the cargo door to the helicopter. When he leaned down to kiss her on the cheek, Dean felt a twinge of envy.

. . .

An hour later, Dean lay prone on the dirt above the embankment that led down to the fenced area, just out of view of the observation post. The boxy A-2 machine gun was in his right hand. His pockets were stuffed with small grenades; on his back over the protective armor was a wide but narrow rucksack. Inside were extra clips for the boxy gun and his two pistols, a backup com device, flares, rope, and a kind of sling made of rope they'd use to carry Martin out if he was hurt. He also carried a .22-caliber Ruger Mark II with a sonic suppressor—aka silencer—strapped in a holster at his chest.

In Dean's opinion, the gun would be almost useless unless placed right on a victim's head, assassination-style. Although it was admittedly an excellent weapon in its proper application, its small and relatively slow bullets wouldn't so much as bruise someone wearing body armor.

Far better, Dean thought, to have MP-5Ns with suppressors—at least you'd have a chance of putting down the person who heard you.

A good quiet crossbow—there was a weapon these high-tech junkies should look into.

"Thirty seconds, baby-sitter," Karr hissed in his ear. He sounded like he was hyperventilating already.

Dean's doubts flooded into his veins, replacing his blood with fear. It was a suicidal plan.

He'd done crazy things before. The whole reason he was here—the whole reason he was working for Hadash, if he was still working for Hadash—was a crazy foolish plan.

One that had paid off handsomely.

That didn't make this one any less ridiculous.

Karr leaped up. Dean followed, nearly tripping as they started down the embankment that led to the fence. A twenty-foot-wide swath had been bulldozed around the fence, both as a perimeter road and to make it easier to see and shoot anyone there. Just as they reached it, Karr pushed a button on his handheld, igniting a C-4 bomb he had set amid the gas cans in the back of the pickup, which they had parked on the northwestern flank of the fence.

Dean pushed himself sideways, got up and reached the fence, then fell through the hole Karr had already cut. He put the fencing back as carefully as he could, using the tape Karr had left to get it back into place well enough to withstand a cursory glance.

Meanwhile, gunfire, cannons, tracers ripped into the blackness. Even the ZSU-23s fired, their four-barreled volleys sounding like the pounding of a giant tin drum. There were sirens and flares, shouts in the distance. Dean pushed toward the supports for the guard tower on his right. Lights were switched on, searchlights—they were playing on the area in front of the fence, the embankment they'd just come down. Dean moved toward the black hole Karr had disappeared into, knowing he could count on only a few more seconds.

Bare seconds—but where the hell was Karr?

He could feel the lights coming, one playing across the interior of the yard errantly, another more purposefully. There was a second explosion, this one in the woods beyond the embankment where they had come down. Automatic weapons began to bark from the guard towers.

Dean felt the skin in the soft spot behind his jaw prickle with electricity. He ran forward at full speed, forgetting for a second that he was running into a minefield. He saw a shadow on his left that had to be Karr, began to dart toward it, then suddenly felt himself upended, flying in the air. He crashed against hard ground, cowering instinctively, sure the next thing he felt would be oblivion.

"Don't get ahead of me, baby-sitter," said Karr, who'd reached out and upended him. "We're real close to the mines."

The guards stopped shooting. They concentrated their lights outside the fence, where the truck continued to burn.

"Sucker's still going," said Karr. "Guess we'll have to walk if the chopper goes down, huh?"

"More likely fly to heaven," said Dean.

"Hey, speak for yourself," said Karr. "I'm going to the other place. Reservation's all set."

He knelt down, holding what looked like a miniature boom mike out in front of him. A thick wire ran to his back.

"First mine's two feet in front of you. Then there's one, um, on the left—shit, these guys are not fucking around. I've seen checkerboards that were in a looser pattern."

It took nearly twenty minutes for Karr to pick through the minefield. By then, things had calmed down to the point where the guards weren't firing randomly and they weren't shooting off flares willy-nilly. Sooner or later, there would be a thorough perimeter check. A careful look would find the hole in the fence. They needed to be in the building by then.

Karr waited next to a four-foot Cyclone fence for Dean to catch up as he cleared the end of the minefield. Just beyond the fence was the main road in. About fifty or seventy yards to the right was a row of buildings that would block off the view of the guards inside the gate, but with time getting tight Karr decided they'd have to take a shot at crossing the road and not being seen. The Bagel's infrared or IR camera showed that there were only two guards at the gate and another two between them and the target buildings. Get past them, and they could get into the buildings without a problem.

Then the real fun would begin, since they didn't know for sure which building Martin was in. The Art Room had assigned percentages to the possibilities, though they hadn't explained the formula they used to come up with the figures. The building on the left was marked at 70 percent; the building on the right, 30. Karr's gut refused to let him make a call, so he'd go with the Art Room's numbers.

According to the Art Room, there had been no more than six or seven people in both buildings at the time their bugs had run out of juice. That struck him as optimistic, but you never knew—they were due for one good break somewhere along the way; maybe that would be it.

Dean finally crept next to him.

"OK, baby-sitter, here's the gig—we run straight to that building right there, one at a time. First guy runs, other guy watches the observation post."

"That's a hike," said Dean. He thumbed right. "Why don't we head that way? We can sweep around, just be exposed on the right there."

"We can't afford the time, and besides, the barracks will be able to see us anyway, so it's not that high a percentage," said Karr. "At least here we know it's just the one or two sets of eyes."

He looked at the image from the Bagel; there was a truck coming from the barracks area, behind them to the right. "We'll wait for the truck to clear. It's got troops in it. If they go to the gate, that's where the guards' attention will be."

"OK."

"If you start shooting, remember the contingency plan."

"Which contingency plan?"

"Every man for himself," chuckled Karr, hunkering down as the truck's headlights swung up the road.

41

Lia punched the button on her handheld several times, frustrated that they had lost the feed from the Bagel. That didn't mean it had been shot down or run out of fuel—reception was notoriously difficult in the Hind.

But it wasn't good. Lia pushed against the restraints of the gunners' cockpit. It was a tight squeeze, even for her. With the missiles and gun pod loaded on the stubby wings, she was paranoid about hitting the switches on the panels, even though the gear was fully safed.

Karr had gone too far this time. It was uncharacteristic— she was the one who took chances, not him, not like this. Jesus, he was out of his mind.

Dean's fault. Karr obviously thought he had to impress the old fart.

Not that Dean was old, actually. Or a fart. Not a fart at all.

"How we doing?" Fashona asked over the interphone, or internal communications set.

"They're working their way to the building, but I've lost the feed from the Bagel. Can you get higher?"

"I don't want to show up on the radar. We're just barely out of coverage range as it is."

"We're five miles away and five feet off the ground."

"That would be twenty. The radar is definitely on and scanning."

"I'd like to see what the hell is going on."

"Relax. Karr knows what he's doing."

"It's not him I'm worried about."

"Hots for Charlie Dean, huh? He's a hunk."

"Screw yourself, Fashona."

"Physically impossible, though many have tried," he said. "You want me to go over the target list again?"

"Why don't you suck on a grenade?"

"If I go, you go," he told her.

"That may be an acceptable trade-off."

42

Dean threw himself against the cement bricks of the building wall, his pulse thumping in his throat. The night glasses blurred so badly all he could see was one dark shadow around him.

"Up, up," said Karr in his ear.

Easy for him to say. Dean put his hand out and moved to the left, fishing for the nylon rope Karr had left for him. He found it finally, took a breath, and started pulling himself upward.

"Jeez, Louise, what's taking you?" hissed Karr. "I had to get up without a rope, and I gotta weigh about fifty pounds more than you."

"The fucking guard just about saw me."

"Relax. I would've nailed him."

"Fucking Ruger's bullets would've bounced off his head."

"Only if his skull's as thick as mine. Come on. I'm ready to go through the roof."

Dean pulled himself over the low rise at the edge of the roof, then immediately began hauling up the rope. Karr had already taken out what he claimed was a silenced Makita portable saw and started cutting. It may in fact have been a Makita—it was blue—but it looked more a small wastepaper basket with a five-inch saw blade than a battery-operated skillsaw. It wasn't completely silent, but Dean didn't hear the high-pitched hum until he was about ten feet away.

"Here we go," said Karr, standing up. He smacked his foot down against the cutout—and promptly fell through the hole.

Dean swung the A-2 forward as he leaped forward. After two steps he dropped knee-first into a slide and pushed the nose of the gun into the hole ahead of his face.

Karr lay sprawled on his back eight feet below.

"Don't shoot me yet, baby-sitter," he said, groaning and cursing as he rolled over and got to his feet. "Luckily, I landed on my head."

Dean pushed his legs over the edge of the hole and jumped down, then crouched and scanned the unlit hallway. At the far end, Karr paused by a set of double doors made of glass. He put out his hand, signaling for Dean to stop. Then Karr took a large device that looked like the plunger head from a plumber's helper from one of his vest pouches and put it against the glass. A wire ran from the device; he plugged it into his handheld.

"Ssshhh," warned Karr as Dean crept toward him.

"That some sort of bug?"

Karr didn't answer. The device used a set of microphones to pick up sounds, calculating distance in roughly the same way a submarine would use passive sonar. The closed stairwell and the glass were a perfect medium, though it could also work reasonably well through a single-layer wall.

"Clear now." Karr stood and, while still looking at the handheld screen, dusted the door hinges with silicone. It may have helped, but the heavy door still creaked on its hinges.

They stopped at the bottom. Karr handed Dean his A-2, then took the pistol out.

"Two guards, coming toward us. Walking. I don't think they know we're here," he said.

"You better hit them in the face."

A smile poked up the corners of Karr's mouth; then he was through the door. The bullets made a light popping sound as they came from the pistol—two bullets, two guards on the ground.

Square in the forehead, both shots.

"Good work," said Dean.

"I may not be as good as you, baby-sitter, but I can hit what I'm aiming at every so often."

"I didn't say you couldn't."

"Basement door," said Karr, pointing all the way down the hallway. A steel door sat next to the main entrance. He started moving toward it, then stopped as a set of headlights swung across the front of the building. When the lights faded, Karr trotted forward, then threw himself down and slid the last ten feet on his belly, possibly to keep from throwing a shadow that could be seen through the front glass, though Dean thought Karr might just have done it for fun. He put his plunger up again, fiddled with the handheld, and cursed.

"Door's too thick. Doesn't resonate enough."

"Let's search the rest of the place first," suggested Dean.

"Nah. If I'm putting a jail in here, it's going downstairs. Place looks like a lab or something, doesn't it?"

Dean hadn't seen inside of the rooms—they were all closed—so didn't hazard a guess.

"You don't have some X-ray machine that can see through the walls?" he said instead.

"Stinkin' bean counters cut it out of the budget," said Karr. He took a grenade from his belt, thumbed off the tape. Dean still held his gun. "Hopefully, we don't need this."

"Agreed."

"Ready?"

"Ready."

"Sure?"

"I'm sure."

"Sure you're sure?"

"You gonna bust my chops all night or what?"

"Only as long as necessary, baby-sitter." Karr jerked the door open, pushing himself across and into the opening. Dean waited until he started to retape the grenade, then slid over to follow.

The basement was a long low-ceilinged room crammed with machinery. Several tables were tarped; others had racks of what looked like oscilloscopes and discarded computer gear. They walked the length without seeing any sign that prisoners were kept here.

"Shit," said Dean.

"Yeah, all right. Let's check out the first floor."

The doors to the rooms were locked by card-readers. Rather than fooling with the locks, Karr put his listening device up, scanning the room sonically.

"You sure that's good enough?" Dean asked.

"As long as he's breathing, we'll hear him. These doors aren't that thick."

"What if he's dead?"

Karr shrugged and moved on. At the last door he pulled down the gear and took out a small drill, punching through the screws that held the mechanism together. Dean tensed, his adrenaline once more starting to pump.

"There's no one inside," said Karr. "I just want to see what the hell they do here."

With the cover of the lock off, he examined the circuit card, then reached into his pants pocket and pulled out a set of alligator clips. One of the LEDs on the reader mechanism flashed a few seconds after he began probing around, and the door lock clicked open. Dean started to push inside, but Karr held him back, nodding toward the floor. The goggles picked up two fuzzy IR beams. The room was filled with several dozen servers and storage devices, along with two workstations.

"They have the room alarmed but not the hallway?" said Dean.

"Pretty interesting, huh?" Karr took out a small digital camera and began taking pictures.

"What do you figure's in those computers?"

"Could be porn."

Dean wasn't sure whether he was kidding or not. He followed Karr back upstairs, where a similar search revealed equally empty rooms, though no more computers.

"I was afraid of this," Karr said. "Let's go next door. Get on my back."

"Huh?"

"I'm going to lift you out of the building," he told Dean. "Unless you think you're strong enough to pick me up and let me drop the rope to you."

Dean scowled but said nothing, climbing up the bigger man's back and then balancing precariously as he was lifted by the heels up through the hole in the roof. He felt a little shaky; fatigue was starting to get to him, and he was hungry besides. He managed to crawl out of the hole, then stopped a few feet away, resting for a moment before going for the rope. He was too old for this shit, too old.

"Dean!" said Karr in his headset.

"I'm moving as fast as I can," answered Dean.

He looked up. Two guards stood five feet from him, the laser targeting dots from their AK-74s crisscrossed on his chest.

43

Karr didn't have time to figure out how he'd missed the guards outside when he'd checked the UAV image before they started down the hallway. He ran back to the stairs, Dean's gun in his left hand and his in his right. He got down to the first floor, slung the second rifle over his shoulder, then pushed out. He ran into the computer room they'd examined earlier, jumping over the security system's detection beams. He just barely kept his balance.

There were no windows, but there was a door that led to another room. It was locked. Karr threw his shoulder against it, but it stayed put. With no time for finesse, he took out the pistol and bored out the lock mechanism.

This room had two windows. He pushed the door shut behind him, then ran to them quickly. Dean was saying something in English over the com system; it went dead before Karr could figure out what it was.

The windows were alarmed, but it was a simple wire system, easily defeated with a clip and wire set. He pushed the window open, then paused, checking the Bagel scan carefully. He saw now why he'd missed the sentries—there was a ladder up the side of the roof, hidden by an overhang. They were making for it now.

It was on the opposite side of the building, away from Building Two.

Karr pulled up the cursor and clicked it on Dean's IR

profile, prompting the computer to memorize it. It could now locate him at will.

Assuming they didn't kill him first, of course.

Building Two had a set of steps that led to a steel door in the basement. Karr ran to them, once more using his .22 to blow out the lock. But this door had a dead bolt or something else securing it: it jammed when he tried to get in.

There came a time in every show when you had to play the luck card. Tommy Karr hated to play it this early, but there was no other choice. He ran up the steps, glancing at the feed from the Bagel—the sentries were coming around the side of Building One. He bashed the nearest window with his gun and then dived inside the building, rolling in the darkness on a surprisingly thick and relatively soft rug.

Like a pig in shit, he thought to himself, jumping up.

44

"What the hell's going on, Karr? Where are you?" Lia hissed.

"Building Two. Aren't you watching?"

"I'm still trying to get the feed from the Bagel."

"Just use the sitrep. Did you get all the weapons loaded?"

"Of course."

"Did Fashona bitch about the jacks?"

"Is the pope Catholic?"

Specially designed trolleys and hydraulic jacks were used to load the weapons pods onto the wings. While these machines did all the heavy lifting, they had to be positioned just so beneath the hard points; it was not a job for an impatient man, and inevitably left the pilot in a foul mood.

Lia clicked into the map, which showed Karr's and Dean's positions. Dean was on Building One, moving toward the side.

Christ, the bastards were going to throw him off.

"We're coming in," she said.

"Just hold on," Karr told her. "Let me find Martin first."

"They're going to kill Dean."

"Relax. They'll question him before they kill him."

"Jesus."

"Don't go postal, honey."

"Postal? You're fuckin' hyperventilating."

"I'm out of breath. Look, you guys have to stay on schedule or you'll get nailed by the SA-6. Wait until they take out the van. I'll get Martin, then I'll bail out Dean."

She bounced back to the sit map, which showed the team's location.

"Karr."

"You have ten minutes. You can't sit tight until then?"

She was worried about Dean. She was *really* worried about Dean.

Would she have worried so much about Karr?

Damn straight.

Maybe.

"Take out the guns, then get the two guards on the inside of the gate, in case they have shoulder-launched SAMs," Karr reminded her.

"I know my fucking job."

"Then do it," he said. "Gotta go."

His channel remained open. Lia pressed the mike button for the helicopter's interphone. "Ray—"

"I heard," said the pilot. "The SA-6 van blows in seven and a half minutes."

"God, they'll be dead before we get there."

"Probably not."

"Shit, Ray, *go*! Let's go now—we can take it out ourselves."

"If you want to get out and push, be my guest. If not, we do it the way Tommy drew it up."

"If Dean and Karr die in there, I swear to God, I'll never talk to you again," she said.

"Yeah, well, they ain't going to die, so don't get your hopes up."

45

Dean moved down the fire escape–like ladder as slowly as he could. Every five seconds of delay would increase Karr's chances of getting away, which in turn increased his own odds of survival. Finally, the man above him had enough and began stomping at his fingers to make him go faster. Dean jumped the last two rungs and pretended to crumble to the ground, but the Russians were having none of that—the man who'd gone down first put his rifle about two inches from Dean's face.

Dean had surrendered the .22 and his combat knife, along with his pack and all of his grenades. He still had a small Glock hideaway strapped to his calf and another under his vest. But at the moment there was no way he could get them before being perforated.

The Russian said something, probably telling him to move forward to the front of the building, where there was a vehicle. Dean didn't have to pretend not to understand; he stood with his hands out, as dumb a look on his face as he could muster—which was pretty dumb.

"I don't speak Russian," he said.

The Marine said something that sounded like "pash-lee, pash-lee," which Dean recognized as Russian for "let's go." As he started to move, the Marine behind him decided he wasn't moving fast enough and slammed his rifle butt into Dean's kidney. The American fell to the ground, this time not faking it. The Marine went to jab him again, this time with the barrel end. Instinctively Dean grabbed the gun.

He realized this was a big mistake about half a second before it fired.

46

One minute, Stephen Martin was having a glorious wet dream, banging two models on a pristine Aruba beach. The scent of sunscreen mixed with tequila and the heavy odor of women in heat.

The next minute, he was being pulled out of bed by his undershirt, dragged across the cold cement floor.

"Fuck," he mumbled as he tried to grab whatever had him. "Jesus. Let me wake up."

He jerked his elbow into something hard, then felt himself spinning backward. His head slammed against the cement.

What the hell were the idiot Russians doing now?

"You better be fuckin' Martin," said a voice in English. American English.

"I am," he muttered. He realized he was still dreaming, but damn—*damn*—this felt real. He was lifted up and tossed down, carried over someone's shoulder.

Not a dream. The man carrying him ran from the room, down the hallway to the steps.

"What's going on?"

"I'm rescuing you. How the hell are you still alive? You a cat?"

"Put me down."

"Sshhh."

Martin's rescuer paused at the base of the stairwell, glanced at something in his hand, then started running up the steps, taking them two at a time. He paused again at the top. Two men lay sprawled on the floor above.

Martin pushed his torso off the man's back, trying to twist down. The man was large, with hair so blond it nearly shone. He had a handheld computer in his left hand and a long, boxlike gun in his right.

NSA!

"Hey, are you from Desk Three?" asked Martin.

"Let's save the songs for later, OK? We still got to get the hell out of here and I don't know if the place is bugged."

"There are five hundred troops here, and scientists."

"The troops are mostly gone, and I'm not worrying about any eggheads. Can you walk?"

"Yes."

"Nice underwear," said the NSA op, putting him down. "You look good in white."

Martin felt himself flush. The man studied the handheld, which seemed to be getting a live video feed. Martin realized it must be a surveillance arrangement showing what was going on outside.

"OK, when I say go, you go, OK? Run right behind me. When you see the helicopter, run for it."

"Helicopter?" asked Martin.

"Get ready."

47

As built, the Hind used a reasonably accurate, if somewhat kludgy, KPS-53AW sight, aiming its chin gun via a pair of control wheels and a primitive optical aiming set. Missiles were aimed with an ocular that looked something like what might be found on a microscope circa 1960.

The Poles had kindly removed these quaint, if obsolescent, devices before selling the chopper to Petro-UK. And while some—Fashona specifically—claimed to prefer some of the old muscle, the items the NSA wizards had selected to replace the original weapons were a vast improvement.

Six Hellfire missiles—considerably more accurate than the original AT-2 Swatters, or even the AT-3 Spirals fitted on E models—sat on triple rails that rode the outside of the winglets. Two GAU-13/A Gatling 30mm cannons, fitted into slightly modified Pave Claw GPU-5/A pods, sat next to the Hellfires. A four-barrel development of the highly successful GAU-8/A Avenger designed and fitted exclusively to the A-10 Warthog, the guns spewed 30mm armor-piercing and high-explosive incendiary versions at a rate around twenty-four hundred a minute. Not that you'd actually keep your finger on the trigger that long.

Last but not least were the two rocket pods. Here the Hind went native—the weapons were Russian 142mm S-5K rockets that could penetrate roughly nine inches of armor at about four thousand yards.

Which was maybe nine times as thick as the armor on the skins of the two ZSU-23s that Lia had zeroed in on the aiming reticule as the Hind popped up over the fence. The RWR sounded in the cabin behind her, indicating that the SA-6 radar had found and was locking on the helicopter. A half-second later, a space-launched missile known simply as a Vessel flashed down from above, smacking through the radar van at the opposite end of the compound like a Pedro Martinez fastball dividing a bowl of jelly. Three seconds after that, two more Vessels collided in the air opposite the east fence, temporarily drawing everyone's attention from the approaching Hind.

As tracers from the ZSUs began arcing in the air, Lia got the launch cue from the targeting computer. Her first rocket missed high, sailing into the dirt directly behind it. The second rocket obliterated the top two barrels of the antiaircraft gun on the right. The third and fourth missiles, fired from the other winglet, took out the ZSU she'd actually been aiming at.

"Swinging around!" yelled Fashona, ducking the front of the helicopter.

Lia moved her thumb down on the joystick, selecting the left cannon pod only. She could see one of the sentries raising his gun toward them.

She pressed the trigger and erased him.

The helicopter stuttered in the air as the big gun reverberated and its stream of gas pushed against the tail. Fashona threw the Hind sideways, spinning around. As he did, Lia saw a tank or armored car moving near the bank of ZSUs she'd targeted earlier. She selected the Hellfires, locked, and fired.

"I thought we were saving the Hellfires until we're sure they're out of the building," said Fashona as the vehicle exploded. "Otherwise you should've used them on the guns."

"Just find Charlie, huh?"

"Troop truck, coming out of the barracks." She selected the cannon, then stopped when she saw something else moving behind it.

"I'm on it—shit! Another armored car."

"Hellfire the motherfucker."

"What kind of language is that?" she asked, locking and launching the missile. "You can't use Hellfire as a verb."

48

As soon as Karr heard the Hind he shoved open the door. Two Russian Marines stood in awe about five yards away, staring in disbelief as the helicopter raked the compound with rocket and gunfire. Karr's A-2 cracked twice and both men fell over as if they'd been sawed in half.

"Go! Martin! Go!" he yelled, moving out from the doorway. He did a quick turn, made sure the way was clear, then reached back and pulled the bewildered rescuee out from the door. He pushed Martin along the alley, then across the back to Building One. He got him down and glanced at the handheld display from the Bagel—the Russians and Charlie Dean had disappeared somewhere. One of the Zeus antiaircraft guns began firing from the far end of the base. Karr knew from the briefing that it wouldn't be able to hit the Hind, but he also knew Fashona and Lia should have taken it out.

"Up the ladder, up the ladder!" he yelled to Martin. "Go! Go!"

Martin started to complain. He hadn't put on his shoes, and his feet were cut and bleeding.

"Just get the fuck up *now*," Karr said, grabbing his shirt and pushing him toward the ladder as two Russians came charging down the road. Karr leveled his gun and fired four bursts, missing with all as the men threw themselves to the ground. That was good enough for now, though—he jumped on the ladder and climbed up so quickly he nearly knocked Martin off at the top.

The compound rocked with gunfire, rockets, and secondary explosions. Karr saw one of the men he'd missed coming down the alley and fired another burst, cratering the man's skull.

"Fashona!" he yelled as the helo whipped toward them. "We're on the roof. Put down a line and haul Martin up."

"Don't have ropes," said Fashona. "I got no crew, remember?"

"Fuck me."

"I'd love to, honey, but you're not my style."

"Shit. I don't trust this roof. Can you land in front of the building?"

"Yeah, if Lia can stop playing with the stinking cannon."

The helicopter whipped around about twenty feet from them, tilting on its axis as the cannon on the right side of the fuselage roared. A truck at the far end of the compound caught fire.

"All right, I'm going to send Martin down. I'll cover him from here, then go and get Dean."

"We'll cover him," said Lia. "Get Dean and let's get the hell out of here."

Karr whirled around to Martin. "You gotta go back down the ladder. Helicopter's coming for you.

"I-I can't."

"Yeah, man, you go now," said Karr. He spotted a car moving down the road from the area of the SAMs. "Go! I'll worry about the car."

"What car?"

"Go," said Karr. He pushed him toward the ladder, then burned the entire magazine—more than eighty bullets were left—tearing through the front end of the vehicle. By the time he was done, the remains would have fit in a coffee can.

He pulled out his handheld to look for Dean as he slammed in a new ammo box. Karr hit the Bagel's control screen, pushing the small UAV closer toward the base. Then he went back out to the view screen and from there directed the computer to find the image he'd earlier associated with Dean. It took several long seconds; finally, the screen popped into map mode and a white box outlined three figures running toward the main gate.

The Hind swept in from behind him, shooting its cannon as it did.

"Lia! Watch out for Dean!" yelled Karr. "Don't fire at the gate."

"Where is he? I'm not getting a feed with the locator system."

"He's near the gate."

As Karr looked down to update the position, the screen went blank.

49

The three bullets the Russian fired hit Dean almost square in the chest. It was a good thing—the NSA body armor not only kept them from penetrating but absorbed some of the impact as well, spreading it through its high-tech cells. Still, his breath drained from him and Dean curled with the pain, just on the edge of consciousness. Two of his ribs felt like they were broken, and when the Russians jerked him to his feet he stood there paralyzed, nearly in shock.

One of the Marines finally pushed him toward the gate. Dean stumbled forward, his head off-kilter. Though he knew it couldn't be true, it seemed like six or seven helicopters were flying overhead, supporting a company of ground troops attacking from all sides. A dozen Russian Marines scattered in small knots on the other side of the fence, firing toward the surrounding tundra and nearby town, though Dean knew there wasn't anything there.

Soon, very soon, the Russians were going to decide he was the cause of all this misery and take a little revenge. Dean tried to slide his hand in beneath his vest to get one of his hideaway guns, but his ribs screamed with pain. One of the Russians put his hand on Dean's back and shoved. As he did, the Hind loomed above, a dark, angry cloud of gunfire. Smoke and dust whipped into the air. The fence, only a few yards away, erupted. The metal seemed to jump into the air. Dirt, rocks, cement chips, metal, gunpowder—the air became thick with debris. Dean dived to the ground. In the swirling tornado he grabbed his calf, fishing for the small Glock strapped there. By the time he found it, he was choking and couldn't see. He rolled to his hands and knees and started crawling toward the helicopter.

He'd gone about five yards when he realized it wasn't the helicopter, which was now somewhere overhead and firing again. Something moved on the ground to Dean's left and he rolled again. An assault rifle started firing a few feet away from him—he could hear it but couldn't see the muzzle flash.

Turning onto his left side, he began pushing himself through the dirt, away from the gun. By turns the night became green, then red, then yellow and purple. Shadows furled into immense balls of blackness, then disintegrated. The helicopter came back, skimming in toward what remained of the gate. Dean saw Karr running toward it. As Dean started to follow, he realized it wasn't Karr but one of the Russians.

The Glock made a soft popping sound in his hand, and the recoil was so sweet he wasn't entirely sure in the chaos that he had actually fired. He pressed the trigger again, and the man turned.

Dean threw himself to the ground, but the Russian didn't fire at him. Dean pushed forward, swimming more than crawling. His hip burned; something had hit him there. He shook his head, trying to wave off the pain. He'd suffered far, far worse.

He had to get out of here soon, or the next thing that hit him would take his head off. But now where was the Hind?

The thing to do, the only thing to do, was get to a clear open space and wait. They would come and get him. They would.

They were kids, but they would come and get him.

Shit. What he really needed was a company of Marines.

He'd settle for a squad. Shit, one guy, Bill Wiley maybe, humping over the fence.

Thirty years ago, maybe. Not now, not here. This wasn't a Marine show. For better or worse, this was the kids' game.

For worse, definitely worse. They were blowing it big-time. Them and their high-tech bullshit toys.

But wasn't it his fault for going ahead with a bullshit plan? He knew it was bullshit and had said so.

Like Vietnam.

Either everybody around him was dead or they were pretending to be. Dean reached as gingerly as he could beneath his vest for the other Glock. Holding one in each hand, he started walking toward the main road, trying to sort out the battlefield. The buildings were almost dead ahead, the SAMs and flak dealers up to the right, out of view, though he assumed they were the source of the flames and black smoke curling through the flare-lit haze. Behind him were the barracks. He could hear vehicles coming from that direction, or at least thought he did.

Maybe get to the buildings, out on the roof, above all of this shit where they could see him.

So what happened to the stinking locator thing, huh? Where's my beacon to beam me back aboard the mother ship?

As he started across the road toward the buildings, Dean felt the ground rumble. He looked to his left and saw something crashing through what was left of the main gate.

It was a BMP, a tracked armored personnel carrier with a cannon and a machine gun, one of the vehicles that had left earlier to check out the diversions. One of the guns atop the vehicle began firing. Dean dived into the dirt, diving, diving, diving, swimming down, and cursing himself for being a fool, for being a hero, for being here at all.

Then the ground spit him up. A volcano erupted where the gun had been. Tossed in the air by an explosion, Dean found himself diving into the dirt near the building where he'd originally been captured.

"All this time, you haven't moved like two feet," shouted a voice in his ears.

Where?

"Up! Up!"

Dean looked up and saw the ladder at the side of the building. He grabbed it, started to climb.

"They're coming."

Four loud explosions pushed him upward. Dean knew it was Karr, knew the explosions must be the NSA op's A-2 firing, but couldn't see anything except the suddenly grimy night in front of him. One of his eyes had welded itself shut, and the other was half-blinded by the flash from the BMP's explosion. He climbed as best he could, diving onto the roof and belatedly realizing he ought to make sure it was still there.

It was. He got up and went back to help Karr. But the NSA op didn't need any help—he kicked his feet over the top of the roof, saw Dean, and grinned. Then he whirled back and worked his A-2 like a drill hammer, smacking the reinforcements that had been following the BMP.

When the loud crack of the A-2 stopped, Karr threw down the gun and turned back toward Dean. The roof had started to shake. The Hind loomed over the side of the building, materializing like a train in thick fog.

Dean reached for the door—it was folded open—but then saw he'd never get it. Instead, he wrapped his arm between the two struts of the landing gear on the right side, barely holding on as the Hind whipped sideways off the roof. He turned to look back to Karr, but something kicked him in the side—the kid was dangling on the other strut.

The helicopter dipped down and the air around it seemed to catch on fire. Rockets leaped from the pod on the winglet, so close the exhaust burned Dean's cheeks. He knew he was letting go; he knew he was dead. He felt his soul looping around, spiraling toward heaven.

Then he was sprawled on the ground.

Karr laughed at him, picked him up, and settled him into the chopper, almost gently.

"Not bad for a geezer," Karr shouted. "You're doing OK, baby-sitter. You're doing OK."

50

Rubens strapped himself into the seat as the helicopter's blades whipped into a frenzy. The Sikorsky—a civilian version of the Blackhawk—was detailed to Admiral Brown, who was sitting across the aisle checking his "clean" or unsecure E-mail. It tipped forward and pulled into the sky, headed back to Crypto City.

Rubens had gotten what he wanted—complete operational control of the mission. It was an important victory, even a historic one. But it did have certain risks. The CIA could be counted on to harp on any failure. Blanders was definitely on the road to becoming an ally, but he still had axes to grind, especially on this. And as covert operations of any nature always carried with them a high potential for failure, there was an enormous downside.

But this was what Desk Three had been established to do. This was the direction they'd been heading in all along. This was the way wars would be fought in the future. Collins was simply a distraction.

Rubens had boxed her out fairly well, actually. But she would no doubt return another day.

The Russian president was going to owe his life to William Rubens when this was all over. What a deliciously ironic thought.

The most pressing order of business now was to finger the coup leader. Bib and his people had to do better. *Had* to.

Rubens took out his own small computer and pulled up the E-mail program. He'd be spending all his time over the next few days in the Art Room; best to get the routine driftwood squared away. He'd have to run out to his house, button it up for an extended absence.

No time. Use the phone program. That's what it was there for.

Karr and his people—he needed them in Moscow. He shouldn't have let Karr stay out in Siberia to look for Martin.

Good God, he'd completely forgotten about Martin!

Panic overtook him for a moment. What was it Pound had said in the *Cantos*? "I am not a demigod—I can't make it cohere."

Rubens took a breath. Of course he could make it cohere. This was why he wasn't in *banking* or lounging around some silver beach in the Caribbean. *This* was the highest intellectual pursuit possible. He was master of the most powerful forces in the most powerful nation in the history of the world.

Pound was a schizophrenic anti-Semite and no one read his goddamn poetry anyway.

"It went very well," said Brown. "A historic moment."

"Yes."

"I expect Central Intelligence will be out to scuttle us. That Collins—she seems to have it in for you. There's a history there?"

"Yes," said Rubens, trying to make his voice sound noncommittal. "She was with the Special Collection Service."

"She ran it, didn't she?"

"A few years ago—before your time."

"And she would have preferred if Desk Three were set up the same way, with a CIA officer in charge. Preferably her," said Brown. Then he added, "There is a personal element as well."

Rubens smiled before answering. He was starting to actually like his boss, or at least believe him competent.

"I think Ms. Collins is professional enough to overcome any personal difficulties when dealing with situations as they develop," Rubens told him.

"Nice answer," Brown said. "We'll hold them off. I expect the DDO will end up working for you."

"She'd quit first."

They fell silent for a moment.

"The hearings into Congressman Greene's death are set
to begin next week," Brown said after checking through a
few more notes on his handheld.

"Yes."

"They won't interfere with this." Brown said it as a state-
ment, not a question.

"Certainly not," said Rubens.

"I assume you're doing a little checking into the situation."

Was it a trap? The death of a puny congressman—what
was that next to this operation?

Or did Brown think Rubens was somehow responsible?

Preposterous.

Though of course if he had truly wanted Greene dead,
well, then he could accomplish it, surely.

"I have been, well, somewhat busy with this," said Rubens
noncommittally.

When Brown didn't say anything else, Rubens decided to
change the subject. He hadn't had a chance—more accurately, he hadn't taken the opportunity—to inform the admiral that Martin might still be alive. He did so now.

"I thought we were sure he and others died," Brown said.

"Reasonably sure," said Rubens. To him this was a major
distinction, though the admiral frowned. "But we picked up
a voice and we're looking into it. If he is alive, we'll try and
recover him."

Brown's brow knotted. The compartmentalization of the
agency and the operating rules for Desk Three gave Rubens
the authority to proceed on the mission without informing
Brown; nonetheless, the admiral's expression made it clear
he would have preferred an earlier update.

"Can we get him back?"

"Certainly. If it's him," said Rubens.

"He'll have compromised Wave Three," said Brown.

"To some extent," admitted Rubens. "We had already begun to revise the program as a precaution, however. One way or another, we have to assume it was compromised."

"Powers survived the U-2 hit," said Brown. "Despite everything."

He was referring to the infamous shootdown of a U-2 flown by Gary Powers on May 1, 1960. According to agency lore, the U-2 (which was part of a CIA program at the time doing NSA work under the Green Hornet program, which captured radio and signal intelligence) had been rigged with explosive gear that was supposed to make it impossible to survive a bailout.

"We'll debrief him thoroughly," said Rubens. "If it's him."

Brown nodded, though it seemed a very reluctant gesture.

51

By the time they reached their destination on the bank of the Ob River, the sun had started to rise. Dean sat curled over the back of the Hind's seat the whole time, sunk deep into sore fatigue. He'd loosened his bullet-proof vest to take some of the pressure off his bruised ribs, but didn't bother looking at his hip; it hurt enough already.

Too old, too slow: Dean thought about what had happened in the compound. His body had done all right—his reactions had been slower certainly than when he was young, and he hurt a hell of a lot more, but overall he'd done all right. What hadn't done well was his head. For one thing, he hadn't properly checked the roof coming out. Worse, his head had scrambled in the middle of the fight.

That was a fatal problem. He'd seen it happen to a very good captain in Vietnam, early in his tour there. The man led them into an L-shaped ambush, tried to flank the enemy through the thick jungle, lost a quarter of the force in a cross-fire.

Time to quit.

Karr and Stephen Martin stood against the side of the helicopter, peering through the smallish windows. Karr had just finished grilling Martin about what had happened, how he had escaped the plane, how he had been captured, what he had said.

Dean hadn't heard it all, but he could piece together the

highlights. Martin had crawled through a small access hatch with a parachute he wasn't supposed to have and left the plane after pressing the destruct sequence. He assumed the others had gone out as well. He hit his head when he landed but apparently managed to walk some distance before two men with guns appeared in the darkness not far from a road. He'd spent some time in a police station or military office— he believed it was the former—before being blindfolded and taken to the base where he had been rescued. He'd been questioned every day since but hadn't told them anything.

Even Dean knew that must be a lie. Martin's fingers shook and he kept blinking; the Russians had obviously broken him.

"OK," said Karr, turning back from the door. "We're landing."

The Hind dropped precipitously a few seconds later; Dean thought his head would hit the ceiling. Karr slammed the door open, then prodded Martin out. Dean, legs shaky, felt like he was falling to the doorway. He jumped lightly onto the ground; the shock reverberated up his side, jostling his ribs so badly he winced.

"Go," Karr ordered, pointing toward the riverbank a good distance away. Then he jumped back into the helicopter, leaving Martin and Dean alone.

"They leaving us?" asked Martin.

Dean shook his head, though in truth he wasn't sure. He started walking through the high grass. Martin eventually followed.

Just as they reached the shore the Hind's engine roared. Dean turned and saw the helicopter jerk upward into the air—and then burst into fireball. It skittered about fifty feet ahead, then, still burning, keeled over and went into the ground.

"Jesus," said Martin. He took a step toward the black smoke of the wreckage, then stopped. "What the hell?"

Dean stared at the fuselage, feeling as if he'd been hit in the back of the head. He checked his gun, took the safety off—whoever had shot the Hind down was nearby.

Three figures came out of the smoke, running toward them. Dean started to level his gun.

"Is it them?" said Martin.

The question probably saved their lives. Belatedly Dean realized that the NSA ops had blown up the helicopter, rigging it hastily to look like it had crashed. The wreckage probably wouldn't fool an expert, but the odds were that no one would care enough to send an expert to investigate.

Why didn't he realize that's what they were doing?

"Get the lead out," said Karr, trotting up like a maniacal JV football coach on the first day of practice. "We got to get moving."

Martin fell into a jog, but Dean, his hip burning and his ribs aching, simply walked. A small boat was hidden about fifty yards farther up the riverbank. It was very small and settled near the gunwales as the first four members of the group boarded. Dean looked at it doubtfully.

"Come on, baby-sitter, there's room," said Karr. "Sit next to Lia in the stern."

Dean's boots sank into the mud as he reached for the boat.

"Push us off first or we'll be stuck." Lia was holding the engine up out of the muck at the shore.

Dean splashed clumsily into the water as he leaned against the side of the Vessel. He managed to get in without swamping it, falling to the bottom with his pants sodden, while Lia slapped down the engine. She cursed and pulled the rope starter, getting a few coughs but no ignition.

"Choke it," said Karr.

"Yeah."

"Come on, like you'd do to your boyfriends."

"Fuck off," said Lia, wrapping the starter string around her wrist and pulling harder. The motor ripped to life, then died. It took three more pulls before she got it going.

"What happened to your leg?" she asked Dean as they began slowly moving against the current.

"Bullet got my hip."

She put her hand down on it. Dean winced, trying not to cry out with the pain.

"Bullet's in there?" she asked.

"I don't know."

"Did you look?"

Dean shook his head. "I don't think it went in. It didn't feel that bad."

"You've been shot before?"

"Not really."

He was lying, actually; he'd been hit twice in Vietnam but for some reason now didn't care to admit it. Old news— or an admission of being old, washed-up.

"Let me see it," said Lia.

"It's OK."

"How do you know?"

"I do."

"If you haven't looked, and you've never been shot—"

"I suppose you have," said Dean.

"Three times," she said.

"She has that effect on men," said Karr.

"Screw yourself, Karr," snapped Lia.

Karr threw up his hands as if he'd touched a hot plate, then went back to scouting the riverbank. "Don't beach us, Princess."

"Screw yourself." She looked down at Dean. "I'll look at it in the van."

"Is that where we're going?" asked Dean.

"We have a van—or should have a van—about two miles up the river."

"It'll be there," said Fashona behind him.

"We requisition vehicles in case we need them," said Lia.

"What do we do if it's gone?"

"It'll be there," said Fashona.

"Karr will carry us," said Lia.

The van was waiting, as Fashona had promised, and unlike the outboard engine, it started on the first try. They drove it about five miles to the outskirts of a village, where a Mercedes truck sat near the road.

Dean, sitting on the floor next to the rear door, heard Karr tell Fashona to keep going.

"What's wrong?" asked Lia, leaning over the space between the driver and passenger seat.

"Tire marks in the dirt," said Karr.

"We can scan it," suggested Lia. "Probably it was just someone looking to steal it."

"Not worth the risk," said Karr. "We'll just drive this to Surgut."

"Fuel tank is just a regular tank," said Fashona.

"So we stop," said Karr.

"A long haul," Lia said.

"Well, you can click your ruby slippers anytime you want," he told her.

Lia slid around and plopped down on the floor. "How's your hip?" she asked Dean.

"It's all right."

She frowned at him, then pushed along the metal floor to look at it.

"Pull down your pants," she ordered.

"Yeah, right."

"Oh, don't be a sissy," she said, reaching for his waist.

Dean let her undo the button at his waist and leaned over to make it easier for her to slide the top of his pants down. Her hands felt warm.

"It doesn't hurt anymore, really," he said.

"You're burned and cut up a bit," she said. "You'll live."

"Gee, thanks, nurse."

She let go of his leg abruptly. Now that he had it exposed, Dean figured he might as well clean it and asked if they had anything to do so. She seemed almost reluctant to get the first-aid kit, which was under the passenger seat. Dean took it from her, using the hydrogen peroxide to clean the wound. It burned and frothed immediately, which he took as a sign that the stuff was doing something. Then he daubed Mercurochrome on the wound.

"That shit doesn't do anything, you know," said Lia.

"It's an antiseptic," said Dean.

She waved at his hand. "You'll be fine."

"Thanks for the sympathy."

"I didn't know you wanted sympathy." She seemed genuinely puzzled. "You don't seem like the type."

"You guys might as well try and get some sleep," said Karr from the front. "As soon as we get to Surgut, we're taking a plane to Moscow."

"Then home," said Dean. He lay back on the truck floor, feeling very old and very tired, glad the mission was over.

52

A metal desk dominated the office, sitting precisely in the center of the small space. The desk itself measured no more than a meter and a half across; its shallow bank of drawers barely accommodated a full pad of paper. Photographs and citations had once covered the walls of the office, but now only their shadows remained, spots of cream against the dull yellow mass. It had been years since the office was occupied; its last owner had reviewed farm reports for a defense secretary, his identity now as obscure as his job had once been.

The bank of offices here was regarded as unlucky by some of the building staff, not because they were small and had limited electrical and phone services, but because a jilted lover had tried to commit suicide by setting herself on fire in the hallway. She had not succeeded, but even so, there were rumors that her ghost walked here at night.

The assassin did not care for such rumors, nor did he contemplate the size of the room or the simplicity of its furnishings. He cared only for the window, which looked over the courtyard of the building where his target would be two days hence.

The room connected to the hallway via another room the exact same size. The hallway door and most of this outer room could not be seen from the room with the window the assassin needed. This was a problem; it made it possible for someone to enter the outer room and ambush him while he was at his post. The glass panel on the door made a dead bolt impractical; it would be child's play to cut through the glass. Keying the dead bolt would delay his escape, and besides, the glass panel was large enough for someone to climb through.

Difficult, surely, but then, the assassin was himself an expert in difficult things.

There was a solution. From one of the two large bags he'd brought, he removed a large oval lock that looked precisely the same as the others on the hallway. Five buttons made a circle around a central switch; the buttons had to be pressed in a certain order to open.

Except that here, pressing any of the buttons would ignite a small C-4 charge in the lock. As would breaking the thin wire tape he placed around the window. The only way to safely open the door was with the inside latch.

Door secured, the assassin went back into the room with the window he wanted. He climbed on top of the desk and sat with his legs crisscrossed. He did not think about his task; the job was simplicity defined and did not require thought. He did not think about his surroundings; they were not worthy of thought. He gave himself over entirely to thinking about his young son, who was now five.

He had not seen the boy for nearly a year. As he stared now at the light patches on the wall, he reviewed the boy's entire life, or at least what he had known of it. He smiled at the mischief, berated himself for losing his temper three times. It occurred to the assassin, as it had occurred to him before, that his outbursts of anger were his own fault and not the boy's; he regretted yelling at him. He could take solace in the fact that he had never spanked the little one in his entire life—though perhaps many would see that as a personal flaw. The assassin did not mind such opinions; to him, being known as an indulgent father was hardly a disgrace.

When his reverie reached the boy's last birthday, the assassin began to laugh. He remembered how his son tried in vain to push a large piece of cake into his mouth. The assassin laughed, remembering the little boy's tears when he finally realized he could not have it all.

And then, for a moment, the assassin cried as well.

He sat on the desk a few minutes longer. Then he slowly unfurled his legs and began setting up his post. He would now think of nothing except his mission for the next two days, or as long as it took.

53

Sherlock Holmes once used the absence of a dog's bark to solve a crime. One of Bib's teams had used the absence of communications to provide another list of possible ringleaders of the coup, presenting it to Rubens on his return to Crypto City.

Unfortunately, the technique worked better on the page than in real life. The analysis pegged two possible military leaders as the top choices. But neither had made the earlier lists of likely conspirators—Oleg Babin, the equivalent of an American four-star general in the Far East command, and Ilya Petrosberg, a defense ministry official who had been with the Marines.

Rubens still favored Vladimir Perovskaya, the defense minister himself. So did the CIA and nearly everyone else who had an opinion.

They could plan to freeze out all of the top suspects, but that would spread their resources. And there was always the problem of inadvertently freezing out loyalists who might be useful.

Rubens stared at the paper on his desk. As so often in intelligence, the problem wasn't so much getting information—there were reams and reams of it. The problem was sorting through and analyzing it, then making the right guess on what to do about it.

He had no choice. He'd freeze everyone on both the main

list and this new one. In the meantime, he'd give Bib another push. Had they looked for patterns in the use of ciphers or communications devices? Something had to stand out.

There were other developments. British MI6 was starting to make discreet inquiries. The damn Brits were always sticking their toes in where they didn't belong.

The direct line to the Art Room buzzed. Rubens picked up the phone.

"Boss, we got him," she said. "Martin. Tommy and his guys are bringing him back."

"I'm glad he's alive," said Rubens, though of course the exact opposite was true. However, if he had to have survived the crash, it was far better that they had him than the Russians. It would be easier to assess the damage to the program with his account.

"He claims he didn't tell the Russians anything about Wave Three," added Telach.

Even Rubens had an extremely difficult time stifling a laugh of derision. Of course Martin had been broken; it was absurd to think otherwise. It was just a question of how much time the Russians had had to interview him.

"I will be down shortly," he told Telach. "Have Karr and his people arrived in Moscow yet?"

"They're en route."

"Tell them to move more quickly." Rubens hung up and glanced at his watch. There were seven minutes left until the scheduled hourly update on Bear Hug. The update involved a secure conference call with the NSC, agency, and military leaders connected with the operation. While he could take the call in the Art Room, he'd never make it through the security chamber in time. He'd have to take the call here, then go downstairs.

He thought again of the things that needed to be cared for at his home. The African violets must be watered, and he should change the thermostat and phone settings. He'd also want to put on the random lighting pattern that made it seem as if the house were occupied.

Rubens picked up the gray phone and called home, where

the house's central computer system could be accessed through its phone mail system. He hated using the gadget. The phone menu was exasperating, and not too long ago he'd managed to tell the lawn sprinkler system to keep itself on 24/7; he returned home just in time to prevent a mud slide.

The machine answered on the first ring, indicating he had a message. Rubens hit his code to check. The machine greeted him and then began playing a message from his cousin Greta.

"Hi, Bill, I hope you're well. Call me, OK?"

It had been left a few hours before.

Call her?

She never, or almost never, called to chat. It had to be the investigation. Was something going to come out?

Was that what Brown had been getting at earlier?

There were no other messages. Rubens hung up, then punched his cousin's number. The phone rang three times, four—he started to hang up, not sure what sort of message to leave. He couldn't tell her to call him here.

"Hello?"

"Greta?"

"Bill?" Her voice sounded tentative, very un-Greta-like.

"Are you all right?" he asked.

"Oh yes, I'm OK. Have you heard the news?"

"What news?"

"There's going to be an inquiry into Congressman Greene's death. There's a special congressional committee."

That was it?

"I had heard that, yes," said Rubens. "Are you concerned?"

"Concerned? Of course I'm concerned. I'm worried."

Maybe she did do it, he thought. Perhaps she felt pressure to confess.

That would end the rumors and contain the potential damage. A good solution.

"I'm sure you have nothing to worry about," he said in his most soothing voice. "If you need anything, I'll help any way I can."

"Thanks."

"You expect to be called as a witness before the committee?" he asked.

"I don't know. I guess."

Rubens thought of the scene playing on Fox. They'd cut from the live feed to the studio, where one of the commentators would point out that her cousin was William Rubens, the most important spymaster since . . .

He was not a spymaster.

Most important since whom?

"They're all grandstanding," said Greta. "They have their own agendas."

She stopped speaking, probably on the verge of tears. As Rubens thought of what to say next—as he considered what formula might get her to gush out a confession—something odd occurred to him, something unprecedented.

He felt sorry for her.

"I feel like I'm in a vise," she said.

"Washington is like that," Rubens told her. He glanced at the small clock on his desk—it was almost time for the conference call.

"Do you have anything to worry about?" he said. It was blunt and crude, but with the time constraints it was the only way to proceed.

"What do you mean, William?"

"I mean that, unless you're ashamed of something, I wouldn't worry about all this," he said, backtracking. "It's nonsense."

"I'm not ashamed of anything."

"See?" Rubens pitched forward in his chair. Better to leave things in as positive a light as possible. "It'll work out. Look, Greta, I have to go. Do you need anything? Anything at all? Do you want to just talk?"

"No, thanks. Thanks. I appreciate your support."

"It's nothing. If you want to talk, let me know. I'm busy, but I'll help. I promise."

"It's good to have family."

Rubens hung up, feeling more guilty than he would have cared to admit.

54

Malachi Reese cursed and slammed on the brakes about half-way down the parking lot aisle in Lot 2D. Some stinking SOB had parked in his spot. He threw the Honda into reverse without bothering to figure out whose car it was; security would do that, and besides, he was running late as it was. The problem now was where the hell to park.

The handicapped section. There were sixteen spots in the lot, mandated by federal law—even though no one with a handicapped license had clearance to park here.

Sixteen other scumbags had gotten there first. This really was a serious alert.

Malachi wheeled back, the heat shield in the Honda clattering as the engine jerked on its mounts. He almost parked on the sidewalk but at the last moment saw a spot near the fence. He raced a Neon for it—*as if*—leaving a good patch of rubber on the hot asphalt as he screeched in. Out of the car, he ran to the facility entrance, trotting in place as the security guards—who had seen him leave only a few hours ago—wanded him and did the retina thing.

Inside, Malachi dialed his MP3 jukebox to the Clash's "London Calling." The hunt for a parking spot had made him feel particularly nostalgic.

There was an extra set of security guards downstairs in the hallway leading to Conference Room Three, where he'd been told to report. Malachi didn't know them, which meant they dished major hassle over his MP3, making him put it under an X-ray and then passing it through the bomb sniffer gate twice. By the time Malachi finally entered the briefing room—a small auditorium with thirty seats, about twenty of them filled—they were well into the operational briefing, with an Air Force colonel Malachi didn't recognize talking about "the asset limitation list." Malachi saw Terry Gibbs, one of the other platform jocks, sitting in the second bank of seats. He slid behind him and poked him in the back.

"You're big-time late," whispered Gibbs.

"Some asshole parked in my spot," said Malachi, pulling up the LCD video screen at the side of his chair. He flicked it on: channel A featured a map of the greater Moscow area, with red stars all around it. Malachi recognized the stars as defense installations without having to tap the screen for IDs.

"So like, I have to lose my day off because we're going to bug the Russians again? Shit, Frenchie could have done it." Frenchie was an Air Force captain named Steven Parlus.

"Take off the earphones and listen to what the colonel's saying," said Gibbs. "Look around. You're not flying the platform. They want you on the Birds. Kelly's unavailable and Duff asked for you. You missed Rubens."

"The F-47s? Kick-ass."

Malachi pulled out his ear buds and started paying serious attention. The F-47Cs, sometimes called Birds, were Mach 1.5–capable UFAVs, or unmanned fighting aerial vehicles, capable of carrying weapons as well as "mission pods"—signal and image–capturing gear. The remote planes were an outgrowth of Boeing's successful F-45 program for the Air Force, which had provided considerable pointers for the satellite-controlled NSA force. They generally worked in packs or flights of four and required several remote pilots, along with a full relief team.

"This unit here is our prime concern," said the colonel, tapping at a base northeast of Moscow. The legend identified the unit there as 593, a fighter aviation regiment of MiG-35 "Super Fulcrums." The MiG-MAPO next-generation fighter was based on the MiG 1.42, itself a development of the MiG-29.

"Yes," said Malachi, as if he'd just hit a three-point shot at the buzzer. Those close enough to hear him snickered, and the colonel giving the presentation stopped speaking and looked toward him.

"Is there a question, Mr. Reese?" asked the colonel.

"No, sir," said Malachi. "Just saying we're going to kick their butts."

"That's not the idea, Reese," said General Tonka, standing up from the front row. Tonka was another holdover from Space Command. "Russia is a member of NATO, an ally— no unauthorized dogfighting, no unauthorized anything."

Tonka's nickname was, naturally, Truck, though he was built like a slim walking stick. He'd flown combat in the Gulf. He gave the room one of his best stares, then turned back to Malachi and pointed at him. "I know you're a cowboy, Reese. Don't fuck up."

"No, sir," said Malachi. "Not on purpose."

Two hours later, Malachi joined the flight crew in Control Bunker C, a separate underground facility with its own power supply, ventilation system, and communications network. It linked to the Art Room via three separate dedicated lines, each of which was always on. Malachi was second pilot, essentially the copilot in a four-man crew that also had a pilot, navigator/weapons officer, and radar/ECM man. They could control from two to eight planes with the help of a bank of computers and a dedicated satellite network. This could be augmented by J-STARS and AWACS aircraft; eventually, specially equipped Raptors and Strike Eagles would also be able to tie into the network.

"Look who the cat drug in," said Train—officially known as Major Pierce Duff. Train had cut his teeth as a young lieutenant flying F-16s in the Gulf War and was regarded as one of the top remote pilots in the service. This was his team,

and Malachi—or "Mal," as they sometimes referred to him—
swept his torso down as a gesture of respect.

Kind of.

"He was probably making it with some ho in the elevator," said Riddler, who worked the radar and ECMs, or electronic countermeasures. Riddler's real name was Captain
George Thurston.

"Got me," said Malachi. "Where's Whacker?"

"Getting updated disks on the weapons sets," said Train.
"More programming code from your people."

"Hey, I just work here. I'm not one of them," said Malachi.

"Yeah, he's a mutant alien form of fungus," said Riddler.

"Actually, bacteria. I've evolved." He slid into his station,
which was dominated by a large flight stick. Most often the
remote planes were directed through verbal or keyboarded
commands. While the pilots could take direct control via the
stick, the transmission delay could amount to more than two
seconds, which made guiding the planes a difficult art. You
had to think ahead, anticipating not just the plane but also
the control lag. Combat situations were especially treacher-
ous.

Naturally, Malachi prayed for one.

"The planes are due to be off-loaded at Nöbitz, Germany,
in four hours," Train told him. "We have to be ready to take
them off the ground as soon as they're fueled."

Nöbitz was an airfield near Altenburg in the southern part
of the country, once used by Soviet forces during the Cold
War. It had obviously been chosen for security purposes, not
proximity to the target area—it was a good hike from there
just to the Russian border, let alone Moscow.

"We're looking at a two-hour cruise to get on-station,"
added Train. "We get there, we stagger back to tank. We're
looking at a twelve-hour window at the moment."

Malachi whistled. That was a long time for the robots to
stay aloft, even with refueling. It would also be a considerable strain for the crews.

"I want to run through a couple of mission bits on the

simulator first," explained Train, "practice ingress and egress and at least one refueling. Then we break, get a real brief, come back, and do it."

"Sounds hot," said Malachi. "What kinds of weapons are we carrying?"

"Still to be decided," said Train. "Probably AIM-9s, AM-RAAMs, and Paveways, full mix." So equipped, the planes could be used for either air-to-air or air-to-ground attacks.

"Hot dingers," said Malachi.

"One more thing, dude," said Major Duff, leaning over to Malachi's station. "No music. For anybody."

"Shit. Serious?"

"Serious. Whacker threatened to break out his Barry Manilow collection, and I just can't live with that over the interphone circuit for twelve hours."

"Agreed," said Malachi, pulling out his ear bud.

55

Karr decided on his own authority to have the plane land at Kirov, not Moscow. He told the Art Room it was because of a peculiar challenge by an air controller, but the real reason was that he had doubts about Martin.

He'd checked Martin's identity with the portable retina scanner and there was no question it was him. Karr had gone over Martin's story with him several times; while it was obvious that he was hedging about what he had told the Russians, that was to be expected—no one wanted to admit he'd been broken, even if it was obvious. The details about Martin's escape from the plane checked with what the technical experts had predicted, and there were no inconsistencies or inexplicable gaps.

Yet Karr was still bugged.

Normal procedure called for a transfer out of Moscow via an antiseptic protocol that minimized other contacts. But that would jeopardize one of the safe houses and possibly the people who had set it up. Karr had to get the team into Moscow right away, which implied further complications for holding Martin. He might end up with considerable knowledge of the network in the city, which presumably he hadn't had as an equipment operator.

Karr couldn't leave him in Kirov, however. He had no people there, not even CIA agents who might be roped into the job. There was no safe house. Foreigners were often monitored when they checked into hotels. And it would take quite a while to arrange a pickup.

What was it that made him feel uneasy? The fact that Martin didn't seem all that happy in the first few minutes of the rescue?

But that could be explained by the fact that he had been sleeping and didn't know what was going on. Martin would already have passed countless background checks, lie detector tests, all sorts of investigations.

Still.

The pilots of the Fokker 80 were Brits who were only too happy to land at Kirov, since it would save them considerably on the use fees and fuel.

The pilots did a lot of work for the CIA. They probably had been set up in business by MI6, though that wasn't entirely clear, since the British intelligence agency actually used different freelancers, all native. The only thing Karr was reasonably sure of was that the pilots wouldn't sell them out to the Russians, the Chinese, or anyone from the Middle East.

That, and their plane was reasonably fast and spacious.

Karr had told them the team was a group of American businessmen who'd gotten sick while looking at oil sites in Siberia. The odds on them buying that story were about the same that a snowman would last a full day on a Miami beach.

"OK, up and at 'em," he told the team camped out in the well-appointed passenger cabin.

"Moscow already?" asked Fashona, unfolding himself from the seat.

"Kirov. Let's go."

"Kirov?" said Lia.

"Hit the road. Up, Martin. Let's go, Dean, shake it. Come on."

They got a rental car and began driving toward a collection of tall buildings on the highway, one of which bore a Holiday Inn logo. Karr found a nondescript semi-Western-style no-questions-asked motel—its Russian name translated literally as "small name"—at the edge of an industrial complex. The motel had what amounted to a coffee shop at one side; he told the others to go in and get something to eat while he talked to the Art Room.

"Why aren't you in Moscow?" demanded Rockman, the runner, when he came on the line.

"I have questions."

"I need you in Moscow right away. Where is Martin?"

"He's around. He's what I have questions about."

Rockman didn't answer for a moment. "We need you in Moscow. Deliver Martin to the embassy and we'll find someone to take him back."

"I want to keep him sterile."

"Sterile? You're sure it's him, right?"

"Yeah," said Karr. "I'm sure."

"Look, we have something of a much higher priority than Martin," said Rockman.

"Can I have Dean take him back?"

"You're going to need Dean."

"My ESP isn't working all that well tonight," said Karr.

"We'll tell you the game plan when we're ready. Your line's not secure enough."

The satellite system connecting Karr with the Art Room used four different and independent encryption systems; the NSA itself would have trouble reading it.

But it was theoretically possible.

The only more secure system—aside from going home and speaking in person—was located in a Moscow safe house.

"Do what you can with Martin," added the runner. "Put him on ice if you have to. That's your call. But we need you in Moscow. And we'll need your whole team."

"All right," said Karr.

56

Two cups of coffee—actual, real coffee—and Dean felt wired. He had a hard time sitting in the restaurant booth, let alone concentrating his thoughts. He wanted to get back home and sleep for a week, if not more.

Lia had on her pissed-off scowl and Fashona kept jerking his head back and forth. Martin seemed to be in a fugue state, possibly so mentally wasted that he couldn't process information anymore.

Dean had been on a mission in Vietnam rescuing a South Vietnamese village official from the Vietcong. They'd gotten the man back alive—he'd actually been left when the small unit retreated as the Marines moved in. That guy had had the same look Martin did now, completely spaced. The gooks hadn't hurt him physically, but their taking him screwed his head so badly, Dean had doubted he lived more than a few weeks after his rescue. The first cold he caught would kill him.

Same thing with Martin. He slumped in the corner of the booth, eyes wide open, but body stiff, as if its joints were welded in place.

Dean could've ended up like that, too. Still might.

"Wow, you're a cheerful bunch," said Karr, sliding into the booth next to Dean. "Jesus, only Dean looks like he's awake."

"You're talking pretty loud," said Lia.

"You don't really think they don't know we're from out of town, do you?" asked Karr.

"What's the drill?" asked Fashona.

"The drill is, we have about an hour to get to the airport," said Karr. "Our tickets await."

"Why'd we get off the charter?" said Lia.

"Complications." Karr looked at Martin. "Stephen, you figure you're all right to travel by yourself?"

Martin didn't seem to hear. Lia kicked Karr under the table so hard Dean felt it. He looked over at her; her brow was furled as if she were trying to send a telepathic message.

Karr ignored it. "Yo, Stevie?"

"I'm OK," said Martin.

"I'll give you the route when we get there. Come on, let's do it." Karr threw a small wad of crumpled rubles on the table. "Anyone looking for souvenirs can get 'em at the airport."

Karr didn't bother checking in the rental car when they reached the airport. He'd booked Martin on a flight to St. Petersburg and from there to Sweden and then the UK; the rest of them were going to Moscow. Karr took Martin along to the gate—he'd booked two seats just so he could do so—while the others checked in. Their flight was already boarding.

"He'll have to catch up," said Lia.

"You know where we're going?" said Dean.

She rolled her eyes instead of answering.

Their seats were next to each other. The airliner was a Tupolev Tu-154, somewhat similar to a Boeing 727 with a comfortable, if nondescript, cabin. But after the Fokker the interior seemed dowdy and crowded. Lia jerked her legs away as Dean's foot accidentally brushed against hers. She seemed to have recovered from her brief try at being human and was back into full-bitch mode.

Dean briefly fantasized about what she might look like without her clothes. He remembered the skirt she'd worn when he first saw her—very nice, though even in the baggy pocket-laden pants she was a knockout. One of the attendants was a blonde with a model's body and soft blue eyes, but she looked bland by comparison.

Obviously he needed real sleep.

"Shit," Lia muttered. The plane had filled up; Karr's seat was empty.

"You think we should get out?" Dean asked.

"He can take care of himself."

"Just checking."

She twirled her finger around the bottom edge of her shirt, working out her anxiety or something.

They were taxiing back from the gate as Karr bounced down the aisle, his shit-eating grin lighting his face.

"Hey, homes," he said, pointing at them and then plopping down next to Fashona in the row in front of them.

"You cut it close," said Lia, leaning forward.

"Nah. I would've caught up on the runway if I had to."

"Is Martin OK?"

"A question that won't be answered until two hours from now," said Karr. "Though I'm fully prepared to guess the answer now."

Karr pushed his seat down so abruptly the top cushion caught Lia in the face.

"Shit," she said.

"Oops. Sorry." Karr gave her one of his shit-eating grins. "Better get some sleep. We may not have a chance for a while."

Neither Dean nor Lia slept on the short flight, but Karr snored so loudly Fashona poked him once or twice in the ribs to get him to stop. Dean found himself admiring, even envying the kid, simply for his ability to relax.

Dean dragged himself down the ramp after they landed in Moscow. The others walked through the terminal with the self-assured quickness of regular travelers, but Dean moved slowly, diverted by sights and slowed by his fatigue. His ribs and hip had stopped hurting, and while he had an assortment of scrapes and bruises, there didn't seem to be anything wrong with him that rest wouldn't cure. Though it was night, there was a certain excitement in the terminal. Dean began to feel curious and, thinking about the city, wondered if he might come back someday as a tourist.

He had learned to sort the clothes. Karr was dressed in a fairly standard Russian style—simple brown pants and shoes, a couple of shirts that were obvious under the pullover, a slightly worn but clean suit jacket that didn't match the pants. But he still stood out as a foreigner who dressed like a Russian. So did the others.

They took a black-market taxi into the city, all four of them cramming into a ten-year-old Toyota Corolla. Dean stared from the window, expecting gold spires and painted domes, symbols of the city's exotic flair. For a while, he was disappointed. From the highway Moscow looked a lot like any other city at night—lights and traffic, big boxy buildings in the distance. Finally, a quartet of gold-painted domes loomed above the shadows, glinting in the wash of nearby searchlights. Then they seemed to move back, hiding amid the more mundane facades, gray with the night.

They got out in front of an apartment building on a block that could have been in Queens, New York. Karr led the way to the door, then abruptly turned around as the taxi drove out of sight. He double-timed across the street; Dean found himself running with the others down an empty sidewalk, into a building and then through a courtyard, out through another building, and once more to the street. Karr stopped short at the door, letting the others catch up before pushing it open and walking calmly down the stoop to the street, walking along to a small bus stop. Dean was still catching his breath when the bus appeared, a large yellow box that stopped in the middle of the street and held up traffic while they boarded. Lia grabbed his hand; Dean looked at her in surprise, then realized she had slipped a ticket into it. He watched her insert hers at the end of a small box and then pushed a large round knob at the other end; he did the same, validating it, then followed Lia to a seat about halfway down the aisle.

Three stops later, they all got off. The houses here were two-family townhouses and seemed quite new. Small by U.S. standards, their sides were made of prefab cement panels and their fronts brick, though those might have been prefabbed as well.

Karr went up the walkway of number 442 and slipped a key into the door.

"Hang tight," said Fashona, grabbing his shirt as Dean started to follow across the threshold. Karr stood just inside, a small probe in one hand and his tiny computer in the other. He laid his hand in the middle of a photograph on the wall before reaching for the light switch. As the others watched, he walked inside and to the right, entering the kitchen. A minute or so later, several other lights came on and Fashona nudged him forward.

"Home sweet home?" Dean asked as Fashona walked into the living room and plopped down on the couch. Dean fell into the thickly padded seat across from it.

"Never been here before," said Fashona. He promptly closed his eyes and went to sleep, his head nearly 180 degrees to his body as it leaned on the back cushion.

Lia locked and bolted the front door, then went into the kitchen, where she started taking pots from the cabinet. Karr, meanwhile, trotted up the stairs. He came back about ten minutes later.

"When are we going home?" Dean asked.

"Not sure we are, baby-sitter. I'll let you know when I find out what the hell is up. Don't look so shocked. Go grab some of that coffee Lia's making. Fill about half the cup up with water before you pour in her sludge, that's all."

Dean got up and went to the kitchen, where Lia was in fact watching the black liquid drip through a Braun coffeemaker.

"Be done in a minute," she said.

"What's going on? Were we followed?"

"We have another assignment," said Lia. "But we don't know what it is yet."

Dean leaned back against the counter.

"I don't have another assignment," he said. "I'm done."

She shrugged.

He could go to the embassy, tell them he had to talk to Hadash. That would get him home pretty quick.

Karr lumbered down the stairs and into the kitchen a few minutes later. He had a half-sheet of paper in his hands, which looked as if it had come from a thermal fax machine. He turned on the stove burner and set it on fire.

"Eyes only," he told Lia.

"Screw you."

"There's an empty bed in the back." Karr turned to Dean and winked.

"Think twice, big man," said Lia, pulling down a coffee mug.

"No time anyway," said Karr.

"What's going on?" asked Dean.

"You and Princess are going to go join a CIA team near the Kremlin," he said.

"What?" said Lia.

"You're going to help protect a VIP."

"Fuck that."

"She really is a gutter mouth, isn't she?" said Karr to Dean. "Remember that when you kiss her."

"What's the story?" Lia had her hands on her hips. Her face was shaded red.

"Part of the Russian government is going to revolt. We're going to stop it."

"How?" asked Lia.

"Just focus on your little bit or you'll go all to pieces like me," said Karr. "Then you'll smell like me and God, you'll never get a date."

"Is this for real?" asked Dean.

"Shit, no, I make this kind of stuff up all the time."

"What are you going to do? Sleep?"

"I have a few things to run down," continued Karr. "Including making sure Martin got where he was going. I doubt he did. I'll catch up."

"Shit," said Lia as the coffee splattered on her hand.

"Better drink the coffee quick," Karr said. "Spooks are sending a car over. You have to pee, Dean, you better do it now."

"Who are we protecting?" Lia asked.

"Alexsandr Kurakin," said Karr.

"The fucking president?"

"I'm not sure how sexually active he is," Karr told her. "So use your judgment on that. I'd definitely bring protection, though, and I'm not talking about Charlie Dean."

57

Alexsandr Kurakin studied his suit in the full-length mirror, examining the way his cuffs fell, adjusting and readjusting his tie. Then he leaned forward, making sure that his thick hair was precisely in place. If he was vain about anything connected to his appearance, it was his hair, still admirably thick at fifty-eight. He found a few errant strands and worked them into place with his fingers.

As a young man, Kurakin had been fairly handsome. Now he was perhaps "more distinguished than pretty"—to use the words of an Italian magazine that had profiled him recently—but he could still cut a charismatic figure on television.

He would prove so once again this evening. By then, this suit would be stained, most likely with blood. His hair would be disheveled. But everything would be accomplished.

Not everything, not nearly. The Americans would be angry about losing their spy satellites, even though Perovskaya and his aborted coup would be blamed. Kurakin would face reprisals, even after persuading the American president that it was Perovskaya's plan all along. There would be a storm, certainly; the only question was how severe.

The Russian congress—well, they would rage furiously, but they were already impotent, and in assuming martial law he would depose them anyway. The military would fall behind him, following the initial confusion. The units that had been moved on Perovskaya's authority would, unfortunately, suffer some consequences—but then, their leaders were not particularly loyal to begin with, which was why he had chosen them. Another storm, but only a brief one.

And then, the deluge. But under his control. Martial law would sweep away the obstacles. First, the rebels in the south would be dealt with. The Chinese would stand aside or be punished severely. They would see this and probably not even have to be threatened.

He needed a military victory to seal his position, and so defeating the rebels—or at least plausibly claiming to—was critical. And then, quickly, perhaps even simultaneously, the next step. The forces that had made Russia a chaotic asylum for thieves, gangsters, and lunatics would be crushed without mercy. The criminals would be dealt with summarily. Russian society would be restored.

After that? Democracy? Too far in the future to tell.

He had hopes. He was still an optimist at heart, an old believer.

Kurakin stepped back from the mirror. There was a knock on the door—his bodyguards. It was time.

58

Johnny Bib kept twenty-three voices in his head. Exactly twenty-three. Twenty-three was a beautiful number, a prime with mystical qualities and associations. There were twenty-three ages of man, twenty-three major rules of life, twenty-three important places in the world. Eleven was a good number, and seventeen, and as far as his personal preferences went, Johnny had always felt something for 103. But twenty-three was sublime.

One of the voices told him now that he was wrong about the coup. He heard it quite clearly as Rubens and the CIA people on the conference call debated whether the movements they had observed meant the coup was under way or still in its preparatory stages. Clearly, as Rubens argued, it was the latter; the intercepts made that clear. Johnny was about to cite the statistics to back up his superior when the voice broke into his thoughts and told him he was wrong.

He was shocked. Rarely did he get anything wrong. He sat silently in his seat and waited for an explanation, but the voice did not offer one.

Where was the error?

The voice didn't say.

"Where was it?" Johnny asked.

Realizing he'd spoken out loud, he glanced up immediately, looking to see if anyone had noticed. He could not tell anyone about the voices, since they would not understand,

Rubens especially; they would think him more than usually eccentric, even for the NSA.

Every pore in Johnny's body opened. Sweat flooded into his clothes. His shirt was so wet he glanced down to make sure the pinstripes weren't bleeding into his skin.

But no one seemed to have noticed.

"Latest, Johnny?" asked Rubens.

"I—"

"You mentioned a possible time window for the attempt on Kurakin, based on the driving distances and one of the intercepted schedules."

Rubens was prompting him. Johnny liked Rubens; he was one of his few intellectual equals at the agency and obviously was trying to help him now.

He couldn't let Rubens make a mistake.

"It's wrong," said Johnny finally.

"What?" said Rubens.

"Wrong."

"Perovskaya, the defense minister—you had new information about him?" asked Rubens.

Johnny nodded his head, though he wasn't covered by a video camera and no one could see him. The intercepts seemed to point to Perovskaya. He was in contact with three of the obviously rebelling military units. There was additional traffic, not yet decrypted, between his secretary and two other units, as well as an order from his office to a key Moscow infantry unit allowing extra leave. Johnny had told Rubens all of this before the secure conference call.

Wrong, said the voice again.

Where?

The voice wouldn't respond.

"Johnny, are you with us?" asked Rubens.

Johnny began to nod.

"OK," said Rubens. "Keep at it. Brott, any updates on the Air Force?"

Johnny listened for a few seconds to the force analysis, then abruptly took off his headset and left the Art Room. He had to find his error, with or without the voice's help.

59

The first thing Dean noticed about the CIA officers was that they smelled like they hadn't taken showers in about a month. They were dressed almost identically in dark blue suits. Creases checkered the clothes like bizarre spiderwebs. Both seemed to have tried shaving a day or so ago, with mixed results.

Using an apartment several blocks from the Kremlin as a command post, the two men were coordinating eight surveillance teams trying to find an assassin believed to be targeting Russian president Alexsandr Kurakin. Two of the teams were currently inside the Kremlin.

Dean shared the common Western misperception that the Kremlin was a single building; in fact, it was a complex of roughly ninety acres that included a number of Russian government buildings as well as old cathedrals and ancient palaces, many of which were open to tourists. The president's office, formerly in the Senate, had been moved the year before to the Arsenal, displacing the Kremlin guards; it was off-limits and equipped with a variety of devices to disrupt surveillance and eavesdropping, including a copper skin inside the president's suite that made it almost impossible to place a conventional bug or fly there.

Nonetheless, the CIA could track Kurakin's position to within a few feet, even within his office suite, by using a variety of sensors, both preplaced and handheld. ("Handheld" simply meant that the devices were mobile and placed into position for a specific task; in this case it included a van's worth of equipment that homed in on microwave frequencies.) The NSA had penetrated the computer that kept the president's appointments calendar, which was not in code or cipher. But knowing where he was and would go was not the same as being able to protect him. While it was not difficult to get inside the Kremlin, getting close to the Russian president was at least as hard as it would be to get close to the American president.

"We'll know when they get him. That's the only thing I guarantee," said the officer-in-charge, Al Austin. He had flaming red hair and a sardonic, almost demonic, laugh. His breath smelled of coffee that had been made a week before and continually reheated. "They want us to catch his bullet. It's a friggin' joke."

Austin was exaggerating his assignment for sarcastic effect, but not by much. They were to detect any "actual physical threat" against Kurakin and pass the information back to the Art Room, from which it would then go to the White House and back to Kurakin.

"Why don't we just have the post office mail him a letter?" said Dan Foreman, the other agent. He was bent over a laptop screen on the floor; three other CPUs were piled nearby. Four twenty-inch flat screens and one that had to be at least thirty-six inches were arranged on a low table against the wall. The large one showed a grid map with position markers on it; the others had a variety of data and, in one case, a video image. A satellite dish sat next to the window, nestled among thick cables that ran to the roof above.

"How do we know they want to kill him?" asked Dean.

"We don't," said Austin. "Who're you?"

Dean told him he was on temporary assignment for the NSA and had been shanghaied.

"Welcome to the friggin' club," said Austin. "We'll have a little ceremony later where we prick our thumbs and mix our blood."

"If I were going to kill the president, I'd use a Secret Service agent," said Dean.

"No shit," said Freeman. "But if you have a way of infiltrating Kurakin's bodyguards, let us know. We've tried. Believe me. Bastards won't even have a drink."

"They're almost all related to him. The two who are with him all the time are cousins he grew up with," said Lia. "I doubt they'd give him up."

"Nah. Anybody's going to kill him, they'll *Oswald* him," said Austin.

"Meaning what?" asked Dean.

"Sniper. Oswald—Lee Harvey. Get it?" Austin shook his head. "Jeez, Lia, your boyfriend's slow."

"I thought she was queer," said Foreman.

"That's just what she told you to get you off her back," said Austin. "Probably the nicest letdown you ever got."

"What's the intelligence on the sniper?" asked Lia.

"Intelligence? There is none," said Austin. "Talk to your friggin' boss. This is his show."

"We can check his route, places he's going to be," said Dean.

"I see the agency continues to maintain its high IQ standards," said Austin. "How high can you count, Charlie Dean?"

"He uses both hands, which is twice as many as you do," said Lia.

"Yeah, one of 'em's always occupied," said Foreman.

"I used to be a sniper," said Dean.

"Yeah, I once studied law," said Austin. "Look, Lia, you guys want to help, spell Foreman on the sit map, OK? He needs some sleep. I do, too."

"I hadn't realized you were a couple," she said.

"You're just sharper than a pickax today," said Austin. "Excuse me while I take a shower."

The grid map on the large CIA flat screen was a dedicated locator map tracking the Russian president and IDing, when possible, those around him. The information was correlated from a number of inputs that were being routed into a satellite in geosynchronous orbit and then downloaded into a pair of satellite dishes the size of television receivers on the roof. Under other circumstances the information would have been sent to the CIA "bunker" inside the Moscow embassy, but since the Russians knew about the bunker it was likely they would take steps to isolate it when the coup started.

The Russians also knew about the satellite, and so there were two contingency plans in case its transmissions were blocked. One involved an elaborate routing system through secondary satellites and telephone lines; the other, even more desperate, called for a special balloon launch from the Zamoskvoreche district. The fact that the balloon would fly over the Church of the Resurrection added nothing to the odds in favor of success.

Additional signal intelligence interpretation was being handled back in Crypto City and provided on an as-needed basis.

"All we have to worry about is what happens outside the Kremlin," she told Dean. "Inside is moot—unless we're part of his security team we'll never be close enough to detect something before it happens."

"So we look for the sniper."

"Yes," she told Dean. "They already have."

"You think they know what they're doing?"

Her answer was to pound the keyboard of one of the laptops. A map of the city appeared with several dotted lines in yellow.

"He has a meeting at the new Education Building down here at two P.M. These are his likely routes. After that, he's supposed to go to a senior citizen housing project for a dedication. He'll be there at five."

"What's it look like?" asked Dean.

She pounded the keys again. A 3-D view appeared on the screen. Dean leaned down to look at it, brushing lightly against her arm. She didn't react; neither did he.

"That would be a pretty good place for an ambush," he said.

"Where would the sniper be?"

"I'd have to see it in person."

"Let's go there," said Lia.

"I thought we were going to watch their gear."

"Bullshit on that. I guarantee they've had more sleep in the past forty-eight hours than we've had in a week." She went to the door of the bathroom, listening for a moment before pushing in. Dean, who was standing behind her, saw Austin sitting naked on the toilet bowl.

"Hey!" he said.

"We're going to check the housing site for snipers. We'll be back."

"Shit!"

"Yeah, I can smell it from here."

60

Malachi had flight control of the second plane in the two-plane element, wingman to Train's lead. They flew a sucked echelon, a formation that had Malachi's F-47C riding a sixty-degree angle off Train's tail. Their altitudes were offset as well; Malachi tracked 5,000 feet higher than Train, who was at 35,000 feet. Their indicated airspeed was pegged at 580 knots, a bit under Mach 1.

The two MiGs approached from the southwest at high speed. According to the RWR, they hadn't spotted the two Birds—but they had a perfect intercept plotted out.

Interesting coincidence.

"We'll bracket," said Train.

"Roger that."

"Intercept in zero ninety seconds."

"Roger that."

Malachi leaned forward in his seat, heart thumping so loudly it could have set the beat for Fat Joe. Their formation was aggressive—arguably too aggressive for manned fighters since it limited defensive maneuvering and made it easier to cull off one of the fighters, usually the wingman. But the unmanned planes were designed to be aggressive. The formation allowed them to concentrate their attack in a variety of ways, most of which a pilot in a teen jet—an F-15, for example—would have salivated over.

The top screen of Malachi's cockpit area showed the enemy planes coming toward them, rendering them as red double triangles. The screen had a yellow bar and letters at the top, telling the pilot that his Sidewinder AIM-9 M missiles were ready. Just as in a "real" plane, the all-aspect Sidewinder would growl when it sniffed the MiG in the air ahead. Either Whacker or the pilot could make the call on when to fire the missile; in this case it was Malachi's decision.

Malachi felt the muscles in his forearm and fingers starting to freeze on him. He glanced sideways toward Train and for some reason was reassured by the veteran pilot's quizzical stare.

"Break," said Train.

Malachi leaned on his stick a little too hard, then got befuddled by the transmission delays. The plane dropped two thousand feet as he backed off, and now he started to fall behind it—the nose of the small robot pointed too far east, then too far west as he found himself wallowing through the turn. He was a far better pilot than this—far better—but he lost his concentration and then his target; if it weren't for the dedicated sitrep or bird's-eye-view screen sitting between the two flying stations, he might have lost himself as well.

He wasn't that far from where he was supposed to be. He started to nudge back on the stick, and the enemy plane came across the top edge of his screen. The Sidewinder growled, but Malachi hesitated. The target pipper included a distance-to-target reading that told him he was 3.5 miles away, which was at the far end of the Sidewinder's range.

He was gaining on the MiG. If he could hold off a few seconds he'd have him.

"Fire Fox Two," Train called his shot on the lead plane. Fox Two was a heat-seeking missile.

Train added something else, but Malachi lost it as the MiG he was attacking jerked to his right, aware that he was being hunted. Malachi went to follow but lost the MiG as it started a series of zigging turns—though it was extremely maneuverable, the slight time lag in the control system made it impossible for the F-47 to stay with the MiG. Instead, Malachi backed off his throttle, waiting for the MiG to commit to a real turn. That was stock MiG strategy—use his plane's extreme maneuverability to cut inside his pursuer, ending up behind him in what would have looked like a swirling ribbon if the movements were painted on the sky.

Rather than following him, Malachi would aim at the point where he came out of the turn, hoping to nail him there. A larger plane, of course, would never be able to make that sharp a cut. The MiG moved left, then right, then left, committing itself. Malachi went for the gas—

"Fire Fox Two," said Train.

A second later, the lead plane's missile flashed into the side of Malachi's screen and merged with the tailpipe of the other plane.

"Splash two MiGs," said Riddler from the back.

"Fuck," said Malachi as the screen blanked. The simulation over, he put his head over the back of the seat.

"You took way too long," said Train, who had swiveled to the side.

Malachi nodded. "Yeah."

"You had trouble on the bracket," said Whacker. "You went at it too hot and you got sucked into a pursuit. There's too much lag in the controls. That second is a killer. Use your missiles. You could even have launched the AIM-9 when the MiG first started to cut. At that point I think you would have gotten him."

"He would have gone to flares and stuff."

"Yeah, but you would've had a shot."

"I sucked," admitted Malachi. "I got the jitters when we picked them up."

Train stood up. "All right, guys. Take five. Germany should be ready for us soon. You OK, Reese?"

"Yup."

Train had the option of flying both planes in a combat intercept; the computer would actually take the wingman position, following a prescribed routine based on Train's movements as well as those of the bandits and a tactical library. But Malachi had shown a million times that he could beat the computer.

A million times in simulations, that is.

"Malachi, you all right?"

"Major, I'm kick-ass OK," he said. "Just need a quick kick from Speedball and I'm set."

"Speedball?"

"Music group," said Malachi, taking the MP3 player from his pocket. "Only on break. I promise."

61

Karr stayed in the shower until his toes wrinkled. The hot water washed away seven thousand miles' worth of grime, then ground away at his skin, shaving off several epidermal layers. Back in the kitchen in fresh clothes, he made a whole pot of very strong coffee and sat at the table, reading an old issue of *Car and Driver* stowed here at his request. The magazine was several years old and he'd already read it cover to cover perhaps three dozen times; one of the cars it featured was no longer even offered for sale. But he read it eagerly, even thoughtfully, his mind absorbed by details of the Mazda RX-8's cornering ability and a rant about how hard you had to mash the Z car's gas pedal to get it *really* moving.

Between the coffee and the shower, Karr decided he was awake enough to forgo a stimulant patch; the time-released amphetamine made him feel a little too jumpy and he'd only used it once since coming to Russia. It allegedly wasn't habit-forming, but he figured that was complete bull. His concept of the body as temple for the spirit did not preclude trading vodka shots, eating double cheeseburgers, or forgoing some of the precautions they preached in health class, but he was enough of a control freak to dislike operating in a submerged haze of consciousness.

He closed his magazine and got up from the table. He retrieved a large metal attaché case from the bottom cabinet next to the stove, opened it, and took out a laptop. Then he went back to the table, pulled out the chair he'd been sitting on, and got down on his hands and knees, feeling carefully for the right tile—he could never remember which of the four beneath the table it was. Finding it, he pressed on one corner and tried lifting it with his fingernails, but they weren't quite long enough. He tried two more times—he'd actually managed to get it the last time he was here—then gave up and got a pair of knives whose thin blades were hooked slightly; he jostled up the tile with a flick of his wrists, retrieving a large coaxial cable from a compartment next to the plug.

The system took a while to boot up and then check itself. Karr poured himself a cup of coffee in the meantime, sliding back into the chair. As the test pattern came up, he took out his satellite phone and called Blake Clark in St. Petersburg, an MI6 contact whom he'd asked to meet Martin when he arrived. The British agent answered the phone with a sharp "Clark." Glasses clinked in the background.

"How'd my package do?"

"Arrived and left."

"Take the flight to Finland?"

"Said you'd told him there was a change in plans," said Clark.

"Yeah. Which plane?"

"You didn't tell me I had to baby-sit the chap."

"He's gone now?"

"At least an hour."

"You're sure he got on a plane."

"He didn't come out of any of the entrances. My people were watching for him."

"Thanks, Blake. I owe you one."

"Actually, if we're keeping track, you owe quite a bit more."

Karr hit end, then keyed Bori Grinberg. Grinberg answered on the first ring.

"Da?" Grinberg's accent—and language—always started out somewhere around Berlin but could range over to Paris, up to Kraków, and back to Moscow depending on the circumstances.

"It's Karr. So?"

"Meter never moved." Grinberg's English had a Russian tint to it, which made Karr suspect that he was in fact Russian, though definitive information was impossible to come by. His first name was Norse—but names meant nothing.

"You're at the terminal?"

"Da."

"OK, I need you to walk through the building, back near the gate, rest rooms, all that, see if the marker was off-loaded. Keep the line open."

"Walking."

Karr had slipped three pimple-sized "markers" onto Martin's clothes before packing him onto the aircraft. The markers contained radioactive isotopes, chosen for their uniqueness and ability to excite the detector Grinberg had in his hand. Karr had told him to wait at the airport and see if the meter flipped.

Grinberg was a freelancer believed to retain ties to Russian intelligence. Karr found him valuable nonetheless, though admittedly he had to use some precautions—such as, in this case, not identifying whom Grinberg was looking for.

Unfortunately, to get Grinberg to do the job, Karr had had to blow one of his equipment cache points in St. Petersburg. Such points were difficult to come by, and replacing it would take several days of angst—not to mention a trip to St. Petersburg, a city he didn't particularly like. It also meant he compromised all of the technology in the cache, which Grinberg could be counted on to help himself to.

Which was why all of the technology—the most notable items beyond the tracking gear were some eavesdropping kits and a pair of stun guns that looked like wristwatches—had been purloined from the Russians themselves.

"How we doing?" he asked Grinberg. He could hear him walking through a crowd.

"Nee-yada."

"You trying to say 'nada'?"

"Da."

"You have to work on your slang. But before you can do that, you have to figure out your nationality, *ja*?"

"Hai!" he said.

"I haven't heard Japanese from you before. Thinking of moving?"

Grinberg let off a string of Russian curses, apparently aimed at someone who had bumped into him in the airport. It was already clear to Karr that Martin had in fact boarded an airplane—that or bribed Grinberg and Clark to make it look as if he had—and so he turned his attention to the laptop. After clearing himself into the system, he initiated a program that put him on the Internet, spoofing a German gateway into thinking he was in Düsseldorf. From there he accessed a file on a server and downloaded a program to his laptop's prodigious RAM—there was no hard drive. With two keystrokes Karr hacked into the reservation system controlling flights out of St. Petersburg, a destination he had chosen specifically because he found this system so easy to access.

"Ne rein," said Grinberg.

"French, right?" said Karr, recognizing the phrase for "nothing." "No trace anywhere in the airport?"

"Nope."

"Now comes the hard part—I'm going to give you a plane to check out."

"Plane?"

"Yeah. Actually, it's still at the gate. I know the flight." If Grinberg didn't find the markers on the plane, then Martin had to be still wearing them, which would make the next step considerably easier. Karr keyed his computer and saw that the flight would be leaving in exactly forty-five minutes. "I need you to check the trash and then the plane—they won't have vacuumed it."

"Mon dieu."

"Yeah—uh, you'll find a ticket waiting at the gate. Round-trip." He hesitated, waiting for the screen to refresh. The hack was perfect, but the system wasn't particularly user-friendly—he had to enter Grinberg's name with an asterisk before each letter. He screwed something up and it came out as "Grinnberg," which he figured was close enough. "You're misspelled in the computer, just so you know."

"They will ask for my credit card," said Grinberg.

"So give me the number and it'll be there."

"You're going to make me burn a good card?"

"You buy them by the hundreds, don't you?"

"Karr—"

"Come on, plane's boarding. It's worth another thousand euros. Going into your account now."

Grinberg got the card out quickly. Dean put in the number, then told him he'd call back in about forty minutes, by which time he expected him on the plane.

Twelve flights left St. Petersburg in the hour or so since Clark had lost contact with Martin. Karr looked through the different passenger lists, looking for single passengers paying cash and added to the manifest at the last minute. He found three likely candidates on three different planes—one flying to London's Heathrow Airport, one to Poznan in Poland, and one to Moscow.

London wasn't worth checking out, Karr decided; if Martin really was coming west he would have taken the flight Karr had arranged. Poznan was in central Poland, not particularly handy to anything—which would make it a clever choice. But if Martin was being clever, he would have simply bribed someone and taken his ticket, gambling that the airline wouldn't bother matching passengers.

Not a good gamble these days, but maybe worth the risk.

Nah. Not after everything else he'd been through.

But Moscow seemed too easy.

Karr backed out and went over to an airline Web site that helpfully provided flight information. The plane from St. Petersburg was due in about an hour.

Tight, doable.

Easy, though. But maybe he was due. He did live a good life.

62

Certain habits are so ingrained that they are impossible to change—the way a man sucks in the last swirl of beer at the bottom of a glass, the way he moves over a woman when making love, the way he squints into the high sun when he's been up too long for too many days running.

Among Charlie Dean's many inherent habits was one of considerable benefit under the current circumstances—the ability to look at a site and read it for the best possible sniper locations. Standing at the chain-link fence around the construction site Kurakin was scheduled to visit, he spotted a dozen great ones, another four or five good ones, and even a few marginal ones that might be chosen for specific reasons. Dean wanted to check them all.

Lia held him back. "Hold on. We have some work to do first."

"Like?"

"For one thing, figuring out how to get past the guards at the gate. For another, eliminating some of the possibilities. At least a few will be covered by video devices our friends have already planted. So are the entrances."

"The guy could've come in days ago."

"We'll check everything out that needs to be checked," said Lia. She crossed and began walking up the street, part of a residential area in southeastern Moscow.

"You're going in the wrong direction," Dean told her.

"You know, Charlie, sometimes I wonder how you get your clothes on right in the morning."

"You know, I think it's about time you and me had a talk," said Dean.

"Not the birds and the bees again."

"You always have to be a wiseass, huh?"

A look of regret flickered across her face but changed quickly into a sneer. Lia quickened her pace.

"See, I don't think you are an asshole," said Dean.

"You've been wrong before."

"Not about that." Dean tried to grab her arm, but she pulled away, then spun, and put her finger at his throat.

"Don't fuck with me, Charlie. Let's just get it done, OK? This is a shitload more important than anything you've ever done."

"You don't know what I've done."

"I know everything about you. Everything—Khe Sahn, the highlands, the lowlands, California, South Africa. I know your fuckups and your successes. I know how many medals you have, and how many people you killed. I also know how many got killed saving your ass. I'm not going to be one of them."

She whirled away before Dean could find something to answer.

Lia found a small park two blocks up from the housing site. A few mothers were watching kids and talking; she sat on a bench out of earshot, then took her handheld out and punched into the SpyNet portal. It took almost a minute for the system to register and authenticate her; Dean, still sulking, trudged over slowly and sat down.

She wondered if he kept doing things to piss her off on purpose.

"So?" he asked.

"Hang tight," she said. She thumbed in the most recent satellite picture of the site, then had the computer render it as a schematic. After she deleted the topo lines, she showed it to Dean. "Use the stylus to highlight the places you wanted to look at."

"Kind of small," he said after taking the computer.

She took it back and pulled down the zoom. The area was now displayed on four screens. As she started to show him how to go from screen to screen, she noticed that one of the women in the distance was looking at them.

"Put your arm around me," she told him.

"What?"

"Charlie, do you need an instruction manual on that, too?" Lia leaned into him and he finally figured it out.

A little too well—he leaned down and kissed her.

Not unpleasantly, though she pulled back to break it off. The old biddy who'd been watching frowned and moved on.

"In the line of duty," he said quickly.

"Four screens," she told him. "Use the compass arrows."

She continued to lean on him. She might have admitted it felt good—but only under severe torture.

"I think I have them all."

"Don't *think* you have them—*have* them."

Lia waited as he went through the screens again. Probably she wasn't *really* attracted to him—he was too old and at times a bit obtuse.

Good-looking, though, with the chiseled shoulders and arms she liked, tight butt, soft but deep voice. He'd be good in the bedroom but probably—certainly—get too attached.

No, she probably wasn't really attracted to him, except in the most theoretical sense. The *problem* was that she didn't have sex enough. This stinking assignment—her fucking life since what, joining the Army?—had turned her into a nun.

Just about.

Karr was nice but too nice, too up all the time; he never turned that bullshit smile off. And Fashona—very nice guy, very not her type.

"Done," Dean said. "Want me to explain?"

Stuff like that. *That's* what pissed her off.

She pulled the computer away and reduced the magnification. Then she sent the image back to the system for analysis.

"Just because there's no one there now," said Dean, "doesn't mean they didn't set up already."

"Really? You think?"

"You want me to help or not?"

The screen came back up. Out of the nearly three dozen places Charlie had identified, only six had had IR readings over the past twenty-four hours. Two were covered by the video cameras the CIA agents had planted, and another was near a microphone.

"These images are made every ten minutes," she explained. "So it's conceivable that someone very, very fast could get in and out without detection. But the approaches are being monitored, so really we're down to four spots."

"What if they came in a couple of days ago?"

"OK. That screen will take a little longer," she told him. "The schedule was only set yesterday."

"They may have staked out the site a month ago."

"Possible," she said. "But not probable."

Extending the analysis to sixty-four hours—that was the longest period available—yielded two other sites.

"I gotta tell ya, I don't trust all this high-tech shit," said Dean when she showed him.

"What do you mean?"

"I mean, you guys have been smoked twice. It never works right."

"Hold on—when were we smoked?"

"Getting Martin out."

"How?"

"You didn't know where he was."

"Well, shit, this isn't a movie. You think we could have gone in with four people—four people, only two of whom were on the ground—without all our gear? Jesus."

"How come you didn't know where he was?"

"He doesn't have a surgically placed locator," she told him. "Just like you don't. You lose your gear and we lose you. Even then, the system has gaps. Shit, nothing's perfect."

She realized she was talking way too loudly and took a moment to lower her breath. "How would the Marines have done it?"

"Well—"

"That was rhetorical, Charles. I'm not looking for an answer." She stood.

"I bailed you out at the car place."

"Yes, you did. Thank you."

Dean got up, standing close to her. "You don't say it like you mean it."

One or two of the women on the playground were staring. Lia turned and looked up into his face. "You know?"

"What?"

Good question, she thought. What?

Dean put his hand on her shoulder.

"Let's just do our jobs, OK?" she said.

"Fine with me."

"Then we'll go our separate ways."

"Perfect."

"Start by removing your hand."

Dean pulled it back with an exaggerated sweep. Lia shook her head and sat down.

"All right," she said. "We have to get in and check these sites."

"There are a couple of good windows and the roof in the apartment block," said Dean, sitting back down as well. "They're at the far end of the range, but possible."

"We'll check them, too. First we get into the site, get that out of the way."

"How?"

"Technology," she said, jumping from the seat. "And a little T and A."

63

Rubens stood at the front of the Art Room, adjusting his headset as he waited for the Moscow assassination team to check in. The Art Room was establishing full contact mode, connecting with the CIA's situation room and the Tank at the Pentagon as well as its field teams and supervisors. Hadash paced nervously below the big screen, sweat pouring down his collar.

"Five," said Al Austin, the CIA supervisor in Moscow. He was at a post near the Kremlin, running the crews keeping tabs on Kurakin and trying to prevent—or at least detect— an assassination attempt.

Two other teams finished the check-in, reporting from surveillance posts that were covering secondary access routes to the capital. Their efforts duplicated that of the NSA's own sensors, but in an operation like this there was no such thing as too much redundancy.

"All right, now that we're all on the line, we're going to run through the latest intelligence," said Rubens. He introduced Segio Nakami, who ran down the analysis on the latest intercepts.

Nakami was Johnny Bib's second in command. Johnny had insisted on hunkering with the crypto people, who were working furiously to break down a new cipher that had appeared in the military intercepts. While finding the keys and decrypting the messages would yield considerable information, they would settle for any discernible patterns of its use that would yield information related to the coup. Rubens agreed that Johnny was more valuable there—and besides, he was acting a little peculiar even for him.

Nakami explained that sixteen different military units had been positively linked to the coup; several others had been ordered to their barracks. All of the orders had emanated from the defense ministry, again pointing to Perovskaya. The one odd thing was that they were in a cipher that had been discontinued some months before, probably because the Russians suspected the Americans could read it easily. This was probably simply a mistake, added Nakami, though they were open to other interpretations.

No one gave any.

All of these units would be cut off when the coup began. Piranha—a virus designed to disable the military computers— would be launched from the Art Room at the push of a small button on Telach's console. Two other virus attacks were also ready. Communications disrupters—basically very large vans containing equipment similar to that carried by electronic warfare planes—were stationed near the military bases and in several key Moscow locations. These would be used to throw a blanket around the city and the rebelling units.

Other resources had been mobilized to monitor the spread and effect of the attack. Besides the existing sensor and satellite net, four Navy ships and nearly a dozen "joint" project aircraft were either loitering or standing by to launch. A schedule had been worked out to feed them onto stations piecemeal, hoping not to attract too much attention. And of course there was a large number of sensors already on-line to help monitor what was going on.

The individual units gave their own short briefs. The CIA people were more than a little testy, mostly reflecting Langley's pique that this wasn't "their" operation. There also was some unvoiced but nonetheless discernible resentment that they were putting their own necks out for the Russian president—a not unreasonable emotion, Rubens thought.

Austin began complaining that he didn't have enough

people to cover Kurakin and managed to detour into a complaint that the NSA team that had been sent over had left without telling him where they were going.

"Are you saying, Mr. Austin, that you can't handle the assignment?" asked Rubens. Rockman had briefed him on Karr's concerns and the latest developments; once again the field officer had instinctively followed the right course of action. But that was why Tommy was there.

"No," said Austin. "I can handle it fine."

"Then do so."

"We have movement," said Telach, raising her hand a few feet away. "Infantry division near Tula."

"We have one unit moving," said Rubens, swinging his mike down in front of his face and addressing everyone on the common circuit. "We wait for another unit to confirm. Then we move. As planned."

He put his hand on Rockman's shoulder, listening as Telach relayed information about the contact. It was an eavesdropping bug; that was not enough to go on.

"I'm bringing up a satellite image," she said.

A satellite photo filled about half of the massive screen at the front of the room. The infantry base was laid out like two half-wheels, with barracks as spokes and vehicles parked in large lots to their right. It took Rubens a few seconds to orient himself to the images; at first glance he thought the barracks were the vehicles.

"This picture's ten minutes old, for reference," said Telach. "Here's the most recent, ninety-two seconds ago."

Another image flashed on the screen to the right of the first. They seemed identical—and in fact were, as Telach showed with an overlay.

A fresh overlay thirty seconds later confirmed that the unit had not in fact moved.

"Have the unit on the gate check their equipment," Rubens told her. "No more false alarms."

64

Karr took a slug from the tall bottle of Coke, watching the escalator from the corner of his eye. A brunette with big-time knockers blocked his view momentarily; he had to physically step back and pry his eyes free.

And as he did, Martin got on the top of the escalator, eyes scanning the crowd nervously.

Karr took a few steps forward, putting himself just beyond the view from the escalator. He hung back as Martin descended. The meter he held in his hand beneath the newspaper sent a strong stream of clicks through his earphone. Martin was still wearing the markers.

Following him would be child's play. Karr hoped to get at least a rough idea where Martin was planning to go next before grabbing him.

Rather than heading toward the airline reservation desks to Karr's left, Martin continued straight ahead, walking in the general direction of the street. Somewhat surprised, Karr followed along leisurely.

Moscow. So that probably meant one of the intelligence agencies.

Or not. A *mafiya* connection, a relative, a car rental place that wasn't as conspicuous, another airport, a safe house, the Army, the Navy, the U.S. embassy—any of a million places.

Karr began trotting as Martin reached the door. A father and a small boy pulled their suitcases in front of him; he nearly fell as he spun out of the way. Karr tossed down the soda bottle, running flat out now.

Martin was walking up toward a car.

Black-market taxi. Another break. He ought to play the lottery today, truly.

"The city," said Martin to the driver in Russian.

"Ckopee!" added Karr, grabbing the door and pushing Martin in with him. "Hurry!"

The driver started to look back, but his eyes caught the hundred-dollar bill Karr had dropped onto his seat. He responded the way any taxi driver would—he hit the gas.

"We are in a hurry, aren't we, Stephen?" said Karr.

"Yes." Martin couldn't have looked more stunned if Lenin had come out of his tomb.

"Boy, you know, it's awful funny," said Karr. "I thought you were supposed to take a plane over to—was it Finland? No, that wasn't it. I think it was Sweden. Yes, as a matter of fact, it was."

"There were problems," said Martin. "I was followed."

"Uh-huh."

"I was on my way to the embassy."

Karr leaned back against the corner of the seat and the door. He stretched his legs as much as he could, which wasn't all that much. "I'll give you this—you're not as dumb as you look. But then again, neither am I."

"Why do you think I'm dumb? I was on my way to the embassy. What would you have done?"

"Embassy. OK." In Russian, Karr told the driver to take them to the U.S. embassy. The driver started to protest that he didn't know the way until Karr reached into his pocket and pulled out another hundred-dollar bill. "My friend can direct you once you're in the neighborhood," he said. "He says he knows it."

"I'm not sure I do," said Martin.

"Beautiful place. Bugged all to hell by Russians. Pretty clever, the Russians."

Martin didn't answer.

"How long have you been a scumbag? Did they turn you, or were you born that way?"

Martin remained silent.

"Do me a favor, Stephen. Lock your door. The embassy's in a pretty high crime area."

Martin made a face but reached over and locked it.

Largely because he did, Karr was ready when he pulled the gun on him a minute later.

"I was kind of hoping you were telling the truth," Karr said. "Even though I knew it was a fantasy."

"Screw yourself." The gun was a small .32-caliber revolver.

"Did you have the gun here, or did you get it past the detectors somehow?" said Karr. "I'd kind of like to know, because I'm always looking for new techniques."

He was also wondering if Martin had been met by someone at the airport, which would mean they were probably being tailed.

Martin didn't answer.

"I'm kind of hoping you don't shoot me," said Karr.

"Start praying." Martin's hand twitched, but not so much that Karr was going to risk rushing him.

"Come on now. I did save you. Even if you didn't want to be saved."

"Stop here," Martin told the driver in Russian, looking at Karr.

The Russian started to protest; they were still on the highway and a good distance from the central city, let alone the embassy. Martin said they'd paid enough money for him to stop anywhere they wanted. He kept his eyes on Karr's the whole time.

"Aim for the heart," Karr told him as he raised the gun. "If I'm going, I want to go quick."

"I know about your vest."

Karr jerked his right arm upward as Martin pushed his hand forward to fire. His hideaway Glock was in his hand and he fired point-blank, the bullet crashing against Martin's left shoulder just as he fired. Karr had loaded the gun with rubber bullets—he wanted Martin alive—but even lead wouldn't have stopped Martin from pressing the trigger.

But Karr had succeeded in throwing off Martin's aim. His bullet flew forward, shattering the plastic shield between the passenger and driver compartments. Shrapnel flew into Karr's face and his eye caught fire.

The car turned sideways, jumping a curb. Karr felt a hard thud against his chest, then fired the Glock again.

65

It was amazing what two shirt buttons could do.

Dean watched Lia loosen them, then walk up to the plain-clothes detectives at one of the side gates to the complex. She had foreign press credentials saying she was a Singapore television correspondent. He tagged along, bodyguard/driver whose job was to keep his mouth shut. Her spiel was all in Russian, but the outlines were in a universal language:

"You're cute; I'd like to see what's inside so the TV cameras don't get tripped up; you're cute."

"Sure, but I have to frisk you first."

"Go for it."

Dean was frisked, too, though considerably quicker. They'd stashed their weapons; the guards seemed more interested in Lia's cosmetics than her handheld or the small satellite phone, both of which looked like normal business items.

Dean wondered how the Russians could be taken in so easily, allowing access to a restricted area in exchange for a chance to cop a feel. But there were other people inside looking at the sight lines, and one of the guards walked with them as they went. So probably they thought, What's the big deal? And let's squeeze a little tit if we can.

Which angered him. Feeling more than a little protective, he glared at the Russian as he led them around to the area where the press would be allowed to stand—a good fifty feet at least from the president's path.

Lia stumbled and grabbed the Russian's arm; as he pulled her up, Dean felt a stab of jealousy. He watched her flirt a bit more, then turn back toward the gate. Baffled, he followed her out. Lia paused and gave the guard a kiss, then began bantering with his partner and finally kissed him, too.

"What the hell was that all about?" said Dean, following as she walked back up toward the street. "Jesus. We didn't even get close to any of the spots. And what was that about kissing them?"

"Jealous?"

"Why did we go in there and not see anything?"

"Wait." She glanced at her watch, then took out a small folding set of opera glasses from the handbag she'd brought with her. The bag—the first Dean had seen her carry since he'd met her—seemed almost foreign.

About a half-block up, she turned and looked back. "One down. One to go. Watch them while I check the layout again," she told Dean, handing him the glasses.

Dean peered through the small case. The first detective had slipped back into his chair and nodded out. The other was laughing at him but looking a little tired himself. He reached into his pocket and took a hit from a flask, then ran his hand along his collar.

"What'd you slip them?" Dean asked.

"It's similar to what guys give dates to knock them out and rape them," said Lia. She looked at her handheld, clicked one of the keys twice, then put it back in her purse. "Except it's faster."

"How'd you get it in them?"

"I don't think I'm going to tell you," she said, heading back toward the gate. "Just in case I need to use it on you."

None of the spots Dean had picked out were pre-set for a sniper. Lia placed what looked like a thin brown elongated pebble at each one. There was a tiny hole at one end where a wide-angle video cam could survey the area. The rest of the rock was a wireless transmitter set to come on at irregular intervals. It took more than an hour for them to go to all the spots Dean had picked out; they had to work around the dozen or so other security people who were overseeing the area.

When they returned to the gate, the guards were still sleeping. Lia walked back up the block to a tree, then took what looked like a tampon holder from the purse and gave it to Dean.

"What am I supposed to do with this?" he said.

"Just hold it."

He held it doubtfully in his hand, as gingerly as if it were a hand grenade. Lia took a small compact from the bag and took it apart, leaving the mirror. Then she took the case back, pulled it, and pushed one part onto the compact shell.

"Give me a boost," she told him. "To the branch."

Dean gave her a foothold with his hands. She grabbed the tree limb with one hand, pulling herself up as she held the contraption in the other. Her legs swung and her shoe almost hit him in the face as he looked up to make sure she'd made it.

It might have been worth the view. He wondered what she'd look like in a long tight skirt.

"Get your rocks off, Charlie Dean?" she asked when she jumped down.

"I'm just trying to figure out what you're doing."

"The transmitters in the flies are very low power. This picks them up and uploads to a satellite. The data is then fed through a computer which will look for anomalies—in other words, if anything changes, the program will sound an alert. We have to call our friend Mr. Austin and let him know it's set so he can bring it on-line. It's probably overkill, but you're the sniper expert."

"You don't think they're going to scan the site before the president comes?" asked Dean. "They'll find the bugs."

"I think they'll be looking for bombs, not surveillance gear," said Lia. "But that's why we used the low-powered flies. They're very difficult to detect, especially if there are other systems in the area. One of the people we saw inside was from the BBC service, so you know the media will have a feed. And then there are the security people themselves."

"Any one of whom may be an assassin."

"These guys, maybe," said Lia. "But hopefully Kurakin's people will be on top of them. There's only so much we can do. Come on—let's go check the apartments."

"You got a nice butt, you know," he said, following her.

"So do you, honey."

66

The taxi screeched and spun and collided with something as Karr tried to grab Martin and avoid the bullets at the same time. He jerked up and bent forward, twisting with the impact of the shots against his armor. He found himself falling out of the car as the door swung open with the collision. The edge of the door smacked his head and he rolled onto the pavement, everything black for a second. He managed to get one eye open, his right, saw feet running away. Karr crawled and then got up, began running toward the blurry image. A car swerved to avoid something—maybe him—and slammed into the taxi and then another vehicle that had also stopped.

They were on a highway overlooking a ravine. Martin ran along the shoulder. Karr pointed his gun and fired. The gun clicked, but he pulled the trigger several more times, somehow not convinced that it was empty.

Martin went over the guardrail a few yards ahead of him, pushing down the shallow embankment and running along a garbage-strewn streambed. Rats scattered as he ran.

"It's no use," shouted Karr. "You know you can't get away, asshole."

Martin kept going. Karr followed. About halfway down he lost his footing on the slick rocks and slammed the side of his head as he fell. He pulled himself up in time to see Martin duck to the right past a large culvert pipe and disappear. Not sure now whether Martin was armed and planning to ambush him, Karr walked forward cautiously. As he did he changed the clip in his gun, loading his spare, which had real bullets.

"Martin, come on now. What's your story?" said Karr as he came forward. He had his gun aimed at the spot, hoping to provoke Martin from his position. When that didn't work, the NSA op bent low, looking to see if he might squeeze through the culvert pipe; it looked too low and narrow. He edged to the side, then threw himself across the space, gun steadied by his two hands, expecting to see Martin aiming his own weapon point-blank in his face.

Martin wasn't there. Karr's shoulder crashed hard on a sharp rock and his head banged against the ground, but there was so much adrenaline flooding through his veins that he didn't feel any pain. He pulled himself up and began walking along the crevice that held the long pipe, not sure exactly where Martin could be hiding. He managed to wedge himself up at a spot about halfway down, climbing to the top. His eyes had cleared now, but the side of his head and the front of his neck were sticky with blood.

Karr felt Martin behind him, waiting for the best chance to fire point-blank into his head. As he reached the top of the cement pipe he spun around, leveled his own weapon, saw nothing. He spun back so fast his head began to float, but Martin wasn't there, either.

A trail ran through the scrubby grass on the embankment opposite the pipe. Karr leaped across, climbing up seven or eight feet to the top.

A ravine lay down the other side. At its foot was a train yard.

Someone ran from the base of the hill.

Scumbag, thought Karr, starting down after him.

There were voices above. Martin's contact?

He couldn't take any chances now—he'd have to kill the asshole.

Martin had about three hundred yards on him, but Karr closed the gap to about a hundred quickly, following as Mar-

tin ran beyond a row of empty freight cars and then onto a
train bridge.

"Give it up, dickhead," Karr muttered, complaining to
himself and feeding his anger and adrenaline. The bridge had
a two-by-six down the middle of the rails for workers; as
long as you didn't look down, it was a relatively easy run.
Martin was tiring; by the time he reached the end of the
bridge and jumped off to another embankment, Karr was
only a few yards behind.

Until now, Karr had been pretty oblivious to what else
might be going on in the yard. But as he began to slide down
the hill he saw a pair of tractor-trailers coming down the
road that ran along the base. Martin reached the roadway just
as the second passed. He tried to jump on the back but
missed or slipped, falling to the pavement.

Karr leaped down to the road and reached to grab him as
a third truck appeared. The driver laid on its air horn; Karr
scooped at Martin but missed. As the truck barreled toward
him he threw himself backward and fell out of the way.

He was sure he'd find Martin flattened in the middle of
the road when the trailer passed. Instead, Karr saw him running along another run of railroad tracks.

"What are you, Superman? Jesus." Karr crossed the road
as Martin doubled back to the left and disappeared.

Finally running out of breath, Karr walked to the track.
There was yet another embankment off the side where Martin
had gone. A road ran across at the base of the hill.

Martin lay at the edge. Superman had tripped and knocked
himself out.

Well, there was a break, thought Karr; he'd managed to
get Martin alive after all. A quick shot from the syringe he
had in his pocket and they'd head for the embassy.

Karr started sidestepping down. When he was ten feet
away, Martin jumped to his feet. Karr didn't even get a curse
out of his mouth before the son of a bitch began running
back up the opposite embankment.

There were cars on the road above. Karr couldn't take the
chance that one of them was waiting for Martin.

"Stop!" he yelled, aiming his gun.

Martin swung back, his .32 aimed at Karr's face. The agent brought him down with a bullet square to the chest.

"Suck," he said as Martin tumbled down past him dramatically. Karr momentarily turned his attention toward the road above, expecting someone to come over the side. With one eye on Martin, he edged up the hill, trying to see whether the bastard did indeed have a tail.

If he had, he'd fled. The road was empty.

Martin lay spread-eagled below, his face toward the sky and his legs sticking back up the hill.

"About fucking time," Karr told Martin when he reached him. There was a black circle of blood on his shirt, but Karr took nothing for granted. He stomped on Martin's right forearm, wanting to make sure the bastard was really out before he lifted him up and out.

It was only then that Karr conceded that Martin was probably dead. Cursing himself, he bent down for a pulse.

Nothing.

But then, this guy had been written off as dead before. Karr got down on his hands and knees and checked again.

Dead.

All that stinking work and he managed to croak anyway. It would have been easier to nail him back at the Russian Marine base.

Karr rifled Martin's pockets. There was nothing there except for a small key and a pocketknife.

Karr rose and took some pictures with his miniature digital camera. Another truck was approaching on the road where he'd almost gotten run over. As it passed, he fired two bullets point-blank into the dead man's skull, just to make absolutely sure, then got the hell out of there.

67

He checked his watch. Two hours were left now before his target would come. The security people were already in place, most of their sweeps already done.

The assignment itself was straightforward. He was not concerned with completing it.

Afterward—that was a more difficult problem. For certainly his employer would not want him to complicate the delicate situation.

He had no doubt he could make it out of the building. Beyond that, the difficulty would increase.

His wife and son were already safe. When he eventually joined them, a deal would be arranged—the money he was owed in exchange for silence.

He doubted his employer would concede easily. But that was a problem for later.

It was possible, of course, that he would not be followed, that the rest of the money would arrive in the accounts as promised. Unlikely, but possible. The assassin by necessity planned for the alternative.

Something moved on the street. The sniper looked down from his perch toward the street as a garbage truck moved slowly past.

Two hours, no more. He rolled his head around his neck, listening to the joints crack, then sat back to wait.

68

In the hands of a skilled operator, the SVD Dragunov guaranteed a hit at 800 meters. They gave themselves another 400 meters to work with, but even so, came up with only two rows of apartments with a view of the main speaking area that weren't already under CIA surveillance.

Lia produced a new set of IDs ostensibly showing that they were with state security. They were let into six apartments and picked the locks on two others without finding anything.

The roof was already staked out by Russian security personnel. Lia exchanged some quick and heated comments with them as Dean looked around; if there was a sniper setup he didn't see it. The building blocked any other sight lines for at least a mile.

"I still think his own security people are the problem," said Dean as they left.

"More likely this is all just bullshit," said Lia.

When they reached the car, Lia took her denim jacket from the back and pulled it on, initiating the high-tech com gear that connected her to the Art Room. She got in the car and started talking. By the time Dean got in, the conversation was over and she had more than her usual frown on her face.

"Trouble?" he asked.

She didn't answer.

"It must be a pain in the ass having them in your ear all the time," he said.

She still didn't answer.

"Where we going?"

"To go hold the CIA's hand," she said. "They're getting nervous now that things are heating up."

"We ought to check out the other site first," said Dean. "Near the building they're dedicating."

Lia began threading her way through a set of narrow streets. They weren't particularly crowded, but progress was slow anyway. As they waited in a queue to turn, Lia reached to her pocket and took out her handheld. She put her thumb in the middle of the screen, then held it on the steering wheel and wrote something with the stylus. As they turned the corner, she gave it to Dean.

"Pull down the satellite image of the area," said Lia.

"How?"

She walked him through the steps, which involved initiating a program and then using pull-down menus. She had already stored the site images; the toolbar included buttons to update and review them. The checkbook program Dean used for his business back home was more difficult to use.

He studied the images.

"They can secure it pretty easily," Dean told her.

He began playing with the resolutions. It was like a miniature video game, the computer cobbling different views based on its data. The 3-D screen was difficult to see except at an angle; the lines and colors were clear, but the screen was simply too small for much detail. It seemed to him likely that the president would arrive at the rear, where the position could be covered by security better than the front. He would come in through a courtyard that could be easily controlled. That put three buildings within the eight hundred or so yards within which the Dragunov was effective.

The roofs of these buildings were very steep, which meant that only the insides were suitable for a sniper. Since they were government buildings, presumably they could be easily inspected. According to Lia, the CIA people had done just that and had surveillance cams in the hallways, though they couldn't be accessed by the handheld.

Dean pulled out the resolutions, looking at the streets and trying to psyche out the route a motorcade would take. As he didn't know anything about Moscow traffic patterns, it was all a jumble. Even if the guy weren't riding in a well-protected limo, there looked to be at least a dozen different ways for him to get to either of the sites; no sniper would take a chance on picking out one without reliable inside information.

No. If he was setting up to kill Kurakin, he'd have to take him either at one of those appearances, or back at the Kremlin.

If Dean were doing it, what would he do?

The construction site offered a lot of opportunity. But the security people would know that and set up a good net. Even if he got his shot he'd never get away.

The Education Building, the site they were looking at—he'd have one good shot in the courtyard. But again, the security people would have it psyched out. They'd draw a circle around the rifle's range just as he had, find the three buildings, and watch them.

Unless you nailed him on the street leading to the back courtyard. Hit him through the car with a tank gun. Or Barrett. The .50-caliber bullet could get through an engine block and would probably make it through the roof of the reinforced Mercedes Kurakin used.

Or maybe not.

As a young Marine Corps sniper in Vietnam, Dean had worked primarily with a Model 70 Winchester—personalized, of course. In the callused hands of a professional, it ranked among the most accurate rifles ever produced, as long as it could be properly maintained and fine-tuned. He could hit his mark at a thousand yards, give or take. The M40A1 that replaced it was more dependable primarily because its fiberglass stock didn't constantly pull the barrel out of line like the wood. The weapon of choice among the current generation was the M24, a somewhat lighter gun than its pred-

ecessors. But given the best circumstances, none of these
weapons would guarantee a hit beyond the thousand yards
or so of Dean's day.

A Barrett 82A1, however, could make a kill at 2,000.
During the Gulf War, the .50-caliber rifle adapted from the
M2 machine gun had been used at least once to kill a man
at 1,600 meters—roughly a mile.

Move the range.

If they moved the range out to 2,000 meters, the courtyard
entrance would be in range of another office building.

Two, in fact.

"What kind of access to weapons would this guy have?"
Dean asked Lia.

"What do you mean?"

"Could he get a Western rifle?"

"It's best to assume he could get anything he wanted,"
she said. "Why?"

"We've been thinking of a Russian gun. They're accurate
at eight hundred, a thousand meters. If he used a long-range
American weapon he could almost double that."

"And still be accurate?"

"Accuracy depends on the shooter, and there are always
trade-offs. But yes."

Lia found a place to park. They checked the first site again
using the new range criteria; there wasn't a tall enough building there.

"So basically, we just extend the circle on the Education
Building," she said.

"These two buildings," Dean said, leaning close to show
her.

She gently leaned her head against his chest as she examined the screen.

"Let's do it," she said, pulling up right and hitting the gas.

69

The satellite image showing the troop movement came into the Art Room about ten seconds before the translated intercept was delivered, and in that small space Rubens feared that they had missed something, that their massive network of sensors and stations had somehow failed to pick up the command for the coup to begin—or worse, that they *had* picked up the signal but failed to interpret it properly.

But then it was like the start of a thunderstorm, information pouring in from every direction, more units starting to move.

"We have confirmation," said Rubens, looking at Hadash. "Launch Piranha. Initiate the rest of the attacks."

Hadash nodded. Telach pushed her button. The Piranha unit, ensconced in its own bunker in another part of Crypto City, unleashed the viruses. Within thirty seconds, Russian computer systems began to overload and fail. Meanwhile, the jammers began disrupting communications, and the other virus attacks were launched.

"Time to alert Kurakin," Rubens told Hadash.

Hadash nodded. He told the aide on the other end of his phone line to put President Marcke on.

"They're putting through the call now," said Hadash. He listened for a second, then relayed a question from President Marcke. "Where is Kurakin?"

"Still at the Kremlin," said Rubens.

"Negative," corrected Telach. "He's just getting into his limo to go out to the Education Building. We have that marked in sector three. He has a passenger."

"Who?" asked Rubens.

"We're working on it," said Telach. She had to practically shout to make her voice heard over the din. "But we think it's Vladimir Perovskaya, the defense minister."

"Can't be," said Rubens. "He's orchestrating the coup."

70

Dean craned his head upward, not so much looking at the buildings as absorbing them into his brain. If he were the sniper, where would he be?

He was a sniper a million years ago under completely different circumstances, called on to do completely different things.

If he were the sniper, where would he be?

The buildings had about equal views, if the simulation on Lia's handheld computer was accurate. So Dean would opt for the apartment building—there'd be less coming and going during the middle of the day.

Three, possibly four rows of windows would have a shot. Which would he take?

Dean would go to either the most obvious place, which would be dead center in the top row, or a considerably more obscure spot at the left side of the building, where the window offered a narrower view but probably just as good an angle.

His position would depend on all sorts of things, starting simply with access.

If he were the sniper, he'd think about how he was going to get away. One of his instructors had pointed out, aeons ago, probably on the first day they met, that you weren't *really* successful unless you lived.

"How do we get in?" Dean asked Lia when she returned

from casing the block. There was nothing suspicious.

"We just go in," she told him. "Why this one?"

"Because it's an apartment building," said Dean. "Less people to run into."

"No, it's crammed with people," she said. "These especially—they get four or five families to an apartment. You could have six people in a room. He couldn't chance someone coming in, even if he took the others hostage."

Dean shrugged. Lia played with her handheld for a few seconds. "That building is mostly vacant."

"How do you know?"

"It's on our inventory of government buildings."

She turned the screen toward him, but Dean didn't bother looking at it; he'd already turned to examine the building.

A little higher than the apartment building, different angles but essentially the same choices.

Lia nudged him toward it. "We only have time for one. Austin says Kurakin's on his way." She began to trot; Dean fell in alongside.

Was this the ultimate irony: two Americans—hell, the entire NSA, CIA, and God knew who else—working to save the life and government of a Russian president?

In Dean's day, the Americans would have applauded if there was a coup; they might even have engineered it.

This *was* Dean's day. Still. He was in it as deeply as he'd ever been.

The door was carded. Lia took a card with a set of wires on it from her pocketbook. She inserted the card into the reader, the wires hanging down, then attached what looked like a small, thin travel clock to the wires. There was a loud buzz; the lock popped on the door.

"Which floor?" she asked, trotting toward the steps.

"Top," said Dean. "There's no elevator?"

"I doubt it works," she said. "Come on."

Dean was huffing by the third floor, and there were twenty-something to go. On the fifth landing he stopped for a breath and looked through the doorway. There was an elevator about halfway down.

"Hey!" he shouted to Lia. "Let's check the elevator."

"Go ahead!" she yelled, still running.

He walked out into the foyer, still huffing. As he punched the button, someone emerged from an office a few doors down. Dean tried to turn his grimace into a smile as the man approached, praying the man wouldn't say anything that he'd have to respond to. As he reached to punch the button again the elevator door opened. Dean stepped in and jabbed the button for the top floor.

As the doors started to close, the man began to shout and run toward the car. Dean hit the close-doors button, pretending at the same time to put his hand out as if to stop the car. The man jammed his hand against one of the doors but failed to hold it; he jerked his hand away and they traded puzzled looks as the car began to move even before the doors had fully closed.

While it sounded more like a garbage disposal than an elevator, the car actually moved swiftly toward the top floor. As it rose, Dean took out the small pistol Lia had given him in the car and made sure it was loaded and ready. The doors opened and he walked into the corridor calmly, trying to orient himself and calm the adrenaline that charged around his skull.

There were a dozen doors nearly on top of each other lining the hall. Dean counted off five and stood outside the sixth. He put his hand on the knob gingerly, expecting, knowing, it would be locked.

Except that it wasn't. And now that it was moving, now that he had the knob in his hand, the door seemed to ease inward on its own—he was committed; there was no way to wait for Lia, no way not to jump inside the room gun-first, left hand coming up to steady his aim.

Nothing.

Dean's heart pounded in his mouth as he slid along the wall, angling to keep the open doorway on the left in view. He could see a window, something moving—he dived forward into the space, hitting the floor and just barely keeping himself from shooting a shade.

Dust lay thick on the faded floor linoleum. Dean rolled up, started back to the hall—and walked right into Lia's pistol.

"Fuck," he said.

"Fuck yourself," she said. "Shit."

They looked at each other, catching the same breath, catching something besides fear and surprise and anger in each other's eyes.

"Shit," repeated Lia.

"Shit." Dean pushed away, back into the hall to the next door. "This one."

"No, there's no one up here. I've seen the scan. You're it."

"Shit."

He stood over her, peering down at the screen. "The building's clean?"

"No—we can only get this floor from the satellite. We're going to have to look at the others. And listen, don't go springing open any more doors. They may be booby-trapped."

"Let me see that 3-D again," he said. He took the hand-held from her as the view flashed up. "This office—let's look at that," he said, pointing to a window on the seventeenth floor at the far end of building. "There's an air shaft right next to it—see the roof?"

Lia didn't answer. Her hand was once more at her ear. "Car's about three minutes away, maybe less," she said, loping for the stairs.

71

Alexsandr Kurakin leaned back in the Mercedes, listening to the defense minister babble on about the Navy's needs for an aircraft carrier as if Kurakin were some second-level bureaucrat who didn't know a machine gun from an anchor. For the past two years he had endured such mindless lectures silently, nodding when appropriate, pretending that Vladimir Perovskaya was a military genius. They were now within sight of the Education Building and it occurred to Kurakin that he no longer needed to listen to such lectures.

"Aircraft carriers are obsolete," he said. "The American carrier battle groups can be sunk or disabled within an hour after I issue the order. The real difficulties are their satellites and missile systems, which will soon be rendered impotent. I have already given the order."

Perovskaya finally stopped talking. His jaw lowered slowly as he stared at the president in complete disbelief.

Kurakin began to laugh. One of the phones on the console between the two men rang. Kurakin picked it up.

It was his chief of staff. The president of the United States had an urgent personal message and wanted to talk to him directly—now, right now. It was more urgent than possibly could be believed.

Kurakin could believe it. But while he had expected the Americans to discover the coup on their own—indeed, he had planted the clues—he had not expected a warning.

Touching, in a way.

"Well, the president of the United States," he said, turning and looking at Perovskaya. He gave a snort of derision, which the defense minister didn't react to. He held his hand over the mouthpiece; they were just turning into the complex.

"You go in without me," he told Perovskaya. "Keep the old comrades entertained until I catch up."

72

Karr had climbed out of the train yard when a pair of police cars sped past in the opposite direction. He waited until they were out of sight, then jogged quickly down another road, treading his way into an area of small shops and apartments.

About a mile from the train yard he found a table outside a small shop and sat down to take stock of his battered body. His pants were ripped in two places and his ankle was swollen; otherwise his legs were all right. His stomach was fine. His chest and side hurt like hell, but to check on the damage he'd have to take his shirt and vest off.

No sense doing that. Just see really big bruises. If there were *real* damage there, he'd be dead, most likely.

His head felt as if it had been taken off and put back on at an odd angle. He touched the skin near his right eye—the one he thought he could see out of fairly well—and nearly screamed with the pain. He didn't dare try it on the other side.

The shop where he'd stopped sold secondhand clothes but also did a little bit of business in the morning and afternoon selling tea and drinks quite a bit stronger. A middle-aged woman noticed that he was sitting outside and came out to see what he wanted; she started to tell him that customers ordinarily came inside to get what they wanted but stopped abruptly, obviously put off by his face.

"Bandits," he told her in Russian. "But I'm OK. Scared 'em away with my face." He smiled. "Tea?"

She nodded, then backed through the door. Karr had to check in but decided he'd have to wait until she reappeared with his drink.

Some parts of Moscow could be Brooklyn, New York. In fact, some parts of Brooklyn probably seemed more foreign than parts of Moscow, more Russian at least, stocked deep with émigrés who were consciously and in some cases desperately trying to re-create what they liked about their homeland. Here people weren't trying to hold on to anything except what they needed to do to get by. Dean watched a woman push an immense baby carriage up the nearby hill, stopping every few moments to take a break and talk to her passengers—a pair of large mutts, not children. Two workers shared a cigarette as they passed across the street.

The woman came out with his tea, along with a bowl of warm water and a washcloth. She wanted to wash his wounds. As gently as he could, Karr told her no, he was fine. "I'm OK; I'm OK," he insisted. She was almost in tears as she went back inside.

Rockman answered in the Art Room when he punched in.

"Hey," Karr told him. "Give me Rubens."

"All hell's breaking loose," said Rockman. "We're under way."

"Yeah. Give me Rubens."

"Fuck, man. We're busy."

"He wants to talk to me."

"Fuck."

"Just do it, runner."

"Mr. Karr, quickly," said Rubens.

"I had to shoot him," said Karr. "No doubt about him being a scumbag. I'm guessing it went back some, too. They must've had a pretty important reason to blow the penetration on Wave Three, don't you think?"

Rubens didn't say anything. Obviously, he'd already figured that out.

That's why he was the boss.

Black* 337

"Sorry I bothered you," said Karr.

"Wait for Rockman," said Rubens, going off the line.

As he waited for the runner, Karr looked up and saw that the woman was now peering at him from the doorway. She had a bag of ice in her hand—and a bottle of vodka in the other. Karr waved her over. What the hell.

Karr jerked away as the ice touched the side of his head, but the woman's soft grip on his chin turned him back.

"Thanks," he told her, forgetting for a moment and speaking in English. He repeated it in Russian, adding that she was an angel; the woman smiled and told him he was welcome.

73

Rubens pointed to Rockman, signaling him to take the line back. As he turned back toward Telach, Johnny Bib ran into the room.

"They're using fractals," shouted Johnny, arms flying crazily. His head bounced back and forth; he seemed to be having one of his fits.

Perfect timing.

"Excuse me, Johnny," said Rubens.

"Look," said Bib. He shoved some pictures in Rubens' hand. "They're at the base of the photos, these sequences down here. We're working on them, but the significant thing isn't the cipher, it's the pictures."

"These pictures are of Perovskaya," said Rubens.

"It's a setup to discredit him. They've just started to circulate. From the president's office, with information about a coup."

The pictures showed the defense secretary and a young male in bathing suits. Perovskaya had his hand around the man's waist, reaching toward his crotch.

"Oh," said Rubens aloud. "Oh."

Rubens realized why it wasn't clear who was behind the coup. Even before Martin had turned up alive, it had been obvious the Russians were hiding something important concerning the Wave Three target—now he knew what it was.

He turned to Hadash.

"Perovskaya's the assassin's target," he said. "Perovskaya, not Kurakin. Kurakin set it all up."

"Why would he do that? He could just fire the defense minister."

"Yes," said Rubens. "It's a cover—the Wave Three target—we must strike the lasers immediately. This was all arranged by Kurakin to cover an attack on us."

74

The car pulled into the lot flanked by two larger limousines carrying the security people. The assassin slid his finger ever so slightly against the edge of the trigger.

This was the difficult moment, the point at which time suspended itself. The moment could stretch to an infinity.

The reticule—the American scope used crosshairs rather than the pointer familiar on older Russian devices—was zeroed in on the left side of the car. He had a good, clean view, would see his target's face clearly before firing.

One shot. Then out. He could feel the people who'd been sent to get him already working the building, waiting for him to come. They'd have the entrances guarded, be on the roof. But he was ready.

One of the bodyguards knocked on the car window, then moved away. There were others nearby, six or seven people, bodyguards and aides now trotting through the courtyard from another vehicle, a small bus. He ignored them all, waiting for the door to open. Finally, it cracked. His target put his foot on the pavement, hesitated.

There was a noise in the distance as the moment floated in its infinity. A bodyguard moved. The target remained in the limo. The assassin's finger remained steady on the trigger.

75

Lia ran full steam to the door, then stopped abruptly. She reached not to the knob or lock but to the glass, pushing the side of her head against it. Then quickly she took her knife out, started to pick at the lock.

"Back!" she hissed at Dean, sliding down the wall. He threw himself to the floor as she whipped her knife at the glass.

The doorway exploded. Dean jumped up and ran, following her inside, shooting blindly, knowing that the sniper would be somewhere near the window in the front of the room.

But he wasn't—this room connected to another, just beyond.

The sniper loomed at the side, an MP-5 in his hand. As Lia fell to Dean's left, a bullet spun Dean so fiercely he slammed against the wall.

God, Lia.

Dean saw the sniper retreat—not from the apartment but back to his post, starting to sight his weapon. He wedged his left arm beneath him and fired his pistol with his right, knowing that the bullet would miss.

It did, but the second caught the sniper in the side. As he fell against his gun he fired, and the room reverberated with the report of the massive gun.

Dean's third bullet struck just at the lambda where the

rear sections of the bone came together. Fragments flew through the sniper's brain; by the time Dean's next bullet caught the assassin in the spinal cord he was already dead.

Dean's first instinct was to look through the man's scope to see what was going on. Something grabbed him as he bent toward it.

Lia.

Lia?

"No prints," she said.

"You're OK?"

"He just got my vest. Come on. Let's get the fuck out of here."

"Did he hit or miss?"

"Just go—we can't do anything about it now." She pulled him toward the outside room.

"Wait," he said. He nodded back at the sniper, who had crumpled sideways to the floor, one hand still up on his gun. "There are people waiting for him."

"How do you know that?"

"He chose this room because he could escape from it without being stopped. The question is, how?"

76

Malachi Reese felt his head starting to pound as the flight crossed east toward the Urals, rushing toward a group of four MiG-27s that had just taken off from Nizhni Tagil. The planes were fighter-bombers, old but fully capable of dropping several tons' worth of munitions on any number of targets, military or civilian.

At the moment it wasn't clear where the MiGs were headed or even if they were part of the coup; their unit had not been ID'd earlier and so escaped the general jamming and confusion campaign. The Art Room was trying to sort it all out, but at the moment their orders were to shoot the MiGs down.

Train had the two lead F-47Cs, both of which were armed with Sidewinders and AMRAAMs. Malachi had the second half of the group, which were flying with laser-guided Paveways for ground attack if needed, along with a pair of Sidewinders each. Malachi would take over as Train's wingman when the flight closed to attack. The computer would handle the two planes configured for ground attack, basically holding them as reserves against these relatively weak opponents.

The lead planes were at 60,000 feet, moving at Mach 2; they'd intercept the MiGs in about five minutes.

"I want to go to active radar to get us an attack vector," Riddler told Train. He needed permission because the radar would make it easier for the MiGs and other Russian assets to detect them. Thus far they had not been seen by the defenses.

"Roger that," said Train. "You awake over there, Malachi?"

"Wide awake."

"Get into Two and take my wing on my mark. Go to autoflight first."

The step-by-step instruction was unnecessary, but Malachi took no offense. He took control of his fighter as Riddler activated the radar in Bird Four. The precise plot found the MiGs slightly closer and faster than they had thought, moving at 500 knots at flight level twenty-five degrees to the south of Bird One's nose. The planes were flying a combat trail; from above it would look like a somewhat disjointed string.

"No data on weapons," said Riddler. "Still looking for their radar. Negative on that."

The MiGs gave no indication that they "saw" the Birds' radar or even knew the planes existed. Malachi's hand tensed on his control stick. Missing his music, he started to play a vintage Clash song in his head, "Police on My Back," as mixed and rehashed by XtaVigage, thrash rappers from Miami.

"Bandits are beginning a turn east," said Riddler. "Accelerating."

Malachi had them on his screen, four red triangles that moved in slow staccato in the lower right quadrant.

"Stay with me, Malachi."

"On you."

They traded quick updates on speed and position, accelerating slightly. They were beyond visual range; the AM-RAAMs could be launched at will.

"They may be heading back to their base," said Riddler. "Getting data now on instructions, voice instructions. They may have an order to return back."

"Whacker, ask Desk Three if we're cleared to shoot them down. I want a direct yes."

"Yeah."

"Hang tight, guys," said Riddler. "Hang tight. Their altitude is dropping."

Malachi leaned forward in his seat as they continued to close the distance on the bandits. Whacker had opened a small pop-up target data screen on the main flight view; the computer had designated and locked its tracking mode on the bandits. A white box at the center of the screen plotted where Malachi should be in the formation; he was pushing forward a little too fast and a little high, and the computer began blinking the box to scold him.

"Break off the attack," said Riddler. "We have confirmation that they're returning to base."

"Desk Three says not to fire," said Whacker.

"Shit," said Malachi.

"Enough of that," said Train. "We'll maintain our course eastward and make sure they do land. Get me a vector to their base."

77

As Rubens started to tell Telach he needed to talk to the Bird strike team, something exploded in the right corner of the picture on the screen at the front of the Art Room. Realizing he was seeing the assassination attempt, Rubens stopped and focused on the screen, where a video feed from a CIA-planted video fly covering part of the courtyard was now being displayed. The view was partly blocked off and de-layed a second and a half because of all the encryption and the routing, but it was clear enough for him to see Perov-skaya standing a few feet from where the bullet had hit, his arms jerking up out of shock.

For a moment, Rubens worried that there would be an-other shot. Then the bodyguards started to move, pushing the defense minister back into the car and out of the frame.

"Lia and Dean got the assassin," said Rockman, nearly shouting. "He got the shot off, but they got him. He's down."

Rubens turned to Hadash nearby. "Tell President Marcke to ask to speak to Perovskaya. Otherwise, they'll kill him. He was the target—if Kurakin wants him dead it must be to our advantage that he's alive. Quickly."

Hadash started to relay the message. On the screen behind him, cars whipped by. The video transmission suddenly stopped—the Russians must've turned on a wide-spectrum jammer.

Rubens turned to Telach. "Where's the Bird strike force?"

She hot-keyed a sitrep map onto the now-blank main screen. It showed the four-plane flight almost over the Urals.

"Put up the Wave Three target. And the laser facilities themselves."

The planes were sixty-three miles to the southwest of one site and another hundred miles farther west of the other. The command bunker, the target of the Wave Three mission, was in the middle.

Take the two sites. Now.

"Telach, what channel is the Bird commander on?"

"What's going on?" asked Hadash.

"Two-two-alpha," said Telach.

"Listen in," Rubens told him.

78

"He had a way to use the air shaft," Dean told Lia. "It runs along this wall somewhere."

"How do you know?" asked Lia.

"Because if he chose his spot according to what the best sight line was, he would have gone higher."

"Maybe he thought there were people there."

"There weren't, remember?"

"Maybe this door was easier to fix."

"Nah." Dean looked at the wall where the air shaft would be. It seemed solid, but maybe there was a trapdoor or something. He put his ear against it and began banging with his fist, looking for a hole.

"No," said Lia.

"They'll be waiting at the exits."

"The roof?"

"Check with your gizmo."

She fiddled with her screen while Dean looked for a hollow spot. There didn't seem to be one, nor was there a closet.

So what was the dead bastard thinking? Maybe it did have to do with the door or the interior; maybe there was no partition in the other office.

Dean stepped out of the office, trying to put himself in the assassin's head. He knew his business very well. The only thing that had tripped him up was something so far out of the range of possibilities that he never could have foreseen it—American agents trying to save a Russian president's butt.

He'd definitely have had a slick way out.

The next office was on the corner of the building. Dean went to the door; it was unlocked. This office was very similar to the other, except that it had a window on the side. Dean stood in the middle of the room, his mind blank, as if the solution would just float into it. There were footsteps in the hallway—Lia's. He turned, saw something coiled behind the door.

A short run of chain and a spike.

"What's going on?" said Lia.

"It's like a fire escape." Dean grabbed the chain and went to the window. It opened easily. He looked below the ledge and found a small, deep hole; the spike went in easily. The chain fell to the ledge of the window below.

"Downstairs," he said, turning back into the room. "His way out is downstairs. You go first."

"Me?"

"Yeah, come on—the chain's held by a spike. I'll hold it up for you, then come out myself."

Lia looked at him doubtfully but went to the window. Dean closed the door behind her, locking the latch. She was already outside by the time he got back, hanging off the ledge and trying the chain.

"I think it'll pull right out," she said.

"Yeah, probably," said Dean.

"It only goes down to the next floor."

"Yeah. Go." He dropped to his knees and bent over, grasping the chain with both hands and trying to brace himself against the wall. "Go!"

"Hey."

He looked up. Her face was next to his.

"Good luck," she said. She leaned forward to kiss him.

He gave her a peck in return. "Go."

"Some kiss, Charlie Dean," she said, disappearing. "Work on it."

She looked small, but her weight nearly pulled the chain

out of his hands. He kept his head up, not watching. He heard her break the glass and the pressure released on his fingers.

Dean heard something in the hallway outside as he rose. The spike had bent slightly, but it was still in place. He slid over the side and started down. As his shoes hit the top pane of the glass he could feel the chain slip. He felt for the opening with his feet, got into the office, and tugged the spike out, letting the chain fall to the ground.

"Here," said Lia. She was on the opposite end of the room, pulling at the wallboard. A piece of thick cellophane tape came off in her hand, revealing a seam; Lia pulled back and the board fell to the floor, revealing the metal of the air shaft. She started tapping to try to find the opening; Dean gave it a kick with his heel and the metal caved in on the side and bottom. He cut two of his fingers trying to get it out of the way; finally he just let it fall down the shaft.

"Up or down?" asked Lia.

Dean looked into the shaft. It was about three-foot square, a tight squeeze for his shoulders.

"Down, I think," said Dean. "Because they'd go to the top, thinking he might run up the stairs."

"Hold on," said Lia. She took her handheld out, staring at it.

"Come on. Screw the high-tech crap." Dean got into the hole and started downward. "We can't wait."

"They're above," she said. "Four men on the roof. At least two others on the top floor."

"Good to know we figured it out," said Dean. He sidled his way downward, slipping every third or fourth move. He soon realized that there were small connecting ducts and irregular joints that made it easier to get a grip; he began using them and made safer, though slightly slower, progress. For about the first fifty feet he descended in darkness. Then a pin of light played downward—Lia had retrieved a small flashlight.

It wasn't much help at first; all it illuminated was more darkness. Finally the light made a kind of arrow below; it was the panel he'd kicked in, blocking their way.

Dean pushed it aside with his foot but couldn't get it quite far enough away. He slammed it with his heel, but even though he bent it, the panel stubbornly continued to block the path. Finally he tried wedging it down, putting most of his weight against it. It slid a few feet, then got stuck again. Even with all of his weight he couldn't budge it.

"Son of a bitch," he said.

"Sshhh," she hissed.

Dean kicked at it, then began to try to squeeze past. His legs hit something else.

They were at the bottom.

So where the hell was the door?

Was there a door?

"That flashlight," said Dean.

"They're up there."

"Give me the light."

She dropped it. He saw it at the last second and grabbed for it, but it kicked off his fingers and bounced on the ground. He had to contort his body to reach it; as he started to examine the shaft he heard the growls above them, curses in Russian.

Dean spotted a crack in the wall and pushed against it, but the metal didn't give. He threw his head back and hit the wall—it gave a little.

He turned and looked at the metal behind him. It seemed solid, and while it did flex when he put his hand against it, there was no opening that he could find.

"Here," Lia was saying. "Here."

She was a few feet above him, in a hole.

"It's here; it's here," she said, leaning down. But instead of trying to pull him up, she turned toward the top and fired her gun.

The rumble nearly broke his eardrums. Dean pushed upward, squeezing through the hole just as gunfire erupted down the shaft.

They were in a basement. Lia had another flashlight. No larger than a cigarette, its light played along the walls as she looked for some sort of opening. There were stairs upward, obviously back into the building. Another set led to the side, probably to an alley. Lia started for it and Dean began to follow, though he knew the Russians would be watching it.

"This would be a good time to call for backup," he told Lia.

"I already have."

Lia had reached the door when Dean saw a piece of plywood against the far wall. He ran to it and pulled it away.

There was a grate in front of a hole. It didn't fit right; he pulled it away and tossed it down.

"This way," he told Lia, ducking inside.

79

Rubens began speaking even before the Bird commander acknowledged.

"The lasers are going to target our satellites. They have to be taken down. Ms. Telach will give you the coordinates."

"We can't just attack," said Hadash. "We have no proof."

"If the lasers take out the network, we'll be blind for six months, if not eighteen," said Rubens. "We can't risk that."

Hadash sputtered. "We need the president's authorization."

"You have it," said Marcke over the Desk Three com system—Telach had cut Hadash's line into the Desk Three circuit.

"Thank you, sir," said Rubens. "Gentlemen, stand by for Ms. Tellach's instructions."

80

Whacker plotted strikes on both sites, splitting the flight in two. The IP, or initial point, for the bombing run on the first was ninety seconds away with the gates flooded; the second was fifteen seconds beyond that.

"We won't have the fuel to recover," said the navigator–weapons officer.

"Roger that," said Train. "Punch them in. Malachi, you drive to the second target. Whacker, I want you to sit on that one and take it. I'll launch on the first."

"Good," said Whacker. He touched his screen, automatically inputting the suggested courses into the flight system. The computer presented the information immediately to Malachi, essentially giving him a dotted line to follow to the target site.

"Ground intercept radars are up," said Riddler. "We have an SA-6 battery, an SA-2."

"Jam them," said Train, who had the threat icons on his screen. "Malachi?"

"I have control; I'm on course," he told the flight leader, jacking the throttle.

"Talk it up, talk it up," said the leader.

"Sorry," said Malachi, belatedly realizing he'd forgotten to acknowledge the earlier order. "On course. Uh, ninety seconds to IP. I have both planes. Shit, I'm spiked!"

Either alerted by the earlier encounter or placed on active

alert because of the coup attempt, Russian defense radars were now lighting up all across the country. One had just managed to find Bird Two, "spiking" or locking onto it at very close range. Riddler was already working to break the contact with the onboard ECMs.

"SA-2 site is on us," Riddler told Malachi. The original radar that had found the flight had handed off the information to another radar, which was being used to direct high-altitude SAMs. "We have a launch. Two missiles."

The SA-2 was a rather old missile—early versions were actually used, with great effect, in Vietnam. Malachi didn't worry about them, confident that the electronic fog being poured into the sky by Riddler would confuse them.

The SA-10b battery that fired a few seconds later was considerably more worrisome.

Riddler let out a string of curses as data flowed in about the launch. Six missiles were in the air, all aimed at Malachi. Riddler cursed and complained that the gear must be screwing up because the SA-10bs—they might be compared to a late-model American Hawk, with a bigger warhead and more extensive range—seemed to have come from nowhere.

"Relax," barked Train. "Everyone on their game. Focus."

Malachi's threat screen flashed red as the missiles continued to home in on the robot aircraft. Bird Four, which Malachi had locked into an offset trail about four miles behind the other plane, remained clean.

No-brainer. Two was carrying all air-to-air missiles and could be readily sacrificed. Four was now thirty seconds from the point at which he would start maneuvering to launch his weapons.

Riddler cursed in his headset. Malachi lost track of what was going on around him. He jinked and tossed chaff from Bird Two, trying to make it harder for the SA-10b's onboard guidance gear to close in. Then he pushed his head a few inches from the flight screen and gave control of Bird Two to the computer to fly a "defensive evade" as he took Bird Four into the target.

Riddler barked a new warning, but Malachi was committed. He dipped the wing hard, pivoting nearly ninety degrees as he dropped five thousand feet in a half-breath, playing the stick with a bit of body English to keep his nose precisely where he wanted. In a "real" plane, Malachi would have blacked out from the g forces, and in fact that robot's wings briefly exceeded their maximum stress factor as the speed whipped up.

"I don't have a target," warned Whacker. The weapons officer was looking at a large screen split into three parts. Similar to Malachi's main screen, the top showed a computer-generated picture of the area ahead, with an octagonal reticule at the bottom indicating his current aim point. The bottom left screen was a simplified grid where the target and missile would be shown as a box and triangle respectively; the right was a specific target box, complete with continually updated target information.

"Stay with me," said Malachi. The target area was on the right. The altitude ladder continued to bounce down; he was through 25,000 feet and needed to level off, but the robot was responding sluggishly.

"I don't have a target," repeated Whacker.

Malachi turned up the volume on the imaginary song playing in his head—"Kll Ants" by Z—and blew a wad of air out slowly through his mouth, hanging with the robot as it began to slow, finally answering his tug on the throttle. One of the missile batteries had spiked him—all sorts of warnings were buzzing, but it was all background noise, all diversion.

The target was a blurry red rectangle in the right corner of his screen. He nudged toward it. The robot's tail flew upward—something had exploded below it.

He struggled to hold the plane on course. His eyes were now less than an inch from the screen.

"I'm on it," said Whacker. He switched on a laser beam to guide the missile to the target, locked the data into the Paveway V in the F-47C's belly, and launched.

With the missile away, Malachi began to pull up. The laser designator in the recently updated system did not have to stay on the target after the missile was launched, which made it easier for Malachi to take evasive maneuvers as anti-aircraft systems continued to track him. He shut down the active radar gear, released his last bale of chaff and some flares for good measure, and zigged right. Just as he began to check for Bird Two, his screen flashed—the bomb had exploded.

But not on the target.

"The Russian laser took out the Paveway," said Whacker.

Before Malachi could respond, his flight screen blanked. Bird Four had just been shot down.

81

Rubens stood in the middle of the Art Room, staring at the screen. The Birds' position was displayed on a map of central Russia, along with their targets.

He had nearly been fooled. Kurakin was a very wily enemy.

There was, of course, the possibility that the Birds would fail. There would be enormous consequences if they did.

Rubens folded his arms in front of his chest. There would be enormous consequences if he was wrong about the lasers as well, but that was a possibility he did not entertain.

82

The computer flying Bird Two had done a better job than Malachi, managing to avoid all the missiles on its own. Malachi struggled to reorient himself as he took the stick from the machine, but he was rattled; he had trouble locating himself relative to the laser site.

Train's first strike on his site had also been turned back. He still had both of his planes and was already lined up for a second try.

"Malachi, get down low where the radars won't see you and make your attack from there," said the flight leader.

"I lost Bird Four."

"Improvise."

He may have meant to use the remote aircraft's cannon, but Malachi decided instead he would use the AMRAAMs, which were still loaded in the belly.

Then he decided on something better.

"I'm going to kamikaze the son of a bitch," he told Whacker. "You can stay with Train."

"Malachi, you're being spiked!" warned Riddler.

He rolled the Bird downward, falling into a spin as he plunged from fifteen thousand feet. He recovered and then slid south at about five thousand feet, coming through to four thousand, to three thousand, his heart pounding like the piston of an old steam engine roaring down a Rocky Mountain grade. Riddler tried directing him away from the radar coverage, giving him a graphic on the threat screen that portrayed it as purple blossoms in a 3-D landscape. But he switched it off verbally; it was distracting and the stinking radars were all over the place.

And so were the flak guns. The screen lit up with a thousand water fountains, all spurting toward him. An array of ZSU-23 and larger ZSU-57 antiaircraft guns, radar and optically guided, sprayed lead into the sky before him. Malachi was running through a volcanic field, plunging past the gates of hell.

There was definitely a song in this.

The altimeter ladder at the left side of his screen had descended to one hundred feet, and the indicator was still rolling downward. Malachi's entire body moved backward as he lifted his nose, trying to slip under the radars but not hit the earth. He had an open plain in front of him, strings of tracers and black strings—he was through the guns, past the worst of the antiair. Something grabbed at his right wing; he jerked the stick back, overcorrected, did the wrong thing, cursed, felt himself lose the plane.

"You son of a bitch, hold still," he said.

The computer blared a warning, insisting that he was going to collide.

Then he had a blank screen in front of him.

"Shit," said Malachi. He pushed back in the seat, exhausted, humiliated.

No one said anything for a good thirty seconds, maybe more.

"They're down! They're down!" shouted Riddler. "I have a visual from one of the satellites. You hit the mother square on."

A picture appeared in the middle of Malachi's main screen. In one corner was a building with what looked like a blotchy cloud right over it. It was the laser complex exploding.

"Splash Site One," said Train as Malachi stared at the laser he had just hit. "Both sites are down. Both sites are down—kick-ass, boys. Mal, help me get Two to a good self-destruct; then let's break out the beer."

83

The passage Dean and Lia found extended into a long, dark tunnel. They had to crouch as they ran, but the passage was clear and dry.

Dean heard the faint rumble of machinery ahead. After they had gone a hundred yards, Lia grabbed his arm to stop him; she needed to catch her breath.

"What is this, a sewer?" she asked.

"I don't know."

"Where does it go?"

"Hey, you're the one with the magic map," said Dean. "You tell me."

"I'm not getting anything," she said. "The Russian jamming is cutting down on our signal strength, and down here there's just too much interference."

"That's what I've been saying about high-tech bullshit," Dean told her. "It's useless when you need it most."

"We wouldn't have made it this far without it, cowboy."

A flashlight beam played across the roof from the direction they'd started in. Dean pulled Lia with him, turning off the flashlight at first even though the tunnel was pitch-black. He had to turn it back on; there was no way to see otherwise.

The tunnel began running downhill and angling slightly. After they'd gone another twenty or thirty yards, Dean saw an air shaft or something ahead; light played down it. Lia ran to it, but the shaft was barely a foot square, too narrow for even her to crawl up.

"They're close," he hissed. He could hear their pursuers walking into the tunnel behind them.

Ten strides later, Dean nearly collided with the wall as the tunnel took a sharp turn to the right. Twenty yards beyond that, it split in two.

They went left. The machinery noises were very loud now.

Behind them, one of the men cursed. A gun fired twice and the ricochet of the bullet cracked in Dean's ears.

"Maybe they killed each other," said Lia.

"Yeah. And maybe we hit the lottery."

"Door." Lia pointed ahead. A metal door stood above a cement-block step on the wall ten feet ahead. In the middle of the door was a sign with Cyrillic letters. Lia pulled a small lock pick from her pocket and worked at the lock as two more gunshots echoed through the tunnel. They sounded louder.

"They're panicking," said Dean. There was light now back near the V, small flashlight beams.

Lia undid the lock and pulled the door open. Dean nearly fell backward as a rush of steam blew out into the passage.

"Come on," said Lia, grabbing his hand and pulling him through. They were in a machinery room. The temperature had to be over a hundred degrees. The noise was deafening.

Lia pulled him along to a catwalk, then down a flight of steps. She let go at the bottom, disappearing to the right. Dean followed her into a long tiled hall, turning into an archway as she did, then stopping short on a narrow cement ledge, suddenly in the darkness.

When his eyes adjusted, he saw he was in a subway tunnel. There were lights every fifty feet or so and a flood of white maybe two hundred yards on his right.

"Come on!" yelled Lia.

Dean took two steps, then watched her jump off the ledge. His heart nearly stopped.

"It'll be faster on the tracks," she explained. "Come on! Come!"

Dean froze. All he could think of was horror stories about people getting run over after falling onto train tracks or frying when they touched the third rail.

"Charlie Dean, get that lovely butt of yours in gear!" yelled Lia, turning back and seeing him frozen. "Don't be a sissy wimp."

"Sexist pig," he answered—but only in a mutter; he was suddenly out of breath.

Dean crouched.

Shit, if she could do it, so could he.

Unless there was a train coming.

He checked, saw nothing.

Still short of breath, Dean jumped down. He landed in a crouch and tumbled over, his face hitting something hard and cold.

It was the rail. It seemed to be humming.

Sure that a train was coming, he jumped to his feet and ran in Lia's direction. Bullets whizzed by him—two Russians had just burst out into the tunnel.

Fortunately, they didn't have a good angle from the ledge. By the time they got down on the tracks, Dean had reached the flood of light—a station on the outskirts of the city.

Lia had already climbed on the platform. She reached down and grabbed Dean's hand, helping him upward as the Russians fired again.

A half-dozen people stood on the platform, their faces a study in disbelief. Lia and Dean began running toward the stairs. Then she stopped. A man in a long black raincoat appeared at the top of the steps, one hand on his ear and another in his pocket, obviously holding a gun.

"This way," said Lia, running past the stairway along the platform.

The men who'd been in the tunnel were out now, yelling at the man on the stairs. They were all chasing, converging around the steps as Lia pushed her head down and started to run. Dean threw himself forward as well, following as she threw her hand on the stair rail and pirouetted onto the steps. He looked up to see a large blond bear throw her to the side.

Dean pitched his arm to slug the bastard, but before he could connect, the giant threw him aside, laughing as the off-balance American fell against the steps and then rolled down onto the subway platform.

Karr.

"Hang tight, Charlie Dean," said the NSA agent, spinning around at the steps. He had his jacket, a box—there was a massive roar, the sound the metro engine might make if it exploded in the tunnel.

Two men fell off the platform.

Karr yelled something as the echo of the A-2's gunshot dissolved into the roar of a train screeching into the station. Dean saw people backing away, then getting on the train. They looked pale as the doors closed.

"Come on," said Karr, bolting up past them as they continued to hug the railing. He'd thrown away the jacket, giving up all pretense of hiding the A-2. "Those fuckers have radios. Come on!"

"How the hell did you know where we were?" Dean asked.

"Had the Art Room track the locators. Can't beat the technology, Charlie. It's what I've been telling you. Now if we could use it to hail a taxi, we'd be home free."

84

Rubens slid into the backseat of the director's car, snapping on his seat belt as the door closed behind him. The Russian "coup"—and Kurakin's plot to blind the American defense system—had been quashed three days ago, but he was still drained. They'd only stood down from their high-level alert twelve hours before.

The Russian defense minister had gone public with the whole story, not coincidentally announcing his candidacy to oppose Kurakin. The president maintained that it was Perovskaya who was trying to subvert democracy, and claimed that the president's bodyguards had successfully intervened to thwart an attempt on the defense minister's life.

There was sentiment at the White House that some of the NSA data should be released, proving that Kurakin was a liar. But Rubens had argued vehemently against that. It would make it clear exactly how extensive the Russian communications network and defense system had been penetrated. Things were always best left murky.

In the convoluted world of Russian politics, it wasn't clear that Kurakin's attempt to short-circuit the electoral process would actually harm him. It might even help him. The photos of the defense minister and the young lad had not yet surfaced. It was possible that Kurakin was holding them in reserve.

There were some who wanted to tip Perovskaya off to

their existence. Perhaps that would be the play; Rubens had not yet given the matter much thought.

The Russians had protested the strikes on their laser weapons. But since they were loath to admit that they had such weapons—which would have been tantamount to saying that Kurakin had lied when he said they didn't—all they could do was mutter a few terse words to the secretary of state about the "unexplained" destruction of facilities "east of the Urals."

The secretary had made sure to look very perplexed as he promised to look into the matter.

Martin's death made it impossible to know how badly Wave Three had been compromised. Wave Three was too important a technology to keep on permanent hold, but its use now had become highly problematic and would have to be rethought.

As for Martin himself, a full-blown investigation was already under way to determine what damage he had done, and to answer such questions as whether he had been turned or come in as a spy. He was a contract agent, a technical expert recruited for his skills, and not one of Rubens' Desk Three people—but that was hardly a consolation.

Problems for another day.

"Congratulations," said Brown as the car started away from the White House. "I think your report was very well received."

"Yes."

"A new era in warfare." Brown smiled as he repeated the president's phrase. "An exaggeration, but not unappreciated. 'A new era in covert action and intelligence gathering.' That was more accurate. Tired?"

"Yes," admitted Rubens.

"It's better that it happens this way," said Brown.

"Agreed."

"No sudden doubts?"

"No, sir, no doubts at all," said Rubens.

"I mean, because it's your cousin."

"No," he said, and yet he suddenly wasn't sure.

"She'll expect us?" asked Brown.

"Not us, no. But I think it much better if you're here."

It had been Brown's idea to come along. The suggestion could be interpreted as an offer of friendship. Surely it was— his boss seemed to genuinely like him.

Did he, though? Why? What would Admiral Brown, NSA director, get from a friendship with his second in command— a second in command whom he hadn't chosen?

Ammunition to dump him?

A paranoid thought, surely. But paranoia was necessary to survive. Suspicion was the most important quality a man could have.

Greta was waiting in front of the restaurant just as they had agreed. As the driver pulled up, Rubens pushed the button to roll down the window.

"There you are," she said.

"You might want to get in," he told her.

Greta blanched. Nonetheless, she reached for the door. Brown, meanwhile, got out and went to sit in the front. The driver lowered the glass partition as he got in.

"I don't believe you know my superior, Admiral Brown."

"By reputation only," said Greta.

She gave him the sort of smile a politician gives a constituent whose face he can't place. Brown smiled at her, then said something to the driver. The partition went back up as the driver pulled away.

"I've figured out how Greene died," said Rubens.

Greta didn't answer. Rubens took this to mean that she knew as well. Probably she had known from the beginning.

"Why would you sleep with a congressman?" he asked.

It was a bluff—Rubens had no evidence of an affair, nothing to back it up. But he also felt strongly that it must be so. It was the only motivation if Greene had in fact been murdered.

Which he believed must be so.

"Oh, it was years ago. Back when I worked at HUD. I was young."

Rubens let it pass, though he knew she must be lying. Either Greene's talk about firing her was a smoke screen to cover up the affair, or it was intended as blackmail to keep her from breaking it off.

"I've never really been able to control Jack's passions," said Greta. "He's not like us. It's so—well, he was a mistake, wasn't he?"

Rubens said nothing.

"How long before this comes out?" she asked.

"There are FBI agents en route to search your house, though I doubt they'll find anything," said Rubens. "They'll question Jack, of course. He should be in custody by now."

"The media?"

"I couldn't say. I thought you'd want to be informed."

"I appreciate it," she said, smiling as if it might actually be true. "Where are you taking me?"

"Wherever you want."

Rubens felt an impulse to say something encouraging. Assuming Jack kept his mouth shut, prosecuting the case would be difficult at best, even with all the pressure from Congress. As yet, there was only circumstantial evidence that the guitar had been tampered with. Acting on Rubens' hunch, however, the FBI had uncovered travel records showing that Jack had been in New York at least once when the band was. They were interviewing possible witnesses there, as well as reinterviewing people who had been at the party.

The FBI agents had also realized—and Rubens had known, though not made the connection—that the CEO had started his life's work as an electrical engineer.

An honorable profession, surely, one that supplied much useful knowledge about how to cause freak accidents.

A coincidence, no doubt.

It had taken the coup for Rubens to see it all, though it had happened right in front of him. The misdirection play, the obvious pattern overlooked—intelligence was more a matter of imagination than data. If you couldn't imagine something happening, you couldn't understand what you were looking at.

"Maybe you should drop me off back at the office," said Greta. "I'm going to resign this afternoon. Go out on a high note. Faithful wife, all that."

And strongly imply that he was guilty. A perfect outcome, surely.

Rubens buzzed the driver, who took a turn back toward the government buildings.

"Did you know about it in advance?" Rubens asked his cousin as they drove.

"You think I'd tell you if I did?"

He smiled. "If I wanted to, I could find out."

"I bet you could."

85

"Is there anyone here for Flight 102? Flight 102 for New York?"

The flight number didn't register until the woman added the destination. Dean put up his right arm sheepishly, wincing not from shyness but from the stiffness in his arm. His whole body still hurt, unused to the workout of the past several days, and stiff from a succession of puddle-jumpers whose seats were little more than folding chairs with seat belts. He'd arrived at Heathrow Three after eighteen hours of airplane flights. Ostensibly the tangled course he'd followed from Moscow had sanitized his trail, though Dean strongly suspected the convoluted track—he'd been in Poland, the Czech Republic, Austria, and Norway—represented some sort of bargain fare bonanza for the NSA.

But at least for the flight across the Atlantic he was taking a *real* airline.

"Your flight is boarding now, sir," said the attendant with an English accent. "Could you step this way?"

Dean shambled over to the ticket counter with the cover luggage he'd been given and told the clerk his name. The man had a bit of trouble with it at first; Dean spelled it twice.

"Oh, excuse me, Mr. Dean—here you are. Sorry, sir, quite sorry—Catherine, could you please escort Mr. Dean to the gate upstairs? I'll make sure they know you're coming."

An attractive young woman appeared at Dean's right.

With a deferential smile she led him toward the escalator up
to the gate level. Dean followed along through a side door
of the security checkpoint, over to his own personal detector.
He gave the woman and two guards a bemused smile as he
emptied his change into a small Tupperware container, then
stepped through the boxy gate. The attendant beamed back
at him every few feet as she treaded him through the crowded
duty-free shopping area. Finally they made it to the moving
walkway, a long hall with windows looking out at the airplanes.

"Thanks. I would've gotten lost back there," he told the
woman as she stepped onto the walkway ahead of him. She
just smiled. "I think I can find my way from here," he added
when she didn't get the hint.

"Oh, not to worry, sir," she said indulgently. "We're almost there."

She was short, but she had a quick pace and he had to
push his stiff legs to keep up as they dodged more leisurely
travelers. He'd slept for nearly twenty-four hours in Moscow
at the end of the operation, but he still felt exhausted.

He also felt very, very old.

They hadn't said good-bye. Lia and Karr and Fashona
were gone from the safe house when he woke. In their place
a dour-faced CIA agent took him to breakfast at McDonald's,
then drove him to the airport after supplying him with baggage, a proper passport, and travel documents, along with a
list of his flights. The man hadn't even bothered to introduce
himself.

He hadn't known where the others were and, in fact,
didn't seem to know who they were, or at least didn't admit
knowing. When Dean asked what had happened to them the
CIA agent merely shrugged. "Assignment, probably," was all
he said.

Dean would have liked to say good-bye. He'd come to
like Karr—hell, it was hard to dislike Karr, even though his
goofy smile could get on your nerves sometimes.

And Lia—Lia he liked a lot, though not necessarily for
her personality.

Actually, her personality *was* attractive, underneath the tough-girl thing she did. But she probably had to play it that way or she wouldn't survive. She was a good kid.

A good *woman*.

Dean's mind wandered as they made it to the end of the walkway. His guide picked up her pace, strolling down the long hallway toward the departure gate. She had nice legs and beautiful hips—but she wasn't as pretty as Lia.

"Here you go," she said, sweeping her hand out as they reached the gate area, a separate waiting room off the passage. "Have a nice flight."

"Thanks," said Dean.

The last of the passengers were just getting past a final security check at the far end of the room as he entered. A familiar voice seemed to hit him on the side of the head as he came in the room.

"Just turn the damn thing on, for christsakes. You never heard of an on-off switch?"

Lia DeFrancesca was standing to one side of the door leading to the boarding tunnel, shaking her head as a ham-fisted guard tried to turn her handheld on to make sure it was really a computer.

"Here," she said, grabbing the computer from the guard. "God. On. Off. On, off."

"She's always cranky in the morning," said Dean, walking up. "And in the afternoon. Pretty much around the clock."

Surprise flickered across her face when she turned her head to him, but only for a second.

"Stuff it, Charlie Dean." She turned back and disappeared down the runway.

"Lovely personality," Dean said to the attendant.

The airline employee nodded, then took Dean's boarding pass.

"Oh, yes, sir," he said, his voice gaining a little snap. "You'll want to get aboard right away, sir."

Dean took the ticket back. At the door to the airplane, the attendant took the pass, smiled, then led him inside.

"Champagne, sir?" she said, standing to one side at the head of the first-class section.

"Uh, champagne, sure," said Dean. He started toward the back of the plane.

"Your seat's right there, sir," said the attendant. She smiled and pointed toward a wide, thick, soft first-class seat.

"Really?" said Dean. He hadn't bothered looking at the pass downstairs.

The attendant turned her head slightly in a way that suggested either utter servitude or well-disguised contempt. Dean opted to believe it was the former. He turned and started to back into the seat, feeling more out of place than he had even in Siberia. He'd never flown first class before.

"Try not to act too much like a rube," said Lia, who had the seat next to him. She was wearing her denim jacket over a short black skirt and chiffon top so thin he could see the delicious outline of her breast. It was going to be a great flight.

"Fancy meeting you here," said Dean.

"Yes," she snapped. "What luck."

The attendant poured them champagne and the video screens began showing the preflight warnings and service advertisements. The other passengers settled into their seats.

"A whole bottle of champagne," said Dean admiringly. He turned to Lia. "A successful—uh." He stopped, not wanting to say "mission" where he might be overheard.

"A successful what, baby-sitter?" she said.

"Don't you ever give it up?" he said.

She smirked. Then she leaned toward him and gave him a kiss.

"Hey, none of that," boomed a voice behind them.

Karr poked his head over the seats.

"Karr, what are you doing here?" asked Lia.

"Chaperoning, obviously."

"We're all on the same flight?" asked Dean.

"Duh," said Lia.

"Some coincidence, huh?" said Karr, sliding back down. "I guess we're all supposed to go to the same place."

"Life's full of coincidences," said Lia.

"You know, I've never flown first class," said Dean.

"I couldn't tell," said Lia.

"This the way you guys always travel?"

"Yeah, right," said Lia. "We're lucky we're not shoveling coal in the bottom of a boat."

"So how did we end up here?" said Dean.

"That's actually a pretty good question," said Lia. They both turned back to Karr.

His only answer was to smile and sip his champagne.